CONFESSIONS ABOUT COLTON

CONFESSIONS ABOUT COLTON

OLIVIA HARVARD

wattpad books **W**

wattpad books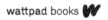

Published in Canada by Wattpad Books, a division of Wattpad Corp.
36 Wellington Street E., Toronto, ON M5E 1C7

www.wattpad.com

First Wattpad Books edition: March 2020

ISBN 978-1-98936-510-6 (Hardcover original)
ISBN 978-1-98936-511-3 (eBook edition)

Names, characters, places, and incidents featured in this publication
are either the product of the author's imagination or are used fictitiously.
Any resemblance to actual persons (living or dead), events, institutions,
or locales, without satiric intent, is coincidental.

Wattpad, Wattpad Books, and associated logos are trademarks
and/or registered trademarks of Wattpad Corp.

Library and Archives Canada Cataloguing in Publication information
is available upon request.

Printed and bound in Canada

1 3 5 7 9 10 8 6 4 2

Cover design by Michelle Wong
Images © Noah Buscher via Unsplash
Typesetting by Sarah Salomon

CONFESSIONS ABOUT COLTON

PROLOGUE

Whenever Colton Crest told me a secret, I did everything in my power to take it to the grave. That was how our friendship was.

There was an eerily trustworthy quality about him. He had the kind of charisma and charm that almost hypnotized you. It was as if he had given you a key to the universe and it was your sole responsibility to protect it. And it was a comfortable feeling knowing that Colton would return the favor. He would be the most understanding person, no matter how vile or poisonous the secret was, and lock it securely in his memory.

We told each other everything, knew every ugly detail. Well, that's what I had thought. But one thing Colton never told me was why he disappeared.

It stirred a hell of a lot of commotion. Hampton High was the worst, like you'd expect any high school to be. Students started rumors, teachers gave out false information, parents gossiped. Some said he went to jail, others announced he was abducted.

For a brief period, a Facebook page was created, solely dedicated to many conspiracies surrounding Colton's disappearance. A whisper would bounce across the walls of study hall and the story would be posted by the final school bell. It was absolute rubbish, but people were addicted to it, refreshing their browsers to soak up fabricated nonsense.

Colton had such an active role in the community that it was almost impossible to find a resident that didn't know about him. He was an honor student, part of the school leadership team, president of the science club, captain of the cricket team. On weekends he would volunteer to deliver hot food for Meals on Wheels, and he started a campaign to reduce local littering and promote recycling. He was a model citizen.

No one knew where he had gone.

Not even Colton's family had a clue about their son's whereabouts. Whenever they were asked to address the issue, they dismissed it and repeated the same monotone explanation: he was visiting relatives. But you could see the distress in Mrs. Crest's eyes, the haunting shadows that were tattooed there as her motherly instincts told her to prepare herself for the worst.

When Colton's disappearance reached a month, it was still the same. Rumors continued to spread like wildfire, residents greedily feeding off false tales like leeches.

Someone told me he was scouted by an agent and they flew him from here in Australia out to Hollywood to film a multimillion-dollar movie.

I heard he's on the run because he beat a guy up so bad that the guy almost died.

Apparently somebody kidnapped him, and the reason his family hasn't notified the police is because the kidnapper is threatening to kill Colton if the Crests tell anyone. There's a huge ransom and everything.

This continued for yet another month, but by this time, the Crests seemed a lot calmer. They had obtained some information, but they seemed unwilling to share. This didn't particularly bother me at the time. He was my best friend, and I trusted that he'd take care of himself. If his folks were calm enough, then I was calm too.

The days continued to pass. Sunday, Monday, Tuesday, Wednesday, Thursday, Friday, Saturday.

I went to school; I did my homework. I went through my normal routine and did my best to be patient. I knew Colton would come back.

It was a Sunday the day Colton Crest came back to town—when I heard the unexpected knock on my door . . .

"Hey, have you got a beer?"

I stared at him as he shrugged off his jacket and went into the kitchen, raiding my fridge like he always did. The fact that he'd just turned up at my place like he hadn't been missing for two months was unbelievable. But alas, there he was. He hadn't shaved in a while, and he was missing his usual smile, but he seemed to be physically unharmed.

He pulled out a six-pack and pushed past me to bring the drinks out onto the pergola. I followed, my eyes glued to him as I picked up a beer. Colton remained calm, pulling out his pocket watch every now and then to study the time with unnerving fascination. The watch was a classic piece of him and there was never a moment he didn't have it hooked onto the back loop of his jeans. The family heirloom was priceless, both in financial and sentimental value. I watched as he placed it back in his pocket before I took a swig of liquid courage, letting it quench my dry throat and ignite a fire in my stomach.

Then I got down to business.

"Where have you been, man?" I asked him. "And quit the bull about being with family."

He smiled and tipped his bottle of beer to his lips. "Stop trying to play detective, Elliot. Some mysteries can't be solved."

I never asked him again after that. I guess I didn't want to push him to a point where he'd disappear again. So I kept quiet. But although my silence was ensured, it didn't apply to the rest of the school. When Colton returned to class, questions were asked and the story of his reappearance had him at the height of his high school fame.

†

"We thought someone was holding you hostage or something," Marcus said. Colton and I were standing by his locker the morning of his return to school.

Colton laughed, turning his back on the conversation to open his locker. "Seriously? That's what you guys thought?"

"We didn't know what to think."

"You're about to be sorely disappointed. I was just out of town visiting relatives."

"The teachers weren't even sure about what happened to you. Some said you'd dropped out or transferred," Marcus insisted.

Colton let out a dry laugh and closed his locker. "Yeah, that's Hampton High for you. The right people knew where I was. This town is just too small—people talk too much."

When he turned around, his attention focused on something behind our classmates. Without saying anything, he beelined in the direction of the school notice board. Among the advertisements for after-school activities and lunchtime meetings was a missing person poster with Colton's face on it.

Colton plucked it from the board, and his lips simply twitched into a small smile. "Black-and-white photos really are ominous, huh?" Then he laughed. "Honestly, though. If I ever go missing for real, please do not use my high school yearbook photo. It does absolutely nothing for my assets."

Silence followed.

"Oh, come on. It's kind of funny how dramatic everyone was over this," he said. Colton turned to me and nudged his elbow into my side. "Elliot, man, you've been quiet all morning."

An uncomfortable laugh escaped my lips, but my tone was deceivingly amused as I said, "You're having way too much fun with this."

Colton grinned. "Don't worry, I'll be sure to keep everyone in the loop next time I go visit family. In the meantime, I'm going to head to history, if that's okay."

Colton tucked the missing person poster between the pages of his textbook and walked away.

†

This continued all through the months leading up to the night before graduation. I took Milo for a walk that evening. We took our old route at the back of the house, keeping close to the park behind my neighborhood, then headed onto the street, where we made a shortcut toward Lake Mason.

The sun was just over the horizon, the sky performing its grand finale of color transitions. The streets were empty, the late spring air was fresh. Other than my dog's excessive panting as he worked his stubby legs, everything was tranquil.

But as soon as we reached the edge of the water, Milo went absolutely mental. The hair on the back of his neck stood high in alert as he barked hysterically at something by the dock. At first, I thought there was another dog or a bird he wanted to chase, but when he started pulling me toward the water, I realized what had gotten him so on-edge.

There was a body floating in the lake.

"*Shit*," I whispered to myself as my fingers searched my pockets for my phone.

It was disturbing to be confronted with the sight, but for some reason, I was propelled forward by a sick curiosity. Like witnessing a car crash, horrifying and terrible, but impossible to look away from. I walked closer, making my way toward the wooden slats that made up the dock. Milo's barks began to mix with whimpers, his tail dropping low.

But as I got closer, my footsteps faltered. The descending sun's light fell upon the back pocket of the deceased's jeans and reflected off a shiny surface. It was blinding for a split second, causing me to look away. A sinking feeling settled in my stomach and my insides churned uncomfortably. There was only one object with a surface as polished as that. My hands shook, and Milo's barks were replaced by silence. I suddenly felt lightheaded.

I forced myself to look up, to ensure my imagination wasn't getting the better of me. But as I got closer, the unsettling feeling in my stomach crawled its way up my throat and left a sour taste on my tongue. I recognized the royal blue logo of our school jersey covering unnaturally gray skin. My heart quickened when I saw the pocket watch for sure, and I knew it was him.

Colton Crest was dead. And I had found him.

DENIAL

After the police and ambulances arrived, the evidence unfolded before me. Someone escorted me away from the scene so the police officers could surround the area with barricade gates. As that was happening, a special marine unit was called in, and a couple of officers went out and collected the body, struggling to balance the weight of the passenger as they hauled him onto the boat. It rocked uneasily, threatening to tip, but soon enough, it balanced itself out and arrived back on the shore.

Seeing his pale and lifeless exterior should have been proof enough that it was him, but my brain told me otherwise. I came up with every single excuse for what my eyes were seeing. It was just a hallucination, a pure figment of my imagination as a result of pre-graduation excitement. I was mistaken and it was someone else, a stranger who looked similar. It was all a dream, and at any point, I would wake up and attend my graduation ceremony with my very-alive best friend standing beside me.

When his pocket watch and personal belongings were removed

from his person to be inspected, I didn't blink. When they found his identification in his wallet, which would confirm it was him, I still didn't move a muscle. I was paralyzed. This was all a huge misunderstanding, a practical joke, an end-of-year showcase of hilarity. It was a stunt, an act, a gag. Colton wasn't dead.

Colton wasn't dead.

Colton wasn't dead.

Colton wasn't dead.

My older sister Cass was calling my name, faint and distant, an annoying hum in the background.

"Elliot?"

A strange silence engulfed me, deafening my ears and causing me to wrap my arms around my head and hunch in defeat. My surroundings dimmed until I couldn't identify where I was. The scenery had become a blur, and my body felt numb.

"*Elliot*," Cass repeated when she reached me, pulling me to her. "I'm so sorry . . ."

"He's not dead!" I insisted, throwing her arms off me and backing away. "He's not. He can't be."

"They think he's been in the water for at least twenty-four hours," she whispered carefully, as if her word choice would shatter my sanity. "Elliot, they think he was murdered . . ."

Murdered.

The word sent a jolt of cold shivers rattling down my spine. I was down on my knees, my hands desperately clutching the ground as if I would float away if I didn't anchor myself. My heart was pounding so aggressively it felt like it would jump out with one of my heaving breaths.

The weight of a blanket suddenly engulfed me, and a heavy hand landed on my shoulder. "Come on, son."

I was pulled like a stubborn weed in the garden until I was standing upright and then moved until I found myself sitting at the back of an ambulance. A medic attended to me immediately, taking my blood pressure and checking for any injuries. But they couldn't provide the instant remedy I craved. I needed someone to open up my brain and erase the memory—the startlingly frightening image of seeing your best friend's lifeless body.

Shivering, I wrapped the blanket tighter around myself.

"He's in shock," I heard the medic say to the police officer that approached. "I don't think it's appropriate to ask questions at this time. Give him some time to recover."

I focused on a patch of dirt in front of me that was surrounded by bits of gravel and a few blades of grass desperately trying to flourish in a hopeless situation. The scene was exactly how I felt. From the corner of my eye, I could see a police officer talking grimly to the medic. My sister hovered close by.

"We'll need to get some information before he can go," the officer said. "Let's bring him down to the station, give him a cup of tea until he's ready to talk. In the meantime, may we interview you, Miss Parker?"

My sister nodded curtly and gathered Milo in her arms. Our dog barked manically, his whimpers shrill. The atmosphere was so thick with tension that it was almost impossible to breathe, and Milo sensed the hostility. His little body shook, desperate to do something but uncertain of what.

The police officer escorted my sister away to a more private area, farther from the crime scene. The black-and-yellow painted barricades created a sharp contrast, such bright color wrapped around such a grimly dark backdrop.

When the police officer finished talking to Cass, he helped me into the back of a car. He explained that we were going to Oakland Station for some questioning, but I could take all the time I needed before I was ready to talk. When we arrived at the precinct, I wasn't escorted into an interrogation room, nor was I confronted with intimidating mirrors that would have forced me to stare at my reflection, my features shadowed by a single dangling light from the center of the ceiling that flickered tauntingly. Instead, I sat on a chair next to a fake potted plant and a water cooler.

"Hi, honey. You must be Elliot. I'm Jan, one of the detectives," a soft woman's voice said. I looked at her but stayed silent. "I brought someone for you to meet. Don't worry, you won't have to say anything. He doesn't speak fluent English. His name is Jasper."

The woman glanced down at the golden Labrador sitting by her feet. She made a small gesture and the dog approached me. He placed his soft chin against my knee and I instinctively reached out and touched his fur. Having a therapy dog by my side cleared some of the clouds in my head, melted a few icicles forming in my chest. I felt a little warmer, especially when Jan gave me a cup of steaming tea.

She was forgiving, allowing me enough time to gather myself. However, it was starting to get dark, and I was exhausted. I didn't want to be there any longer than I had to. So I eventually told Jan I was ready to talk. After my farewells to Jasper, I was put in a smaller, more private room and the detective from the crime scene sat me down.

"This will be difficult," he started. "I'm going to ask you some questions that might be upsetting, but I need you to answer as honestly and with as much detail as possible. We'll start off with something easy, though—introductions. I'm Detective Inspector West. Can you please state your full name, date of birth, and address?"

"Elliot Benjamin Parker. August 8, 1997. I live at 53 Cosgrove Drive."

"That would make you over eighteen, correct? Since you're of legal age, this questioning session may be conducted without the presence of a parent or guardian."

"I know."

"Okay, Elliot, can you tell me exactly what happened this afternoon?"

"I found Colton Crest dead."

"And what was your relationship with Colton? If any?"

"We were childhood friends. I've known him since we were six."

"It must have been a difficult thing to witness. Now, I'm going to ask you a few questions about this afternoon. First of all, why were you at Lake Mason?"

"I was walking my dog." My mouth was cotton, my throat sandpaper. Every word was accompanied by the nightmare I had seen. "We were walking by the lake, and my dog started barking at something in the water. I walked down to the dock, and that's where I saw him."

"Do you usually take that route when you walk your dog?"

"I mean, it's been a while, but it's usually where we go."

"Did anyone else accompany you on the walk?"

"I went alone."

"And can you tell me roughly what time you left the house?"

"I don't know . . . around seven at night?"

DI West scribbled something down. "When you got to the lake, did you notice anything strange? Was there anyone lingering around the area?"

"I didn't see anyone there at the time, and nothing seemed out of the ordinary. Well, until I found Colton."

"When was the last time you were in contact with Colton?"

I sifted through my memories and tried to remember the last time I had seen him alive. It was earlier in the week.

‡

Colton was slumped back in the corner of our booth as he swirled his half-empty glass of soda, making the remaining ice cubes rattle. He kept his gaze out the window, constantly scanning the parking lot. His eyes narrowed, sweat gathering on his brow.

"You seem distracted," I said.

Colton turned to look at me and smiled easily. He placed the glass down, and drops of condensation dripped onto the table. "Just stressed," he explained. "Exams were pretty shit."

"Yeah, but they're over now. Nothing more we can do," I said, before picking up my own drink and downing the rest of it. The sweet strawberry fizz was like nothing else.

"I'm ready for this all to be over."

There was something sad about his voice.

†

"Last week," I said. "We were hanging out."

"Did you notice anything different when you were with him? Maybe in his behavior?"

"He was stressed, but I didn't think much of it. It was exam season. We were all a bit on edge."

The police officer hummed. "And you haven't spoken to him in any other form since then? Text messages, social media?"

The questions were necessary, but I was getting agitated. I wanted to go home. "I messaged him a couple of days ago to see if he wanted to jump online and play video games, but I never got a response."

"Was it common for Colton not to respond?"

"Yeah. Sometimes we just don't catch up for a few days. He's not the fastest replier in the world, but he eventually gets back to me. Since he's been back, he's always doing something, usually busy after school with sports and clubs and community service."

My heart leaped and got lodged in my throat. I was still talking about him like he was alive. DI West seemed to pick up on this too. He coughed and shifted in his seat, looking down at some paperwork sitting in front of him.

"Besides," I continued, "when Colton disappeared in May, he eventually came back."

"Disappeared?"

I nodded. Surely his secretive trip away in the middle of the year was connected to his unexpected fate. "In May, he went somewhere for a couple of months. He said he was with family, but something felt off about it."

"What felt off?"

My emotions swirled and filled me to the brim. I hoped my voice didn't betray my frustration. "It was just awkward timing, having such a long vacation during senior year. It was abrupt too. He never mentioned it before he left."

"Did his parents seem okay about this?"

I shrugged. "That's a question to ask them."

DI West sighed and rested his elbows on the table, rubbing his hands together. He stared at me with piercing gray eyes. "Elliot, do you have any idea if he had any type of conflict with anyone? Would anyone want him . . ."

"No," I interrupted. "As far as I'm concerned, nobody was out to get him."

West nodded. "I think that's all for tonight, Elliot. Thank you for your cooperation. Let me show you the way out."

A weight was lifted from my shoulders, and I felt lighter as I floated toward the door. The room was starting to feel hot, my skin felt sticky, and my head was throbbing. I was ready to go home; to try to forget this nightmare. Or, better yet, wake up from it.

DI West opened the door for me and I stepped out, a rush of air brushing against my damp forehead. "Oh, and Elliot?"

I turned, dread sweeping over me like a tsunami.

"I am very sorry for your loss . . . especially with the way you experienced it."

I didn't have enough energy to say anything, so I turned my back on him once again and started walking toward the parking lot. I didn't make it very far before my dad stepped into view. His hair was a mess, socks mismatched and wrapped in absolutely hideous sandals. His eyes were wide behind his round glasses.

He quickly walked up to me and threw his arms around me. He clutched the back of my head and pulled my face into his shoulder. I couldn't help but sink into the comforting embrace. I was exhausted, all emotion was drained out of me, and it was an effort to keep upright.

"I'm sorry, my boy," he whispered. "I'm sorry."

I just held on tighter.

ANGER

I had been to only two funerals in the eighteen years of my existence. The first one was for my grandfather, who had passed from cancer. It wasn't a difficult experience, and I mean that in the most sensitive way possible. It was just *expected*. My family and I had been preparing for months, saying our goodbyes and spending as much time with him as possible. We just *knew*.

Colton's was number two. What made it ten times harder was the fact that I hadn't known he was going to die. Nobody had. This made the pain strike stronger than the last time I had lost someone. The knot in my stomach tightened into a suffocating squeeze, the desperation for closure shredding my insides to ribbons. It kept getting worse, the feeling intensifying, slowly making me feel like I might implode at any sudden movement.

Then a shoulder blade nudged into mine and for a fraction of a second, it gave me a physical sensation—no more pain than a pinch, but pulling me from my thoughts to focus on my current surroundings.

The guy who had bumped me smiled sheepishly, apologized, and joined a group of people engaging in a solemn conversation.

It was only then that I thought, *Who are these people?*

I had known many of them almost all of my life: classmates, family, friends, important members of the community. But in that moment, they were complete strangers. Who were the people that were crying into tissues and exchanging a damp Kleenex or two? Who were the people that were visiting with Colton's family and mumbling generic things like *deepest sympathies* and *sincerest apologies*? Who were the people engrossed in deep conversations, mentioning Colton's name as if he were a brother to them?

It made my blood boil. It made my fists clench. It made my jaw tighten and triggered something hungry and wild and powerful: anger.

"I can't believe he's gone," said Lydia, Colton's girlfriend, joining me by one of the pews. "Who could have done this to him? It's all over the news . . ."

"I don't know."

She brushed a piece of strawberry blond hair away from her face and dabbed under her eyes. "I—I think I'm going crazy. I keep hearing his voice, hallucinating that he's here. It's like he's trying to communicate to me from beyond the grave."

"Doubt it." I kept my voice monotone.

"Maybe I just need counseling," she whispered while staring off into the distance.

"Maybe."

"You're doing that thing again," Lydia said, craning her neck to look at me with her big green eyes.

My teeth clenched, a tick pulsing in my jaw. "What?"

"That thing where you answer in one-word sentences," she said. "I need someone to talk to, Elliot. *Please.* This is hard for me."

Her words buried their way under my skin, latching on and cutting the single thread of control I had left. I turned to her. My anger had transformed into rage, a wild and hungry fire that burned within me. *This is hard for me.* Had she ever considered that it was hard for me too? Equally, if not more? I was the one who'd found his body. I was the one who'd found him *dead*. Lydia had hardly spoken to me after Colton disappeared, and now she wanted to have a huge heart-to-heart about his passing?

"Hard for *you*? It's a *tragedy* for you. It's *traumatizing* for me. I still have nightmares about finding his body in the lake. You can't complain to me that it's *hard for you*."

Lydia's heartbroken face made me instantly feel guilty for my outburst. The three of us used to hang out all the time. At first, it had felt like I was constantly intruding on their relationship. But Colton and Lydia were not only the best duo, they were also great individually. They were my best friends.

Lydia deserved an apology, a sincere one. I couldn't give her that. Not then. So I stood up, brushed past her, and made my way to the exit. The suffocating sensation of being locked in a room full of grief and melancholy was finally set free as I inhaled the warm spring air.

With shaking hands, I ran my fingers through my hair and looked up at the blinding sun until spots appeared. Then I closed my eyes, and the splotches of light danced behind my eyelids. I tried counting them to distract myself. I wasn't sure how long I had been standing there, but it wasn't nearly long enough, when I was interrupted.

"Elliot?"

Cass. The gravel crunched beneath her boots as she made her way over. "It's almost time for your eulogy."

The noise that came out was a grunt crossed with a sigh.

"It won't take long," she insisted, giving my shoulder a comforting squeeze. "You're doing well."

Once we were back inside, Cass disappeared. The sea of faces blurred as I continued down the strip of carpet that divided the room. We were all there for the same reason, but I had never felt so isolated.

The desire to blame fired up within me again and a series of questions flooded into my mind. What was wrong with the universe? Why did Colton have to die? Why couldn't I have taken the walk a day earlier? I could have spotted him sooner, saved him faster. Maybe I could even have prevented his death.

As soon as I stood up at the lectern, a rush of nausea swept over me and beads of sweat broke out on my forehead. I clutched the sides of the stand, allowing my nails to dig into the wood and my knuckles to turn white. Licking my dry lips, I took in the audience sitting there in front of me, their faces wearing a mixture of expressions as they waited for me to make my speech.

I forced down the dry lump that was forming in my throat and the room swung—or perhaps *I* did—as I reached into my jacket pocket and searched for my index cards. There was a button, something that felt like an old piece of gum, a coin, and *finally* my written speech. But when I pulled it out, it was a single piece of paper and not my small collection of notes. Someone coughed from the back of the room, which caused my panicked self to open the paper and place it on the stand. So that was it: a spontaneous moment. But when I smoothed the folded wrinkles of the page, it showed a messy scrawl that was not my own.

> *If you found this letter, it means that my job was successfully completed: Colton Crest is nothing but a memory, a lifeless body, a shell . . .*

Quickly stuffing the piece of paper back into my pocket, I saw the crowd of people blur until they were distorted shapes. My heart raced, stomach clenched, palms dripped. Someone called my name. Asked if I was okay. I wasn't sure. I couldn't concentrate on the voice.

I took a step away from the podium, trying to control my shallow breaths. The microphone only emphasized my suffocation. With a heaving chest, I tried clearing my throat to apologize, to excuse myself, but the words couldn't find their way out.

I had to get out of there. So, without another breath, I bolted.

†

Twenty minutes later, I was finally alone. My dad had followed me out of the church, calling my name, but I ignored him as I got into my car and drove. I had to get out of there.

When I finally found a quiet road, I pulled over and picked up the letter. My thumb ran over the lined piece of paper, feeling the indents of the writer's script. I was having an internal battle about whether I should read the whole thing or not. A part of me wanted to just throw it out, to forget, because I *knew* that whatever was written would destroy me. But a bigger part of me begged to read it, to soak in every word and let it consume me.

A dollar coin sat near the console, reflecting light from the sun, causing its golden exterior to shine. I leaned over and picked it up, letting it slide between my fingers. One side had an image of the queen; the other held a cluster of kangaroos.

Heads, I throw the paper out. Tails, I read the rest of it.

I balanced the dollar on my thumb and flicked it into the air, watching as it spun back down to my palm. Slapping the coin onto the back of my other hand, I took a deep breath.

"Tails," I muttered, staring at the animals printed on the coin.

I tossed the dollar back to where I had gotten it and unfolded the piece of paper. Although my insides were squeezing, and my conscience was begging me to stop, I didn't.

I read.

If you found this letter, it means that my job was successfully completed: Colton Crest is nothing but a memory, a lifeless body, a shell. I'd like to say that killing him was hard, but really, it was the opposite. It seemed almost too easy. You could have saved him. But you didn't. I'll let that sink in.

One thing you should know is that I knew Colton better than you did. You have to be able to recognize weaknesses and target them. I bet you don't know any of his weaknesses. I mean, he was the golden boy of Hampton High, wasn't he? It was expected that he wouldn't have any evident flaws. But trust me, if you had gotten to know Colton the way I did, you'd know that he had plenty.

I'm the only one who has all the answers. I know where he went when he mysteriously disappeared. I know what happened. I know why. But giving out all that information wouldn't be any fun. Let's play a game. I have written six more letters and hidden them in six different locations. Each letter contains a confession. By the time you read the last letter, you'll know who I am. Scavenger hunt, anyone?

Take your time, though. I have nothing but time.

I'll even be attending his funeral. I'm the person you were least expecting.

Now before I finish up and let you tear yourself apart trying to figure out this mystery, I'll leave you with the first confession: I killed Colton Crest.

A couple of days had passed since the funeral and I thought about taking the letter to the police. So far, there hadn't been any advancements in their investigation—or, if there were, they hadn't released any information. Yet there I was, holding a vital piece of evidence and withholding it from the authorities.

I should hand it in.

But the thought of giving up the letter didn't sit right. Would I find a threat in my car the next morning? Would another letter turn up in my mailbox a week later? The part of me consumed by rage desperately needed an outlet. I needed someone to direct my hatred toward and this was the perfect opportunity.

Striking up your own investigation would do more harm than good.

I groaned internally, tired from the constant battle in my head. The letter explained that there were clues to suggest where the next would be found. But there were no signs of riddles or poems or anything remotely like a puzzle. The more I read it, the less it made any sense.

Perhaps I wasn't cut out to be a detective. I took it as a sign to surrender the letter. If I couldn't figure out anything by the end of the day, I'd hand it over.

"Are you hungry?"

I looked up from the letter to see Cass standing at my door, holding a tray of food. Although I was perfectly capable of making my own lunch, she felt the need to baby me. Her older sister instincts (and her unhealthy urge to keep busy under difficult circumstances) were kicking in, but I would have felt a lot more comfortable if she had just gone back to university and focused on her studies. I enjoyed having her around, but I didn't like the reasons why she was visiting.

She had come home to Newtown to be there for my graduation. It was only meant to be for the weekend. Then she had planned to head back to campus to focus on her summer classes. And then I found Colton dead. The school had canceled the ceremony—it was to be rescheduled in a few weeks—and Cass had stayed ever since, trying to provide moral support and warm meals every day.

I shrugged and she entered, placing the tray on my study desk. "Thanks."

"What are you working on?" she asked, nodding at the piece of paper in front of me. "I thought school was officially over."

I reached out and grabbed it, folding it lazily. "Just doing some reading," I answered, shoving it between a couple of books.

"Your eulogy?" she asked tentatively, as if the remembrance of my breakdown at Colton's funeral would ignite another.

"Yeah."

"You really should apologize to the Crests," Cass said, placing her hands in her pockets and rocking back on her heels. "Walking out in the middle of the service wasn't one of your greatest points."

"I know."

She dropped onto the edge of my bed and crossed her legs, nervously tucking a piece of hair away from her face. Her posture was impeccable: back straight, neck poised. That could only mean one thing. She had news—and nothing particularly good.

"What?" I asked, spinning around in my desk chair to face her. She shifted uncomfortably. "Cass?" I prodded. "What is it?"

My sister looked down at her hands and eventually said, "Mom's coming."

"*What?*"

"She's on the next flight out," she explained.

The divorce had happened before I could remember. Cass said she recalled getting pulled out of preschool, but that was about it. According to my father, their split wasn't based on anything dramatic, like cheating. My parents had simply lost their spark of affection and agreed that it would be best for them to go their separate ways. I thought it was one-sided, though, because Dad hadn't dated since then, while my mother, Valerie, had remarried and had three more kids.

She visited at least twice every year, usually on our birthdays and sometimes during the holidays, but other than that, we hardly saw her. She was like that distant relative that everyone has. The one who you share an awkward relationship with and who gives you presents you loathe because they hardly know you. That was the kind of connection I had with my mother.

"Is she bringing Ryan?" I asked. Ryan was the name of her new husband. Technically I guess he was my stepfather.

"No," Cass answered. "He's staying home to look after the kids."

"Why is she even coming?"

"She thinks it might be a little overwhelming for you here. She wants to take you out for a week-long vacation. Anywhere you like, as a graduation gift."

"I'm fine right here," I insisted, cringing at the thought of my mother being around and the thick, unbearable tension that came with her visits.

I wasn't sure if I could handle her presence, especially at mealtimes. She was an impressive cook, but that didn't compensate nearly enough for the awkward silence that consumed us at the table. There just wasn't anything I felt comfortable talking about with her, and I was sure she felt the same. She was my biological mother, sure, but her family in Queensland were the ones she had grown to love and treasure. She'd left when I was barely two; we were almost strangers now.

We'd always had trouble establishing a connection, and there was only so much of a relationship that could form through phone calls and cards in the mail. Cass occasionally called her, but I suppose she remembered more of her than I did. Either way, Valerie never put in the effort to see me, so I never returned the gesture. And I wasn't about to start now.

Besides, I had six more letters to find.

"Maybe a change of scenery *will* make you feel better," Cass suggested. "I don't know about you, but this town just feels so much darker now, even if it is spring."

"I'm not going anywhere, Cass," I answered firmly before I stood, picked up my keys, and swiped the letter out from between the books.

"Elliot! Where are you going?" she called.

But I was already out the door and down the stairs. My dad was in his office, his old typewriter out and a stack of syrup-drenched pancakes next to him. The door was wide open, showcasing a messy display of unorganized papers and a wall of bookshelves filled with paperbacks with cracked spines. Dad looked up at me, startled eyes growing wide behind his glasses. Before he could say a thing, I'd opened the front door and left.

†

"Check out my new socks," Colton said, lifting his leg out from under the table and pulling his pants up to reveal horrendously stretched-out fabric

with clusters of his girlfriend's face printed on it. Lydia buried her face in her hands and made a small, tortured sound.

"That's disgusting," I said.

Colton lifted his index finger for me to wait before he swiveled around in his seat to hike up his other leg. This time when he pulled his pants up, he revealed a stretched-out sock with clusters of my face on it.

"Now that," I said, "is a work of art. Awful picture of me, though. My head looks ginormous."

"They only had one size," Colton said, grinning. He lowered his leg back down. "Now my favorite people are with me wherever I go."

"We're already with you wherever you go," Lydia pointed out.

"It's true. This relationship is a tricycle now, what with all my third-wheeling all the time," I teased.

In all honesty, I didn't mind. I never felt like I was intruding on anything when we all hung out together. The dynamics were comfortable. Every Friday after school, we would go to The Jukebox diner for burgers and milkshakes. And this afternoon was no exception.

"I was thinking we could name our first child Percy," I said, stealing a few fries from the basket sitting between us.

"Child?" Lydia asked, her eyes wide.

"Our?" Colton scoffed. "I believe the child would be mine and Lydia's."

"Are you saying I wouldn't be the godfather? The cool guy who lets the kid have ice cream for breakfast and puppies for Christmas? All I can say is wow. I'm offended to my core."

"What makes you think I wouldn't spoil my kids with puppies and ice cream?" Colton asked.

"Wait, I'm still on the whole having-a-child bit," Lydia said, rubbing her temples. "I won't be mentally prepared to even consider kids until at least ten years have passed."

"Oh, definitely," Colton said. His pocket watch had found its way out again, and Colton cupped its face in his palm. On any other eighteen-year-old, it would have looked ridiculous. But I couldn't remember a time when

Colton hadn't had it. It was just an extension of himself. His thumb ran over the lid and he smiled, leaning to the side to kiss his girlfriend's cheek.

"Time is ours."

$$\ddagger$$

I found myself at the diner again, this time alone, in the exact same booth we always shared, ordering a large chocolate milkshake and side of fries. Then I took out the letter and read as I ate. The words on the page seemed a lot fresher because of the new scenery. The natural lighting from the window made the ink look clearer, and my grease-powered brain helped me see the writing from a whole new point of view.

Take your time, though. I have nothing but time.

Something about those two sentences ignited a spark within me. Time. Whenever I thought of time, I remembered Colton's pocket watch. The gold exterior, the way he always hooked it on his jeans, and the faint ticking sound whenever he opened it and examined the time as if it were a lot more complicated than it seemed. Maybe the next letter was in his pocket watch. But as I was thinking it through, darkness loomed over my booth; a shadow was cast across the letter. Looking up, I saw Lydia, wearing one of her pastel dresses with the church collar and a silver cross around her neck. She had probably just come back from Saturday mass.

"Mind if I join you?" she asked.

I motioned toward the seat across from me. She sat down and tucked her purse in her lap. Reaching out, I pushed the fries toward her. I knew she wouldn't be able to resist. They were her favorite, after all. As I'd predicted, she reached over and grabbed a couple.

"Thanks," she muttered.

I folded the letter away before Lydia had a chance to ask about it. She focused on the food on the table, first nibbling at the small, rejected fries that were extra crunchy from being in the deep fryer too long, then when they were gone, eating the bigger ones and quelling her appetite. It didn't take long for the entire basket to be empty, revealing an oil-soaked paper towel left at the bottom.

"God, that was so good," she said guiltily, looking at the empty tray. "Hey, want to split a second round? I'm meant to be on a diet, but fries get me every time."

She raised a hand to wave someone to our booth. I couldn't find the words to apologize, even though I knew I should. Although Lydia and I hadn't exactly been the closest during Colton's disappearance, that shouldn't overshadow the friendship we had before he left town.

"Lydia," I said. "How have you been?"

"With the diet?" she asked, laughing uncomfortably. "It sucks. I think I gained more than I lost. Comfort food, you know?"

"No," I answered, with a hint of a smile. "I meant how have you been with . . . everything?"

"I've been . . . *coping*, I suppose is the word." She brushed some imaginary dirt off her dress.

"I'm sorry for the things I said at Colton's funeral. They were uncalled for."

"No, no." Lydia shook her head. "You were right, I'd been selfish even before he died. I could have been a better friend. He left both of us."

"I just feel so guilty—"

"We all have things we're guilty of," she answered, something dark crossing her face, before turning to the employee who arrived at our booth. "One large basket of rosemary-seasoned fries, please. And a diet Coke. Elliot, do you want anything?"

Despite Lydia's suspicious behavior, a weight had been lifted off my shoulders and the knot in my stomach had loosened, making me feel significantly better. However, there was still one more apology to make. Whether it was the comfortable and familiar environment of the diner, clearing the air with Lydia, or the awesome food, I found the stress and frustration I had been feeling all week starting to fade. And it was making me feel extremely determined to resolve all complications.

"No, thanks," I answered. "I should actually get going."

"Oh?"

"I'm going to see the Crests. I still haven't apologized."

"You're full of apologies today, Elliot Parker."

"Maybe, but I hope the world is full of forgiveness today," I answered, picking up my jacket. "I don't mean to take off so abruptly."

"I understand," she said.

"Want to grab a pizza sometime later this week? It's been a while since we just hung out. Just you and me." Lydia flinched as if I'd slapped her. "I didn't mean—it wasn't supposed to come out like that."

It took a moment for her to breathe and look up, but when we made eye contact, she forced a smile. "No, yeah, I know what you mean. It's okay. Pizza sounds good."

But her voice told me she was lying—not just about the pizza, either.

I had walked up the stairs to Colton's front door a million times. But before I could curl my fingers around the old-fashioned brass knocker, I swayed and found myself leaning against one of the towering pillars on the porch. A mixture of fast food and nerves was the perfect combination for uneasiness. My forehead rested against the cool exterior of the pillar and, between blotchy patches of black ink that splashed my vision, I could see areas where the white paint was chipping. I took a few deep breaths. The letter had given me a distraction from what was really happening. It was almost like an escape from the real world.

Almost.

The confession had allowed me to view Colton's death from a completely different perspective—as if I were an outsider looking in. Standing in front of his house was too much of a reality punch. It took me a good couple of minutes to gather myself. The brass handle felt cold and hard as I knocked.

Mrs. Crest was wearing an apron with her shirt sleeves rolled up to her elbows. At first, she frowned at me, struggling to identify who I was. She looked tired as she examined me, her faded blue eyes squinting to remember my features. Eventually, she looked almost relieved as it came to her.

"Elliot," she said. "It's so good to see you."

"He-e-y," I choked out.

Mrs. Crest motioned for me to enter. With tentative steps, I shuffled into the spacious foyer of the house. I followed her to the kitchen, where she picked her knife back up and sliced through a carrot with impeccable ease.

"Mrs. Crest, I came here to apologize for last week. It was a selfish move, just walking out during the service. I wasn't in the right headspace, but I know that isn't an excuse."

Mrs. Crest put the knife down and wiped her hands on her apron before coming around and wrapping her arms around me.

"Sorry." She sniffled as she pulled away, wiping her nose on her sleeve. She gave me a shaky smile and returned to the chopping board, but she didn't pick up the knife. She just stared at the vegetables scattered across its surface.

"Do you know what happened to him?" she whispered. At first, I thought she was talking to herself, repeating a rhetorical question. But when she looked up at me with watery, pleading eyes, I knew it was directed at me.

"No," I answered. "But I'm trying to figure it out."

Mrs. Crest laughed half-heartedly. "Colton always loved solving mysteries. He'd watch those black-and-white crime series and always piece together the story before the main character did."

I forced a small smile, worried that if I contributed to the conversation, it would grow into something ugly. Talking about Colton too much ignited a spark of anger, a raging flame of frustration toward everyone. Directed at Colton for not telling me anything. At his parents for not taking better care of him. At myself for not realizing, for not looking out for him. I counted to ten in my head.

Then out of the blue, Mrs. Crest said, "How would you like to stay for dinner?"

She looked like such a mess I was afraid that something bad might happen if I left her, so I said, "Sure."

She smiled, seeming pleased, and wiped her hands on her apron. "I'll just get some meat from the freezer downstairs. I won't be a moment. Make yourself at home, Elliot."

"Not a problem, Mrs. Crest."

Her departure created the perfect opportunity to sleuth. My mind ran back to the time theory. I had been thinking the next letter could be in his pocket watch. . . . But what about other options? There were only two significant clocks in the Crest residence: one in the dining room and the other in the upstairs corridor. I would have to be quick.

On the far side of the kitchen wall was the cuckoo clock. It had once been painted vibrantly, but the colors had faded, and a layer of dust coated the roof. It was almost as if the little bird hadn't come out of its house in years.

Maybe it hadn't.

I lifted a chair from the breakfast bench, moved it over toward the wall, and climbed up. My fingers shook as I started winding the minute hand, heart hammering in my ears. I was desperate to piece the puzzle together, but I wasn't sure what to expect. Would I find another letter accompanied by something? Like a photograph, or a piece of Colton's clothing, or a tissue with a smear of his blood?

I didn't have time to worry about how long to keep winding because once the hand was pointing at the twelve, the small wooden bird sprang out. The mechanics were a little rough and, luckily, the cuckoo didn't sing its song, but the bird was out now, and I had to work fast. I had only a few seconds to discover whether it held a secret. The first place my eyes were drawn to was its beak. Empty.

Soon the bird made its swift departure and it disappeared inside its little house. I then searched the entire front of the clock, from its worn exterior to the design details. But nothing could be found. Trying to swallow my discouragement, I searched the body of the clock. I ran my fingers down its smooth sides, feeling the even texture of the shaped wood as if the physical contact would give me some sort of clue.

And it did.

My hands ran up against something rough underneath the clock, and sharp edges pierced my skin. There was something engraved into the side near the bottom, so I quickly crouched to see if it was a clue. With my face pressed against the wall, and my eyesight adjusting to the lighting, I saw small scratchy letters, making up a short sentence.

THIS CLOCK HAS THE WRONG TIME.

The little cuckoo clock had stopped working years ago. So technically, the time was always wrong. This made no sense as a message to let people know the clock was broken—why not just take it down? It must be from Colton's killer. It must be a clue.

That meant that Colton's killer was someone who had been invited into his house, but that didn't really rule anyone out. Colton had people over all the time. He had hosted club meetings, social events, and school projects at his house over the years. Practically half of our school had been there.

Or maybe someone else had found a letter in their jacket pocket. Maybe I wasn't the only one who had it. Did other people know about the letters, the confessions? Were they trying to lead me to the next clue or pull me further away from it?

A million questions ran through my mind, but before I could comprehend any of them, I heard footsteps on the stairs. I jumped from the chair and rushed it back into place. I didn't know what to do with my hands, where to stand, where to keep my gaze. I shoved my hands into my pockets and prayed my face didn't betray my guilt, because my body sure screamed *awkward*.

Mrs. Crest appeared, carrying a tray of meat in her hands. She looked at me with a slight frown. Her eyes scanned around the room like she was looking for something. Maybe even looking to see if something was *missing*. A wave of panic washed over me as I wondered if I had left anything out of place, anything that gave away that I had been searching her house.

But just like that, the frown was replaced by a warm smile. "How does roast sound for dinner?"

"Sounds great," I managed to choke out.

Mrs. Crest set the meat down on the kitchen counter. "Would you mind giving me a hand?"

"Sure," I said, feeling my heart rate slowly decrease back to normal.

In actuality, I wanted to escape—to go back into solitude and analyze the information I had found. But I couldn't just leave. Mrs. Crest looked like she was starting to suspect something. Walking out now would only make it worse.

"What would you like me to do?" I asked.

"Could you please start off by grabbing a few ingredients for me?" she asked as she washed her hands. "There's some rosemary and rock salt in the spice rack. I need to season the roast."

I did as I was told and walked over to the spice jars, which were lined up alphabetically. Skimming my fingers over the labels on their lids, I picked up the two required containers. But before I turned back around, something caught my eye.

Thyme.

†

Dinner was torture—almost as awkward as dinner with my own mother. However, the fact that I wasn't blood-related to the Crest family was at least an excuse for the uncomfortable atmosphere.

I cut a slice of roast and lifted it to my mouth. The room was so quiet that I could hear my own jaw moving, each chew clearly defined. Mrs. Crest looked across the table at the empty chair where Colton used to sit. Mr. Crest looked grimly at his meal, staring at the vegetables as if they were enemies.

"This is some great cooking, Mrs. Crest," I said, in an attempt to break the ice.

"Oh, thank you, dear," she answered.

The oppressive silence made me shift nervously in my seat. I tried not to draw my attention back to the small bottle of thyme. There was something in there. I was sure of it.

This clock has the wrong time.

Because the letter wasn't talking about a clock *or* time. It was talking about *thyme.*

Although I had gotten one step closer, it also seemed like I had taken three steps back. Did anyone else have a letter? Who wrote the clue on the side of the clock? Was it Colton's killer? What kind of clue would fit in a bottle of herbs?

"Elliot, are you finished?" Mrs. Crest was standing, her untouched dinner in her hand.

I looked down at my half-eaten meal and handed it over. "Thank you."

She took it from my hands and walked to the kitchen, her movements robotic and stiff, her body functioning without the help of her conscious mind. Then she stared out the window above the sink, gloved hands diving into the water, soap suds forming in clusters around her arms. She seemed so lost in her own thoughts that I was worried she might not be aware of what she was washing.

As Mr. Crest stared at his newspaper, I went into the kitchen to help. Not only would I probably save Mrs. Crest from cutting herself on a steak knife while she was washing it, but I would also get an opportunity to grab the thyme and test my theory. When I reached her, I gently placed my hand on her shoulder.

"I'll wash," I said.

She smiled and stepped to the side, grabbing a towel to dry the wet dishes. Sinking my hands into the warm water, I removed a plate and scrubbed it off with a sponge. From the window, I could see the old tire swing in the Crests' backyard with its worn rope, dotted with black-and-white bird droppings. As kids, it had been our pirate ship, our space shuttle, our time machine.

As I thought, my hand dipped back into the water, fingers brushing against something sharp. My natural instincts kicked back in, and I withdrew from the blade of the knife. It was merely a scratch, and it didn't bleed, but it was enough to make me remember my purpose there. One, to make sure no one got injured and two, to get that bottle of thyme.

"Mrs. Crest?" I began.

She looked at me, slightly dazed. She seemed so distracted that I felt like I could have manipulated her into saying anything I wanted. It was the perfect time to ask.

"Would you happen to have any thyme?" I asked.

Mrs. Crest leaned back and looked toward the cuckoo clock. She frowned and said, "That old clock hasn't worked in a long time. I should really just put it away. But I'm guessing it's just past seven, dear. Do you need to leave?"

I took the last few things from the water, being careful that I didn't get nicked, and said, "No, *thyme*. The herb."

"Oh," she said, smiling as I carefully handed her the wet utensils. "Yes, there should be some in the rack over there. Is Cass planning to cook something?"

She seemed to be alert now, and slightly suspicious. I guess I couldn't blame her. When you lived with your single father who didn't know how to cook anything that wasn't already half-prepared, and your only sibling was away at university most of the time, perhaps asking for ingredients was pretty uncharacteristic. But thankfully Mrs. Crest mentioned Cass, which was the perfect lie.

"Yeah, she wants to make dinner one night this week," I said.

"That's lovely."

"My mother's coming to town," I added, to make it sound more believable.

"Oh, that's nice," she cooed, completely eating up the lie. I hoped she wouldn't invite herself over. "When she comes, tell her I said hi and that we should catch up for coffee sometime."

"Will do, Mrs. Crest."

Once I'd pulled the plug and watched the water swirl down the drain, I wiped my hands on my jeans and crossed the kitchen. I pulled the jar out, checked twice that it was the right one, and curled my fingers around it.

"Elliot?"

I turned and swallowed. Was there a hole in my story? A fault in my lie? Mrs. Crest just smiled and pointed behind me.

"Whatever Cass is cooking, tell her it will taste better with a hint of rosemary," she said, motioning for me to take the other herb too.

I let out a silent sigh of relief.

†

Back home, the house was quiet. Cass had disappeared into her old room and Dad was still by his typewriter. Even though he was a writer by profession, and a teacher at one point by extension, he'd never moved to a computer—preferred to clack away at the keys, typewriter ribbon increasingly hard to find these days. The steady sounds of his fingers hitting the keys filled the silent space. With the thyme in my pocket, I was on my way upstairs when I heard him call.

"Elliot, is that you?"

"Yeah," I said, backtracking to his office and peering in.

"Do you want something to eat? Cass made—"

"I already ate," I said, cutting him off.

He nodded and shifted uncomfortably in his seat. There were minimal things that made him feel awkward: discussions about physical development . . . and my mom. So as I entered the cramped, messy space and sat down in the chair opposite him, I knew what to expect before he opened his mouth.

"Your mother's coming to town," he said.

"I know. Cass told me."

"Did she tell you about the holiday she wants to take you on?"

"Yeah."

"How do you feel about that?"

"The father-slash-therapist approach? Really, Dad? Is the head tip really necessary?" I asked.

He stopped looking at me like I was an injured puppy. "Really, Elliot."

"She's stubborn," I said.

"I know." He laughed half-heartedly. "Just like your sister."

We sat there in silence for a while. Then I said, "I can deal with it."

He smiled weakly. "I know, kiddo. I'm just saying you don't have to."

That was what I liked about my dad. He didn't bombard me with comfort or try to suffocate me with affection. But he wasn't completely careless about the situation either. I could rely on him to have my back no matter what.

"Thanks, Dad," I answered. He nodded briefly.

After taking the stairs two at a time, I expected to see my sister in her room, but she wasn't there. Thankful to be alone and not interrogated for leaving so quickly earlier, I went to my room, closed the door, and took out the bottle of thyme. It was smaller than my palm and two fingers wide. I wasn't sure what could be in there, if there was anything at all. A small scroll of paper? A rolled-up piece of a photograph?

Only one way to find out.

Unscrewing the cap, I sat the bottle on my desk, took a deep breath, and gently tapped my finger against the exterior, watching as it tumbled to its side. Fragments of thyme scattered everywhere, showering my desk with dots of green. I dusted my fingers through the thyme, hopelessly searching for something—*anything*—that would push me forward.

Nothing.

Defeat came flooding in in waves, and my shoulders sagged. I rolled the empty glass bottle around the table, flicking it from side to side, trying to figure out my next game plan. As I racked my brain for ideas, I picked up the bottle and looked at it up close.

The brand was generic, nothing special, but it did have a recommendation on how to season a roast. I skimmed over the rest of the writing: the company's name, a "keep out of reach of children" warning, weirdly long directions . . .

> *Directions of use: Through the cluster of gum trees to the south of Hampton High, in the cemetery, is a tree marked with X where further secrets lie.*

This was it—this was the next clue! As I gently twirled the bottle between my fingers, my mind tried to process the next part of the scavenger hunt. I skimmed over the rest of the words and my heart sped up as I read the instructions.

> *Take a shovel and a mask and prepare to dig deep, but alas, be very careful because beneath the dead do sleep. You'll find a box of treasure, marked with teenaged blood. Inside is not nostalgia, but a clue caked in mud.*

‡

The local cemetery happened to be placed on the plot of land directly next to Hampton High. There was enough distance between them to ensure that anyone visiting a gravesite would have privacy and not be disturbed by the hundreds of obnoxiously loud high school kids next door, but they were still close enough that you could see the dotting of headstones from the school's soccer field.

When Colton and I had started high school, we were just scabby twelve-year-old boys who had a fascination with anything dangerous and spooky. The cluster of gum trees between the far side of the south field and the graveyard were just beyond school grounds and sometimes we'd head over there at lunch. In a way, it was mischievous and fueled our rebellious pre-teen phase, sneaking away from the supervision of the teachers on duty.

One time while we were out there, we found a tree marked with an *X*. We decided then and there that the place would be like our secret hideout. Well, *secret* was a stretch. A bunch of other students snuck out there too. But at the time, we convinced ourselves that we were the real discoverers, that the spot was ours alone.

We hid a bunch of "treasures" near the tree, things like a bullet we had found hidden among the dry sticks and leaves and a double-sided coin we'd won from a bet with our classmates. Everything was collected in a little cloth bag smeared with both of our blood. After watching so many dumb movies about blood oaths, we'd thought we were the coolest, picking the scabs on our knees and using our thumbs to mark our blood on the bag. The thrill of the place lasted only a year. The summer after grade seven, we had already forgotten all about it.

I had forgotten all about it. Until now.

In my haste to stand up, I knocked my knee against my desk. The pain was sharp and made me grit my teeth, but it didn't stop me from moving. I limped my way over to my door and hobbled down the stairs. I knew exactly where the place was. I knew exactly what I'd be digging for.

"Going for a drive," I called out to my dad as I swung the front door open.

"Again?" He sounded startled. "Don't stay out too long!"

I ducked around back to grab a shovel from our shed, just in case, and threw it in the trunk. As I got in the car and turned the engine on, I checked the dashboard clock. It was after eight. The sun was starting to disappear beyond the horizon, the town veiled in a warm summer's glow. During any other circumstance, it would have been a great opportunity for a scenic drive. However, sneaking back to the school I had just graduated from to retrieve something buried in the cemetery nearby didn't exactly give off the vibes of a cinematic coming-of-age experience.

For all I knew, I could be digging my own grave. Regardless, there was no way in hell I was going to hand over the letter to the cops now. I was way too deep into the mystery, and it was only the beginning.

There had to be a reason I was being contacted, and I was going to figure out why.

Colton's killer was mine.

If it was anything like the horror movies, I'd find one of Colton's bones or his bloody heart under the tree marked *X*. I reached over and flicked the radio on, turning to a random station and letting the sound of an old guitar melody fill the small space. When I reached a stoplight, I rolled the window down, thankful for the crisp air that filled my lungs. I rubbed my forehead, feeling the slick sweat that had formed against my hairline, and closed my eyes. For a brief, delicious second, everything was quiet. Everything was tranquil.

I would have fallen asleep if it weren't for the furious beeping of the angry driver behind me. I quickly stepped on the pedal, catching the light before it turned yellow.

Focus. One hundred percent concentration was needed if I was going to follow the clues to Colton's killer. This was a guy who had made a personalized label for some damn herbs. A killer with that much creativity was dangerous territory. I had to be prepared for the unexpected.

The Hampton High grounds were fenced in and protected by security cameras, but there was one sliver of gate that anyone could get through. If you timed it right, you could slip past the camera as it rotated to another area. Students would occasionally sneak through there to skip a class or two.

Parking a good distance away, I went the rest of the way on foot. Although I had only graduated a few weeks ago, my high school felt both familiar and foreign. I had been a student, but with a diploma under my belt, I was suddenly a stranger trespassing on the grounds. I made my way toward the back of the field.

I was terrified. Absolutely terrified. I knew what I would be digging for, but what if I found something else?

I had not been to that marked tree since early on in high school, but it was still there, seemingly untouched. Standing in front of it, I took a deep breath.

Three steps to the left. Five steps forward. One more to the left.

I dropped to my knees and ran my hands over the dirt, dried leaves and sticks scratching my palms. The area looked untouched, like no one else had been here. Once the space was cleared, I started digging. The clue had said to use a shovel, but Colton and I never buried things very deep—something the killer must have known. It didn't take long for me to find the top of the bag. With just a few more handfuls of dirt, I managed to pull it out of the ground.

With shaking, dirty fingers, I loosened the drawstring and emptied the contents onto the ground.

The things Colton and I had collected were still in there: the old bullet, the double-sided coin, a few Pokémon cards . . . but there was something new. A silver key.

Attached to it was a yellow plastic key ring stamped with the number 183. When I flipped it over, there was a simple logo advertising a business named Scott's Storage Solutions. I had never heard of it before. I wiped my hands across my jeans and pulled my phone from my back pocket to do a search.

The place was located slightly out of town and provided secure storage units of all different sizes. There were big garage-style rooms for extra clutter and more locker-sized compartments for things like seasonal gear or backpackers looking to stash any extra belongings. Rentals were charged monthly.

I wanted to check it out, but it was starting to get late. Having a sleep-deprived, on-edge teenager covered in dirt arrive at a storage facility to frantically search a locker might raise some red flags. Besides, the administration office wouldn't be open until nine the next morning, and I needed answers as to whose name the locker was under.

I clutched the key in my hand. By this point, it was dark and I was relying purely on the flashlight on my phone to navigate my way around. Now that I had located another clue, I was filled with pent-up energy. Staying still wasn't an appealing option. My hands needed something to do; my legs needed somewhere to go. So I decided to stop by the gym.

There was a bottle of water in the back of my car, so when I returned, I used it to wash as much dirt off my hands and pants as I could. I couldn't get everything off my jeans, but it was a start. Besides, I had some spare clothes in my gym locker.

I hopped into my car and headed out. My fingers drummed against the steering wheel and I kept swiveling in my seat, unable to find a comfortable position.

The gym lights glowed up ahead, its glass exterior showcasing late workout classes, with people doing their cool-down stretches and the last rounds of their weights sessions. I pulled into a parking space and headed inside. The familiar stench of dry sweat mingling with deodorant greeted me in the empty locker room. As I passed the rows of lockers, reserved for gym members only, I stopped in front of Colton's.

"Hey," a deep, booming voice called.

A bulky man with a shaved head stood in the doorway with his arms crossed. A tattooed flock of intricately designed ravens soared out from his shirt collar and disappeared behind his left ear. His stance was strong, as if he was daring me to step forward.

Rick.

He was the owner of the gym, and he was always there; it was his second home. In fact, sometimes people joked that it had become his *only* home after his divorce.

When he scanned my face, his expression softened. "You're," he said, then coughed. "You were a friend of Colton's, right?"

"I was," I said. "How did you know?"

"I've seen you both here together. Haven't seen *you* in a while, though."

"Exams have slowed me down a bit," I explained.

"Didn't seem to be the case for Colton."

I opened my mouth to say something, but I faltered. When Colton had come back, he'd seemed busy. Busier than usual. He would ditch plans last minute, always seemed to be going somewhere after school, was already out in the mornings when I dropped by. He would have plans for the weekends and couldn't jump online to play video games. Was he here during many of those times?

"The bloke was a tank," Rick said, shaking his head like he couldn't believe it. "He was definitely focused on fitness or . . ." He trailed off.

"Or?"

There was a scar on Rick's left eyebrow. When he frowned, it dipped like a lightning bolt about to strike. He looked at me with piercing eyes and pursed his lips before saying, "Or surviving."

I hoped Rick didn't hear my breath catch in my throat.

"Not a bad idea if you ask me. Everyone thinks danger lurks in the city. There are crimes happening every hour. But it's smaller towns people should be terrified about. We all know each other's business, are all somehow a part of each other's lives. We become a tightly knit community, which is why it's so horrific when we realize that one of us has the capability to kill."

It was extremely unsettling. Not going to lie, it scared me shitless. Home wasn't safe. "Thought sure makes you want to sleep with one eye open," I said.

"Tell me about it," Rick said, rubbing his hand across his shaved head. "I haven't been able to rest easy in weeks. I can't imagine what it's been like for you."

"Shit, honestly." I didn't try to force a smile or a laugh. I wasn't going to sugarcoat it. This whole thing was a bloody mess.

Rick's gaze dropped to my jeans, and he stared at the smudged dirt stains on my knees. I swallowed, and my hands reached down in a poor attempt to conceal the mud.

"A word of advice—don't go digging for answers."

"Excuse me?" My voice came out clear and loud, definitive, stronger than I felt. I straightened, trying to appear far more confident than I actually was. An icy shiver ran down my spine and I gritted my teeth to avoid shaking.

"I just think this is a case for the police. Sticking your nose into places it doesn't belong only means trouble. I'm guessing that's one of the reasons your friend encountered such an unlucky fate."

"That's a bit of a bold assumption, suggesting I'm doing any of that," I said. Rick was a big man; he could beat me in a fight without even trying. Was it incredibly courageous or outright foolish of me to be so ballsy?

He stepped forward, keeping his eyes on mine. My gaze was locked on his like a magnet. There was no escape. "Perhaps. Or maybe it's just a really lucky guess." He took a step back. "Be careful."

"Is that a threat?" I dared to ask. It was getting harder to sound sure of myself. My voice came out small, not reaching its potential volume as the words wavered dangerously.

"No. It's a recommendation."

"What's that supposed to mean?"

Rick turned to walk away. But not before he called over his shoulder, "There's still a killer out there, and I don't think Colton was the first or the last person to be murdered."

The following morning, I drove out to Scott's Storage Solutions. I had barely gotten any sleep the previous night. Following my creepy encounter with Rick, I'd gotten into my gym clothes and worked out. But it felt like I was being watched the whole time. I couldn't stop thinking about what Rick had said, and even when I was safely back home again, I was awake for a majority of the night, staring up at my ceiling, my brain a commotion of incoherent thoughts.

But once eight o'clock rolled around, I was out of bed and in my car. It was a short fifteen-minute drive to my destination. I took the back route to avoid the morning traffic. Administration wouldn't be there until nine, but people were able to go in and retrieve their things anytime. Clutching the key in my hand, I stepped out of my car and walked toward the place.

It seemed the area was divided into three sections. Garage-sized storage rooms were to the right and they were all painted green. To the left were some medium-sized red lockers, big enough to fit a person.

And straight ahead was the administration building and a wall of small yellow lockers. They were similar to the size you could find at theme parks or bus stations, with enough room to fit a backpack and other smaller personal belongings.

I looked at the key in my hand. Since the keychain attached to it was yellow, I started heading toward the small lockers. I wasn't sure what I would find, but eliminating the larger lockers made me feel ten times lighter. It eliminated an abundance of possibilities.

But I had also watched enough horror movies to know that the scariest of items had the potential to come in small packages. Maybe I'd find a gun loaded with bullets. Maybe I'd find a finger from another victim. Maybe I'd find a small, dead animal rotting inside.

My insides were twisting, turning, flipping, and squeezing. It felt like I was on a ride, dropping down, except it was never-ending. Once I had found the locker, I tightened my grip on the key. The jagged teeth sunk into my skin. With a deep breath, I inserted it into the lock.

It turned. I pulled on the locker door. And opened it to reveal two things: a manual to assemble a piece of furniture. And a letter.

I didn't wait to get into my car to read it.

Unappetizing thing, time. Or should I say "thyme." In all honesty, I didn't think you'd find the second letter. I congratulate you for your efforts. Perhaps the world isn't as stupid as I thought.

Now I suppose you want more information, considering you dedicated your time—and thyme—to working this out. Where should I begin then? The night he disappeared? Very well. Something you should know is that Colton talked to me before he left town. His face was unshaven, dark circles under his eyes, skin pale. He was a complete and utter mess.

Which was why he wanted to get out.

He didn't have to tell me why, because I knew. It was May

17. You see, if you had known Colton the way I did, you would have known that every year, on the same day, he disappeared. It took me a while to realize this. The first time was chance, the second was a coincidence, but the third was a pattern. And this continued for more years to come. If you were to look at his school records, you'd see a significant amount of absences that happened to fall on the exact same day.

It wasn't always like this. And I bet you're wondering why.

Let's backtrack eight years, to May 17. Colton was ten and had a fascination with trains. But that's too generic. Anyone could have noticed that. He was just a child, after all. But eight years ago, on May 17, Colton made an early transition from childhood to adulthood.

Which brings us to the second confession: Colton watched a man die.

Harrison Noel, aged twenty-three, crossed the street. He had a phone pressed to his ear and a coffee in his spare hand. He was on his way back to university for an afternoon class, talking to his pregnant girlfriend. The roads were clear, no vehicles in sight, the safest opportunity to cross. Then suddenly, a car turned the corner. It happened quickly. A man, a car, a collision, a death.

Colton himself didn't have to tell me the details of the event. A good old newspaper does the trick. It only took his confession of the incident to allow me to dig up my own information. This traumatized little child watched Harrison Noel die. Although there was nothing anyone could have done to save the man, Colton felt responsible, his guilt eating him alive.

And this year was the year he decided he needed closure, so he left town and went in search of answers. He wanted to find Harrison Noel's murderer. Yes, that's right. Murderer. It

seemed like a perfectly unquestionable case of manslaughter,
right? Wrong. Although the incident seemed accidental, in
reality, it was a carefully structured plan.

Colton seemed to be flirting with death.

So I followed him.

And you're about to retrace his steps too—and find out
what he did during his disappearance.

I felt breathless after reading the letter. Colton and I had been friends almost all our lives. Surely something serious like watching a man die would have come up in conversation. At first, I felt betrayed. The letter mocked me, teased me into thinking that perhaps I didn't know my best friend at all. That maybe he didn't trust me.

But witnessing a murder must have brought indescribable suffering, especially at only ten years old. We all deal with things in different ways. Maybe he wasn't ready to talk about it. I had to ignore the taunting tone of the letter. Maybe the guy Colton left town to find killed him too.

I hastily folded the letter back up, placed it in my pocket, and then reached for the instruction manual. It was a double-sided piece of paper, creased where it had once been folded into a tight package. It appeared to be for a very generic-looking table—no fancy compartments or drawers or shelves or attachments. It didn't seem to be anything special.

Until I turned it around.

One particular instruction line had bits and pieces highlighted with a green marker: *Assemble L and M using screws 7, 8, and 9.*

LM789

I repeated the sequence in my head over and over again until reciting it became second nature. When I looked up, I noticed a woman in her mid-thirties walking over to the administration building, coffee in one hand and a bagel in the other. She struggled as she pulled out a collection of keys and unlocked the door. However, it appeared she wasn't exactly having a stroke of luck because she dropped the keys the minute she pulled them from the keyhole.

"Oh drat," she whispered to herself as she realized she didn't have any free hands to pick up her keys.

This was my opportunity to get on the woman's good side. I rushed over as she placed her breakfast in her mouth and tried to shuffle the rest of her things around. Before she could struggle any further, I stepped in, picked up her keys, and pulled the door open for her. She looked over at me with kind brown eyes and shuffled her way inside. After she had dropped her things onto the desk and placed the bagel onto a tissue, she turned to me.

"You are an angel sent from heaven," she said, lifting her arms up to the sky. "Whose dumb idea was it to put a door you have to pull there anyway? Every morning I struggle just to get to my job. All right, love, my name is Dianne. How can I help you today?"

I held up my key. "I have one of your rental lockers and unfortunately, I've lost all of my paperwork. I was just wondering if you could tell me how much time I have left to use it so that I don't incur any late fees?"

"Of course I can, dear." Her voice was as sweet as honey. Dianne's fingers danced across her keyboard for a brief second before she reached her hand out to take my key.

There were a couple more seconds of typing and clicking. She squinted at the screen from behind her glasses. "Let's see. So you rented out locker number 183 last month on the fifth and paid for it to be used for six months. Your key won't be due until the fifth of May next year."

That meant the killer was here back in November. This was all terrifyingly well thought-out. I guessed they had rented the locker out for six months to ensure it would give me enough time to find it. But what if it had taken me longer? Would the killer have come back here to extend the time?

"Is there anything else, dear?" Dianne asked.

"Yes, actually." I snapped out of my thoughts. "This is going to sound ridiculous, but my family actually rented out this locker, and we can't seem to remember which name it was under. Would you be able to let me know so that the same person can return the key?"

"Not a problem! If you give me one second, I can double-check for you. This happens all the time with my husband and me." She clicked away with her mouse. I had to stop myself from shifting from foot to foot, putting my impatience on display, as I didn't want to betray the fact that I was desperate for more information. And a name would certainly get me closer to solving this mystery.

"Ah, here it is. So, the locker was rented out by a Mr. Elliot Benjamin Parker."

My blood ran cold. The killer had used my name. Not only that, but it was my full name. My heart felt like someone had ripped it out from my chest and wrung it like a wet sponge. My other details were probably in the paperwork too, like a phone number or an address or an email.

The killer knew all my personal information.

"That's me!" My voice was alarmingly high-pitched. "It's just strange because I was going through my bank statements and the bill hasn't come through on there."

"That sounds about right. Our records say that you paid up-front in cash. There is a two-hundred-dollar bond, however, so once you return the key to us in May, you should be able to get it back. That is, if the locker hasn't incurred any damages. Are you okay, sweetheart? You look a bit pale."

Dianne's voice sounded distant. My arms suddenly felt icy, so I reached out and rubbed my hands over the goosebumps on my skin.

I choked out a thank-you as I retrieved the key and stumbled my way out. Outside, the warm, summer air dried the sweat collecting on my forehead.

I made my way back toward my car and kept checking my mirrors as I drove. There was a prickling feeling at the back of my neck, as if someone were following me. As if someone were watching my every move.

†

"Elliot?"

Cass's voice woke me from a sleep that I didn't even remember falling into. My neck felt stiff from not moving the entire time, and the rest of my body ached in protest as I forced myself to turn over and look at her. My sister frowned and gave me a disapproving shake of her head.

"It's four in the afternoon," she whispered, stepping into my room and closing the door behind her.

I was still half asleep, so I mumbled, "Leave me alone. I was studying."

"You've graduated," Cass said, sounding irritated. "You've been acting really weird lately, but can you please just have a shower, change your clothes, and pretend to be normal for two hours? I have afternoon tea made. And later, I need to talk to you."

I squinted up at her. "I'm beat. I think I'll sleep through the rest of the afternoon. Call me when dinner is ready."

Cass protested, but I had already curled back up in my bed, the familiar comfort of my mattress welcoming me back to unconsciousness. Just before I could fall fully back asleep, the covers were torn expertly away, and the pillow was snatched from under my head. I groaned, burying my face into the mattress.

"I don't think you heard me correctly," Cass said, her voice rising an octave. "Have a shower, get dressed, and be down for afternoon tea in ten minutes."

"My best friend died," I answered, wanting to disappear. "Let me sleep."

"I know he did. I was there. I'm involved too," she said. "Mom's here."

I flipped onto my back and sighed in defeat. It was only to be expected that my mother would turn up at the doorstep at the worst possible moment.

After a cold and invigorating shower, I changed and headed downstairs. The tension created by my dysfunctional family hit me the minute I got there. I could hear my father constantly clearing his throat, which was something he did when he was nervous. Cass had been cooking, the thing *she* did when she was put in an awkward situation—she believed food fixed everything.

As soon as I walked into the kitchen and stared at the stranger across the table, everyone leaped into their sweet and sympathetic roles. Cass ushered me to sit and passed me a plate of freshly baked scones. Dad poured me a glass of water, and my mother forced a smile. I hated the fact that my family tried to manipulate themselves into thinking we had perfectly normal relationships. They didn't have to pretend that we were okay because I knew that we weren't, and I had accepted our current arrangement. I was eighteen, not eight.

"Hi," I said, taking my seat.

Valerie kept the plastic smile on her face and slid a package across the table. "I got you a little something."

"You shouldn't have."

"Come on, honey," she said, trying to sound affectionate, but the term of endearment sounded like a strangled cry. "I never get to see you."

More like you never want to see us.

"Okay," I answered, not wanting an argument. I tore into the paper wrapping.

It was a book, a thin hardback without the dust jacket. Across the black surface of the front cover, in a silver scrawl, was *A Madman's Message: A book by Gregory Everett.*

"It's just a little something I read in my first year of university. It was such an eye-opener for me, and since you've graduated, I thought it would inspire you." Valerie's smile was broad and unwavering.

"Thanks," I said, trying my best to sound enthusiastic.

Dad, who had been silently sitting at the counter, coughed. "It's a really interesting read, Elliot. I studied it for one of my literature classes, and it's a well-crafted piece of writing."

My mother glanced over at my dad, her lips twitching. They held eye contact for the briefest of seconds before she turned away. The relationship between my parents was like a rubber band—flexible but breakable. They were civil, but they could never quite look each other in the eye. Cass tried to ignore it, scrubbing at dishes that were already clean.

"Anyway," Valerie broke the silence with her overly cheerful tone, "I want to take you for a holiday. Wherever you want, as a graduation present."

"I want to stay here."

Valerie cast a disapproving glare at my father, who shrugged and sipped his coffee. "It'll be good for you, honey. Get some fresh air, a change of scenery, somewhere where it's not so . . ."

"Morbid?" I suggested.

"Delicate," she corrected.

"Like I said, I want to stay here." I picked up a scone, smothered it in strawberry jam and fresh clotted cream, and took a bite, giving myself an excuse to stop talking, even it was only for a few seconds.

She sighed, uncomfortable with arguing with the son she hardly knew. "How about I give you a few days to think about it? I told Ryan I'd be away for a couple of weeks regardless."

The mention of her husband didn't seem to affect my dad much.

He stared expressionlessly at his crossword puzzle and poured himself another mug of coffee. When I returned my gaze to my mother, she looked at me nervously.

"If I get something done, maybe I'll consider it."

It had been four days since Valerie had come to town and she was constantly attempting to organize awkward lunch dates. If she hadn't been so persistent, perhaps I would have agreed to a few. But the fact that she was forcibly trying to squeeze sixteen years of lost time between us into such a short period made her effort seem like a burden rather than a priority. So, with my mother constantly trying to photoshop herself back into my life, it was hard to get into the right headspace to solve the mystery behind Colton's death, which is why I decided to go to the public library.

With the letters in my pockets, I made my way to an isolated desk and started studying. I placed the letters in chronological order and did a quick comparison. The handwriting was the same: messy and scrawled in black pen, the kind with so much ink that if you press hard enough, it bleeds through the pages. The script showed no evident signs of the gender of the writer and was always written on the same blue-lined paper, straight out of a notebook.

Looking at the letters side-by-side, the only thing I could tell was that it was written by the same person, and that person was right-handed. Judging by the estimated quality of the pen and its ability to smudge when wet, there was no way a left-handed person could have written it without the words turning into a black blur. That eliminated one subset of people, but since Colton was the only one I knew who was left-handed, all I had figured out was that he hadn't been the one writing the letters.

The second one mentioned a traumatic event in Colton's life—something I hadn't known about until I had read the letter. It must have been a significant episode if it was included in the confessions. I wasn't sure how legitimate the story was, though. It could have been a work of fiction, introduced to throw me off. There was only one way to find out: research. And what better way to start than taking advantage of the library's resources?

Newtown's history was in the non-fiction section, a single aisle filled with old books of newspaper snippets, photographs, and transcripts of radio recordings. They were organized by year, so I hovered my fingers over the dusty spines until I found the right one. As I flipped through the pages, I scanned the black-and-white images, the small print, the bold titles. Then there it was: the story of Harrison Noel.

> On Thursday, May 17, a local university student was killed by a speeding vehicle. Harrison Noel, aged 23, was crossing the road at 1:00 in the afternoon when the driver accelerated into the pedestrian, resulting in an instantaneous death. It was later discovered by police that Tristan Yanks, the 25-year-old driver, and the victim, Harrison Noel, had gotten into an argument three hours prior to the incident.

There was nothing else about the argument—either the reporters didn't know, or they weren't allowed to publish that kind of information. The only other important tidbit was that the incident wasn't unintentional, and Tristan Yanks had been sentenced to eight years in jail. But as I looked at the dates, I realized he would have been released a few months ago.

Around the time Colton disappeared.

The book in my hands was helpful, but it was not available to check out. So I pulled my phone out, took a quick photo of the page, and pushed it back into its spot. That small newspaper article was a delightful piece of information, but it wasn't nearly enough to satisfy my curiosity. I picked up the book beside it and skimmed through more articles.

Tristan Yanks. What kind of person was he? What kind of family did he have? What sort of childhood did he experience? What drove him to kill?

I went through many books, skimmed hundreds of articles, but I couldn't find anything else. The media had no idea who Tristan Yanks was before he became a murderer. Even a quick google search on my phone didn't show many relevant results. No social media accounts were found, no blog posts about him, no other online articles.

I sighed and put the books back, but as I was doing so, something on one of their spines caught my attention: NF301. I quickly reached for the aged instructions manual in my back pocket and found the same type of code. Two letters accompanied by a three-digit number. It was a library book.

With the paper in my hands, I went searching. At first, it was difficult to navigate. The library was organized in a strategic manner, but because my heart was pounding and my head was filled with a dozen thoughts, I found myself weaving through the aisles like a lost boy looking for his mother in the supermarket.

With some effort and a little wandering around, I finally found the right shelf. I ran my fingers over the spines, looking for the correct combination of letters and numbers, until I found the book. It was called *Room Service*, a book about hotel management written by L. A. Maddison. I wasn't sure if the paperback was a clue itself, but I took note of the title and the author, then sat on the ground and searched through it.

As soon as I opened the front cover, out fell a business card. I picked it up and ran my fingers over the smooth surface. It had a logo and scribbled down at the bottom in the familiar script of the letter-writer was *Bentley Motel, room 102.*

The name sounded familiar, but a quick google search confirmed that it was a motel located in the next town over, Ridgemount.

That was where I was headed to next.

‡

I wasn't sure what to expect when I got there, even though I'd had a forty-five-minute drive to think about it. Still, I parked in front of the row of small cabins, each big enough to hold a bedroom, a kitchen, and a bathroom. I wondered if this was the killer's hideout. Perhaps I had been led there to get murdered too.

I gripped my hands more tightly around the steering wheel, not letting go until my knuckles turned white. If it wasn't the killer's hideout, then what? Was I going to open the door to see something beyond my nightmares? Was it just a trap? Was it simply an empty motel room?

As I sat and stressed, a woman rounded the corner. She was wearing a dark purple coat that swung around her ankles. The collar was up, obscuring most of her features, and she kept her hair down and around her face to prevent any more recognition. If she was trying to draw attention away from herself, it wasn't working.

She paused in front of room 102. Sunk down in my seat so she wouldn't see me, I watched as she pulled out a key card and inserted it through the slot until the door clicked open and she disappeared inside. What now? All I knew was that the motel room was currently being occupied by a woman in a purple coat. I wished Colton was there. He was extremely good at reading people, always discovering the smaller details just by watching how they acted.

†

"God, Mrs. Prestwidge has been sad recently. Sadder than usual," I said.

The air that Wednesday morning was crisp, and we had just finished doing our annual cross country run at school. We sat on the grass with our water bottles, waiting for the rest of our classmates to finish the course.

"She's going through a rough time with her husband," Colton said, lying down.

"What? You said that with weird confidence. I didn't know you were her confidant."

"I've exchanged about eight words with her," Colton said, laughing. "She took off her wedding ring a couple of weeks ago. Her eyes have been puffy, which suggests she's been crying a lot."

"Jesus. And you got all that just because she's not wearing her ring anymore?"

"It's the small details—like wedding rings that signify marriages, or religious symbols to indicate spirituality. You can tell a lot from how a person acts. When people feel awkward, they start shifting, they can't make eye contact, they might bite their lip."

Colton listed all the ways people behave when they're feeling certain ways—or when they're trying to hide when they're feeling certain ways. I listened half-heartedly, my mind already distracted by the ham and cheese sandwich I was going to have for lunch.

Colton was still rambling when Lydia finished her run and she approached us, looking a bit wobbly. "Oh my God," she wheezed, placing her hands on her hips and bending over to catch her breath. "Running more than eight hundred meters shouldn't be a thing."

"Sounds like the run went well," Colton teased. He was still on his

back, arm across his eyes to shield away the light. With his other hand, he grabbed his water bottle from the ground next to him and lifted it up for Lydia to take.

She eagerly took it and drank deeply.

"Anyway, what was I saying?"

"You were talking about reading people," I said. "And I was about to tell you that you watch way too many mystery shows."

Colton laughed. "Sounds about right."

Lydia dropped down next to us and wiped her hand across her sweaty forehead. Strands of strawberry blond hair stuck to her flushed skin.

"I think reading people is an interesting skill," she said, breathing heavily between her words. Colton lifted his arm and looked at her, a soft expression on his face. He reached out and gently placed a hand on her knee.

"It can be very beneficial."

✝

Very beneficial indeed. If only I had listened more carefully that morning.

Colton was a detective at heart, an observer of detail. Within the short ten seconds the woman had appeared, he probably would have noted her approximate shoe size or a significant bulge in the pocket of her jacket. He'd know exactly what to do. Hell, he'd probably march right up, pound on the door, and start an interrogation.

But Colton was dead, and I didn't have his help. I had only ideas of what his methods would have been if he were in my current situation. With that in mind, I grabbed my keys and got out of the car. There was determination in my steps that felt oddly empowering as I walked toward the motel room. Before I could second-guess myself, I knocked.

I wasn't sure what to expect, and honestly, I wasn't prepared. What if the woman was committing a crime inside? What if she was the killer and was expecting my arrival, holding a gun pointed at my forehead? What if there was another body? I wasn't sure what was behind the door.

But I sure as hell wasn't expecting to come face-to-face with my sister.

"Elliot," she said, eyes wide.

"*Cass?*"

"How did you know where to find me?"

I wasn't trying to.

"This is *your* motel room?" I answered instead. "Why do you *have* a motel room? Don't you have your own apartment on campus?"

Cass frowned, nibbling at her bottom lip. "How about I fix you something to drink?"

She was avoiding my questions, and even though I didn't answer her, she cut through the room and walked toward the far side, where the kitchen area was. Silently, she put the kettle on and took out a small tin of hot chocolate. I followed her in, in a daze.

"How much do you know?" she asked with her back to me, as she found a couple of mugs. When I didn't instantly reply, she added, "Colton must have explained."

Honestly, at that point, I couldn't have cared less why Cass was there. What I wanted to know was how my best friend knew about my older sister's motel room. It was disturbing and confusing, and I needed to sit down.

"He didn't," I answered, a sour taste forming in my mouth.

"Oh." Cass stilled for a moment. Then she asked, "Would you like something to eat? I think I have a packet of assorted cookies in the cupboard."

"No."

"Would you prefer something savory?"

"No."

"How about—"

"*Cass!*" I yelled.

She stopped moving and finally turned, the only sound between us coming from the hissing kettle. She focused her gaze straight ahead, looking through me rather than at me, as if ignoring the problem would eventually cause it to disappear. Then, slowly, her eyes met mine.

"I know what you're thinking."

"Enlighten me."

"You think I killed him."

Surprisingly, the thought hadn't even crossed my mind. She hardly knew Colton, and they were civil, always engaging in polite conversations about school and the weather, but their relationship barely skimmed the surface. However, after the letters and the clues had led me to the motel room, it made me reevaluate Cass and Colton's relationship.

"I want to know what you're doing here," I answered.

Cass turned her back on me and continued making our drinks, then arranged a couple of cookies on a plate. She was silent as she placed them on the table, and although she was quiet, I didn't push any further. By the look on her face, I could tell she was going to say something. If I pressured her, she might change her mind and bite her tongue.

She pulled one of the chairs out and sat down, wrapping her hands around her mug. "Earlier this year, there was a fire in my building."

I took the seat across from her and listened.

"It was some stupid incident with a hair straightener left plugged in by one of the girls on our floor." Cass shook her head, remembering. "It got out of hand, and eventually, we all had to evacuate the building. It was late and we were tired, so my roommates and I decided to chip in for one of these cabins for a couple of nights, just until we got the all-clear that we could go back."

I was still waiting for her to mention Colton. So far, he didn't fit into the story.

"We were granted permission to go back after one night, so the girls went ahead in the morning while I stayed to make sure nothing was left behind. We were just going to give the key back early, but the night before I left, Colton turned up. I don't know how he found me, but he was there." Her voice had dropped to just a whisper, as if the memory was so dark and haunting that saying it out loud would unleash something terrible. "He looked like shit, Elliot. Absolute shit. And he was freaking the hell out, saying he needed to get away. I—I didn't know what to do."

"What *did* you do?" I asked softly, tearing my gaze away from the contents of my mug.

She took a shaky breath and closed her eyes. "He said he needed somewhere to stay for the night and asked if he could have my room. Since I was leaving anyway and the room was already paid for, I agreed and gave him the key. I let the staff know and they didn't seem fazed. I guess business isn't that great. I—I didn't think it was that much of a problem. I thought it was just a fight with his parents, a way to escape from them or something. That was the first night of his disappearance."

There was a twisting sensation in my stomach—a feeling I knew too well, but it still caught me off guard every single time. It was sharp and painful, something that couldn't be soothed with medication or warm beverages. It needed answers and time and understanding to conquer its battle.

"I didn't think much of it at first. I went back to my apartment, attended my classes. But I guess I was starting to get worried, because at the end of the week, I went back to check on him, only to find that he was gone. Management said the room was occupied only for a couple of nights. He had packed his things and left. After a few more weeks, I came back into town, and it was only then that I realized he had been missing for three weeks and counting."

"You saw him the night he disappeared . . ."

"I know," she whispered pathetically, taking her hands away from her mug and burying her face in her palms.

"Have you told the police?"

Cass shook her head. "No," she muttered between her fingers. "I can't."

"Why?"

She looked up at me. "I just can't. You have to understand. I just can't."

"So when and why did you come back?"

"I've had the room for only a couple of nights. And I'm here for the same reason you're here. I'm looking for answers."

"I never said why *I* was here."

Cass hesitated, lips parted slightly, momentarily stunned. Then she regained her composure and wrapped her hands back around her mug, gazing into the swirling liquid. She stared down at her beverage for a few more moments before standing up and walking over to one of the twin beds on the opposite end of the room. She reached down and picked up a handbag, fishing through her belongings before pulling out a notepad.

"Only one person occupied the room after he left it. It was during September," she said, flipping through her notes. "But other than that, this place has been deserted, so I booked the room again for another couple weeks. I was thinking there might have been a clue that Colton had left somewhere. It would have been so discreet that the cleaners didn't notice it. He was always so . . . meticulous."

"Meticulous?"

"I read, all right? Don't look so surprised."

"I'm not surprised about your vocabulary. I'm surprised about the context in which you used it. Like you knew him," I answered, watching as she stiffened, eyes staring at the notepad but not reading the words.

"It's a simple observation. You don't have to be friends with someone to know their intelligence."

"You have to know them to some degree."

Cass shrugged as if to say *end of discussion*. "So other than your accusation about my choice of words, what do you think about what I've discovered?"

"Honestly, I'm thinking a million things at once," I answered.

"Tell me one."

"First of all, I'm wondering how the hell you even got that information."

"Easy," she answered. "This motel is old school. The owners still haven't passed on management to the newer generations, so bookings are still hand recorded. The room where they keep the keys is in the back office, so while they retrieved mine, I quickly flicked through the listings. I didn't have enough time to go through the details, but I didn't think anything else was really that relevant."

"When did you become such a good sleuth?"

I wasn't sure if it was a compliment, but Cass took it as one. She smiled as if I had said something else entirely. "Learned from the best."

"Colton was the best."

Cass stilled.

"I should go," I said, standing up so quickly that I knocked the table and caused my mug to jitter. Some of the liquid inside splashed out. My sister jumped up and tried to find some tissues. As I was turning to leave, I noticed two key cards on the counter. If she had two, did that mean someone else was sharing the room with her? I didn't have time to think about it. Instead, I picked one up and clutched it in my hand.

When Cass turned around, she looked like she wanted to say something, but she pursed her lips and forced a smile.

"I guess I'll see you later then."

"I guess," I replied.

Then I was out the door and headed toward my car. I sat there, switched on the radio, and tried to let the music and advertisements distract me from my hurricane of thoughts. The key card sat heavy in my hands, weighed down by the fact that I had just stolen it, and I didn't have much time before Cass figured out it was missing. I closed my eyes, and the sound engulfed the small space.

"It's Friday, so head on down to Mozzarella Sticks for our two-for-one pizza deal. You don't want to miss it!"

I hadn't realized how hungry I was under the advertisement came up. A fresh pepperoni pizza sounded good, maybe with some garlic bread. My mind reeled back to seeing Lydia on the weekend at The Jukebox, and I realized how much I missed her.

Picking up my phone, I dialed her number. It took three rings before she picked up. A faint *hello* came from the other line, but it was mostly drowned out by the sound of rattling and a string of incoherent muttering. She had dropped her phone. It was something so simple, a common mistake, a moment of clumsiness, but it made me smile. She hadn't been herself since Colton died, and that simple slip-up gave me a glimpse of the old Lydia, the one I had found to be missing.

"Sorry about that," she said, once she retrieved the device.

The realization that I missed my friend had me momentarily stunned, so when I heard her voice, I didn't answer right away.

"Hello?" she repeated. Then a little louder, "*Hello?*"

I cleared my throat and straightened in my seat. "Uh, hi."

There was a pause. "Elliot?"

"Yeah, hi."

"Hi."

"I was wondering if you'd considered my offer." Lydia stayed silent on the other line, so I added, "The one I made at The Jukebox? About pizza?"

"Oh," she answered slowly. "Yeah, I remember that."

"Would you like to go down to Mozzarella Sticks? I'll pay."

I waited for her response.

Finally she answered, sounding much brighter. I could hear her smiling. "You know what? That actually sounds great."

"I'll be there in an hour."

†

Mozzarella Sticks was one of two pizza places in town, and even though it was slightly more expensive, it was by far tastier—especially the garlic bread, which was always complimentary if you got two pizzas. We ordered two large pepperonis, and while we were waiting for them to come out of the oven, our garlic bread and drinks arrived.

"I almost forgot what carbs taste like," Lydia said, tearing off a piece of garlic bread and devouring it.

I laughed as she reached for a second piece. "Slow down, there."

"Sorry." She grinned sheepishly before dropping the last bit of bread into her mouth. "This diet is literally killing me. I was so hungry yesterday, I was tempted to eat my sweater."

"Appetizing."

"Compared to lettuce? It's the equivalent of chocolate." Lydia picked up her glass of iced tea and took a sip.

"You look a lot better," I said. It was true; she had more color in her cheeks, a purpose in her step, a glimmer of light in her eyes.

"I've been keeping busy." She placed her glass down and licked her lips. "You don't look so bad yourself."

I laughed humorlessly. "I've been keeping occupied too."

As soon as the pizza arrived, Lydia picked up a slice, the cheese stringy as she pulled it away. For a few moments, we ate in silence, the only conversations coming from those around us—flirtatious comments, laughter, a shout.

It was good to be with someone. Being with Lydia gave me a sense of normalcy, and I was grateful for that after spending the last few days trapped inside the letters and what they meant.

"I heard your mom was in town."

The feeling slowly disappeared. I picked up my drink and avoided eye contact, taking a large gulp to quench my dry throat before I said, "She is."

Lydia looked at me for a long moment, calculating what was appropriate to say next. Eventually, I decided to save her from the discomfort.

"She wants to take me on a trip."

"A trip?"

"Anywhere I want."

She reached up to her neck to fiddle with the silver cross resting above her collar. "As a graduation present?"

"She likes to call it that. But really, if Colton didn't die, I'm pretty sure she wouldn't have offered."

Lydia seemed much more composed now when I mentioned his name. She didn't flinch or tear up or purse her lips.

"Well," she said, finally looking at me, "if you need to get away, you're always welcome at my house."

"Thank you."

We both finished eating our pizza and drank our beverages until all that was left was ice. The conversation remained light, talking mostly about what we wanted to do now that we had graduated; plans had changed since the start of the year because Colton had been a significant factor in our futures. Originally, we had organized a gap year where we would travel as a trio, but he was the glue that had kept us together, and now that he was gone, both Lydia and I had been considering different paths for the upcoming year.

Lydia decided she wanted to go to the city and start university. The new scenery, fresh faces, and distraction would do her some good. As for me, I planned to defer for a year and piece together the mystery that Colton had left behind. But I didn't tell her that. Instead, I made up an excuse about working and saving up some money.

"Did you hear about the camping trip?" Lydia asked, once our plates were cleared and we were splitting a chocolate lava cake to kill more time. She was picking at it, and even though I was already full, I didn't want to leave just yet.

"No. What camping trip?"

"Graduating class is organizing a camping trip. Kind of like one last gathering to remember Colton," she said, placing her spoon down.

"When is it?"

"Date hasn't been announced yet, but I'll let you know. It'll be a good night."

With my stomach filled and my head a lot clearer, I was inspired to continue with my investigation. When I answered Lydia, my response applied to more than just the camping trip.

"Yeah," I said. "It will be."

I couldn't stop thinking about the room key, so at one in the morning, I found myself sneaking out my window. Although I was past the age where my father would be concerned about what I was doing at God knows what hour, the rush of adrenaline was still prominent.

But the thrill of doing something no one else knew about was surprisingly addictive. Plus, I didn't want Cass to know. It was her motel room I was going to, after all. After quite a painful and awkward shimmy down the trunk of the tree, I headed for my car. There was something about driving at night that was both inspiring and frightening. It was like a dark, silent world waiting for you to discover the secrets of the universe, but with danger lurking within shadows and around sharp corners.

With the window open for the cold night air so I could stay awake, my mind drifted to the letter, which had led me to the motel business card, which had led me to the motel room. It had to have more significance than what I was seeing. Besides, I needed to be as alert as possible once I got there.

After the long night drive, I finally made it to the Bentley Motel. I decided not to park in the actual parking lot. Instead, I pulled up across the street next to a fish 'n' chips shop and killed the ignition. Reaching over, I opened the glove box and started sifting through all the junk. The contents consisted mostly of old assignments, chocolate wrappers, and a couple of stray pens. But among the mix, I managed to find the key card.

I got out of my car and started to walk. Other than the wailing of a child a few doors down and a man having a late-night cigarette, the place was deserted. It was dimly lit, enough for me to navigate my way around, but dark enough for something to emerge from the shadows and drag me off into the abyss. It gave me the creeps. I shoved my hands into my pockets and speed-walked until I was standing in front of room 102.

When I inserted the key and opened the door, a part of me expected someone to jump out from the darkness with a machete and threaten to decapitate me. But when the door swung open and the lights flickered on, the room was exactly how I had left it. My mug was even still on the coffee table as if Cass had been in a rush to leave and had forgotten to put it in the sink.

I walked over to my barely touched beverage and looked into it. The liquid looked murky. I turned away. I wasn't sure what I was looking for, but I was determined to find something. The bedside table drawers were filled with nothing interesting, the usual essentials provided: a local phone book, a Bible.

The kitchen area—if you would even call it that—was just as dissatisfying. The counter was filled with some mismatched crockery and cutlery, the fridge empty other than some milk, and the cupboards held some everyday things, like bread and some travel-sized spreads of butter and honey.

But although nothing was sticking out, I didn't get discouraged. Instead, I started looking in various other places, such as the bathroom cabinet, which harbored nothing other than a couple of rogue Band-Aids and some dust.

I checked the shower curtain for any hidden messages or hidden compartments within the folds. I looked at the toilet, only to find some immature graffiti. I searched within the pages of the Bible and the phone book, looking for anything to fall out as I flipped through, anything highlighted or circled, but they were both pretty long and eventually, after two paper cuts, I decided to stop.

The furniture got my attention next. I looked over it, under it, skimming through every surface, pulling it apart and seeking something more. But it was hopeless.

I felt hopeless.

Sinking against the wall between the two twin beds, I sat on the floor, defeated. Was I wasting my time with a mystery I couldn't solve? Was following the clues just a death wish? Was the letter I found going to say that I was the next victim?

I groaned, scrubbing a hand down my face. It probably didn't help that Cass had already had the chance to search the place thoroughly. Maybe she had found something. Either way, it wasn't looking like I would be finding any clues.

As I was about to push myself up, my fingers scraped against the baseboard. The surface was rough, as if someone had hacked at it with a knife. I turned and examined it.

CT + LR

NOT ALL BLADES ARE FOR CUTTING.

Then an object beneath the bed caught my eye. It was such a simple place to hide something, so clichéd that it had completely slipped my mind to look there. Reaching over, I pulled it out.

A journal. It was small, pocket-sized and leather-bound, big enough to write down lists and ideas in. *This is it*, I thought, my heart racing. Then I opened it.

At first, I was in such a hurry to absorb every single detail each page held that I couldn't comprehend what was written. But after I forced myself to control my breathing, I started from the first page.

The Curious Case of Colton Crest

I recognized the handwriting.

Cass.

I quickly flipped through the other pages, not sure what I was looking for. There was all sorts of information about him since he had disappeared. She had bullet-pointed some key events from the night Colton had knocked on her door; she had recounted the day that she found me at the lake, when I had discovered his body; she had written details about the funeral.

But why? I didn't have time to think because I heard a voice right outside the door.

"I couldn't sleep. Yeah, I'm here right now."

It was my sister. I'd be toast if she caught me.

Since I was crouched down, she probably hadn't seen my shadow, but there was absolutely nothing I could do about the light. The artificial yellow glow stuck out like a sore thumb, and it was too late to fix that. I quickly dropped onto my back and started shuffling under the bed, being sure to place the journal where I had found it—under the bed, but with a corner poking out.

The door clicked open and I curled up, making myself as small as possible. Cass walked in and silently shut the door behind her.

"There's just so much on my mind. My conscience is eating me alive." She sounded tired. "I hate lying to him. I can't keep something this big from him, he's my brother. . . . No, you're right. . . . But *they* came to *me* . . ."

I stayed completely still.

"When should I tell him? I'm getting way too involved in this. I mean, he was his best friend. He deserves to know." Silence as she waited for the person on the other end of the phone. "I suppose. But the minute things start to get out of hand, I'm telling him everything."

I watched as her shoes came closer. My breathing stopped.

"Hey, did you come by this afternoon? . . . Oh, nothing. I must have forgotten to switch the light off, that's all. I'm just getting my journal, then I'll be out of here."

I watched as she lowered into a crouching position, her fingers reaching under the bed to find the book. I was holding my breath, my heart pounding so hard that it was the only thing I could hear. I was sweating uncontrollably, and I was pretty sure I was turning a flattering shade of purple from all the panic.

Hurry.

Cass finally got hold of the journal and stood up.

Thank God.

"Hey, one more thing . . . did I happen to give you the spare key when I saw you this afternoon?" Her feet walked around the bed. "I can't find it." She paused. "No? Shit. I hope I didn't lose it."

There was another brief second of silence. Since it was so quiet, I could hear murmuring on the other end of the phone.

"No, Elliot wouldn't . . . shit. He wouldn't find anything here, you know that. We searched the place top to bottom. There's nothing." She sighed. "Yeah, I'm leaving now. I'll see you later, okay?"

Cass hung up, but she didn't instantly leave. Instead, she walked around the motel room, tidying up, emptying the contents of my mug down the sink and quickly washing it. Then she finally started heading for the door, switching the light off before exiting.

I stayed in my hiding spot until the headlights of her car shone through the curtains, thinking about the conversation and the journal, a million and one questions and theories running through my head: Who was the person on the other end of the line? What secrets were they keeping? Could they be involved in the murder of Colton?

My brain was scrambled and my head ached. Eventually I scooted out from under the bed but stayed lying on the carpet, looking up at the ceiling as I tried to get my breathing back to normal.

Then I remembered the graffiti.

Not all blades are for cutting.

I knew where the next letter was. The ceiling fan.

I dragged a chair over and started inspecting the blades. One by one, I looked, eyes examining, fingers searching until I reached the last one. There it was. Neatly folded and taped onto the fan. The letter.

It was hard not to rip the whole thing off at once. After slowly peeling the paper from the blade, I blindly pulled the chair back to its place, not bothering with putting it in its original position, and headed out the door in the dark.

Pocketing the letter, I stepped out into the cool evening air. Everyone had returned to their motel rooms by now, so there were no late-night smokers feeding their desperate cravings for one last cigarette, and all was quiet, no wailing cries of babies to be heard. Not even the dogs were awake.

But even though I couldn't see anyone, that didn't mean I wasn't being watched. So, with my hands in my pockets, I walked back to my car, fast enough that I could break into a run if necessary, but slow enough to not draw attention to myself.

As I crossed the street and reached my car, I pulled out my keys. Inside, I locked the doors and, with shaking fingers, opened the letter.

> *Interesting. Very interesting.*
>
> *If you found this letter, then you have successfully followed my clues again. And although I shouldn't flatter myself, they weren't very easy ones to decipher. Because if they were simple, that would be an insult to me. Killers have crafty*

minds, after all. The ones who get away with it anyway.

But once you realize that your job was completed almost effortlessly, then you have to have a little fun, right? Get back into the race, the hunt, the arena. That's what fuels people like me: the adrenaline, the thrill, the rush. Mind games happen to be my specialty, and if I could do it to Colton, I can do it to anyone.

Interesting. Very interesting. Isn't it?

Want to know something else that's very interesting? Then stick around, because I have another confession: Colton Crest may have been a hero in high school, but anywhere other than your shitty little town, he was known as Daniel Heckerman. That was how he got so much information when he disappeared.

But to pull off a secret identity, you have to learn how to lie.

Lies: beautiful and intricate sentences. You can convince anyone of anything if you know how to lie. And Colton Crest sure knew how. Just ask Alexandra Yanks.

✝

Alexandra Yanks? Yanks, as in a relative of Tristan? The person who supposedly murdered Harrison Noel? Why would Colton seek her out? For how long did he have a second identity?

Who was the real Colton Crest, and did I really know him?

Apparently not.

Stapled to the back of the letter was an extra piece of paper. It was significantly smaller and considerably thinner, with jagged edges on one side. Flipping it around and detaching it, I realized it was a Woolworths supermarket receipt. The one on Gersbach Road in Ridgemount to be exact.

DAIRY FARMER'S MILK
HOMEBRAND PLAIN FLOUR
ELBERT'S FREE RANGE EGGS
STARLEM BUTTER
HOMEBRAND CASTOR SUGAR

Scrawled on the back, in the same script as the letter-writer's, was a short message.

> Hope you've got a sweet tooth. The Ridgemount farmers
> market, every Saturday from eleven a.m. to one p.m.

†

I woke up to the sound of my phone ringing. When I lifted my sleepy head from the steering wheel, the harsh light of the morning sun made me blink. I hadn't moved since parking my car at the side of the road in Ridgemount, just a few blocks away from the motel. My muscles were stiff, and they screamed in protest as I stretched.

"Hello?"

There was silence for a split second. "Hi, sorry, did I wake you up?"

I rubbed my left eye with the heel of my hand, trying to bite back a yawn. "No, no, it's fine. What's up, Lydia?"

"I didn't mean to bother you," she said quickly. "It's just that your mom has been calling my house non-stop. She's been trying to reach you all morning. Where are you?"

"Do you know if she called the house phone?" I asked instead, hoping she wouldn't notice me sidestepping her question.

"She didn't say. I'm guessing she did."

I hoped my dad was still sleeping and that Cass hadn't gone back to the house.

"I should probably call her," I said, sighing.

"You ignored my question, you know."

"I did? I'm sorry, I was out for a drive before dawn this morning. I'm actually still out." Colton wasn't the only one who knew how to lie.

"That doesn't explain why you sound like you just woke up," she answered.

"I'm tired, Lyd."

She stayed quiet.

"I'll call you later, okay?" I said.

"Okay," was her only response before hanging up.

Lydia was definitely suspicious, and she never hung up before saying goodbye, which meant she was pissed too. And everyone knows it's a guy's dream for two women to be mad at him. Opening my door, I stepped out and stretched on the path. Then I dialed my mom's number, trying to clear the drama with at least one of them.

She must have been waiting for my call because she answered halfway into the second ring.

"Elliot, I've been trying to reach you for the past two hours."

Her tone was a mixture of hurt, confusion, and anger, but because she knew she couldn't pull the Mom card on me, she didn't know how to approach the situation. I hadn't spoken to her properly since the day she'd arrived in town. There had been a couple of awkward phone calls that consisted mostly of generic conversation topics and a lot of uncomfortable silence, but that was all.

"I was out," I said.

She sighed softly and took a deep breath, and when she spoke again, her voice was back to overly perky. "I was hoping we could get lunch together."

"I've already told you—"

"I know you've said you're busy, but I want to spend some time with you. I haven't been in town for years, so I want to visit some of your favorite places with you."

"Right." I couldn't help the bitterness in my tone. "I have some errands to run, but how about I pick you up at your hotel around one?"

"That sounds wonderful. I can't wait to see you."

"Where are you staying again?"

"The Bentley."

I grew still, eyes flicking across the road. "In Ridgemount?" My tone was slightly accusatory, so I covered it with confusion. "Why are you staying there?"

"It's a bit of a drive, I know." She sounded sheepish. "But I also know Cass goes to university there. I thought she'd show me around campus, but she's been busy. I better let you go. The faster you finish your errands, the earlier we can have lunch."

We said our final, awkward goodbyes, and I quickly jumped back into my car. I switched my phone to silent and tossed it into the passenger side. If my mom saw me, she'd start questioning me, and I didn't need the stress of that, so I turned the ignition on and pulled away from the curb.

‡

I didn't drive very far before my stomach started grumbling. Up ahead was a turnoff sign for a supermarket, so that's where I decided to go. A pack of chocolate chip cookies was on sale and so was the chocolate milk. They weren't the most nutritious of choices, but I craved the sugar. After I weaved my way around the bakery and toward the refrigerators, I circled back to the cashier.

I dropped my things on the conveyor belt and fished through my pockets for my money. The cashier greeted me with a monotone voice. I watched as his tattooed hands scanned the barcodes on my breakfast items and lazily dropped them into a plastic bag.

"Five dollars seventy. Cash or card?"

"Cash," I answered, handing over the money.

He dropped the coins into the register, ripped my receipt and dropped it into my bag. With a voice that matched the boredom in his expression, he handed me my stuff and said a lame, "Later, dude."

"Hey," I said, stepping back. "How long have you worked here?"

There wasn't a lineup, but my eyes skimmed toward the end of the belt just in case someone had stepped up. The guy behind the counter gave me a strange look—the most emotion he had expressed all morning—and cracked his knuckles. For a moment, I thought he was going to punch me, but he dropped his hands to his sides and raised an eyebrow.

"Couple of years. Why?"

"My friend used to be a regular in this town."

"Yeah? What's his name?"

"Colton Crest."

His face didn't register any recognition. But then I remembered what the letter had said: *Colton Crest may have been a hero in high school, but anywhere other than your shitty little town, he was known as Daniel Heckerman.*

"Daniel Heckerman?" I tried instead.

"Oh, Daniel!" He smiled, nodding. "Great bloke."

"Did he come here often?" I repeated.

"*Heaps,*" he answered. "He was the life of the town. Everyone loved him. When's he coming back anyway? It's been ages."

"He's dead."

"No."

I didn't know what else to say. "He is."

"You're fucking with me, man."

"I'm really not."

"Holy shit."

We stayed in silence for a few more moments. I waited for him to register the news, but he just kept shaking his head in disbelief.

"I wonder if Alex knows. Man, she's going to be so bummed."

"Alex? As in, Alexandra Yanks?"

His eyebrows rose. "You know her?"

"Heard of her," I lied.

"She's famous for her cakes. If you're in town for the day, you should go down to the farmers market at the park across from the library. She sells the best cheesecake. Seriously, they're so fucking good. But man, I can't believe Daniel's dead."

I was trying to keep up with the conversation just as much as the cashier guy was. How did Alexandra Yanks know Colton?

"I wonder how Tristan is going to take the news."

"Tristan Yanks?"

"Are you sure you were Daniel's friend? Because you sure as hell don't seem to know much about him."

Tell me about it.

"I thought I knew him," I answered honestly. I didn't know why I was telling him this, but if I wanted him to open up, then I figured I had to as well. "But I guess his life was more complicated than it seemed. I guess that's how he got murdered."

"Murdered," he repeated, not meeting my gaze. When he did, he pursed his lips, then raked a hand through his hair before he said, "Shit. I thought he OD'd. Christ. Okay, look, I'll tell you what I know about him. But you didn't hear it from me, okay? I don't want to be the next one dead."

"Hey, Tina!" cash register guy hollered across the supermarket. His co-employee turned around and looked at him in confusion. "I'm going for a break."

Tina frowned and looked like she was going to say something, but he was already making his way toward the back of the store, ignoring customers who brushed past us with questions. He led me through the staff room, his tattooed fingers running across the lockers, and out the back door.

"Before we get down to business, I'm Bones."

"Bones," I repeated.

"Bones," he said again, showing me the knuckles on his right hand. His name was written across them in an antique font.

"Elliot."

Bones just nodded and reached into his back pocket to pull out a cigarette. He placed the stick between his lips and grabbed his lighter, but before he lit it, he said, "Do you mind?"

I'm pretty sure he would have gone ahead and done it anyway, so I just said, "Go for it."

"Sweet." He flicked the lighter and lit up the cigarette, inhaling deeply before exhaling a cloud of smoke. "I actually met Daniel here a couple of years ago. He was with Alex, Tristan's mom."

One, he visited prior to this year? Two, he was with Tristan's mom?

It was like doing a dot-to-dot puzzle with the numbers missing. All I had was a confusing combination of randomly drawn lines and missing information; I was struggling to see the bigger picture.

"At first, I was, like, 'Wow, this is dope. I didn't know Tristan had a little brother,'" he continued. When he saw my confused expression, he said, "They were practically identical. Honestly, everyone we met thought the two were related."

"Are they?"

"What? No. They aren't *really* related," Bones said, giving me a sideways glance before exhaling another breath of smoke. I hadn't realized I had spoken out loud. "They were like blood brothers. Best of mates."

I wasn't sure if it was the secondhand smoke or all the information getting thrown at me, but I was struggling to breathe.

"Daniel used to come to the local markets a lot, and that's how he met Alex. Eventually he started working for her. They were out one morning picking up things for Alex's bakery stall. That's how we met. Dude, you look like you're about to puke," Bones said, giving me a worried glance.

I refrained from dry heaving and managed to choke out, "I'm fine."

He took one last long drag from his cigarette and dropped it to the floor, using the heel of his boot to crush it. Then he started waving around, trying to get rid of the stench, but it had already consumed me, and it was all I could smell.

"You want some water?"

Pull yourself together, man.

I straightened and shook my head. "No, I'm all right."

"When Tristan was released, Alex instantly introduced him to Daniel. They pretty much did everything together after that. Tristan treated Daniel like his kid brother. Anyway, this one night, Tristan invited me and some other guys over for a beer. I had just gotten off my shift, and I bought a six-pack for the occasion. But when I got there, his garage doors were open and they were yelling. Tristan was fucking pissed. You should have seen him. I hadn't seen him that mad since . . . well, since he killed Harrison Noel."

"So what did you do?" I asked, worried about what was going to follow.

"I got the fuck away from there, man. Trust me, you would have done the same." He ran a hand through his thick hair. "Look, Tristan's my mate and everything, but it's no secret that he has anger management issues. I'm not saying he killed Daniel, but . . . just be careful around him."

†

Checking the dashboard, I took note of the time. It was just past twelve. I hadn't realized I had spent so long at the supermarket talking to Bones. Even though I almost suffocated from the secondhand smoke, the information I had gotten was well worth it.

That meant that the farmers market—which Bones had said was located at the park across from the library—would be open for another forty-five minutes. I wasn't particularly sure what I was planning to say to Alexandra. How I was going to approach her, how I was meant to direct my questions.

What *did* I want to know?

How was I supposed to say it?

Yeah, hi, you don't know me, but my best friend got murdered and now his killer is taking me on this wild scavenger hunt, taunting me to piece the mystery together, and what do you know, you're supposed to be a clue. Would you mind sharing what you know?

Yeah, because that would go down smoothly.

The farmers market seemed to be a pretty big thing within the small community of Ridgemount. Cars surrounded the block and pedestrians crossed the dangerously busy streets. Spring had been pretty cold the past few weeks, but the weather was warm that day. The sky stretched out in an endless blue hue, the wind no longer harsh and biting. It was as if the heavens had granted the small town a pleasant atmosphere so they could enjoy the festivities.

Since it was so busy, I had to park a couple of blocks down and walk the rest of the way up to the park. It was overwhelmingly packed; people explored the grounds in clusters, deep in conversation and laughter. I wish I could have enjoyed the scenery. Stalls were set up across the grass, from beaded jewelry to fried foods, secondhand books to fresh produce. Guitarists sat on stools, microphones pressed to their lips as they entertained crowds of people, and artists sat barefoot on the grass, sketching portraits of various visitors.

It would have been a pretty good day, but I was there for a purpose: I needed to see Alexandra Yanks.

Once I dropped my donation into the volunteer's hand, I stepped deeper into the park. Because the space was predominantly a field, the sky wasn't obstructed by twisting branches. Instead, the only trees circled the perimeter of the park, giving shade to tired families with kids hyped up on sugar.

Bones had mentioned Alex's killer cheesecake, plus the letter referenced a sweet tooth, so I beelined to the dessert stalls. There were three helmed by women, all with equally delicious-looking pastries. They all looked around the same age too, and I wasn't sure which one to start with, so I lingered around some customers, pretending to decide which cake to select.

"Alexandra!"

The woman in the far left stall turned, searching the crowd until her eyes focused on someone behind me. They exchanged snippets of conversation, keeping it brisk and light until Alexandra handed her friend a cupcake with whipped cream topping and they said their goodbyes.

"I'd recommend a slice of caramel pie."

I turned and found myself in front of a girl. A beautiful one. Hair spilled down her tanned shoulders in waves of gold, her brown eyes shining under the spring sun. I watched, mesmerized, as she carried a tray of cupcakes behind Alexandra's stall.

"Don't tell me you're not a caramel fan."

"Is that a crime?"

"No, but it's definitely an insult," she answered. "Try a slice of the caramel pie and I promise you'll change your mind."

"It's that good, huh?"

"Amazing. I'll even let you in on a little secret. If you flatter her enough"—she nodded toward Alexandra—"she'll serve your pie with vanilla bean ice cream."

Alexandra, who had just finished with a customer, walked over to me, wiping her hands on her apron, and gestured toward the sugary goods.

"What would you like, honey?"

"Um," I said, "a slice of caramel pie? Please."

Her smile showcased a gap between her two front teeth as she sliced into the moist crust. Once she'd cut a good-sized triangular segment, she placed it on a plastic plate and handed it over.

It took me a moment to realize that she was waiting for me to do a taste test. Hesitantly, I stabbed my fork into the corner of the pie. The crust crumbled and gave way to a smooth texture inside. As soon as my tongue hit the sweet pastry, I was a goner. Caramel was not something I was a fan of, and even though the beautiful girl with the blond hair had warned me about how delicious it was, I was still taken by surprise.

My sounds of appreciation must have been pleasing to Alexandra. "How is it?"

"Probably the best pie I have ever eaten. Can I buy the whole thing?"

She laughed, even though I was serious, and said, "Wait, let me get you a scoop of my homemade ice cream. It complements the flavor perfectly."

Alexandra ducked under her stall and pulled a cooler out. Ice cubes rattled together as she rummaged through and pulled out a plastic takeout container filled with ice cream. Then she grabbed a scoop from a tub of water, shaking it dry before plunging it into the soft vanilla. I held my plate up and she reached over, dropping the spherical scoop on top of the pie.

It was the perfect addition to an incredible dessert, and the mixture between warm and cold, smooth and crumbly was indescribably good. As soon as I was done, I refrained from licking my plate clean and instead dug around in my pockets and pulled out my money.

But before I could request another serving, the golden gleam of the coins brought me back to Colton's funeral. I remembered sitting in my car after ditching the service and flipping the coin. The coin that I had let decide my fate. I promised myself another slice of pie *only* if I figured out how the hell I was supposed to talk to her about Colton.

"Didn't I tell you?"

I looked up and saw the girl from earlier, grinning at me with satisfaction. "Definitely the best."

"Do I maybe get a thank-you for introducing you to the love of your life?" she teased, nodding at my empty plate.

"Do I maybe get a name, so I can do so?"

She smiled. "Eliza."

"Thank you, Eliza."

"You're very welcome . . ."

"Elliot."

"You're very welcome, Elliot."

"Eliza, could you please give me a hand?" Alexandra called as she stacked empty trays together.

"Better get packing. We've got to get everything into the pickup before everyone else heads out. It gets crazy busy at closing time. If you're ever around again, be sure to drop in and buy something. I recommend the fudge brownies next."

As she turned, I blurted, "Wait!" I didn't want to leave without a single answer. "Do you need a hand?"

Eliza smiled. "Really? That'd be great."

We walked over to the back of the stand, where she formally introduced me to Alexandra, who, after expressing her thanks, handed me a crate filled with cream doughnuts to pack up.

"How long have you worked for Alexandra?" I asked as Eliza passed me a couple of crates. I gently placed them into the pickup truck and turned for the next batch.

"All my life," she answered, smiling at me. "She's my mom."

I hadn't known to connect the dots earlier. Now when I compared them, I could see a striking resemblance. They had the same eyes, although Alexandra's were decorated with wrinkles, and even though her hair was now silver, I had no trouble seeing her with the once-golden waves of youth. But now that I knew Eliza was a connection to the Yanks family, I suddenly had a new way to reveal the secrets of the past.

"Thanks again," Eliza said as we got the last of the equipment in. She locked up the back and secured everything into place. Then she reached into her pocket and pulled out some cash.

"No," I said, refusing to take it. "It was my pleasure."

Eliza insisted one more time, but when I didn't take the money, she pursed her lips. "At least take *something*. How about the rest of that pie?"

Food payment was my weakness, so I allowed her to retrieve it, wrapped up in a box, and hand it over. "Thanks."

"No, thank *you*."

This was it. I needed to say something, to make sure that we'd see each other again. To ensure I'd get answers.

"Since you introduced me to the pleasures of caramel pie, how about I introduce you to something you're bound to love?" I suggested. "It's only fair."

Eliza smiled. "What did you have in mind?"

"How about lunch tomorrow?"

Wait, lunch? Shit. My mom.

By the time I got back to the Bentley, I was forty-five minutes late, with three missed calls from my mother. I wasn't sure which room was hers, so I slowly cruised around and finally found her sitting outside with a frown.

I parked in front of her. "Sorry, the traffic was hell. Forgot how long it took to drive out here." It didn't surprise me how effortlessly the lies slipped out.

Valerie stood, dusted off her jeans, and forced a small smile. "It's okay, honey. I understand."

Just as my mother stepped into the car and put on her seatbelt, her phone started ringing. She seemed slightly alarmed by the vibrating device sitting in her purse and ignored it uncomfortably. I didn't think much of it as I pulled away from the hotel and onto the road, but half-way down the street, it started ringing again. Out of the corner of my eye, I could see her clutch her bag closer, fingers twirling through the many straps and buckles.

"You should answer that," I suggested.

Valerie looked up at me, confused, trying to calculate the meaning of my tone. She reached into the leather compartments of her bag, and after some fumbling around, she found her phone. Her eyes recognized the number on the screen and she hesitated. Although her body was angled so that I couldn't directly see the device, I knew exactly who it was: Ryan.

Her other family was a tender subject, and something we never directly discussed. She'd invited us to her wedding, but my father politely declined to attend on my behalf. I was six at the time and for a kid, going to a wedding meant sitting down for hours just to see two people kiss. Only Cass went, but she was bribed with being a flower girl and was more interested in wearing a dress and eating cake.

I knew about Valerie's kids too. She'd tried showing me pictures one Christmas. I was thirteen, and it pissed me off immensely. I didn't refrain from displaying my disgust, and she got the message clearly and never showed me photos again. It was frustrating knowing that only one family could win so much of her affection that she'd show them off. I doubted she had shown her other kids pictures of me and my sister.

Valerie hesitated before sliding her finger across the screen. "Hi, honey."

There were some incoherent words from her phone, and I tried not to listen in on the conversation, but it was difficult when we were in such a confined space. My fingers itched to reach over and switch on the radio, just to have something else to listen to, but I didn't want to make it any more awkward.

"I'm having a great time," she said, sounding a little too cheery. Or maybe that was really how she spoke to him. Maybe he made her that happy. My fingers tightened on the steering wheel.

"Elliot and I are on our way to lunch," she continued. "He says hello."

When I did nothing but purse my lips, her voice dropped a little.

"He's driving. I shouldn't be pestering him. He needs to concentrate, that's all."

Guilt surfaced again and I swallowed it down.

"Yes, well, tell the kids I miss them. I'll call again tonight, okay? I love you too. Okay, talk soon."

As soon as she hung up, a silence fell upon us. It was so thick I had to reach over and wind down my window, desperate for the rushing feeling of air, both to fill my suffocated lungs and to cool my sweaty forehead.

Valerie put away her phone. She looked like she was going to bring it up, but then she apparently decided against it. Instead she said, "So, where are we going?"

Good question.

"Honestly, I've never really been to Ridgemount, so I don't know any good places. I've only come down a few times to visit Cass, but we usually eat on campus."

"How about we go to the shopping center food court? I need to pick up some new soap anyway. I never trust the products motels provide."

Saturday afternoon and the small parking lot was jam-packed with vehicles; we found a spot only after circling a few times. Valerie talked to me about all sorts of things the whole way as we navigated through the weekend crowd, like a new show she'd started watching, and how some of the fruit here was much better than back home, and how she'd found some wool in a nearby shop and was suddenly inspired to teach herself to crochet. It was strange—I couldn't work out which I preferred: silence or too much conversation.

As we reached the food court, she asked me what I'd like to eat. I awkwardly gestured in no particular direction, and her gaze followed my limp hand toward the kebab stall. Once I'd ordered my lunch, she didn't hesitate to pay, even when I protested.

"Please, Elliot," she said, gently pushing me away from the cash register and pulling out some money.

She then crossed the food court while I picked a table. She found the sushi bar and ordered herself a tray and a side salad with some sort of dressing that smelled amazing. But before we dug in, she stopped me by placing her hands in mine. At first, I thought she wanted me to pray.

"I'm not really religious . . ." I mumbled, pulling my hands back.

She looked momentarily confused before she let go, rummaged through her things, and pulled out a small bottle of hand sanitizer. She reached over to my hands again and squeezed a little onto my palms.

I looked down at the small drop of purple liquid. It smelled like berries and slid across my skin. The gesture was so maternal, and it seemed to be second nature to her. I imagined she did things like this for her other children all the time. However, it was so foreign to me . . . but I'd be lying if it didn't make me feel warm inside. I looked up and watched as she rubbed her own hands together, oblivious to my staring.

"I've started painting again," Valerie said. "It's funny, actually. A publisher reached out to me and now I'm in the process of illustrating a children's book."

"Oh?"

"I used to paint a lot when I was at university, and I made a lot of friends because of it. One of them actually lives here in Ridgemount. She works at the library. I popped in the other day, and they're redoing the children's section. They're painting the walls with different book characters and animals and all sorts of lovely things. She wants me to do a piece."

"What are you going to paint?" I asked.

"I don't know. There are so many possibilities. Did you know that when you and Cass were babies, I did something similar? I painted your bedroom walls with all kinds of magical things. There were characters from books and movies, and creatures from my imagination."

"I don't remember that," I said quietly.

Her smiled faltered slightly. "It was a long time ago. I suppose you don't. Your sister used to tell me stories about you drawing. Do you still draw?"

I frowned. "I haven't drawn since I was like eight."

Valerie shifted in her seat. "I just . . . I thought you might still enjoy it."

"I don't." I sighed. "I wasn't very good at it anyway."

"You know what they say—practice makes perfect."

"Sure, but my drawings looking abstract when I had no intention of them being so kind of killed my dreams of becoming a world-renowned artist."

"Oh, Elliot," she said.

"Don't worry, it wasn't that much of a tragedy. When I turned nine, I wanted to be an astronaut and that dream died pretty quickly too. I've definitely changed what I want to be more times than I can count."

"What do you want to be now?" Valerie finally asked.

Everything was different, and I didn't have a clue. Although my future was still a draft, now that my best friend—one of the main characters in the story of my life—was gone, it felt like I had to erase it all and write something new. Just thinking about it drained the remaining life out of me. Despite that, however, I knew there was one thing I desperately wanted to be in my future.

"Happy," I finally answered.

Valerie's gaze softened. Her shoulders sagged slightly and she swallowed. "Elliot . . . I really am sorry about what happened to Colton. I can't imagine experiencing that kind of loss." She took a deep breath. "And I'm sorry I haven't been a very good mother over the years. I should have been there for you, not just to support you during your losses but to celebrate your triumphs too. No matter how big or small."

It was the first time Valerie had properly apologized. It was the first time she had acknowledged her absence. In a strange way, it felt comforting knowing that she recognized I'd needed her while I was growing up. That there were times in my life where I'd needed a mother.

"I really am sorry, Elliot. I hope you believe me."

"I believe you."

It was true; I did believe her. I appreciated her apology, but there was a lot of healing required. I wasn't quite ready to forgive her yet. I gave her a reassuring smile. Then we ate. We were quiet as we finished our meals, lost in our own thoughts. For once, I didn't feel uncomfortable.

†

When I dropped my mom off and said I had a good time, I wasn't lying. The trip back home was slow, and I had to keep the windows down so I wouldn't pass out from fatigue. But I managed to make it back home in one piece. My dad's study door was open, so I dropped my keys back into my pocket and peered inside. There he was, lying right in the middle of the floor, glasses on, eyes shut, barefoot, with his arms sprawled out.

"I think yoga requires a little more effort than that," I said, leaning in the doorway.

He opened one eye. "I have writer's block."

That explained everything. Dad always did weird or spontaneous things when he was stuck with his writing: random road trips, strange diets, experiments in sleeplessness. He described it as his way of overcoming the barrier. Cass argued that he did it because he was just a severe procrastinator.

"Enjoy your meditation," I said, turning to close the door.

"Elliot."

I paused. "Yeah?"

"Do tell me next time you decide to sneak out of the house."

Busted.

"Sorry, Dad."

"You're eighteen now. I trust you to make mature decisions, and I think we have come to a stage in our relationship where we can overcome these discussions without arguments or punishments. I'm willing to turn a blind eye on this little incident if you make me some two-minute noodles."

My dad was a champion.

"Chicken- or beef-flavored?"

"Chicken. I love your sister, but I miss the simplicity of microwavable foods. I don't know how much longer I can handle eating things I can't even pronounce." He smiled at me sheepishly.

"Don't let her hear that."

"I'll try. Oh, and Elliot?"

"Yeah?"

"Your mom called. She was looking for you this morning."

"I know. She found me."

He pushed his glasses farther up his nose. "How'd it go?"

"Surprisingly well."

"You're okay?"

"I'm okay. I'm going to make those noodles now, all right?"

"All right." He closed his eyes. "Thank you."

I half-shut his door and made my way into the kitchen. Cass was sitting at the counter, laptop in front of her, fingers furiously typing something. She frowned at her screen, then deleted whatever she had written. Once she saw me, she pulled out her earphones.

"Where have you been?"

"With Mom," I answered, taking out some noodles.

She looked like she was going to say something else but thought better of it. "Okay."

The small notebook I'd discovered last night was sitting on the benchtop. Instinctively, my sister wrapped her hand around the leather binding and placed it on her lap.

"What's that?" I asked, forcing myself to sound calm as I took out a bowl.

"Just some study stuff. I'm doing a project."

"A project. For university?"

She hummed in agreement. "Been working on it all night."

"You must have gotten to sleep late last night." I kept my eyes on her.

She met my gaze. "I did."

We held eye contact for a few more minutes before I turned back to what I was doing. Cass decided she didn't want to be interrogated anymore, so she packed up her things and left the kitchen. She was hiding something. And I wondered what I'd have to bargain for her to tell me what.

Worried that I had offended her, I decided to call Lydia that night. "Hey, Lyd."

"Elliot."

I wasn't sure if she was still pissed about that morning, but I decided to apologize anyway. "I'm sorry about this morning."

She surprised me by saying, "Don't be."

"I went for a night drive. I wasn't in the right headspace. Then I fell asleep on the side of the road and woke up there this morning."

"Where did you go?"

"Ridgemount."

There was quiet for a few seconds.

"Must have been quite an adventure," she finally said.

"It was. I had lunch with my mom today." There was something about Lydia that made me want to tell her everything: about my day, my life, my family. Anything that was on my mind.

"I'm worried about Colton."

Lydia looked up from her book and squinted at me. We were sitting in Lydia's backyard one afternoon in spring. She was relaxing under the shade of the only tree in the garden. I was rocking myself on her tire swing. We had invited Colton to come over to hang out, but he had bailed on us. Again. He had been doing it a lot recently.

Lydia and I still hung out sometimes. Besides, her mom was making spaghetti carbonara for dinner and I couldn't resist. It just tasted so much better than my dad's version. Granted, my dad's version came from a frozen pre-made packet and all he needed to do was chuck it in the microwave and press Start.

"I know what you mean," she said. "This is the third time this week he's said he's too busy to hang out."

"No luck with getting him to go on dates?"

"Nada. I really wanted to go to the botanical gardens on the weekend. They have a free flower arranging class available for students." She pouted. "Ever since he came back, he's seemed . . ."

"Different?" I finished. "Kind of paranoid? Stressed about really little things?"

"Exactly." Lydia sighed. She folded the corner of the page she was reading and closed the book. She tossed it onto the grass beside her and placed her face in her hands.

"What do you think happened when he was gone?"

"I don't know," she whispered. "But it must have been terrible if he can't tell either one of us."

What trouble could he have possibly gotten into while he was away? I lowered myself until my back was resting on the swing. I spread my arms out and let my hands flop. Looking up, I could see patches of sky and sunlight peeking out from the cluster of leaves and maze of branches.

"Do you think he killed someone?"

"Elliot!" Lydia shrieked and I felt her fist hit my calf. "Colton would never hurt anyone, and he's definitely not capable of murder."

"But what if it was self-defense or something? He's watched so many mysteries that he probably knows how to kill someone and properly dispose of a body."

"If it was self-defense, he would tell the police. There would be nothing to hide. For all we know, maybe it was family stuff he was dealing with. Maybe one of his grandparents is sick."

It was possible, but it still didn't explain why he didn't tell us. "Why keep that a secret, though?"

"People deal with that kind of thing in different ways. Maybe he's just working out his feelings. When he's ready, he will tell us everything. We just need to respect his decisions."

"You'll defend him until the very end," I said, teasing her. "He doesn't deserve you."

"People will do anything for those they love," she whispered.

I snorted and flipped around again. This time, my stomach sunk into the middle of the tire swing. I placed my hands on the ropes holding it up.

"I'm not sure I believe in love."

"Love isn't exclusively romantic. You can love family and friends."

"Okay, then. Let me rephrase. I'm not sure I believe in romantic love. I mean, just look at my parents. They were divorced before I can even remember."

Lydia gave me a smile. Just seeing that extremely small lift of her lips was warm and hopeful and encouraging. "You're not your parents. Just because their relationship didn't work out doesn't mean yours won't. Besides, their marriage wasn't a complete waste of time. Something wonderful came out of it—you."

Although her speech was sweet, it didn't completely revolutionize my beliefs. It was, however, a very uplifting thought, and I couldn't help but smile back. "You really are something else, Lydia Potter."

"You're blessed to have me as a best friend," she said with a laugh.

I was serious when I said, "I really am."

†

"Elliot?"

Lydia's voice was quiet and she sounded far away. I could tell her *almost* anything. Not about the letters. Anything but the letters.

"How did it go?" she asked.

"Surprisingly well." I leaned back on my bed, propped myself up with my hand behind my head and looked up at the ceiling. "Not as torturous as I thought it would be."

"Really?"

"Really."

"Then I'm happy for you. Hopefully, there'll be more of those to come."

"I'm not hoping for anything. My expectations are still low."

"Such a pessimist."

"I'm a realist. There's a difference."

"Does the realist have anything going on tomorrow?" she asked, her voice lighter, more cheerful.

I thought back to Eliza and our lunch date. "My morning is free. What did you have in mind?"

"Sunday mass." She paused. "I can practically hear your internal groan. I know it's not an ideal way to hang out, but I've found it surprisingly comforting, you know? I thought maybe you'd like to join me."

I hadn't stepped into a church since Colton's funeral, and I wanted to avoid doing so for as long as possible. But Lydia seemed to find serenity in the space. Maybe I could too.

"Okay," I said, trying not to sound so reluctant.

"Do you want me to pick you up?" she asked.

"No, I'll drive and meet you at the front. I'll need my car. I have lunch plans."

"With your mom again?"

I didn't want to mention Eliza. Not yet. So I lied. "Yeah."

"I hope it goes as well as it did today," she answered.

There was a small bell-like noise in the distance, accompanied by a vibrating sound. Lydia shuffled around on the other line, probably looking at the notification on her phone. I waited patiently until she returned.

"Sorry about that. I just got a text from one of the girls from school. We've been organizing that memorial camping trip for Colton, and she just messaged me the final details."

"What night?"

"This Friday, at Darion Rock. It's the park near the church."

"Are we allowed to camp there?"

"Charlie's dad is on the board and he's giving us permission. Just for the night. We have to be packed and have the area cleaned up by six in the morning, though. Bring a sleeping bag and some food. That's all you're going to need."

"Got it," I said. "Want to go down together?"

"I'd like that," she answered quietly. Then she stifled a yawn, and I heard the creaking of springs as she lay on her bed.

There was silence after that. I was almost sure she had fallen asleep. Then she spoke. "Elliot?" she muttered sleepily.

"Yeah, Lyd?"

"Is it getting easier for you?"

Her voice was so soft, so fragile, full of vulnerability, but at the same time, demanding the truth, needing the strength and power of reality. I could have lied. I could have told her I was slowly getting better, slowly learning to accept it. That I was beginning to come to terms with things. But it was a lie even I couldn't believe, and I didn't have the motivation to convince someone else to believe it.

"No. It's not. To be honest, it's getting harder."

"Just making sure."

"Making sure of what?"

But she had already fallen asleep.

†

The following morning, I met Lydia at the front of the church. She slid from her car, wearing another sensible, pastel-colored dress, hair tied back with a ribbon. As soon as she neared, I tugged a piece of her hair.

"Don't you look as cute as a button."

"Shut up," she answered.

I followed her into the church. I don't know why, but I wasn't expecting that many people to attend the Sunday morning service. So needless to say, I was slightly alarmed when I saw the horde of parishioners hovering within the small spaces between the pews.

Parents with well-dressed children exchanged polite words with the elderly. Young couples loitered and engaged in soft conversations. And then there was Lydia and me. Two barely graduated teenagers who stuck out like a highlighted passage in a textbook of words and no pictures.

And even though no one seemed interested in us as we made our way toward the center of the crowd and chose a place to sit, I still felt like everyone was watching. Flashbacks of the funeral overwhelmed me. It didn't take long for Lydia to notice my discomfort; the excessive sweating and ragged breathing were pretty obvious indications of my panic. But she didn't say anything. Instead, she reached over and took my hand. It was such a simple gesture. But it made me feel immensely better.

The warmth of her hand was soothing, acting as a reality check. She was an anchor that kept me grounded before my fears consumed my mind and threatened to drive me insane.

I squeezed her hand back.

Then the service began. The priest stood behind the small podium, raised his hands, and did a few polite nods toward a couple of the regulars.

"Welcome—" His voice boomed out of the microphone in a menacing growl.

Startled gasps echoed through the small church, and a ripple of murmurs erupted through the crowd. Even Lydia jumped slightly in her seat, fingers unconsciously squeezing mine.

"Oh, I'm terribly sorry," the priest muttered sheepishly, placing a hand on the microphone and stepping backward. "It seems we have a few technical issues."

Without the microphone, his voice was soft yet powerful. It had been significantly altered by the device, which had made him sound almost demonic. His "welcome" had been scratchy and unnatural, like the moan of a suffering creature.

Because of this, the service was delayed by ten minutes while the microphone was replaced. It took some fumbling before it finally worked, but once it was functioning properly, the mass was back on track.

Lydia kept her hand in mine through the whole thing.

☦

Once the service was over, Lydia let go and there was that awkward second of I-don't-know-whose-sweat-is-on-my-palm-but-I'm-just-going-to-casually-wipe-it-off. We didn't look at each other. Lydia rummaged through her purse—probably for a sanitizer or a tissue.

"The confessional box will be open for the next twenty minutes for anyone who would like to talk," the priest reminded everyone as people started shuffling to the doors, probably ready for an early lunch or a late breakfast.

Lydia stopped going through her things and looked toward the corner of the confessional box. "Do you . . . do you mind if I—"

"Go for it," I said. "I'll wait here."

Lydia stood up and made her way through the maze of pews toward the box. I stayed back and decided to explore. I circled my way through the small space and looked at the variety of different pamphlets that sat near the doors, the beautifully carved statues, the images made by the stained glass windows. The late morning sun shone through broken segments of colored glass, leaving a multicolored image on the carpet. It was utterly mesmerizing.

Without the church being so crowded, the place felt much more comforting, much more welcoming than on the other few occasions I'd been there. The first two times were funerals, which, needless to say, weren't the most favorable memories. Then there was the Sunday mass with Lydia I was at now. During the service, the refined room had made me feel claustrophobic; too many people were staring and talking. And even though we weren't mourning the death of anyone, I had still felt suffocated.

Seeing the church almost deserted suddenly had me looking at it in a new light. The passion poured into the expressions of the perfectly carved marble statues was phenomenal, an attention to detail that I had failed to acknowledge. Even the furniture was in pristine condition, which I would never have thought possible.

"Elliot."

Lydia gently touched my shoulder. I flinched, so startled that I almost fell face-first into the sill of the stained glass window. "Sorry," she said, embarrassed, instantly drawing her hand back to her side. "I've, um, finished."

"How was it?"

"Good, I feel much better. You should try it."

I looked at the confessional box skeptically. "Nah."

She shrugged. "Okay. Maybe some other time."

We started heading to the doors. "Actually," I said, turning to look behind my shoulder, "maybe it would be a good idea . . ."

I had a lot of confessions to make. You were meant to confess your sins, and I wasn't particularly sure if the things I was doing were considered as such, but I did kind of want to vent to someone and a priest seemed like a good idea. I'd heard he wasn't allowed to judge or tell anyone else, and it wasn't like I could tell Lydia or Cass or my dad.

Maybe telling someone would make me feel a little less tense. Lydia waited for a moment, head tilted, a piece of hair spilling down to curl around her cheek as she watched me try to decide.

"Yes," I confirmed, straightening a little. "I think I'll do it."

I marched down toward the box before I could change my mind.

"I'll wait right here," Lydia called after me, her voice bouncing across the high ceiling in a ripple of echoes.

Before I could chicken out, I stepped into the confession box. It was smaller than I'd thought it would be. I wasn't expecting it to have a couch or a coffee table with complimentary cakes and tea, but I had expected a little more space to move.

Sitting down on the small bench located on the side, I said, "Forgive me, Father, for I have sinned."

I wasn't sure if that was what I was meant to say, but it sounded legit, and that's what people in the movies did. I heard the rustle of robes on the other end, but the priest didn't speak, so I took this as an invitation to continue.

"I've been lying to a lot of my friends and family. My friend was murdered almost a month ago, and I'm trying to piece together the mystery. I don't know who to trust, so I haven't said anything to anyone. Sometimes . . . sometimes I think I'm losing my mind."

I kept talking, he kept listening, and it felt surprisingly good. I refrained from mentioning my relationship with the killer and how they had been blackmailing me with letters about my deceased friend. I wasn't sure if a priest's vows of anonymity during confession applied when he was questioned by the police, so I kept my information to myself. Not that he knew who I was, because of the screen that divided us. But if the authorities ever decided to question him, I would be easily identifiable as the kid who'd found his best friend dead. After all, nothing particularly exciting happened in my town, so the story of Colton's death was a tale everyone knew.

Then, through one of the small slats that let my voice project to the other side of the box, a slip of paper, no larger than a business card, tumbled out. There, in the center, were five words:

COLTON CREST IS LONG GONE

"I'm so sorry. One of the lovely parishioners brought a pitcher of homemade lemonade, and I wasn't able to visit the bathroom before the service this morning. Were you waiting long?"

The priest—the *real* priest—had returned and settled down on the opposite side.

But all my mind could comprehend was: *The killer is here. And I just told them my confessions.*

"Son? Are you okay?"

"Fine," I said, backing out of the box, my voice trembling slightly. "I—I have to go."

"Are you all right?" the priest called after me, his voice concerned.

But I kept running, scanning to see if Lydia was hurt. I raced over to her and grabbed her to confirm she was unharmed. She was surprised to see me in such a hurry.

"Elliot. Are you okay? What's going on? What happened?"

"Have you been here by the front entrance the whole time?" I pulled her outside. When she didn't answer immediately, I repeated myself. "Lydia? Have you?"

"Yes," she finally answered. My fingers unconsciously squeezed hers tighter and she let out a little yelp but didn't tell me to let go. "Why? What's wrong?"

I looked at the church, eyes skimming back and forth. "There has to be another exit. Is there another one? Damn it, Lydia, answer me!"

"There's one to the side and one out back," she said, clearly frightened by how spooked I was. I felt bad for speaking to her in such an impatient manner, but I needed to act quickly.

Colton Crest's killer was here. And I was about to hunt and capture that bloody bastard.

"Where's the side door?" I asked, my eyes skipping back and forth between both sides of the church's structure, in case someone emerged. I kept bouncing on the balls of my feet, fidgeting as I felt time wasting away.

"There." She pointed to the left side of the building and I instantly started walking toward it. She followed.

"Lydia, I need you to guard the back exit," I said urgently, looking back at her briefly to show her how desperate I was. "If someone comes out—not the priest—I need you to follow them. Please, Lydia, please promise me you'll do this. It's important." She nodded, her face pale, and ran off toward the back of the church.

This was it. I was about to uncover Colton Crest's killer. I ran as fast as I could to the side door, but what was I going to do once they were cornered? Demand answers? Beat the hell out of the person? Call the police?

As soon as I reached the door, I saw nothing—no pieces of evidence on the ground, no stray hairs caught on the side of the doorway, no signs of forced escape or struggle.

Hesitantly, I crept forward. I tried to keep my footsteps light, my movements fluid, breathing controlled. What if the killer was *right there*, just beyond the door?

It was then that I realized I wasn't scared. I was furious, my blood boiling. This person—this asshole—killed my best friend and was now taunting me with handwritten letters, with confessions and head-twisting riddles, mocking descriptions, and sick hints. They had been driving me insane.

I was livid. And I wasn't going to hesitate to display that.

As soon as I stepped into the church, my eyes skimmed in every direction, looking for someone, anyone. Making sure they weren't lurking within the shadows. It was like doing a hidden-object game, searching for anything out of place.

I laughed silently, humorlessly. The killer would have loved that. Another game.

I searched the furniture, the statues, the pews for anything out of the ordinary. Perhaps something left behind, a wisp of hair, a piece of a disguise that wasn't properly concealed. I was frantic as I scanned everything, trying, so desperately, to find any sign of the killer.

Where are you? Goddamn it, where are you?!

"Elliot."

I spun and saw Lydia. I was breathless, my chest heaving.

"You're yelling," she said softly, but her voice echoed through the church.

"Is something the matter?" the priest asked, appearing out of nowhere. I wondered where he'd come from and how long he'd known I was there. He took one look at my panicked expression and added, "Is there someone I can call?"

"No," I said, a little too harshly. "I'm sorry, we're just leaving."

I walked over to Lydia, took her hand, and gently dragged her out. I wanted to punch something. How the hell did the killer manage to escape so quickly?

Outside, I let go of Lydia's hand and stalked toward my car without another word. I quickly unlocked it and slid into the driver's side. I let the door slam shut and hit my hands against the steering wheel.

"Asshole," I yelled. "I hate you. I *hate* you!"

I pressed my forehead against the wheel and sat there, trying to control my temper. I knew I was acting like a twelve-year-old, but I was so damn frustrated.

After a few seconds, someone opened the passenger side door and climbed in. I didn't have to look up. I could smell her strawberry shampoo.

"I thought you'd left."

"You thought I was just going to leave you out here by yourself? You look like you're about to kill someone with your bare hands."

I laughed humorlessly. "That sounds appealing."

Lydia didn't say anything. She shuffled in her seat and gently shut the door. "What's going on, Elliot?"

"God, Lydia, I'm so sorry," I said, wanting to reach out and hold her. I hesitantly lifted my hand, but she flinched. My jaw clenched in embarrassment. I gripped the steering wheel instead.

"What's going on?" she repeated.

"A lot," I answered, staring out through the windshield.

"Like?"

"I can't tell you."

Telling Lydia would just complicate things. What if she told someone? What if the killer went after her? What if she got hurt because of me? I couldn't stomach the possibilities.

"Not yet," I added. "I just need more time."

"More time," she repeated, looking through me as if I wasn't there at all.

"I'm sorry, Lyd—"

"You sound like Colton."

"What?"

Before, Lydia had been gazing through me as if I were transparent. But now she was staring at me with such desperate intensity, as if I was the only thing left in the world and if she blinked, I'd cease to exist.

"You sound just like Colton," she repeated. "He was always muttering about time. It stressed him out so much."

"I know," I whispered, remembering the day he'd reappeared at my doorstep. The way he'd studied his watch so closely.

"Do you know what frightened him most?" she asked.

"No."

"He nearly told me once. That night—" She stopped herself then and pursed her lips. "I just wish I had known what he was so afraid of."

"Me too," I muttered.

She redirected her eyes back to me and they were filled with wavering tears. "I gave Colton all the time in the world and that wasn't enough. I'm not going to make the same mistake again."

I opened my mouth, but nothing came out.

Lydia opened the door. "I'll call you later, okay?"

I should have said something, anything. But I didn't. I let her walk away.

✝

I went home and stewed in my room, thinking about the killer slipping through my grasp—completely forgetting about my plans with Eliza. Well, until she called me around noon, an hour after our designated meeting time.

"Is this how you treat a girl on a first date?" Her tone was playful, but it still made my stomach sink with guilt.

"I'm so sorry," I answered, scrubbing a hand down my face. "I've had a crazy morning."

"Enlighten me."

"How about over a second attempt at a first date?" I suggested.

"I'd like that. How about coffee?"

"Coffee sounds good. There's a great place a couple of streets down from—"

"Actually, I was thinking of coffee at my house. What do you think?" I thought it was a brilliant opportunity to snoop around. "That way, if you stand me up, I won't feel so bad. I'll be at home."

"I'm so sorry about that. I swear I'm an extremely charming person."

"I'll believe it when I see it. Do you want to come by tomorrow? Say, around ten?"

"I'll be there on the dot."

"I'm expecting nothing less. If you're not here on time, I'll just assume you don't like me," she teased.

"I better get there at nine forty-five, then."

She laughed. "I'll see you tomorrow, okay? I'll text you directions."

As soon as she hung up, I threw my phone onto my bed. I was overwhelmed, and I wasn't sure if I was grateful or stressed because of the distraction. Colton's murder was consuming my life, and I couldn't escape it. I wondered, if the roles were reversed, would it have affected him as much as it was affecting me?

Probably not. But that didn't stop me from mentally bargaining with forces that couldn't change anything.

BARGAINING

The directions that Eliza gave me led me to a patch of private property, a windy dirt road, and a ranch-style house. It was the kind of house that you always saw on television or read about in books, with its timber staircase leading up to a wraparound porch. A rocking chair sat to the left side, beside a small coffee table holding a mug of what seemed to be now-cold tea and a hardcover book with a missing dust jacket.

Everything made me feel uneasy. Something felt . . . *staged*. But maybe I was just nervous. I shoved my hands into my pockets to stop them from shaking and headed up the stairs. Pausing at the front, I took a deep breath before deciding to knock. However, as I raised my knuckles, the door swung open.

Eliza seemed to be in motion, a mission on her mind, but as soon as she saw me, her footsteps came to an abrupt halt. Her sudden pause in movement caused the loose, white material of her dress to swing around her knees and the wilting flowers in her arms shook, petals falling to rest beside her bare feet.

"Hey, I wasn't expecting to see you here this early," she said, lifting her hand and examining the thin gold watch on her wrist. "You're fifteen minutes early."

"Like I said I'd be."

She opened the door wider and stepped to the side. "Come on in. I'll make you something to drink. I just have to throw these out."

The inside of the Yanks residence looked like a dollhouse; it had all the essentials, but it lacked character. I felt uneasy as Eliza exited behind me. Suede couches surrounded a coffee table in the living room, the glass top showing no signs of use. Not a single coffee ring or speck of dust. I ran my finger across the surface to make sure. Spotless.

The large window on the left side of the room was open, heavy scarlet drapes pulled back so the sun could illuminate the room. A soft breeze brushed my arm as I crossed to look at the frames on the mantel above the fireplace. But they didn't hold family pictures. They held words. Poems, quotes, passages.

"My mom's into that kind of thing."

I nearly knocked over one of the frames as I turned around and faced Eliza.

"I'm sorry. I didn't mean to scare you." She laughed and then nodded behind me. "She was never a family portrait kind of woman."

It disappointed me that they didn't have any photographs, which meant I still didn't know what Tristan looked like. Maybe I had been passing him in the streets all this time and I was unaware. The thought made my head spin.

"How about something to drink?" Eliza offered when I didn't say anything.

"That'd be great." My voice came out forced, my throat dry.

I followed her into the kitchen and dropped into one of the stools at the counter. Sitting in the center was a batch of shortbread cookies. The kind that looked like they would crumble and melt in your mouth.

"I know I technically offered coffee on the phone, but in all honesty, I'm more of a tea person," she said, leaning across the other side of the counter.

My lips twitched into a smile. "I'm not much of a coffee fan either."

"I was hoping you'd say that, because I can't brew a good cup to save my life. What would you like instead? Water, peach iced tea, lemonade, hot tea?"

"Iced tea sounds good."

She plopped some ice cubes into two slim glasses, poured the tea in, and slid one over to me. As soon as my hand wrapped around the beverage, I downed half of it without taking a breath. It was cool and sweet and instantly relieved my thirst. Then Eliza offered me some cookies and they were even better than I'd expected.

"Are you a university student?" she asked.

"I will be. I was meant to take a year off to travel but . . ." *My best friend got murdered.* "Things changed."

"I wish I had taken a gap year. I went straight to university. Just finished my first year."

"What do you study?"

"Criminal justice."

I wondered if Eliza had picked that particular area of study because she was genuinely interested or because she'd felt obligated to look out for her older brother. If Tristan ever got into any more trouble, she'd understand all the legal ramifications and could possibly find loopholes that would ultimately allow him to dodge a bullet.

"Everyone thinks proper strategizing will let you get away with anything. But if you think about it, familiarizing yourself with the law? It could allow you to get away with murder." She had a sly grin on her face as she picked up her glass and took a drink. "I'd make an excellent killer."

Her response made my heart beat faster, and not in a good way.

"Better keep that information to yourself. What if I'm secretly a detective?"

"I can think of one way to silence you."

I wasn't a fan of kissing on the first date, but Eliza was smoother than most girls I had dated. Maybe it wouldn't hurt to try. There was a first time for everything. But as she leaned across the counter, close enough that I could see the dusting of freckles on her nose, her house phone rang. She didn't seem alarmed or annoyed. Instead, she leaned back and smiled at me.

"Sorry, one second."

She picked up the phone and walked out the front door to answer.

I wasn't sure how long Eliza would be, but I waited thirty seconds after she'd disappeared before getting out of my chair and wandering around her house. Time was limited, but I started searching anyway. I exited the kitchen and cut my way through the living room until I was in the hallway.

As I looked for clues, I wondered what Tristan Yanks was like. What were his motives? His weaknesses? What made him tick? I wondered if he was in the house right now.

In comparison to the kitchen and living room, the corridor was dark. The only light came from down the hall, where the front entrance was. It shone in broken fragments of pigmented light from the stained glass window above the door. As I scanned the walls, I noticed Eliza was right. Her mother wasn't the family portrait type. There were no pictures of memories of days at the beach or formal occasions or festive holidays.

Instead, there were more framed pieces of writing.

My eyes read through them, trying to absorb and calculate as quickly as possible.

"If at first you don't succeed, try, try again."

Most of them were inspirational quotes. I wondered if they had any impact on the Yanks family when they walked past their walls and read them. The others were segments from books, particularly from classics. I recognized some of the famous lines from high school English class.

However, there was one poem that caught my attention.

> *The ones who seek freedom*
> *Need to get away from the world;*
> *From restrictions, expectations, manipulations.*
> *Freedom is power.*
> *And with it comes self-discovery.*
> *Once you discover yourself,*
> *You can uncover*
> *The secrets of the universe.*
> *Remember to search in all directions.*
> *Because any way's possible.*

It was embroidered using red thread on a piece of white cloth. The letters were thick and loopy, and it looked like it had taken a significant amount of time to complete. But there was something about the way it was written . . .

I leaned in closer and tried to see better through the glass in the poor lighting. Tracing the bottom of some of the words was a thin outline of white thread, I saw. Because of the darkness and the awkward glare, I could barely see it against the white material. But now that it was clear, my heart raced in anticipation.

> ***The ones who*** *seek freedom*
> *Need to **get away** from the world;*
> *From restrictions, expectations, manipulations.*
> *Freedom is power.*
> *And **with it** comes self-discovery.*
> *Once you discover yourself,*
> *You can uncover*

The secrets of the universe.
Remember to search in all directions.
*Because **any way's** possible.*

My heart was thumping against my chest like a wild animal that wanted to break free. That was one of the lines from the previous letter. Maybe the next one was hidden behind the frame . . .

My fingers reached up and skimmed around the edges, but I couldn't flip the picture over and check if my suspicions were correct because just then, the front door swung open. My head snapped toward the entrance of the house. I expected Eliza to step back in, with a smile and flirty comment.

But I instantly knew it wasn't her. Because of the lighting, it took me a moment to make the person out. They stepped into the house, their image altered by the blinding sun behind them. But even then, from the shapes and shadows I could make out, I knew it wasn't a woman. He was tall, broader, footsteps heavier.

"Can I help you?"

Why did his voice sound so familiar? The door swung shut and I had to blink the dark spots from my vision before I could properly see. Fragments of his appearance were slowly revealed: dark hair, broad nose, square jaw. I sucked in a breath, head spinning.

"Colton?"

As soon as I said his name, I realized the mistake I had made. The figure stepped deeper into the house and my vision was much clearer now. His eyes were a shade too dark, his complexion different, lips twisted into an unfamiliar scowl. He wasn't my eighteen-year-old best friend. He was the mysterious murderer Colton had disappeared to search for, Tristan Yanks.

"Can I help you?" he repeated.

The more I looked at him, the more I couldn't shake the image of Colton. Bones was right. They were practically identical. Tristan would have been thirty-three at least, and he looked exactly how I imagined Colton would have looked in fifteen years' time.

"I was just looking for the bathroom."

"Are you one of Eliza's friends?" he asked, uninterested in why I was lurking in the hallway of his house.

His sister returned at the right moment, bumping into her older brother, who was still standing near the entrance. Tristan didn't seem fazed by the collision. Instead, he kept his eyes trained on me.

"Oh, hey," she said to him. "I thought you were out of town."

"Just got back today," he said without looking at her. "My stuff is in the car. Who's your friend?"

Eliza noticed me standing in the shadows of the hallway. She seemed confused at first, most likely wondering what I was doing there, but she smiled after a short moment.

"This is Elliot. Elliot, this is my brother, Tristan."

"Nice to meet you," I answered, trying to keep my voice level.

"Elliot Parker?"

My throat constricted, my breathing stopped, my heart stilled. How the hell did he know my full name? I parted my lips, unable to form any words or sounds. Tristan took this as an opportunity to explain.

"You're that kid who found Colton Crest dead, right?" he said, his tone challenging, questioning.

"Didn't know they'd included a picture of me."

Tristan gave me a half smile. "They didn't. Lucky guess."

My body went cold.

"Eliza, I'll be in the garage," he said, finally acknowledging his sister. And with that, he left.

Eliza looked sick as she watched her brother retreat. She reached up and wrung her wrist. I was too much in shock to decipher her reaction. Maybe she was embarrassed by her brother's behavior. Maybe she was worried. Maybe she knew something. Too many maybes. Too many uncertainties.

"Eliza?" I said.

"I'm so sorry about my brother. That was insensitive of him."

"It's no secret," I answered. "It's okay."

She didn't seem shocked that I was the guy who'd found his best friend dead. She was more concerned about her brother's behavior. I wondered if she'd known who I was already . . . and was that a good thing? Or really, really bad?

"It's not okay," Eliza answered, sounding tired. The thin strap of her dress slipped down one slender, tanned arm and she gently pulled it back up, keeping her eyes away from me. When she looked at me again, she said, "You see, we kind of knew Colton."

I tried to fake surprise, even though this revelation wasn't anything new. I wasn't sure how well I executed it, though. My acting skills were limited to basics I'd been taught in grade eight elective drama. Plus, I was still shaken from Tristan. Everything about him had me feeling uneasy: his appearance, the tense interaction, his voice. Why did his voice sound so familiar?

Why did he *look* familiar? Other than the resemblance to Colton, there was something about him that I couldn't put my finger on. It was like an itch under my skin that I couldn't scratch.

"Kind of knew him?" I repeated.

"How about we go outside and talk? I'll get us some fresh drinks and bring the cookies out," she offered.

Eliza motioned toward the back door, and I held it open for her. The back porch was similar to the front, but it was much wider and had enough room for an outside dining table for six. Toward the right-hand side, there was a hanging egg chair.

Eliza chose one of the chairs at the dining table and sat down. I sat on the opposite side. The fresh glasses of iced tea and cookies sat untouched between us. Finally, she took a deep breath.

"We knew Colton as Daniel Heckerman," she explained. "That was how he introduced himself two years ago."

Two years ago?

"He was sixteen, said he was some kid from a couple of towns over. We met in a similar way you and I did. He was at one of the farmers markets one day. He swooned over my mom's baking and naturally, she was pleased. He ended up being a regular. There was just something about him that brought out the motherly instincts in my mom. I guess she was just having withdrawal. My brother had gone to jail, and she missed having a son to fuss over. Didn't help that he was identical to what Tristan had looked like when he was his age.

"He was such a great person. He really helped my mom out, he was so sweet to me, and he visited Tristan while he was still locked up. Colton was the first person who wanted to get to know my brother since he'd landed in jail. He didn't make assumptions based on information the press had released. He genuinely wanted to get to know him."

I settled deeper into my chair, clinging onto every word.

"What Tristan did cost him eight years. But Colton seemed to make it better for him. Tristan learned a lot because of him. Something his stubbornness always prevented him from doing before. Colton visited him pretty frequently, whenever the prison would allow it. And when my brother got released, they grew closer."

My mind reeled back to the second letter. It had mentioned how Colton decided to confront Tristan about the murder this year. Perhaps he had tried getting closer to Tristan so that he would get answers. Maybe that was why he had been visiting since he was sixteen.

"Something went wrong, though. They were in the garage one night, having a drink. I remember going down there and Tristan was raging. I hadn't seen him so angry before."

Maybe Colton confronted him about the murder that night. He must have lost his shit. Tristan was slowly crawling his way higher up my suspects list.

I was about to say something, but the back door slid open and Mrs. Yanks stepped out. "Eliza?"

Eliza turned around at the sound of her name. "Hey, Mom."

"Hi, honey. I'm sorry to interrupt while you have friends over, but can you help me unload the car? I have some groceries and I'm meant to have fifteen trays of fairy cupcakes baked for an event by tonight," she said.

Eliza turned to look at me. Her lips were pursed, a desperate look in her eyes. She wanted to tell me something else. But she quickly changed her mind about it, her features relaxing as she gave me an easy smile.

"I'm sorry, would you please excuse me for a moment?"

As she stood, I followed. "I should actually get going."

Eliza hesitated, as if she was going to argue. But she didn't say anything and instead led me out toward the front door. Alexandra smiled, recognizing my face from the farmers market, and said a brief goodbye as she started unloading groceries from bags and rummaging through drawers for her baking utensils.

Eliza opened the door for me and leaned against the door frame. "I'm sorry we had to cut this short."

"We'll see each other again," I answered, fishing my keys out of my pocket.

"I don't doubt that."

With that said, I walked down the stairs and headed toward my car. Eliza remained poised at the entrance to her house until I was inside, then she headed out toward the pickup to take out the remaining groceries.

Distracted by the scene through my windshield, I blindly tried to jam my keys into the ignition and missed, so they slipped from my hand and onto the floor. When I reached under my seat, something sliced my fingertip, and I drew back. My reflexes were fast, but my aim was off, so my wrist smacked against the steering wheel, introducing a new pain to my hand.

There was a small cut on my index finger: thin, no longer than a half-inch, and barely scraping across the surface of my skin, but it hurt like a bitch. A couple of beads of blood gathered at the surface of the slice.

Wary of the cut, I carefully reached under my seat again, lifted the right lever and pushed my weight back to slide the seat backward. With a much clearer view now, I could see that scattered across the floor of my car were dozens of pieces of paper, all replicas of the original I had seen in the church.

COLTON CREST IS LONG GONE

I had to get out of there. My finger stung when skin touched metal as I turned on the engine. With my foot on the brake and the car in the right gear shift, I took one last look at the house. There, lurking in the shadows of the garage, was Tristan. He stared me down, completely expressionless. How long had he been there? How much had he seen? There were too many questions and I didn't have enough headspace. Ignoring the howling curiosity in me, I hit the gas pedal, the tires spinning dust as I made my escape.

As I dropped the last of the messages into a garbage bag, someone pulled up behind me in our driveway. Leaning over to the passenger side, I quickly grabbed a couple of stray food wrappers and pushed them into the mix. It was a poor attempt to hide the evidence, but I didn't have much time to think out a proper plan.

"What are you doing?" Cass asked when she stepped out of her car, one hand resting on her hip as she shot an accusing glare in my direction. I gave her a sideways glance, ready to toss out a smart-ass comment or call her the dreaded Sassy Cassy (which always resulted in a punch on the shoulder), but then the passenger side door of her car opened and my mom stepped out to join her.

"Hi, honey," Valerie said, smiling hesitantly. "We just had a girls' day out." She held up her Booster Juice cup as if I required evidence of her whereabouts.

I shut the car door. "Good time?"

"Very," Cass answered, looking at the garbage bag in my hand. "We're just going inside for some tea. Is Dad around?"

"He just left to go to the library. I'm pretty sure he'll be there until closing time. He found inspiration."

"He still writes?"

Cass and I directed our attention to our mother.

"Yes."

"I'm guessing he still writes horror and mystery? Your father never was one to steer away from the comfort of something familiar."

"His stories get darker and more twisted as he goes," Cass said. "The fans seem to love it though."

There was the ghost of a smile on her lips. "When he has writer's block . . . does he still—"

"Do weird things like lie on the ground for four hours?" I finished. "Yeah, he does."

Cass and I exchanged uncomfortable glances. We were used to our father remembering small details about our mother, but when it was reversed, we weren't sure how to handle the situation. My sister decided to end the conversation by gently taking Valerie's elbow and steering her toward the house, asking how she liked her tea.

When the girls had disappeared inside, I tied the garbage bag and headed for the bins. I disposed of the rubbish, making sure to cover it with various other papers and cartons to ensure it was properly concealed. Once the lid was closed, I took a step back. Although I could no longer see the notes, my skin still crawled. The killer had touched those, created them and scattered them across my car floor to taunt and scare the shit out of me.

Bastard. It was working.

‡

For the next few days, I couldn't stop thinking about the framed quote in the Yankses' house—the stitched sentences, the subtle underlining of thread beneath the words. It was all that consumed my thoughts. It was another clue . . . wasn't it?

My head throbbed with theories. I couldn't fathom how Colton had done it. How he had watched all those mystery series and already had three key suspects before half the episode had rolled. How he'd read books and noted down clues as he scanned through the pages and uncovered the murderer before the protagonist did. How he'd understood the way people ticked, how he was able to pick up their motives and interests and the forces that drove them to the point of no return.

He would have known exactly what to do. He would have found the killer by now. He wouldn't be flipping his shit like I was.

The pulsing in my temples increased.

Eventually it became too much and I decided to head out. Grabbing my keys and stuffing a couple of twenties in my pocket, I headed downstairs for some painkillers before I went for a drive. Cass was in the kitchen, following a recipe from a book.

"Hungry?" she asked when she saw me enter.

"No, I'm going to head out. Is Dad home yet?" With Dad at the library a lot these days, it was getting easier to come and go without being noticed.

"No, even though the library closed two hours ago. I figure he went somewhere to eat. He'll probably be back soon, though."

I headed toward one of the drawers by the sink, rummaging through the contents until I found a box of pills. I popped two out and poured myself a glass of water, swallowing them down together.

"What time will you be home?" Cass asked, keeping her back to me as she sliced some vegetables. Although her hands were busy and her head was down, I could tell she was concentrating on my reply. We had both been cautious around each other lately, beating around the bush for information that might accidentally slip out. And because we were constantly on guard, our innocent questions seemed almost accusatory.

"Not sure." It was an honest answer, but as I rounded the counter and saw Cass purse her lips, I knew it was an unsatisfactory one. "I'll call?"

"Don't stay out too long." Cass placed the knife down and wiped her hands on the towel beside her. She stared at me for a moment, then she said, "You know, I wish you'd talk to me. I wish we could talk to each other, there's something—"

"Nothing to talk about."

"There's plenty to talk about. How about the fact that you're hardly home? I barely know where you go sometimes or who you're with." She sounded agitated.

"You don't need to keep tabs on me, Cass. So what if I go out? It's healthier than sitting in my room all day doing nothing."

"But aren't you . . . grieving?"

Her tone was more accusatory now. A surge of anger built up inside me.

"Just because I don't mope around all day doesn't mean I'm not grieving. Maybe keeping myself busy is a distraction until I'm ready to accept that he's really dead."

"Maybe if you just talked—"

"*I don't want to talk.*"

A chime sound followed my outburst, accompanied by a buzzing on the table. Her phone lit up and a text message from someone named "T" glowed. Cass quickly grabbed the device, shoving it into her back pocket.

"I don't want to talk," I answered, trying to keep my tone much calmer. "But maybe you should."

✝

Outside the air was cooler, making it much easier to breathe. I inhaled deeply before I unlocked my car door and climbed inside. As I started the engine, I couldn't help but remember the look in Cass's eyes before I left.

It looked a lot like guilt.

✝

"Cass is just such a pain in the ass, you know? You're so lucky you don't have any siblings."

Colton smiled slightly. "It's because she's at university. You both have different dynamics now, that's why you clash when she comes home during mid-session break."

I had been complaining non-stop to my friends about how annoying my sister was. It had gotten to a point where, instead of talking about it, Colton had just picked me up from my house and driven us to The Jukebox. He'd ordered us two extra-large thick shakes, piled with so much ice cream it made my stomach churn.

"She's so controlling." I groaned. "She goes into my room and tidies up."

Colton laughed. "And what exactly is the problem with that? Mate, I've been in your room—you don't exactly get the job done."

"Hey! I have a system. I know where everything goes, and every item I own has its rightful spot. Charger? Bedside table. Avengers sock? On the third shelf on my bookcase. The other Avengers sock? Top drawer of my desk."

"Why are your socks in such weird places?"

"That's not the point. She's totally screwing up my system. My underwear is now color-coded."

Colton sucked in his breath. "Monster. She's challenging your masculinity by organizing your undergarments."

"That's not the problem. Color-coding things is very aesthetically pleasing. But I have been confronted with the harsh reality that I own far too many pairs of red underwear."

Colton slid my thick shake closer to me. "Drink. Ice cream sweetens the soul."

I took a deep gulp of cold, sugary goodness.

"I hear you," Colton said. "She's not respecting your privacy."

"Exactly." I groaned again. "And Dad hasn't been any help. He's head-over-heels excited that my sister is back home."

"Really?" Colton's eyebrows shot up. "Your dad usually heard you out at least."

"Not this time."

Colton slurped up the remainder of his drink. "How's this? Tomorrow after school we'll head into town and buy you a lock for your door. Don't worry, man, I've always got your back."

†

Without thinking about it, I was on my way to The Jukebox. I didn't know what else to do. It had always been the place we'd gone when I was fighting with my sister. Inside it was warm and smelled like grease, which was both revolting and comforting at the same time. It was perfect. Making my way over, I chose a booth, settled in, and picked up a menu. I already knew that the large chocolate milkshake with extra scoops of ice cream was the only thing on my mind, but I absentmindedly scanned the other options while I waited for someone to take my order.

I didn't have to wait long before a young, slim woman approached my table with a smile and perky voice. She pulled a pencil out from her hair and scribbled down what I wanted. Then, after a few minutes of trying to convince me to order the special—barramundi and mango salad—and me politely declining, she left.

When my beverage arrived, my mouth caught the straw and I took the biggest drink I could muster. It was cold and numbed my tongue, but it was like liquid heaven. I stopped drinking before I could get brain freeze, took a few minutes to savor the chocolaty goodness still lingering on my taste buds and went for a second round. But as I was enjoying my drink, someone called my name.

I recognized that voice. It was Colton's mom. I nearly inhaled my straw.

Slowly I turned in my seat and saw the Crests sitting in the booth behind mine. "Mr. Crest." I nodded. "Mrs. Crest."

Although The Jukebox was a family-friendly diner, not many families actually ate there. It was more of a hangout for high school kids and university students, and the occasional tourist passing through town. Colton's family stood out like a sore thumb.

"I thought that was you. How are you? Come sit with us," Mrs. Crest said.

"Okay," I said, hoping my voice didn't give away how truly uncomfortable I was.

I picked up my glass and shuffled into a seat at their table. They stared at me with wax smiles. Flawless. Practiced. Haunting. I ducked my head, shrinking away from their eyes.

They had already ordered. I kept drinking to avoid any tense conversations and didn't lift my head until their plates had hit the table. I felt like a child with two adults trying their hardest to adopt me, their actions careful and calculated and way too bright.

"I haven't had breakfast for dinner in a long time," Mr. Crest announced, looking at his meal of bacon, eggs, and hash browns.

Mrs. Crest had gone for a burger. The top of the bun was sitting beside the other half, to showcase the cheese-covered patty and vegetable toppings. There were no pickles. Just like Colton used to prefer. As soon as the thought entered my mind, I wondered when I had become so attentive of little details. Had I always been like this? Or was it a result of all the sleuthing I had done over the past couple of weeks?

"Megan, you have to try these hash browns. They have been deep-fried to perfection," Mr. Crest said, holding out a piece on his fork.

His wife quietly declined, delicately placing the top bun onto her burger and picking it up with such care, you would have thought it was a rare glass ornament. I was feeling a bit sick, but I picked up my spoon and started scooping up the ice cream. My theory of keeping something in my mouth to avoid any talking was working, and I wasn't going to back down for my stomach's sake.

"We saw your mother the other day," Mrs. Crest said. "She was with Cass."

"Oh," I said, pathetically. "Yeah."

"We should all go out for brunch. You should come too, and Cass," she continued, then paused, realizing the error in her plan.

If the Crests had just invited Valerie, it would have been fine. Some sophisticated small talk over buttered rolls and eggs Benedict would have had a good outcome. But inviting Cass and me instantly excluded my father, and inviting him would make things uncomfortable between my parents.

"She's probably really busy spending time with you kids, though," she said, trying to reel back her offer.

God, things were awkward.

"Has Cass been using her time well?"

"Sorry?" I said slowly, stretching the word out.

She shook her head to clear her thoughts. "I mean the thyme and rosemary. You said she was experimenting with some new recipes?" she asked.

"She hasn't gotten around to using it yet," I lied. "But I'll return them both soon."

"Take your time."

I remembered the letter, the play on words. Nothing but time. I tried not to shiver and focused on the music flooding through the diner.

Because most customers were between the ages of thirteen and twenty-one, the owners put a heavy emphasis on the music. The jukebox was available for people to choose music, and a few teenagers were crowded around it, trying to decide on a song. Even though no one was particularly interested in the television, it still remained on, turned to the news channel. The sound was muted, but the images were clear, and if you were good at lipreading, it did the job.

Mr. Crest watched the glowing screen with detached interest. I think he wanted something to focus on while he shoveled eggs and bacon into his mouth. Mrs. Crest also kept her eyes glued to the screen, holding up her burger, ready to take a bite but never actually doing so.

While they were distracted by the silent news, I studied them. If I hadn't had anything to compare them to, I would have thought they looked awful. But I had seen them both at some of the darkest points of their lives, and maybe it was the fluorescent lights that altered my vision, but they seemed to have improved, even if it was only slightly. Mr. Crest had bothered to shave recently, so there was no shadow haunting his jaw. And Mrs. Crest had delicately dabbed something under her eyes to reduce the puffiness.

But as I studied her, I saw a shift in her eyes. They became wide, unblinking, and almost glassy. And it only took a breath before that hard glass turned into a wavering wall of tears. Slowly I turned in my seat and followed her line of vision until the TV came into my sight.

A reporter was standing there, microphone held up as she spoke. They were recording an incident live from a town a few hours away. An eighteen-year-old boy had been found outside his house with three bullet wounds to his chest. The headline at the bottom of the screen explained that his drunken stepfather was the cause of his death. I couldn't gather any more information than that.

When I turned back to Mrs. Crest, she was wiping the corners of her eyes with a napkin. Her hands were shaking as she dabbed under her lashes. Seeing another child being murdered had struck a chord in her, prodded at feelings she was trying so desperately to ignore.

"Honey," Mr. Crest whispered, wrapping his arms around his wife, trying to comfort her.

"I'm fine," she insisted, but her voice said otherwise.

"Maybe it was a mistake coming here tonight," Mr. Crest mumbled against the top of Mrs. Crest's head.

"I'm sorry," she tried to say between sobs. "I'm so sorry."

"Shh. It's okay, honey . . ." Mr. Crest looked at me briefly before he cast another worried glance at the woman crumbling in his arms. "Elliot, I'm sorry to have to take off so abruptly, but—" He frowned so deeply that the wrinkles in his forehead had wrinkles. I quickly filled in the silence.

"I understand," I said. "Would you like me to walk Mrs. Crest to your car while you pay?"

He seemed relieved at the offer. "Thank you."

I slid out of the booth and fished around in my pockets for some change. "I'll just grab some money for my milkshake—"

"Oh," he said, shaking his head. "No, don't worry about that. It was good catching up with you, even if it was brief. I'll get it."

Before I could argue, he walked toward the counter with the bills in his hand. Mrs. Crest was still sobbing, her body breaking out in violent shakes as she tried to swallow her tears. I gently took her elbow and helped her to her feet, wrapping my arm around her shoulders when she was upright and directing her to the door.

She continued to swipe furiously at her tears as I held the door open for her to step through, and I quickly hooked my arm around her again to prevent her from collapsing. The light from the diner was the only thing helping me navigate my way through the parking lot, so it took a couple more glances than usual to find their car.

At some point, Mrs. Crest had taken her key out from her purse and she shakily reached out to unlock the vehicle. The lights flashed as her thumb pressed against the remote, and I stepped up to open her door. Taking her hand, I eased her into her seat. I wasn't the type of person to offer comforting words and reassuring phrases, but I felt heartless when I couldn't give her any verbal consolation.

I gently squeezed her fingers instead. But as I was about to let go, her grip tightened.

"Oh, Elliot," she whispered, her voice wavering but desperate. "I'm sorry . . . I'm so sorry."

I opened my mouth to reply but before I could, Mr. Crest arrived.

"Thanks, son," he said, patting my shoulder. "Really, you've been a big help."

"It was really no problem," I answered.

"Be careful on the drive home, okay?"

"Will do, sir."

He clapped me on the shoulder once more before he shut the passenger door of the car and circled back to the driver's side. They both gave me a final wave and wished me a good night before they drove off into the evening.

There was a twisting sensation in my stomach as I cut through the parking lot and found my own car. I couldn't help but think of the Crests—how vulnerable they were, how desperate they were for answers, how broken they were over the murder of their only child.

An idea popped into my head as I thought. I took a deep breath. It was risky. It was dangerous. It was downright fucking stupid. But seeing Colton's parents completely break down had struck something in me. They deserved to know what happened to their son. They deserved answers to their questions. I needed to do this. For the Crests.

I started the engine of my car, my mind made up. I knew the quote I had seen earlier in the week was a clue. And I was going to break into the Yanks residence and steal it.

Half-formed ideas should never be put into action.

This realization came too late. I was already lurking in the shadows behind the Yanks residence, trying to listen for anyone who might still be awake. The drive had taken an hour, and with the windows rolled down and the cool night air slapping my face numb, you would have thought that I would have had enough time to think things through.

And even when I sat in my car a few blocks down for a couple more hours, giving the Yankses a chance to brush their teeth and go to bed, I still couldn't think it through. Every time I blinked, all I would see was Mrs. Crest's face. The sorrow and desperation in her eyes, the pain in her features. It haunted me.

It was only when I was on the back portion of the wraparound porch, pressed against the wall, that I started thinking about how stupid I was. I was trespassing on someone's private property. I was going to steal.

There were so many ways it could go wrong. Was it worth the small chance that I could get away with it undetected?

Before I could think anymore, there was a vibration in my pocket, and although my phone was on silent, you could still hear it buzzing through my jeans. I silently swore and quickly pulled it out, declining the call before it could make any further noise.

Cass was calling *again*. I would bet my money that she was completely pissed that I wasn't answering. And if I didn't die while breaking into someone else's home, my sister would definitely kill me when I returned to my own.

I switched my phone off and put it away.

My hands were sweaty, so I wiped them on my jeans. I wondered if robbers got sweaty hands before they broke into other people's houses. Did they get nervous? Or was the thrill exhilarating? Because honestly, I think the only exhilaration I was feeling was from a build-up of gas from that damn milkshake I'd had at the diner. I desperately hoped I could do this. Being detected by flatulence would just be humiliating.

My thoughts were all over the place. I kept repeating to myself that I could do it. I had driven this far, I had waited this long. There was no turning back.

All I had to do was climb through the window by the kitchen. It was slightly open—enough for me to wedge my fingers inside, hope it wasn't squeaky, and push. It was almost too lucky that it wasn't completely shut or locked, like it was staged that way. A mousetrap with a slice of cheese waiting for that hungry little rodent to snatch up the bait.

I wondered if one of the Yankses had opened it slightly to let the night air circulate. Their neighbors were close but far enough away to give them privacy. Perhaps the family didn't feel the need to lock themselves away at night. They were brave, especially since there was still a killer loose. Or maybe the killer was residing inside.

It was possible that the window was open because they hadn't all gone to bed yet. Maybe someone was still walking around the quiet halls of the house and planned to shut it before going to sleep. Or perhaps they'd simply forgotten about it.

But I had been waiting outside for twenty minutes and still hadn't heard a single sound. Not a cough, not the patter of footsteps, not the creak of a door. I hoped everyone was in their beds, asleep and oblivious to the crime that was about to occur.

Taking a deep breath, I straightened slightly from where I was crouched under the window and tried seeing through the small gap. The moonlight provided my only source of light, so it was weak and there was a lot of squinting involved, but I didn't see anything except for the shadows of furniture.

Next I checked the window. Placing my fingers under the small gap, I gently tried to pull it upwards, testing how quiet it truly was. There was a soft whine of protest as it began to open, but as soon as I had lifted it a few inches higher, the movement was silent and fluid.

I hoisted myself up and into the house. The open window was directly above the sink, so it took some awkward and painful maneuvering to get in without knocking anything over. But as soon as my feet were back on solid ground, I positioned myself into a crouch and listened in the shadows for any approaching noises.

I wasn't sure if I was grateful for the silence or not. Would I have preferred to hear some sort of commotion in the house, just so I knew the family was occupied? Or would the noise have made me uneasy and clumsy?

The beating of my heart soon drowned out the shouting in my head. Being sure to stick close to any furniture that would act as a hiding place, I made my way toward the corridor. I had been in the Yanks residence for only a couple of hours on Monday, but I managed to find my way, even in the shadows.

Clinging to the wall of the hallway, I pressed the back of my shaking hand against my forehead. I was sweaty and breathless, my heart pounding, my head light. When I gulped, it was as loud as a helicopter taking off.

What are you getting yourself into, Elliot?

There was no time for my conscience to start second-guessing things. I straightened and quietly made my way through the framed quotes. It was dark, the only light coming from the window above the front door. It cast a glare on the glass, which caused me to have to look twice at the stitched writing samplers. I struggled as I tried to find the right piece again, my brain trying to make sense of the dim images my eyes were seeing.

Then I found it.

My fingers pressed against the frame. Was there some sort of button that led to a secret compartment? Maybe a clue was wedged between the quote and the wooden back? Was I just overthinking—

As my hand lifted the frame, I felt something taped to the back—a piece of paper. My pulse quickened as I tried to tear it off, my knuckles knocking clumsily against the wall in my hasty attempt. My heart was beating as I fumbled with the paper, my breath quickening. When I finally freed it, I felt an odd rush of relief and fear.

Then I heard footsteps.

Without a second glance at the paper to confirm if it was another letter, I circled around like a dog chasing its tail as I tried to find the quickest escape. The front door was out of the question because the person was making their way down the stairs and had the entrance of the house in their direct line of sight. There was a bathroom located at the end of the hallway, but I didn't know if there was a window big enough for me to squeeze through, and what if there wasn't? I'd be trapped in there.

I was running out of time.

Before the person could round the corner, I quickly slunk into the shadows and made my way back into the living room, hiding behind one of the couches. It seemed like a pathetic place to seek invisibility, but I was panicked, and the number one hide-and-go-seek spot was the best I could do.

From the living room, I could see the staircase, and a part of the hallway and kitchen were directly in front of me. As I sought comfort in the shadows with my beating heart and throbbing temples, I waited.

Crouched to make myself look as small as possible, I was still on my toes, ready to sprint if the time ever came. As I tried to slip the paper into the pocket of my hoodie without it making a deafening crunch, curiosity gnawed my insides. Who was there?

If it was Alexandra, I could probably escape. I was blindly relying on her age to slow her down, but maybe I was wrong and she was secretly a champion athlete. Eliza would be harder. I thought about throwing some furniture as I ran. Putting obstacles in her path would increase my chances of getting out.

But Tristan?

I tried not to think about it. He had killed someone before. I could bet my money he wouldn't hesitate to murder again. Trying to keep covered, I peeked from behind the couch, hoping I could weigh up my competition.

My stomach dropped when I saw Tristan standing at the front of the open fridge, chugging orange juice from a supersized bottle. Even from the back, he looked menacing. I silently cursed myself for slacking off on my workouts and made a mental note to visit the gym. No wonder Colton worked out so much. He had to go up against a guy like Tristan.

Tristan suddenly stopped drinking. He lowered the bottle onto the counter and dropped the lid down next to it. He was unnaturally still. Then, as he reached up, I realized he wasn't having a miniature daydream. He was staring at the open window above the sink.

I stopped breathing.

He reached over and shut and locked it. Without a second glance at the window, he screwed the cap back on the juice and threw it back in the fridge. Then he kicked the door closed and the yellow light disappeared. I didn't dare breathe as he walked away. Did he know someone had broken into his house? Did he know that the trespasser was *still* in his house?

I waited a couple more minutes to ensure the coast was clear. Then I wiped my hands on my jeans and started to straighten from my position, only to be pinned by someone else.

My head slammed against the hard, wooden back of the couch, sending a sickening wave of pain through me. A muscular forearm pressed against my throat, blocking my airway. I felt a momentary surge of panic as I struggled to breathe, my mind working in overdrive to overcome the situation.

Then, before my brain could register what my fist was doing, my knuckles met bone and my attacker let out a grunt of displeasure as my blind shot hit his nose. Tristan loosened his grip slightly and I took the opportunity. I grabbed his forearm and spun around, twisting it with my momentum.

As soon as I was on my feet and Tristan was growling behind me, I leaped up and made a run for it. But he was faster. He dove after me as I hastily made my way around the couch. We both landed hard, chins bumping into the floor.

"Who are you?" he demanded. "What do you want?"

My hood had managed to stay on my head, and I was sure he hadn't clearly seen my face yet. I wanted to keep it that way. I kept my head down and tried to control my ragged breath. I was trapped. There was no doubt we had made a commotion. It was only a matter of time before the rest of his family would come down the stairs and discover what was happening.

"I said *who are you?*" Tristan snarled as he twisted my arm back, using his knuckles to hit me right between my shoulder blades. I bit back a howl of pain. "Better start giving me answers, or blood will be shed."

His right knee pressed against my spine, keeping me down, his grip around my wrist unbreakable. I could feel him shifting his weight, no doubt trying to get a weapon tucked between the folds of his clothes. My heart was beating against the floorboards and I wondered if he could hear the hot blood pulsing in my veins, oblivious to its undeniable future seeping out onto the ground.

But he was struggling to get whatever he was trying to reach. His knee lifted a fraction from my back. Using all the energy I could muster, I rolled onto the arm he was holding, up onto my elbow, causing him to let go before his hand got crushed under my weight. It hurt like a bitch, limbs twisting in unnatural ways. But as soon as he had let go, I used my other hand to get another blow in. Because he was crouching above me, I had access to his throat, so my knuckles went directly to that particular point of weakness.

The darkness helped to disguise my features, I hoped. My hit had managed to knock him off his balance. He was on his toes, bending backward to catch the ground before he went tumbling. Scrambling to my feet, I headed for the front door, not bothering to conceal my footsteps to minimize the noise. I threw it open, Tristan hot on my heels.

"I'll kill you!" he threatened as he raced after me.

My heart was beating with every step, my feet burning as I picked up the pace. Tristan was fast and a gunshot went off behind me. He had speed *and* a weapon. I was as good as gone.

Gasping for air, I tried to feed my suffocating lungs, but every breath felt like poison, burning my insides and sucking me dry. My throat felt like sandpaper as I swallowed, tongue tough and textured against the roof of my mouth.

The Yankses' property was large, and Tristan kept up with me even as I found myself back on the road behind the house. If I got caught, no one would find my body for days. I was in the middle of fucking nowhere.

I kept my pace but turned around, trying to see how close he was. How close he was to killing me. How close I was to dying. But when I looked over my shoulder, trying to see through my tightened hood, I caught a quick glimpse of him retreating into the trees near the front of his property, a gun in his hand and murder in his eyes.

Why did he stop running?

But when I heard the squealing of tires and saw the familiar red-and-blue flashes of light, I knew why he had stayed back. The police car sped to a stop right in front of me.

"Is everything okay here?" A police officer stepped out of the car, directing a flashlight right into my eyes, causing me to put my arm up to block it. My footsteps faltered.

I quickly looked behind me, but I couldn't see anything. Maybe Tristan was lurking within the shadows. I turned back to the officer, who was now shining his flashlight in the direction I'd been looking.

"Yes," I answered, a little more breathlessly than I would have liked.

"What are you doing out at this time of night?"

"My . . ." My brain reeled for an explanation. "My car broke down. I was trying to see if there was any help around."

"Really? You seemed frantic."

"Never really been around this part of town. Thought I was lost," I said, trying to keep my tone level, despite my ragged breathing. My purported reason for running around in the dark was pathetic, so I needed something else to make it sound more believable. "Didn't find any help. A vicious dog found *me*, though."

"Couldn't you have phoned someone?"

I swallowed. "No service."

I knew that wasn't true, considering Cass had called me before I broke into the house. But I hoped I could blame my service company and pray he didn't have the same one. The police officer didn't seem to buy my whole story, but he looked tired. It seemed he didn't want to deal with a rebellious eighteen-year-old at two in the morning.

"If you need any help locating your vehicle and finding your way home, we'll be happy to assist."

"Thanks, I'd appreciate it."

He nodded toward his vehicle. "What was your name again?"

"Elliot," I answered, opening the back door. "Elliot Parker."

The police officer exchanged a look with his partner behind the wheel. She glanced at me through the rearview mirror, frowning.

"You wouldn't happen to be the same Elliot Parker who discovered the body of Colton Crest about a month back, are you?" she asked.

I froze, the strap of my seatbelt in midair. "I—I am."

"Before we find your vehicle, would you mind if we dropped by the station for a few questions?" the other office asked. "It won't take too long."

My stomach flipped. I was a dead man.

†

The room was cold, so I put my hands into the pocket of my hoodie. My fingers skimmed across the paper I had stolen, and I itched to open it, but I left it where it was and instead focused on the officer in front of me. The last time I had been in a room like this was after I'd found Colton dead.

The first time I was there, my statement hadn't been particularly coherent. Denial and confusion had been swimming through me, and the events of that night were masked with fog and blur. This second time around wasn't much different. The memories were distant and out of focus, but at least I was more aware of my surroundings this time, and the voice directed at me. I had been called in to reconfirm my statement, which meant I was thankfully still a witness and not a suspect, enduring an interview and not an interrogation.

I repeated the information I had given the first time, trying to remember details tucked somewhere at the back of my brain.

"Do you remember anything else from that night?"

I shook my head helplessly.

"Do you have any other relevant information that might help us with the investigation?"

The paper in my pocket seemed to multiply in weight. It was evidence.

I potentially had evidence from Colton's killer. The smart thing to do would have been to hand it over and let the authorities handle it. But I had withheld that information for far too long. Because of that, would I then be considered a suspect? Would I become the alleged murderer of Colton Crest?

If I gave up the letters, the clues, the confessions, I wouldn't be able to carry out the investigation by myself anymore. I couldn't figure out the answers, find the truth. This wild-goose chase to hunt down Colton's killer would have been for nothing.

"No," I answered.

He nodded. "Thank you for your time this evening. If you remember anything relevant to the investigation, please contact us as soon as possible."

I was promptly escorted out of the room when the interview was concluded. I took my time on the way out, mostly because I was sleepy, but also because I didn't want to seem too eager to leave and examine the secret paper stashed in my pocket. But as I walked down the hall, I heard voices, and my pace instantly slowed even more.

" . . . Colton Crest . . ."

" . . . signs of struggle . . ."

" . . . head injury . . ."

" . . . blood . . ."

There was a cough behind me. My head turned and I saw a police officer a few feet away. I picked up the pace until I was outside. The cold air was a relief, so I closed my eyes and savored the feeling.

"Do you remember anything?"

I spun. "Jesus Christ, Cass."

"Well, do you?" she pressed, placing her hands in the pockets of her purple coat.

"What the hell are you doing here?" I demanded.

"I got a call. They said you were escorted to the station and that your car had broken down somewhere," she answered, frowning.

"Someone needed to pick you up and bring you home. You've had quite a night. We can find your car later."

"Who's *they*?"

"The police, Elliot. Why are you so damn suspicious?" she shot back.

In arguments, Cass rarely raised her voice. Instead, she lowered it until it resembled something like a hiss. She'd lower her chin and look up at you, venom soaking through her words. Suddenly she'd be a snake. Say the right words and you'd hypnotize her and she'd be momentarily harmless, but one wrong move could result in a poisonous bite. So, to keep the peace, I didn't say anything. It was safer to let her lash out at a distance.

"Just get in the car. I don't want to make a scene," she finally said, crossing the parking lot.

Following her lead, I got into the passenger side and buckled my seatbelt. Cass slammed her door and started the engine, reversing out of the spot and directing the car back onto the road.

"Can you please just answer my question?" she asked after a moment's silence. Her tone hadn't changed much. She was still pissed.

"Why is remembering anything so important to you . . . ?" I asked hesitantly, my voice a little sleepy.

She tightened her hands on the steering wheel and made a sharp turn, causing me to jerk back into alertness.

"Because you don't understand how valuable your information can be. Look, sometimes witnesses and victims can be so traumatized by these types of situations that they block out vital details. You discovered the body and that generates a serious amount of shock, but have you ever wondered why you can't recount anything more, even to this day? Maybe you saw something more, maybe you know something more and your defense mechanism is trying to protect it. Don't you think the reason you refuse to talk or mourn or anything is because deep down, you *know* something?"

"What . . . what are you saying?"

"If you remember anything . . . you need to tell me."

"I need to tell you," I repeated distantly.

"Come to me first, Elliot. Not the police."

"Why not the police?"

Cass looked at me for a brief moment before she returned her eyes to the road. "Because we're family. Family protect each other."

†

When we got home, Cass went to her room, claiming she had a head-ache and needed to sleep it off. Dad was in the kitchen, a fast food bag sitting in front of him, an Angus burger in his hands. The smell was intoxicating. After everything that had happened, my stomach was growling for my attention.

As soon as I was at the table, I snatched a chip from the bag and headed for the fridge, searching for something to put in a sandwich. Ham? Maybe some avocado? Then I was getting the hell out of there and checking out that piece of paper. Just as I was getting out the mayo, Dad spoke.

"Where have you been?"

"Causing trouble," I answered, which was true, but vague.

"That was a rhetorical question. I know where you've been, Elliot. I know you were down at the station. I know how they found you."

I dumped the ingredients onto the counter and kicked the fridge closed. "My car broke down."

"Sit down."

It was a rare occurrence when Dad told either of his kids to sit down. But whenever he did, we knew it was serious and did whatever he asked without questions or hesitations. Dad placed his burger back in its box and scrubbed the sauce from his mouth.

"You know I'm not very restricting when it comes to your freedom, but that's not an invitation to abuse it. This is the second time you've come home at an unacceptable hour in the past couple of weeks. I know you're an adult and I respect you, but I'm an adult too, and you have to respect me. It works both ways, buddy. You have to meet me halfway."

"Listen, Dad, I'm sorry—"

"I'm not finished." He placed a hand up to silence me. "That call gave us a scare, kid. Do you know what it was like hearing the police on the other end of the phone for the second time, saying they'd found you and that you were at the station? Whether it was for an interview to reconfirm your statement or not, it gave us a scare. And I hate to have to do this, but I'm going to have to issue a curfew. Until Colton's murder is solved, you're going to have to be home at ten every night."

"I . . ." My voice trailed off. I was tired and my late night adventures were getting too out of hand. I thought of it as Dad doing me a favor, so I agreed. "Okay."

"I'm sorry. Being a single dad is hard . . . being a dad, in general, is hard. Hell, all aspects of parenthood are hard." He smiled sadly.

"I don't know. I think you're doing a pretty good job," I said.

"Thanks, son. Your sister and I will pick up your car in the morning."

I suddenly wasn't very hungry, so I packed everything up and went upstairs. Once I was in my room, I waited a couple of heartbeats. I listened for footsteps or voices or any other indication that I might be interrupted. But when there was nothing but silence, I pulled out the lined paper. It *was* another letter. My instincts had been right.

Smoothing it out, I started to read.

Cassette tapes can record all sorts of things: songs, stories, secrets. Even confessions. But we'll get back to cassette tapes in a second. Shall we continue with the confessions instead?

July 26 should be a day you remember. It was the day

Colton came back into town. That day was celebrated with such joy and relief and victory, as if he were a soldier who had just come back from war. He was a hero. But he didn't deserve to be. Especially when half the town got the date wrong. The twenty-sixth of July wasn't the day Colton came back into town. It was the date he made everyone believe he did. The truth was, he had been back for two weeks prior to announcing his homecoming. Most people didn't know this. But I did. Do you know who else knew?

You see, Colton was stubborn. It may not seem like such a shocking revelation, considering a lot of people share the same trait, but it was his stubbornness that resulted in a lot of things. For example, when Colton was six, he owned a tire swing. It was always a struggle to get him to come inside. There was a daily protest each time he was on that swing, and only the proper arrangement of compromises would defeat his stubbornness.

Now this may seem like an unsatisfying letter, which brings me back to cassette tapes. I wanted to maximize the experience for you and excite your senses. I thought of making a cassette tape, but hearing my voice would give too much away when I have so much more to offer. Instead, let's hear some different voices. In celebration of advancements in technology, I have created a video. Starring Colton Crest and Elliot Parker, I present to you: confession number four.

At the end of the page was a link. And a password.

Sleep didn't seem like an option when my eyes reached the end of the letter. The sun would be rising soon, and my body demanded rest, but my brain was going haywire. Both the link and the password were a combination of random letters and numbers, dashes and dots. It could lead to any sort of page: an online newspaper article, a blog, a YouTube video. Hell, it could have been a virus. But I had come this far, so sleep would have to wait.

I made my way to my desk and opened my laptop. Once the browser window was open, I started typing. The string of characters seemed to run on forever, but once I had finally gotten it, I pressed Enter, waited for the page to load and input the password. Only one thing appeared on the screen: a video.

It wasn't a blog or part of an article. It didn't have a title or a view count or a scroll bar to load comments. The whole screen was filled with a video, and Colton and I were the stars of the show. The beginning shot was a view from the back of my house, the camera located somewhere high, like on the roof of my pergola. I closed my eyes and shivered. I was disgusted that Colton's killer had set foot on my property, that they had placed a camera and recorded something like this. When had the killer snuck into my backyard? How was the camera installed? How was the person not caught retrieving it?

It was the day Colton had shown up at my doorstep after he had disappeared. The table was covered with beer bottles and we were lounging on the chairs. I remembered that day like it was yesterday. Or so I thought. My mouse hovered over the Play button, and I sat there, at a loss as to what I was about to release. With one last breath, I pressed Play.

†

I was slumped lazily in my chair, a beer bottle in my hand. I admired it with such intense fascination that it looked like I wasn't aware of my surroundings or even who I was with. I lifted the beverage and took a drink, a satisfying burp ripping from my throat. The old Colton would have looked up and given me a high five, grinning as we shared the bond that only a burp could ignite. But the guy sitting next to me was an emotionless shell. He toyed with his pocket watch, opening and closing the lid, always glancing at the time even when it had only been seconds since his last look.

When he finally put it back into his pocket, I spoke. "Where have you been, man? And quit the bull about being with family."

†

My voice was drunker than I remembered.

†

Colton just smiled and tipped his bottle, taking a drink before he said, "Stop trying to play detective, Elliot. Some mysteries just can't be solved."

†

That was all I remembered. Exactly fifteen seconds of the video. I couldn't imagine what the remaining twelve minutes were. I didn't think we'd talked much after. I didn't think I'd asked him any more questions. I didn't think he'd given me any more answers. But all three had happened.

†

"Okay, but can I ask something else?" I said. "Where have you been?"

"You just asked that."

"I know," I answered, straightening in my seat. "But seriously . . . where the hell have you been? Everyone's been freaking out, man. Me, Lydia, your parents . . ."

"Mom knew," My head jerked back.

"Don't look so shocked," he said. "Do you really think she'd let me just take off like that? She would have filed a missing person's report. I told her I'd be gone for a while, she just didn't know why or where."

"And she let you?"

"I'm eighteen, Elliot. I don't need parental consent to do things." Colton pulled out his pocket watch again and glanced at the hands.

"If you're not going to answer where you've been, at least tell me why you just left. If you were in trouble, you could have just called. You know I would have helped you out," I said, placing my now-empty bottle on the table.

Again, the watch disappeared back into his pocket and he smiled sadly. "I know. I'm sorry. I left because I needed answers."

"Answers?"

"Yeah. I wasn't getting them here so I left. It's much easier getting answers from people when they don't know who you are. Or when they think you're somebody else."

"Dude," I said slowly, putting my hands up as an indication for him to slow down, "what are you even talking about?"

"I had a second identity while I was gone."

"Shut the fuck up, man."

"I'm serious."

To my drunk self, this was the coolest shit I had ever heard. My eyes were wide, mouth open in a huge grin, palms upwards, ready to gesture wildly.

"Colton," I said, lowering my voice. "You're like a spy."

He laughed. "I guess."

"What was your spy name?"

"Daniel Heckerman."

✝

This was apparently hilarious to me because I burst out in throaty laughter. Hit with that combination of the cool-spy scenario and the most comedic alter-ego name, I was hysterical. Not to mention inebriated by the alcohol pulsing through my veins. Colton didn't seem the slightest bit drunk, even though there were a lot of bottles on the table. I didn't remember drinking that many, but I guess that's the thing about drinking: you tend to forget things. Maybe that was why Colton was telling me everything. Because he didn't think I'd remember. Because he thought I was too drunk to comprehend.

✝

"Laugh all you want, but it worked."

"You got answers?"

"I did. And secrets."

"Secrets? About what?"

"Secrets about you. And secrets about me. Secrets about a lot of people."

"Secrets about me?" my past-self asked.

Colton pulled out the pocket watch again and watched as the seconds ticked by. When he closed the lid, he looked at his thumb running over the smooth gold surface. Then he suddenly stood, the motion so fast it startled past-me, and I blindly reached over to try to catch the empty beer bottles that weren't even in danger of falling. Instead of putting the watch back in his pocket, he held it and turned for the back door.

"Wait, where are you going?"

"I have something I need to do."

"Colton, you disappeared for months, and you just came back, and what the hell?"

"You're wasted, El. You get bitchy when you're drunk."

"I know. This just isn't fair—"

"You won't remember much of this conversation."

"I will so."

"You're practically unintelligible right now."

"If I won't remember anything, then tell me a secret."

Colton's hand lingered by the door. Finally he dropped it and turned to me. "You think I came home today. Well, that's a lie. I've been back for two weeks."

"And you didn't tell me? Some friend you are," I waved the bottle around.

"Elliot, you're my best friend," he said, looking at me sadly. "I'll eventually tell you everything . . . but if I don't, I know for a fact that someone else will."

"Who?" I asked.

But Colton had already disappeared.

†

The screen went black as soon as the video ended. Then a message turned up on the screen, and panic surged through my body.

VIDEO COMPLETED. FILE
DELETING IMMEDIATELY.

"What? No. No, no, no!" I yelled, not caring that everyone in my house was sleeping.

A bar in the middle of the screen started filling up and yelling at my computer screen wasn't helping. As the bar reached the halfway point, I started clicking furiously with my invisible cursor. When that did nothing, I started typing away at my keyboard, trying combinations, pressing the Escape button with reckless abandon.

My brain was working on overdrive, my heart pounding uncontrollably. I needed the recording for future reference. There was no way I could find another clue with one quick run-through, especially because I was sleep-deprived.

"Elliot," Cass called, knocking on my door.

I frantically looked between my screen and my door. What the hell was I supposed to do?

Cass chose for me. She opened the door and stepped in, sleepily peering at me through half-closed eyes. She wrapped her arms around herself to shield herself from the cold, and stifled a yawn.

A small ball of fur shot past her legs and leaped onto my bed. Ever since the whole thing with Colton, I hadn't been paying much attention to my dog. He had been moping around in my dad's study a lot, sniffing the carpet in search of any extra food he could scavenge. Milo was now all fat and fur, the increase in his already-pudgy size quite evident.

"Do you know what time it is? What the hell are you doing?" she asked.

"Nothing," I said. "I just . . . I just died."

"What?"

I gestured vaguely to my computer. "It was my last life on this game I was playing."

Cass gave me a look like she wanted to both kill me and go to sleep. Thankfully she chose the latter. She paused for a moment, looking at me curiously, as if deciding whether or not she wanted to say something. Shaking her head, she closed my door and returned to her own room. Milo sighed heavily through his nose, trying to get my attention. He had flopped onto his side and was staring at me with big accusing eyes. I felt guilty for neglecting him so much, so I made a promise to take him out more often.

When that was decided, I looked back to my screen. Like the notification had said, the video had been wiped, but there was something in its place.

A GIF of a little girl on a tire swing.

Even though Dad had implemented a curfew, it didn't seem relevant to me anyway. I had been confined to the four walls of my bedroom, watching the cartoon tire swing move back and forth, riding an invisible wind.

The aftereffects of watching the video had been brutal for me. The shock of seeing it, combined with fatigue and near-insanity, had led me to tear down my entire room. If the killer had so easily placed a camera in my backyard, what was stopping that person from putting one in my bedroom? I was probably a hilarious act as the murderer watched from a monitor. I'd never escape.

My room was a disaster by the time I admitted defeat. Books pulled from my shelves, old papers and assignments out of storage, and loose pieces of paper strewn everywhere. Video games were all over the floor, DVDs were scattered on the carpet. It looked like a war zone.

It pissed me off that the killer had so much control over everything. I was a puppet, bending over backward, allowing myself to be manipulated so I could piece together the mystery of Colton's death. I was being driven into recklessness, losing my mind in the process.

Eventually I fell asleep on piles of clothes and fallen pillows. And when I woke up, I cleaned up my mess, placing things back on shelves and rearranging their positions. No matter how hard I tried, I couldn't remember how everything had originally been. That was the thing about destroying something: you couldn't piece it back together perfectly.

For the remainder of the morning, I stared at my laptop, willing the footage to return. I clicked and googled and typed random sequences. The moving image of the girl on the tire swing taunted me, a sickeningly innocent cartoon after a horrifying video. My phone rang and I absentmindedly answered it.

"Hello?"

"Hey," Lydia said. "Are you ready for tonight?"

"Tonight?" I answered distractedly.

There was silence on the end of the line. Then she said, "Colton's memorial camping trip."

Oh. *Oh.* I hadn't even realized it was Friday already.

"Uh," I answered, running a hand through my hair. "I could probably swing by."

"What do you mean 'swing by'?"

"The thing is, I kind of have a curfew," I admitted.

Lydia didn't say anything.

"I just have to leave before ten. Lydia? Is that all right?"

There were some shuffling sounds in the background. She cleared her throat. "Yeah, that's okay. What happened anyway? Your dad is usually so laid-back."

"I guess I've been abusing his trust."

"Is this your rebellious stage emerging?" she joked.

I smiled. "Something like that."

"Okay, but I'm going down early to help set up, so I'll drive myself.

Come find me when you're there? And can you pick up some stuff from the grocery store for me?"

"I can and will."

Lydia gave me a list, and then we said our goodbyes and she hung up. Even though I wouldn't be staying the night, I wanted to do something for everyone else. A lot of people had traveled back into town, cut their holidays short, and postponed their flights just to be there to help support each other.

$$\dagger$$

Around seven, I rummaged through my clothes until I found something and gave it a sniff. Deciding that it would have to do, I put it on and made my way downstairs to get a drink before I hit the road again.

"Elliot, have you seen your sister?" Dad called, scratching the back of his head. He pushed his round glasses up his nose and looked at me with his eyebrows drawn together.

"No," I answered, choosing a bottle of Gatorade and shutting the fridge. "Why?"

"I have a meeting with my publishers about my upcoming work. I figured jeans and a mustard-stained shirt wouldn't shout 'professional,' so I took out my old dress shirts. I'm a disaster when it comes to the iron, though, and I need Cass's help."

"I haven't seen her all day," I admitted.

"Speaking of not seeing people, I've barely heard a peep out of you. You've been in your room all week." Dad opened the fridge and took out a bottle of water.

"Yeah, I know."

"Is this because of the curfew thing?" He ran a hand through his hair, his expression grim. "I'm sorry. I feel like such an awful parent. I don't mean to be so rough on you, kid, especially because of what happened to Colton. I'm not exactly the World's Greatest Dad right now, am I?"

"It's not that," I answered, trying to give my most reassuring smile as I kicked the fridge closed. "I just have a lot on my mind."

Dad didn't seem to buy it. He studied me with excruciating intensity. "You *are* allowed to leave the house, Elliot. I would just be much more comfortable sleeping at night if I knew you were home by ten. Until everything settles down."

I nodded, my gaze down. There was a weight in my chest as I listened to my dad talk about how guilty he felt. But how else was I supposed to explain my behavior? The moodiness, the isolation, the silent treatment . . . These seemed to fit with the natural response toward a parent who'd implemented a curfew.

If only Dad knew what was really going on. I desperately wanted to tell him about the letters, the confessions, the killer. How I was in a one-sided conversation with Colton's murderer. I wanted to get the clues, the scavenger hunt, the taunting secrets, the videos, the stalking off my chest. The lies were eating me alive, and my brain was a ticking time bomb.

"Actually," I said, "I'm going out tonight."

"Oh, good. Where to?"

"There's a memorial camping trip for Colton. I'm meeting Lydia there, dropping off some snacks for the night, maybe sharing a story or two about him."

Dad smiled sadly. "Make it eleven if you stop by the supermarket and grab some pancake mix? We'll have a family breakfast. I feel like I've barely seen both of you kids."

"Thanks, Dad."

He nodded and disappeared out of the kitchen, heading back into his study. And after a quick drink of my Gatorade, I left too, walking out the front door. Outside it was oddly cold for December, so I pulled on my sweater. Then I got in the car and backed out of my driveway.

†

After I had gotten all the stuff on Lydia's list, I drove over to the park. Students had filled up the small lot, and many had opted for parking around the block. I was lucky enough to find a space after a couple of girls wearing sports gear finished their nightly workout and drove away.

As I took my keys out, my phone rang. "Hello?"

"Hey, was that you I just saw pull up?" Lydia said.

"It was," I answered, reaching over to grab the bag on the floor.

"Wait right there, I'll come up."

Lydia appeared as I opened the trunk, her face pale, her cheeks splashed in pink because of the cold. She wrapped her arms around herself and smiled at me.

"Hey," she said. "Need a hand?"

"Yeah, I just have a couple bags back here."

Lydia was staring at something behind me, eyes unblinking. "I went to Woolies," I said, trying to get her attention. "I picked up your favorite gummies. There's a bag of red frogs in there too, just for you." I rummaged through and found the packet, shaking it in all its glory. "I also picked up a bag of sour worms for us to split. I even took out all the blue-and-pink ones and put them in a sandwich bag for you. Am I not the best friend ever or what?"

Sour worms were our thing. Lydia ate only the blue-and-pink ones, and I ate only the green-and-yellow ones. It was our tradition to leave the orange-and-purple ones in the bag and throw it out. Neither of us liked them, and Colton had deemed sour worms unappealing in general.

Lydia usually perked up at the mention of her favorite gummies, but this time she didn't even blink. I probably could have said anything at that point and her reaction would have been the same.

"Lydia," I tried again. "Lyd?"

She slowly returned her gaze to me and gave me a distant smile. "Sorry, what did you say?"

Something was *definitely* wrong. I placed the bag back down and leaned against the car. "Okay, what's up, Lyd?"

"Nothing," she answered, coming to lean next to me, staring at nothing in particular.

"I've known you since we were twelve, Lydia Potter. I know when there's something wrong."

"I have a lot on my mind. I don't know if I can do this . . . Helping to organize this thing distracted me . . . I guess I forgot what I was actually doing. And now that it's really here, I don't know if I can go through with it. Can I really sit here all night and listen to stories about him? Vague narratives of a person these people barely knew? Do they know he broke his little toe when he was seven? Do they know he was scared of clowns? Do they know he'd played the piano since he was ten?"

"Lydia," I said softly.

"Do they know he wasn't as perfect as he seemed? He was just as confused, just as scared, just as batty as the rest of us goddamned fools on this earth!" she screamed, tears streaming down her face.

As I wrapped my arm around her shoulders, she turned and buried her face against my sweater. I rubbed her arm and let her cry until she collected herself enough to talk.

"I'm sorry," she said, pulling away and wiping the tears from her eyes with the sleeve of her shirt. "I don't know what came over me. I just lost it . . ."

"Hey, it's okay. Tonight will be a good night. We're going to eat some good food and we'll remember Colton together."

In all honesty, these words were partly for me too. After everything that had gone on, I found myself not knowing who Colton Crest was. The new picture of him that I'd constructed consisted of false identities, disappearances, and a hell of a lot of lies. Maybe tonight would help me remember the guy I used to know. The one who was insanely good at chess, the one who was head over heels for Lydia, the one who could make anyone laugh no matter how bad their day was.

"It'll be a good night," I repeated, giving her one last hug.

By around nine, everyone was huddled in a group, curled up in sleeping bags, peeking out from tents as we talked about Colton. Stories were swapped, laughter was shared, and we were all having a good time. Lydia and I were sitting together, sharing a blanket and a packet of gummy bears. She was jittery and uncomfortable, but she forced a smile through the conversations and kept busy by chewing on candies.

"Colton was always doing things to make people smile," Lydia said. "Remember when he got all the guys in our class to stand up in the middle of the assembly and do a choreographed dance routine?"

"Or the time he organized breakfast for our history class because our teacher's cat had passed away?" I said.

The stories circled around, and everyone had at least one to share. At one point, Lydia announced she needed to use the bathroom. I helped her up and she walked toward the restroom on the other side of the park.

I didn't think much of it. The minutes ticked by and she didn't return. I tried to keep calm, not to panic, but after twenty minutes had passed, I got so worried that I went searching for her.

The bathroom block was on the opposite end, but the park in general wasn't very large, so it didn't take long for me to navigate my way. When I reached the ladies' room, I hesitated. Rather than barging in, I lingered by the open door and called in.

"Lydia? Lydia?"

A moment later, someone emerged. But it wasn't Lydia. It was Josie, a girl who used to be in my chemistry class.

"Hey, Elliot," she said, looking startled that I was hanging out near the women's bathroom. "Need a hand with something?"

"Just looking for Lydia. Is she still in there?"

"Sorry, no one was in there except for me."

Panic struck me like a lightning bolt. "Thanks," I choked out. "I must have missed her back there."

"Keep your chin up, Parker. I know this must be really hard for you, but you're doing really well. We're all here to support each other."

I had almost forgotten that we were still at Colton's memorial. I was too busy mentally scouting places where my missing friend could be. Josie wandered off back to the camp. I quickly scanned the park. Lydia had seemed uneasy before she'd gone to the bathroom. Maybe she had broken down somewhere. I instantly felt guilty for not showing more concern, for not offering to escort her. What if she'd needed a hand and I wasn't there?

There were no human-shaped shadows lurking around, no signs of movement. I skimmed over the rest of my peers, looking for her head of strawberry blond hair, but I still couldn't find her. I raked my hands through my hair and circled on the spot. Then my eyes landed on the church—her church—and I instantly knew where she was.

†

The air grew colder as I neared the church, some sort of sign that every step I took was closer to something. The wind tore at my clothes, like skeletal fingers pleading with me to stay put, but I shook the feeling away and continued on.

"Lydia?" I called hesitantly, testing the church doors.

They swung open without difficulty and I stepped into the darkness. Reaching out blindly, I tried to find my way inside. I wondered if Lydia could see anything. Was the lack of light comforting? Shouldn't there be a switch or something somewhere? In the foyer area, I started feeling for one.

But as my fingers inched across the wall, a hand reached out and wrapped around my mouth. The person's other hand yanked on the back of my shirt, dragging me backward until I was eaten by darkness.

"Don't make a sound."

"Lydia?" I whispered.

She pressed her finger against my lips. "Did you not hear me? I said don't make a sound," she hissed urgently, irritation coating her words.

I nodded, and she removed her hand, gesturing for me to crouch down beside her. We sat there, our backs pressed against the wall. Both of us were silent, but I could hear the faint sound of her breathing and the psychotic beating of my heart. Lydia's head was turned so that her cheek pressed against the bricks.

I don't know how long we stayed there for, but my knees were starting to ache as we continued to hide, so I shifted, my shuffling feet making a noise. Lydia turned and looked at me with murder in her eyes.

"Do you want to be heard?" she whispered angrily.

Who the hell was this girl, and what had she done to Lydia?

"Why are you so tense?" I asked, hesitantly. I was stepping into unknown territory. I'd either survive another move forward or get blasted to smithereens.

"I'm sorry," she said, deflating. I followed suit and relaxed a little. Nice move, Parker. "It's just—"

One of the side doors groaned in protest as it was pulled open. Lydia instantly fell into silence and urgently pushed me back against the wall. My head hit the bricks and a dull ache throbbed in the back of my skull. She inched forward to peek through the open door and see who had entered. From where I was behind her, I couldn't make out anything, especially in the darkness.

Something caught Lydia's eye and she silently pushed herself off from where we were hiding and crawled into the carpeted area of the church. I kept low and followed her, trying to stay as quiet as possible.

Lydia was a dark smudge hiding between the shadows of the pews. When she saw that I was by her side, she cocked her head toward a cloaked figure. My blood ran cold.

Was it Colton's killer?

The shadow was an unidentifiable blur of black ink, and even as the person slowly progressed forward, there were no indications of gender or body shape or facial features. It was just a silent shadow floating through the church.

If it truly was Colton's killer, I wondered how the dots connected. How did Lydia know to come here? Was Colton's killer stalking her? Was the murderer hunting her, ready to kill her next?

I bit back a snarl. One of my friends had been murdered because of this person. I wasn't ready for another to be taken away from me.

The figure continued walking. A slice of moonlight cut through the dark a couple of feet away. If the person continued walking, I'd be able to identify *something*. Maybe their attire or their eyes or, at the very least, their gender.

Closer. I was on my toes, ready for action. *Just a little closer.* Lydia sucked in a breath of anticipation. *Almost there.*

Now.

The small patch of moonlight shone against a piece of material. And there was no questioning that distinctive purple wool. I knew that coat.

"What the hell, Cass?" I said, standing up from my hiding position. I was livid. Lydia looked up at me, eyes wide because of my outburst.

"We're in a *church*, Elliot," she scowled, standing up to glare at me. But she had confusion and hurt and betrayal in her eyes as she turned around and looked at my sister.

Cass looked between the both of us like a startled animal. Her hand was in her pocket, but it was so deep I couldn't be sure what was stashed in there. A gun? A knife? Hell, if she was the killer, she could have anything in there.

"What are you two doing here—"

Before she could get out any more words, there was some rustling in the back room. The three of us perked up at the sound. This night was getting even more messed up, and I was getting pissed. I needed to direct my anger at someone; I needed to accuse someone. Too much was going on. My head was a hurricane.

What the hell was Lydia doing here? What the hell was Cass doing here? And who *the fuck* was in the back room?

Then a deep demonic voice answered me.

"Forgive me, Father, for I have sinned. I killed Colton Crest."

The voice manipulation was no mistake. Someone was speaking into the broken microphone, the same one used at the service nearly a week ago. It was extremely convenient that it hadn't been fixed because the confession that echoed through the church had enough power to make my bones rattle—and the voice was unrecognizable.

We raced to the back room, but before we were even halfway there, a swift figure in black clothes shot out through the door. The person headed for the closest side exit, their movement a blur of shadow.

My body thrummed with adrenaline. I was so close to uncovering the mystery, so close to getting answers. I could taste the phantom of success on my tongue.

But as we raced after the dark figure, another person ran out from the back room. At first, I thought I was seeing double, but when Cass changed directions and started heading for the second person, I realized we weren't chasing one killer. We were chasing *two*.

Lydia seemed distressed that she couldn't split herself in half and hunt down both people, but she shook herself out of it. Pure determination was etched onto her face as she picked up the pace, maneuvering between pews. Together, we chased the first person, knees knocking into the sides of the hard furniture, bodies twisting sideways to scuttle into the small spaces between the benches.

I was the first to emerge from the church, my eyes searching urgently for one of the killers. Lydia was by my side in an instant, but she didn't hesitate. Instead, she picked up her speed, her eyes glued to the dark figure slowly disappearing in the darkness. I followed her lead.

They were running up the hill and across the road. Lydia blindly crossed the street, barely dodging an angry driver in a black car. He swore and yelled, slamming his palm into his horn, but she hardly noticed the commotion. I circled behind the driver and met Lydia as she sped across the lawns of unsuspecting families.

Up ahead, I could see Cass chasing the second person down. The two unidentifiable figures disappeared toward a path slicing into a cluster of tall eucalyptus trees. The streetlights started to fade at that point. We were no longer under the comfort of their yellow glow, and we were venturing blindly into the darkness.

There was the faint sound of furious footsteps in the distance, dry leaves crunching beneath someone's shoes. I didn't know if it was Cass or one of the mystery figures, but it was my only hope. I continued forward, desperately trying to find the source of the sound.

But the deeper down the track I went, the further astray I felt. I was no longer chasing the whisper of a sound. I was moving out of desperation, hunting something beyond my reach. Lydia seemed to be thinking the exact same thing. Beside me, she stopped, panting, spinning around in helpless circles, trying to find any indication of where the pair could be.

"They couldn't have gotten away that quickly," she hissed into the air. "Show yourselves! I know you're there, damn it!"

But we were greeted with silence.

"They're gone, aren't they?" she whispered to me. "We lost them."

I nodded, even though she couldn't see.

$$\dagger$$

After one last futile look, Lydia and I made our way back to the park. We seemed to drift mindlessly, eyes vacant, movements robotic. Neither of us felt like talking, even though there were so many questions we wanted to ask each other. And where was Cass? I was worried about her.

I wasn't sure how long we had been gone for, but when we reached our group of campers, Marcus, one of Colton's economics class buddies, approached us and answered my unsaid question.

"There you guys are. We've been looking for you for the past hour," he said, glancing between us. When he saw our expressions, he frowned. "Are you two okay?"

"I don't think I can do this," was all Lydia said. Her voice was quiet and croaky as she pushed past Marcus before he could breathe another word.

Quietly, she started packing her things. I watched as she absentmindedly rolled up her blanket, throwing it carelessly into an oversized bag. A few girls crowded around her, cooing and exchanging concerned looks and words of comfort. Lydia brushed them off like flies and ignored their presence as she continued putting things away.

"Elliot," Marcus said, placing a hand on my shoulder. I looked at it, confused. "Did you hear me?"

"What?"

"You look like shit, man," he said. "I don't think I've ever seen anyone that pale before."

"Yeah," I answered distantly, trying to focus on him. "I'm not feeling that great."

"Maybe you should lie down, have a little sugar or something. It looks like you're about to pass out. Hey, Lisa! Can you throw me something sweet for Elliot?"

Lisa looked up from her conversation with her friends. She reached into her big bag of Sour Patch Kids and threw a bunch in our direction. Marcus managed to catch a green one, but most of them bounced off us. One even hit me in the face, and as I reached up, I felt sugar on my cheek.

"Lame, Lisa," he called, rolling his eyes. He held out the treat.

I shook my head. "Actually, I think I might head home."

†

In the parking lot, I headed straight for my car. It had been a long night, so I decided it would be best to just go home and sleep. Cass could take care of herself. Plus, it would have to be nearly eleven, and I had promised Dad I'd be back before then.

But before I could get into my car, someone was calling.

"Elliot! Lydia!"

Cass was striding toward us. Her hair was a mess, curly tendrils sticking to her sweaty face. Her jacket had come undone at some point, the thick wool revealing a dress underneath. There was a wobble to her steps but determination in her eyes. Her feet were clad in a pair of ridiculously heeled boots. It looked like she was walking on the tips of daggers, and by her pained expression, it probably felt like that too.

"Cass." My voice was tired, but there was a hint of relief to my tone.

Lydia slowly stumbled across the gravel, measuring out each step as if the wrong move could send her flying. When my sister reached us, she looked at us both, a million expressions merged onto her face. There was confusion and irritation, guilt and fatigue. A gust of wind plastered new strands of hair onto her damp forehead and she shivered, wrapping her coat back around her.

"What were you doing in the church?" Cass eventually asked. "Do you two know how dangerous it was in there? God, you could have gotten *killed*!"

"Do you know who those people were?" I asked instead. "Did you catch a look at one of their faces?"

Cass let out a puff of irritation. "Stop answering my questions with questions, Elliot." She turned to Lydia with pleading eyes. "Help a girl out?" Lydia just stared back. Cass paused. "If I tell you why I was there, will you two tell me why you were there too?" Cass offered. She took our silence as acceptance and nodded toward her car. It was parked at a weird angle, as if she had been in a rush. Somehow I hadn't even noticed it until she'd pointed it out. "Do you mind if we go in my car? It's cold and I don't really feel comfortable talking about this out in the open."

All three of us slid into her car a moment later. Cass didn't waste a second. She instantly unzipped her boots and pulled her feet free, inspecting the damage. There were holes in her stockings, opening up to reveal fresh wounds. When she drew back her hand, there was blood coating her fingers.

"Cass?" I prompted.

"Sorry," she mumbled, throwing her boots into the back, right next to where Lydia was perched, back straight, eyes unblinking.

My sister sighed, placed her hands on the steering wheel, and gazed out the windshield. "I have a confession. You have to promise that you won't tell anyone."

"I don't know . . ."

"Please, Elliot."

She looked at me with such desperation in her eyes that I remembered the sister I knew. The one who protected her family, and helped around the house, and spent all her money buying special gifts for the ones she loved even though she had been busting her butt for hours at a shitty restaurant with even shittier pay. For once, I wasn't seeing her as the enemy.

"Lydia?" She turned in her seat and looked for reassurance.

"Well . . ." she said slowly. "Okay. Only because if you confess, I'm going to have to too, and if my secret gets out there . . . we'll all be in danger."

I wanted to ask what she meant, and Cass looked like she wanted the same, but she forced a smile and swallowed. "Seems fair. Elliot?"

"Seems fair."

Cass nodded and turned back around in her seat, running her hands down the steering wheel. She kept her eyes focused in front of her, avoiding everything—and anything—in the car. It felt like we were underwater; movements were slow and fluid, time seemed to be ticking through syrup. A lifetime and a half had passed.

"You know how stressful situations make me clean?" she asked.

"After Colton's funeral, I was a mess, so I decided to clean my car. Open the glove box, Elliot."

With my heart beating loudly, I reached over and opened the compartment. There was only one thing in there. Cass started talking again, but I wasn't listening. I couldn't comprehend anything at that point. Because in my hands was a letter. A letter written on the same lined paper, with the same black ink, in the same messy handwriting that I knew so well. A letter written by Colton's killer.

"I'm not the only one . . ." I whispered.

Cass stopped talking and looked at me with huge eyes. "You got a letter too?" she said, voice barely audible.

Lydia snatched the paper from my hands, ignoring our revelation. Her eyes skimmed the words, fingers shaking so violently I didn't know how she could be reading what was written.

"You two aren't the only ones," Lydia said, still staring at the letter. She looked up a moment later, eyes glassy. "I got one too."

My throat constricted. "We all got letters . . ."

We all got letters.

✝

"Wait," I said, ready to burst out in a long speech filled with theories and profanities. But all that came out was an unintelligent, "What?"

"How . . . Why . . . ?" Lydia tried.

"I don't know." Cass lifted one of her hands from the wheel and covered her eyes with it. "I don't know."

"Okay," I said after a while. "Let's start with the letters. Lydia, do you have yours?"

She nodded. "It's in my car."

I pulled my most recent find from the back pocket of my jeans and held it up. "We'll start by comparing notes."

Lydia nodded and got out of the car, hurrying across the parking lot. Cass finally uncovered her eyes and dropped her hands onto her lap.

"It doesn't make any sense . . . ," she said softly.

"To psychopaths like Colton's killer, it makes perfect sense. And we have the opportunity to piece it together," I answered, running my hands over the paper to smooth it out.

"But why *me*?" she asked. "It makes sense that he's tormenting you and Lydia. You were obviously the two people who were closest to him, but I barely even knew the kid. Hell, I'm pretty sure I know more about him now that he's dead than I did when he was alive. Do you think it's because I saw him the night he disappeared? Oh God, do you think everyone he saw during his disappearance got a letter?"

"How did you know to come here?"

"When I came home tonight, Dad said you were out at this memorial trip. With the letters . . . the confessions . . . I thought the killer was planning to hurt you while you had your guard down. I came here to protect you."

"I never have my guard down these days. It's impossible."

Lydia re-entered the car, clutching a piece of crumpled paper in her hand. She quickly shut the door to block out the wind and shuffled into the middle seat so she could lean forward and join the discussion.

"This is my most recent find," she said, holding it out.

Cass and I also reached over, until all three pieces of paper were lined up together. It was the same paper, the same dark ink, the same handwriting. It was real.

"It's official. We've all been contacted by Colton's killer," I said.

"Killers," Lydia corrected softly.

I thought back to the wild goose chase we had all just endured. So much had happened in the past two hours, and now Colton's mystery was even more complicated. Lydia, Cass, and I had all received letters from Colton's *killers*.

"But according to the letters, only a single person killed him," Cass pointed out, running her finger over the written lines. "The person uses the term 'I,' which is singular."

"Maybe the killer is testing us," Lydia said. "Tricking us into believing it was more than one person to confuse us. There's such a distinct voice in those letters, and I don't know about you guys, but in mine, it seemed like the killer was obnoxiously proud of single-handedly getting away with murder."

"It's a test," I confirmed. "Does that mean the killer confessed to someone else in the church?"

Cass shrugged. "If the second person wasn't an accomplice, they're now an accessory."

"Maybe they'll tell the police," Lydia piped up half-heartedly. "Then this whole mess will be over."

As she said it, she realized her words were just wishful thinking. Everything that had happened in the church was for a reason. Colton's killer was an extremely intelligent person, toxic with madness. Everything was strategically planned. This wasn't a spontaneous act.

The three of us sat in silence, lost in our own thoughts.

"How about some coffee?" Cass interjected. "We're pretty much brain-dead right now. A little caffeine will do us some good."

"A latte sounds pretty good," Lydia admitted.

"I guess a cup won't hurt."

†

The closest café was a ten-minute drive away, and none of us had been there prior to that night. Summer had slowly crept up on us, but the evenings were still cool. Inside, the heater was turned on and it didn't take long for the warmth to seep into my skin. By the time our coffees came, my sleeves were already rolled up to my elbows.

"I think we should compare notes," Cass said, using a long-handled spoon to stir her coffee. She peered down into the dark contents of her cup and frowned. I gently slid the bowl of sugar packets over, but she didn't take one.

"If we all got the same letters, we should have been bumping into each other," Lydia said. "There would have been multiple letters at each of the places."

Cass pulled out her copy and placed it on the table between us. My eyes quickly skimmed the written words. Even by the first line, I could tell that the letters were personalized. The only resemblance was the confession. We had each gotten different clues.

"The only parallel is the confession, which means we've all been following different trails. How many letters have you two found?" I said.

"Only three," Cass answered.

"Same here. I've got only three so far," Lydia agreed, opening a packet of sugar and pouring it into the frothy contents of her cup.

"And the confessions are the same?" my sister asked, as she lifted her fingers to count them off. "That the person writing them is the killer, that Colton watched a man die when he was ten . . ."

"And that he had a second identity as Daniel Heckerman and visited Tristan Yanks, the killer who Colton had witnessed hitting Harrison Noel," Lydia finished. She tore another packet of sugar and let the contents rain into her coffee. "They're getting harder and harder to find. It's driving me insane. The next one must be impossible."

"*Almost* impossible," I whispered, remembering everything I'd had to endure just to get the fourth letter. I'd really reached my limits obtaining it, and I couldn't fathom Lydia and Cass doing anything similar. The thought of them in danger made the taste of my coffee ten times more bitter.

"Almost?" Cass's eyes were wide. "You have the fourth one."

I nodded, leaning back in my chair and running my hands through my hair. "You wouldn't believe the things I had to do to get it."

"Oh my God," my sister whispered. "Is that why you were at the station the other night?"

"You were arrested?" Lydia exclaimed, trying to keep her voice down, but her words had a squeaky edge. The news caught her so off guard that she dropped the packaging of her third sugar sachet into her cup and had to fish it back out with a spoon.

"I wasn't arrested. The police just happened to stumble on me that night and pulled me in for questioning."

"Dad and I had to pick up your car in Ridgemount, Elliot. You weren't having a casual drive. Where was the fourth letter?"

Both girls looked at me with wide, curious eyes, a hint of danger hidden behind them. I knew that if I didn't answer, they'd kill me. And if I did tell them, they'd still kill me. I was a dead man either way.

"The Yanks residence," I answered.

"Oh my God," Lydia screeched, swatting my chest. "You idiot. You could have gotten killed!"

She then picked up three more sugar packets, ripped them open and dumped the contents into her cup. I don't think she was aware of how many she had already poured in, but mentioning it would have only pissed her off. Instead, I turned to my sister. She stared at me in disbelief, then picked up her cup and drank down the hot liquid like it was a shot of vodka.

"Oh my God," she said. She tried to think of something else to say, but when she couldn't, she repeated, "Oh my God."

"I got in and out in one piece." Barely. "It's irreversible. Besides, both of you know it's getting harder as we go along. Surely you've had some challenges along the way."

"In comparison, they seem pretty dull," Lydia answered. "I haven't run into any physical challenges other than tonight. I can't say the same for my emotional and mental state. I found my letters in my journal, The Jukebox, and the church."

"And I found mine in my car, my old motel room, and one of the university lecture halls," Cass added. "Tonight has definitely been the only live chase."

I couldn't say my experience was the same, so I stayed quiet. Cass would have been furious if she'd found out Tristan Yanks and I had gotten a few good punches in after I'd broken into his house—which was another reason I couldn't tell her the details. *I'd broken into his house.*

Lydia wouldn't be any better. With all the sugar she was pouring into her cup, she'd be so hyped up, she'd probably punch me in the gut in one of her failed attempts at trying to smack some sense into me. I looked over at her. She was pouring yet another packet of sugar in. How many were in there now? I had lost count. Whatever the digit was, I was sure it wasn't healthy.

I placed my hand on her wrist and she finally looked down at her busy hands. She let the paper wrapper slip from her fingers and dropped it onto the table, dusting off her hands. To make a point, Lydia pushed her full oversweetened cup across the table and placed her hands in her lap to prevent them from creeping back to retrieve it. When I turned back to my sister, she was frowning at her phone.

"What is it?" I asked.

"Dad."

With everything that had happened, I had lost track of time. I pulled my phone out of my back pocket. I had put it on silent so I wouldn't be interrupted during the night. I didn't have to unlock my screen to see a long stream of missed calls.

"I'll call him," Cass said, standing up, phone already pressed to her ear. "But when I get back, the first thing we're discussing is what was in that fourth letter."

She disappeared outside.

Because Lydia had poisoned her coffee with sugar, I slid mine across the table to her. She looked over at it with tired eyes and forced a smile before picking it up.

"You know," she said, "I'd thought of a million different things that might happen tonight, but nothing like this even crossed my mind."

"I know what you mean. I didn't think things could get any crazier."

"Three minds are better than one, though, right? With all of us working on the case, maybe we can piece it together faster." She peered into the cup before taking a drink.

"I hope so."

When Cass returned, she nodded, confirming she had dealt with Dad. "He's not happy, but it softened him up to know you're with me."

"Back to our conversation?"

"Okay, how should I start this? Remember when Colton came home that weekend? He didn't *just* come back to town. He had already been home for two weeks."

"He had been home for that long and he didn't tell anyone?" Cass asked. "Why?"

I filled the girls in on what I had discovered: the confession, the website, the video, the camera installed in our backyard that had recorded a conversation between Colton and me, and how the file had immediately deleted itself and been replaced by a GIF. Lydia stared at me the entire time, disbelief written all over her face. Cass interjected with questions and theories, trying to uncover the answers to questions we had little information about.

"I think he was being stalked," Cass concluded. "Maybe by someone he knew using his second identity."

"He'd been playing Daniel Heckerman for two years," I said, remembering what Eliza told me when I'd first gone to her house.

"Two years?"

"I did a bit of sleuthing." I didn't add anything else.

"A lot can happen in two years," Lydia whispered. "When you're pretending to be someone else, I guess it's easy to open up to people. He must have gotten close to someone."

"And that someone could be the killer."

‡

There was only so much we could discuss before one of us started falling asleep. That person was Lydia. She was slumped in her chair, head lolled to the side. Occasionally she'd murmur an incoherent word to try to contribute to the conversation, but we knew we had lost her.

The three of us agreed on two things while Cass drove us back to the park to collect our cars. The first was that we'd continue searching for the rest of the letters, using my clues since I had gotten the furthest. The second was that we'd discuss everything else at a more convenient hour. Cass made a U-turn and drove off, leaving us standing in the middle of the parking lot. The only sounds came from our classmates on their camping trip.

"You look exhausted. Do you need me to give you a lift?" I asked.

Lydia shook her head. "I'll be fine."

"Are you sure? I don't mind—"

"I'll be fine," she repeated more firmly. "I'm sorry . . . Thank you for the offer, but I think I'd be better off alone tonight. The drive will give me a chance to sort out my thoughts."

I was hesitant at first, but eventually I nodded. "I'll call you?"

Lydia made a sound of agreement, fumbling for her keys. I waited until she had safely buckled up and was on the road before I got into my car and started the engine. As I peered into my rearview mirror, I could have sworn I saw figures lurking in the shadows.

I was being paranoid. Or maybe I wasn't. Either way, I pressed my foot on the pedal and drove faster than necessary all the way home.

There was a knock at my door the next morning. I pulled my shirt over my head just as it swung open.

"Are you ready?" Dad asked.

"Yeah, I guess—"

When I turned around, he was looking at me nervously, wearing a blue button-down. Dad had two options when it came to wardrobe: he was either a slob or, well, *not* a slob. He rarely wore something that wasn't stained or made of fleece. This was one of those special occasions.

"Do I . . . ," he said, running a hand through his hair, "look okay?"

"Yeah," I blinked. "I'm sure you'll impress the pancakes with that shirt. Is that what you were going for?"

He grinned. "Close. Your mother is coming over."

"Why?"

"She's catching the afternoon flight out of here." When I didn't respond, he took it as me being worried. "But she's coming back for New Year's."

"All right," I said.

I wasn't particularly bothered with what my mother did. Christmas was around the corner and I didn't expect her to stick around for a barbecue lunch and a slice of pavlova. I presumed she wanted to be with her family in Queensland. Things had been civil between us, but that didn't mean I was going to raise my expectations. Asking her to stay for the holidays was something that hadn't even crossed my mind. Dad gave me one last smile before he turned to leave.

"Wait," I said. "Don't you think it's going to be a little awkward?"

"Probably," he admitted after clearing his throat. "But she's still your mother, Elliot. She wanted to stop by and say goodbye to you kids before she flew home. It was my idea to have her over for breakfast. You know how I feel about airport food. It's way too overpriced."

It seemed like he was trying to win my mother back. It was an underdeveloped plan, but I'm not sure he knew that. Valerie was a married woman with three more kids. Not to mention that she didn't even live in the same state.

My dad was a writer. He was constantly thinking and creating, structuring sentences like bricks on a building. His sentences were carefully arranged, words prestigiously collected. Plots were layered like cement, strengthening the structure of his narrative. And inside his masterpiece, characters were born and conversations were ignited, each floor adding layers of depth to his creation. In his mind, he had built an estate of fiction.

Transferring this to book form had been a hit, and his debut novel had received its first literary award within its second year of publication. Dad was seen as a genius. But sometimes his intelligence didn't venture far from the pages of his works. Anything to do with women was a disaster, especially if it came in the form of Valerie Scott.

"I'm thinking of doing some French toast as well," he said, forcing me to focus back on him. "What do you think?"

It wouldn't make a difference, Dad, was what I wanted to say. *She's moved on.*

"Sure," I said instead.

He disappeared downstairs, humming an old cartoon theme song. I returned to my bed, lifting the blanket in a poor attempt to make my room look cleaner. When I turned around, Cass was walking past, tying up her hair. When she saw that my door was open, she stopped.

"You look like shit," I said.

"Gee, thanks. You're a real joy."

"I don't look any better."

"It's the hair," she answered. "I go from hero to hobo real quick when my hair is greasy."

"Is that why you have that"—I vaguely gestured toward the ball of hair—"thing on top of your head?"

"Seriously, Elliot, you're an absolute delight this morning."

"Sorry," I answered, stifling a laugh. "Must be the lack of sleep. Feel free to insult me too. I deserve it."

"You look like you crawled out of someone's ass crack."

"Nice."

"Someone's old, wrinkly, sultana-resembling ass crack."

"Brutal."

"And you smell like that person's fart."

"Okay, are you done?"

Pause. "I'm satisfied. For now."

"Do I really look that bad?"

"Yes. I'm surprised Dad hasn't said anything about our appearances."

I followed her out of my room and shut the door. "I know. He's on cloud nine right now because Mom's coming over."

"Oh no," she groaned. "Is that why Dad's wearing that shirt? I haven't seen that thing since he quit his job at the university."

Prior to Dad's successful career as a writer, he was an English professor at the local university. This was before he had discovered that life as an author could guarantee that his working hours required very little effort in the wardrobe department. When he realized that track pants and cotton tees would suffice, his old clothes had gone into storage. But his teaching days were nearly ten years ago, so the fact that he was wearing one of his old button-downs meant this breakfast was practically a celebration.

There was a knock on the door by the time we walked down the stairs. I disappeared into the kitchen while Cass answered, inviting our mother in. She stepped outside to haul in Valerie's luggage, then directed her in.

"Hi, Elliot."

"Hey." I felt awkward calling her *Mom*, and I was pretty sure she'd feel the same if I addressed her as *Valerie*.

"How are you?"

"Not too bad," I answered, watching her shuffle around when my dad acknowledged her with a small smile. "You can put that down somewhere."

"Oh," Valerie said, looking down at her arm clutching her carry-on bag. She slowly placed it in the corner. "I'm sorry for intruding on your breakfast. I was just going to stop by and say goodbye, but your dad invited me over. My two weeks have passed, and Ryan called last night telling me the kids have the flu, so it won't be long until I have four kids to look after. I'll be looking after a ten-, nine-, seven- . . . and forty-seven-year-old." She laughed at her own joke, but when she realized no one else was amused, she sobered and added, "I should be back for New Year's."

"I'm sure it'll be a great New Year's, Mom," Cass said, trying to break the tension. "Maybe we'll host a party this year."

Valerie smiled uncomfortably. "A party sounds lovely. I have a recipe at home for some fantastic meatballs. I'll take care of the snacks throughout the night, how's that?"

"I'll do dinner," my sister answered. "Then we can go outside and watch the fireworks at midnight."

With that decided, the discomfort settled in the room again. Cass looked like she was going to choke on air if she didn't do something, so she disappeared to make coffee. To avoid any more talking, I reached over and grabbed an orange.

"Your father does that."

"What?"

Valerie nodded toward the orange peel on the table. "No breaks in the peel. It's just one endless spiral."

"I'm surprised you remembered," Dad said as he poked his head around the fridge and smiled.

He looked hopeful. I felt sick. My mother studied her hands as if wondering why she had even remembered such a detail and why she brought it up. I offered her half of the orange and she took it, as eager to keep her mouth busy as I was.

†

Breakfast ended straight after the food was gone. There was no after-eating conversation, which I was grateful for. It was only nine in the morning and I was already exhausted just from our morning meal. Valerie delicately dabbed at the corners of her mouth, thanked us, and started her great escape.

Dad followed her outside, the only one who seemed to remain optimistic despite the circumstances. Seeing his ex-wife again was just a reminder of the relationship he used to have. It was broken beyond repair, but Dad was determined to think otherwise.

Cass cleared away the dishes and I got up to help after downing the rest of my orange juice. Stacking the remaining glasses and mugs, I balanced them in a pile until I got to the sink. I gently placed them into the soapy water.

"When should we call Lydia?" I asked, picking up a towel to dry.

"Not today. I'm already looking forward to just crawling back into bed. My feet are killing me, and I haven't been standing for very long."

I looked down at the pillow-like things on her feet and the Band-Aids that covered the backs of her heels. Snippets of the previous night flooded my memory: Cass's ridiculous attire and the inappropriately high shoes she had worn to chase someone down.

"That's your own fault," I said. "Why were you dressed like that last night anyway?"

She turned to look at me, gloved hands frozen, suds dripping from her fingers. She quickly looked behind her to see if Dad was in the room, but we could both still hear him outside, talking to Valerie.

"Not now," she hissed.

"Why not now?" I pressed. "I'm just asking what the special occasion was."

"God, Elliot, I was wearing a dress, not a ball gown." She sighed, picking up a plate and running the sponge over it. "If you must know, I was on a date."

"A date? With *who*?"

"With my *boyfriend*," she answered, exasperated.

"Since when do you have a boyfriend?"

"Since when did you turn into Dad? God, this is the exact reason why I didn't tell you guys sooner. I knew you'd make a giant fuss about it."

Cass had never been much of a relationship person. All throughout high school she'd preferred to marathon *Buffy the Vampire Slayer* with a box of chocolates rather than participate in anything like a date. Her life was dedicated to her studies. And even though she would be turning twenty-one at the end of the month, Dad would have a miniature heart attack if he knew she was seeing someone. He had accepted that his little girl would, in fact, remain a little girl.

"Sorry," I answered. "You guys must be serious."

"Yeah. About eleven months serious."

I tried to hold back my bewilderment. "And you're only bringing him up now?"

"I tried to," she mumbled. "I planned it out and everything. We were going to drive down together, take you guys out to that Chinese food restaurant for dinner. You know, the one with the really good spring rolls? I figured Dad could eat away his feelings if he had to. Anyway, it was around the time Colton disappeared. I couldn't just announce something like that while your friend was missing. Even after he returned, it just seemed like bad timing. I really would like you to meet Trevor at some point, though. Maybe New Year's? I can introduce him to Mom too."

"Trevor as in 'T'?"

"How else do you spell Trevor?"

"No, I mean the letter *T*. Is that the guy you were texting the other night? The one you got all weird about?" I asked.

"That's him. Who else would I be"—realization dawned on her— "*Oh my God.* You thought I was talking to *Tristan?*"

I shrugged. "Could have been him."

"There's no way in hell I would ever want to contact that creep," she answered, shivering.

"He was the one you were talking to that night you came to the motel room?"

"What night . . . ?" Her eyes widened. "That night, I went back for my journal? You were there?"

I rubbed the back of my neck.

"I *knew* I had turned off all the lights! God, Elliot, how many other places have you broken into?"

"That's not relevant." This was not the direction I had wanted the conversation to go in, so I said, "You still haven't answered my question."

Cass dipped her hand into the warm, soapy water and flicked some in my direction. "I know what you're doing, but since you're so interested, yes, that was Trevor too."

"Does he know about . . . everything?"

"No, not everything. He doesn't know about the letters, but he does know I'm trying to piece together Colton's mystery."

"And he's helping?"

"Yes."

"Cass!" Dad called before I could ask my sister any more questions. He wandered into the kitchen. "Do you mind driving your mother to the airport? A taxi might not come in time."

"Yeah, because you were talking too much," I teased.

"Elliot, son, I'm fifty years old and I've still got it with the ladies."

"Okay, gross," Cass said, pulling off her gloves. "I'm going to go now."

She kissed Dad on the cheek and disappeared outside, leaving me with an extremely pleased father, a sink full of dishes, and a couple of answered questions that seemed minuscule in comparison to the bigger picture.

My mom had been gone for a few days the morning my dad found Cass and me in the kitchen. It was early. The two of us were beleaguered by sleep, still not quite awake.

"Why don't you invite Lydia over for breakfast?" my dad offered.

Milo barked at the mention of breakfast, his little tail wagging uncontrollably. I considered it, but only for the brief second before Dad continued with, "I'll cook hot dogs."

My sister scoffed. "Hot dogs for breakfast? That's hardly nutritious."

"It's not about being nutritious," Dad explained. "This is a celebratory breakfast."

"What are we celebrating?" Cass asked. She gathered her hair at the nape of her neck and secured it with the ever-present band around her wrist.

"Elliot got his exam results back," Dad said, reaching over and ruffling my hair. He hadn't done that since I was a child. It felt oddly comforting. "I was thinking hot dogs were an appropriate way to celebrate."

"I don't think that's a good idea," my sister said, scrunching up her nose. "How about this instead?"

She walked over to the cupboard, pulled out a bar and tossed it over to the breakfast table where I was sitting. I picked it up. The ingredients were oats, dried fruit, nuts, and honey. It seemed like an appealing choice, but it was hard as a rock.

I hit the bar against the edge of the table. "Is this what our house is made of?"

Dad took the bar from me and his mouth crinkled like he had just put a slice of lemon in there. "Cass, that's offensive," he said, tossing it into the bin.

My sister reached out helplessly, but it was too late. The bar made its descent into a simmering concoction of wrappers and leftovers. She simply sighed and walked back to the cupboard to get another.

"Honestly, Dad, with your food choices, I'm surprised we even survived," she muttered.

"Cassandra, please, do you not remember party pie Friday?"

"Dad, I don't think that's something you should be proud of," Cass answered, rolling her eyes.

"It made every Friday a party. Of course it's something I should be proud of."

"Yeah, but I hate parties," Cass said.

"And it's the reason I resent pies," I added.

Dad leaned his elbows on the breakfast bench. "Look, as long as you don't grow to resent your old man, I think I'm doing parenting right."

"Party pie Friday is also the reason Cass learned how to cook."

My sister shrugged. "We needed something more than mystery meat to get us through life."

"Exactly!" Dad clapped his hands. "I'm basically an inspiration."

"Speaking of inspiration, shouldn't you be working on your manuscript?" I asked.

"Should, yes. Will I, though? No. I really do love writing it, but I've hit a bit of a bump in the plot. It's a mystery with some romance between my favorite characters. Something I haven't delved into in quite a while."

"Nothing says love like a bit of death involved," I said, deadpan.

"Tense situations tend to bring out lots of different emotions."

"And what do you mean your 'favorite characters'? Don't you mean your main characters?" Cass asked.

"No way, my main character is a bitch," Dad said. "I loathe him."

"Why create him then?"

Dad simply smiled. "Because he has a story to tell."

"I'm on my way to work," Cass announced, looking at her reflection in the microwave to put on her earrings.

"Work?" I asked. "Since when do you work here and not in Ridgemount?"

"Remember how I used to help out the dentist back in high school? The receptionist is on maternity leave, so I've been called in to do her shifts." She took a banana from the fruit bowl and threw it into her bag. "Might as well keep busy while I'm on my summer holidays, which is something I suggest you do too."

"Honestly, I don't know how you can manage all this stress and still find time for a job."

"I need some normalcy to balance out my life. Besides, it's my birthday at the end of the month and I want to buy something nice for myself with my first paycheck."

With all the craziness that had happened, I'd almost forgotten how close her birthday was. And how I still hadn't gotten her anything. My Christmas presents were organized, but I was running out of cash. Maybe a job *was* long overdue.

Cass pulled out a tube of lipstick and a small mirror. Once that was done, she was out the door. With my sister gone, my dad leaned in.

"What do you say to hot dogs?"

I sucked in a breath and pretended to think about it. "I think I'll pass this time."

"Your loss." I stood up to leave, but I didn't get very far before he called my name. "I really am proud of you, kiddo," he said.

"Thanks, Dad."

Once I was out of the kitchen, I headed outside and the first thing I did was call Lydia. She picked up after two rings.

"I was just about to call you," she said, her tone high-pitched. It was lively.

"Hello to you too," I said. Her happiness was infectious. "I was thinking we should go out for breakfast."

"I like the way you think. But how about I make omelets? Pick me up in ten and we'll go to the store?"

"Already on my way."

†

Happiness should be treasured, especially when you're going through a tough time. My exam results had given me a new perspective on my future. One that didn't involve friends being murdered and killers taunting me. I saw a great education and a fresh start.

I should have savored that moment.

Because while Lydia inspected the eggs at the supermarket, I saw Mrs. Crest with a shopping trolley and a forced smile, and my good mood instantly dimmed. If Colton hadn't been murdered, he would have been with us, holding Lydia's basket as she gathered ingredients for her famous omelets. We would have been joking around, celebrating. Her son had gone through everything we had at school, and there was no doubt she knew it was results day.

"Elliot," she said, wheeling her way over. "Lydia."

Lydia nearly face-planted into the aisle at the sound of her voice. She turned and smiled, holding a carton of eggs.

"Hi, Mrs. Crest," she said.

"What are you kids doing here?"

"Just picking up a couple of things for breakfast," I answered, holding up the red basket as evidence.

"Celebrating?"

Lydia and I exchanged wary glances. "Kind of . . ."

"I'm proud of you two," Mrs. Crest said, reaching out and touching our cheeks affectionately. "Colton would have been proud of you too."

She was right. Colton's intelligence was incomparable. He would have whipped both our asses and shamed us with his results, but even so, he would have been more excited about our marks than his own.

"Thank you," Lydia said quietly.

"You deserve a treat," she announced.

Mrs. Crest gently took my elbow with one hand and steered her trolley with the other. She let go of me when I started to follow, Lydia walking on her other side. She led us into the confectionary aisle and smiled broadly.

"Pick anything you like."

"Oh no . . . It's okay—"

"Please." She smiled at us hopefully.

I looked at the arrangement of gummies and chocolates. Then I turned my gaze to Lydia. She shifted uncomfortably. We had been cornered. Although the gesture was kind, I felt guilty, like I was robbing her of something.

"Go on," she prompted. "As much as you want."

Lydia hesitantly reached out and took a pack of gum, strategically picking the cheapest thing there. She held it up and smiled.

"Thank you, Mrs. Crest. You really didn't have to," she said.

"No need to thank me, honey. I'm just so proud of you two." Mrs. Crest reached over, plucked a packet of strawberry-flavored gummies from the shelf and handed them to Lydia. "Don't be shy."

Lydia hesitantly took the candy. While they were talking, I chose a miniature bar of milk chocolate and hoped it would suffice. It didn't. Before I knew it, Mrs. Crest had handed me another two bars. Then she whisked us both toward the checkouts and started loading the food onto the belt.

"Elliot, honey, have you called your mother about the great news?" she asked. "I'm sure she'd like to take you out to lunch or something. She'd be very proud of you. Elliot?" she repeated.

"Valer—uh, my mother went home."

"Oh . . . I'd been hoping we could catch up."

"She'll be back for New Year's," I said, meeting her gaze. "Cass wants to host a party."

"Oh, how lovely." Mrs. Crest beamed. "Speaking of parties, I wanted to ask if both your families would like to come over to our house for Christmas lunch."

Holidays were always the hardest for grieving families, I knew, and this particular one would be the worst. No one wanted to be alone during such a festive season. Christmas was a time for family—and food—but with a significant member missing, in a way, it felt wrong celebrating something so cheerful.

The lunch would ensure the Crests were surrounded by support. Plus, it would be the perfect opportunity to do some sleuthing. All three of us had had some brief discussions since Colton's memorial night, and we'd agreed that the tire swing was the next clue. In retrospect, it seemed so alarmingly obvious, but the video had left me in a shocked state and I'd focused too much on trying to retrieve the footage to see anything beyond it.

The girls agreed that the most reasonable place to start was Colton's house. Even the letter had mentioned the swing and how much he'd loved it as a child. The next letter had to be there.

Lydia stepped forward, took Mrs. Crest's hand, and squeezed.

"That sounds lovely."

"We'll be there, Mrs. Crest."

She smiled, and that single expression alone said more than words ever could.

We said our goodbyes, then purchased our groceries and headed to Lydia's house. I was in charge of making the toast due to my lack of culinary skills.

As Lydia was tossing some other ingredients into her omelet mix, I heard her parents come in.

"He made her so sad, Wendy," Mr. Potter said. His tone was hushed, but there was a furious undertone to it.

"I'm upset about it too, Andrew. But what relationships don't go through hardships?"

"They're barely eighteen. There shouldn't be that much strain on a high school relationship. We still don't know what happened to the boy while he was gone. Besides, we are adults. What we're doing is right."

"When are we going to tell her?" Mrs. Potter asked.

My ears perked up at this and I exchanged a quick glance at Lydia. *Tell her what?*

"Not yet."

"Surely we should give her some time to prepare . . ."

"It'll be fine, Wendy. It'll be fine."

"Mom?" Lydia called out. "Dad?"

The hushed murmuring ceased. A moment later, her parents appeared at the entrance of the kitchen. Mr. Potter's smile was so stretched out, it was as if invisible fingers had dug themselves into each corner of his mouth and pulled his lips to their full capacity.

"Honey," he said, still smiling. He practically forced the words through gritted teeth. "We thought you were going out for breakfast."

"No," Lydia said slowly. "I said I was going to *buy some things* for breakfast."

There was an awkward silence. They knew we'd heard them talking. We knew they knew we'd heard them talking. Mrs. Potter's eyes were like two giant, unblinking golf balls. Her cheeks were flushed pink, and she too had a very unnaturally big smile to accompany such panicked eyes.

"You can join us if you want," Lydia said. Although they were her parents, the offer was half-hearted. She seemed uneasy after hearing their conversation.

"That's quite all right," her dad said. "I woke up early and had some doughnuts and a coffee."

"And I had some herbal tea this morning. I think I'll wait until lunch to eat something."

Silence followed. I stared at the tiled floor of the kitchen, not daring to let my gaze wander elsewhere.

"Okay, well, I'll be in my office doing some work," Mr. Potter announced. He looked at us for a response. No one gave him one, so he cleared his throat and abruptly left.

Mrs. Potter mumbled something about laundry and disappeared just as quickly. That left Lydia and me.

"Not going to lie, that made me extremely uncomfortable," I said.

Lydia groaned, whisking her egg mixture with so much aggression, it was starting to spill from the bowl.

"They think I'm broken or something," Lydia said. There was a touch of bitterness to her tone. "I'm just grieving. It's a difficult process. I try so hard to stay positive and upbeat for them, but it's a theatrical performance, and to be honest, I want the curtains to close."

I reached over and touched her hand—partly for comfort, partly to ensure our breakfast wouldn't be all over the counter before it got into the pan. "I think they're just worried about you. You're their only child. I guess they're just being protective."

"Ever since Colton disappeared in May, they suddenly think he's a bad guy. My dad's the worst." She sighed. "Do you remember that time you came over to my house while he was still missing, and we overheard them talking?"

It was a Saturday morning and I had gone over to Lydia's house to do a school project with her. We were in the dining area trying to do some research. Lydia's parents had just come home, not realizing we were in the house.

"Something is definitely going on with that boy," Mr. Potter said. There was a sharpness in his voice that could have neatly cut through a solid plank of wood.

"We don't know that, Andrew. Don't make assumptions. I'm sure he has good reasons for doing whatever he's doing."

"Sweetheart, she cries in her room some nights, she's so sad. He probably hasn't even explained to her what is going on."

Our eyes met for a brief moment, but Lydia quickly looked away. She conveniently found something interesting in her lap. Her hair fell down over her face, but through the curtain of strawberry blond, I could see her cheeks were flushed.

"Well . . . do you think he's in trouble?" Mrs. Potter asked timidly. It sounded like it was a conversation she was afraid of starting.

"Surely," her husband answered. "Maybe he's gotten into drugs."

"Drugs?" Mrs. Potter repeated, her voice rising to a squeak.

"Drugs are everywhere, Wendy, and they call them all sorts of different names."

"Like what?"

"I—I don't know. Like . . . dandelions or something horrific."

"Dandelions?"

"Or weed! Yes. Weed. Do you see how absolutely ridiculous that is?"

"And you think Colton was involved in . . . weed?"

"No. Probably something far more dangerous."

Mrs. Potter gasped. "Do you think he was dealing it?"

"Maybe. Maybe he got involved in a gang."

"So you think Colton got into a gang and started dealing drugs?"

"I don't know, Wendy. He could have had an affair with some other girl or something. But whatever he's done, it's caused our only daughter distress, and I don't like it at all."

"I'm in the dining room," Lydia called out to try to stop their conversation.

She looked down at the table, scattered with papers and books, like she was focused on our project and hadn't just listened in on a decent chunk of her parents' conversation. I did the same, keeping my eyes glued to my computer screen. An article was up on my browser. I stared at the words.

We didn't speak much for the rest of the morning.

✝

"It's been like that ever since," Lydia said. "It's awkward. They're always talking in hushed whispers. They're keeping things from me."

"We know just how dangerous secrets can be."

"That's what I'm afraid of."

On Christmas we drove to the Crest residence at eleven. Cass grabbed a beer from the cooler in the backyard and disappeared into the kitchen to make a fruit salad for people to pick at after lunch was served. Dad lingered by the barbecue and talked to Mr. Crest.

"Where's Megan?" Dad asked.

Mr. Crest hesitated at the question. "She's upstairs," he finally answered. "It's . . . it's been a tough day for her."

It was warm out, perfect for a holiday lunch in the backyard, but the conversation was steering in an uncomfortable direction, and the heat suddenly made me sick. I opened the screen door and headed inside before I could catch any more of their discussion.

Cass was cutting up some strawberries. "Are you going to have a drink?"

"I'll have one back home."

I had driven my family and given myself the responsibility of taking them home. Dad rarely went out for drinks because he was such a hermit for a majority of the year, and I wasn't sure how much of a drinker my sister was since she'd gone to university, but she needed a day off anyway.

"Have you, uh"—Cass cleared her throat and lowered her voice—"looked around?"

"No. Not yet," I answered, snatching a piece of fruit from her bowl. "Not now."

"It's going to get harder when everyone is here. How are we supposed to do this?"

There was the sound of shuffling feet in the distance.

"We'll figure it out," I said before Mrs. Crest came into view.

Her eyes were red and puffy, her nose pink. Tendrils of graying blond hair stuck to her pale, damp cheeks, and her lips were plastered into a forced, shaky smile. She was an absolute mess.

"When did you kids get here?" she asked, her voice coarse.

"Not too long ago."

"I'm so sorry. I didn't hear you arrive. I was upstairs . . . I was . . . I . . ." She took a deep breath. "I was just . . . freshening up. Are you two hungry yet? I should start taking out the food."

She silently floated around the kitchen, opening up drawers and peering in before closing them and moving to others. Her eyes were distant as she finally found where she was meant to be and started taking food out of the fridge. Salads she had prepared earlier were loaded onto the table, along with a cold, already-carved honey-glazed ham.

"Mrs. Crest," I said. She stopped and looked up at me. "Merry Christmas."

Her smile faltered as she crossed the room and flung her arms around me. She held onto me for dear life and sniffled into my shoulder. I gingerly patted her back until she loosened her grip and wiped her eyes.

"Merry Christmas, honey."

Cass reached over and squeezed Mrs. Crest's shoulder. "We got you a little something. It's under the tree. The one with the Rudolph wrapping."

"That's so sweet," Mrs. Crest said, reaching over to give my sister a hug. "You shouldn't have. I have something for you both too. And there are also gifts for your parents."

There was a knock on the door as soon as she finished talking, so I made my way over to answer it. Lydia stood there with gifts, wearing a Santa hat. Behind her were her parents. Mr. Potter towered over me with his bulky frame, trying to twist his permanent scowl into a smile. Mrs. Potter, a shorter strawberry blond replica of her daughter, stood by her husband's side, holding a big bowl of potato salad.

"Merry Christmas!" Lydia sang.

I held the door open. "Merry Christmas."

She stepped inside and instantly joined the girls in the kitchen. Her parents lingered outside, shifting uncomfortably.

‡

The old tension between the families was still there. Prior to his disappearance, Colton had been the perfect candidate for their little girl, but when he'd unexpectedly left town, they grew convinced it was because he had gotten into drugs or maybe even gotten another girl pregnant. While the Crests were anxious about their son's whereabouts, the Potters wanted nothing to do with it. And even though they hadn't verbally expressed their issues, both parties knew where the other stood. However, when Colton got murdered, the tables turned and distaste transformed into guilt.

We exchanged pleasantries, and I led everyone through to the backyard where Mrs. Crest was setting the table, putting out platters of food, straightening the cutlery, and putting Christmas crackers in front of everyone's plates. Now that everyone had arrived, she had gotten straight to business.

"Hey," Lydia said, poking me in the side with a cracker. "Want to pop one?"

I took the other end and together, we pulled. She ended up with the larger half, so she peered inside and took out a purple paper crown, a little green figurine and a joke.

"Okay, ready? 'What is the best Christmas present in the world?'" she read. "'A broken drum—you just can't beat it!'"

"Classic."

"Oh, come on, it was a little funny."

Lydia rolled up the piece of paper and dropped it back into the empty cracker. Then she pulled off her hat, ran her fingers through her now-messy hair, and set the plastic crown on her head.

"That thing was getting way too hot," she said, holding up the red Santa hat. "Anyway . . . have you . . . ?"

"No."

Her eyes darted toward the tire swing. "When should we : . . ?"

"Not now. An opportunity will open up." I hoped. "We'll just have to be quick."

"In order to do that, we're going to want to plan out specific places to search," she said. "Like the inside of the wheel, or any possible crevices in the tree."

"You don't think it would be up in the branches, do you?"

"That would be problematic, especially with the seasonal changes." She dropped her voice as she whispered, "The killer wouldn't risk the weather. When autumn comes, it would just fall out with all the leaves. And if, by chance, it managed to stay wedged between the branches, it would be completely exposed in winter. Not to mention the wind and rain. No. It's got to be somewhere more secure."

"Under the ground, maybe?"

Lydia chewed her lip. "I don't know . . . that's really stretching my limits."

Digging up someone's backyard seemed easy in comparison to breaking into a stranger's house.

"I'll handle it," I whispered as Mrs. Crest announced that the food was ready.

†

Lunch went surprisingly well. Everyone laughed and talked, smiles were exchanged as the food was passed around the table, and people ate until their bellies were big and round. At first, it seemed that we were playing characters: a big, happy group of friends and family. But as the meal went on, the game dropped, and we found ourselves actually enjoying our time together.

Even Mrs. Crest seemed relieved that everything had gone well. Her cooking had been a success, as had the decorating. And she'd even rewarded herself by piling her plate with seconds. Lately, whenever food had been involved, she never seemed to take a bite. It was good to see her eating.

"Okay, how about some dessert?" she announced as she circled the table and collected everyone's empty plates.

We were all enthusiastic about it, nodding in appreciation as we popped buttons to make room. My dad did a cheer that was a little *too* enthusiastic, but it seemed to make the table erupt in laughter.

Cass helped Mrs. Crest clear the table and refill the cooler with drinks. Then they arrived with an assortment of desserts. The fruit salad my sister made was among the mix, along with some homemade ice cream. There were even some small puddings accompanied with butterscotch cream. But before everyone could dive in—especially into the already melting ice cream—Mrs. Crest appeared by the screen door, looking troubled.

"What's wrong, honey?" Mr. Crest asked, standing from his place at the table and walking over to her.

"There's no pavlova," she said softly. "I forgot the pavlova."

She curled into her husband's side and sobbed. He strategically turned so that his back was to us, making comforting sounds as he held his wife. Everyone at the table shifted uneasily.

"It'll be okay, Megan . . ."

"No, it won't," she wailed. "That was Colton's favorite. I'm a horrible mother. I've ruined Christmas."

She pulled away from her husband and rushed inside.

"I'm sorry . . . ," he said to us before he followed her.

"Andrew," Lydia's mother said softly.

He reached over and patted his wife's hand. "Wendy, we have to do something."

Silence fell across the table.

Then Cass perked up. "You know, I think there's some cream in the fridge. How about we whip up some pavlova? It means so much to Mrs. Crest, and she worked so hard to host this lunch . . . Plus, I can just take some fruit from my salad to top it off."

"That's a great idea," Dad said, clapping his hands together as he stood. "Andrew, how about we run to the supermarket and pick up a base. I'd drive, but I've had one too many drinks already."

Mr. Potter hadn't had anything to drink except for a Coke, so he agreed, and they went through the gate to the car. Mrs. Potter said she'd start whipping the cream, so she disappeared inside to find the beater.

That left Cass, Lydia, and me.

My sister picked up the tubs of half-melted ice cream. "Now's your chance. I'll be on the lookout."

She opened the screen door and headed inside to put the cold desserts in the freezer. I could hear the sound of her voice as she talked to Lydia's mom, keeping her occupied so she wouldn't look out the window.

"Let's go," Lydia said, tugging my sleeve.

Together, we headed to the swing. Lydia circled the tire, running her fingers along the inside, looking for hidden compartments or holes. I searched the trunk of the tree, looking for any nooks or crannies the letter could be wedged in.

Nothing.

Lydia then climbed up a couple of branches and looked around where the rope was tied while I crouched and looked for any signs of the dirt being dug up at the tree's base. The ground seemed to be fully intact, though, and I even tugged on a couple of grass patches to see if they had been loosened.

Again, nothing.

Lydia jumped down and dusted her hands on her shorts. "I couldn't find anything . . ."

"Neither could I," I said, looking at the grass. "Maybe it really is buried."

"Wouldn't be surprised," she said, sitting on the swing. "The deeper we get into this mystery, the harder it becomes."

"There should be some indication of where it could have been buried, though. Like a dirt patch that could easily be dug up or a loose bit of grass. But everything seems perfectly intact." I ran a hand through my hair, frustrated. "It doesn't make sense."

Lydia gently swung herself back and forth. "We must be missing something."

"Maybe obtaining the next letter wasn't meant to be the difficult part. Maybe figuring out the clue was meant to be the challenge."

"And you think we only half-solved it?"

"It makes sense, doesn't it?"

"When you take into consideration the emphasized words, then yes, it makes sense. Do you have any idea what they might mean?"

"No. They're completely random."

We heard a car pull up. Lydia and I exchanged glances and quickly made our way back to the table. Cass peeked out the window, saw that we were back in place, and sagged in relief. We sparked up a conversation to seem like we hadn't just been snooping around the backyard while the pavlova was being made.

It took some convincing, but we finally managed to get Mrs. Crest down for dessert after everything had been set up again. She hesitantly dropped into her chair and looked at what we had done. Her husband lingered behind her, ready to jump in if she broke down again. She was like a ticking time bomb and one wrong move could completely destroy her.

"Thank you . . ."

We smiled and tried to continue with lunch as if nothing had ever happened. The pavlova sat in the center of the table, completely untouched. It was Colton's, after all. Dessert didn't taste as sweet as I'd thought it would.

The day after Christmas, Cass left town with some of her friends from university for an early birthday weekend. While my sister was at the beach, I went over to Lydia's house.

"Come on in," Mrs. Potter said when she answered the door. "Lydia's upstairs. She'll be down in a moment."

I wandered into the kitchen, where I was offered some freshly baked goods. I picked up a blueberry muffin from the cooling rack and it disappeared in three bites. Lydia's mother skimmed through a magazine while I picked up another one.

"Do you like the muffins?"

I nodded. "They're great."

"I'm glad. I've been trying out some new recipes from this magazine. This woman is an exceptional baker."

"Really? Is it that judge from the new cooking show? My sister likes her."

She shook her head. "Her name is Alexandra Yanks. She actually lives quite close to here. Ridgemount, I think it was."

I actually started choking. I inhaled bits of crumbs until it felt like I had half a muffin lodged in my throat. I started coughing hysterically, and Mrs. Potter raced to get me a glass of water. It took a moment for me to clear my airway, but once I had, I looked down at the magazine she had dropped onto the counter.

Alexandra had her own double-page feature in the cooking magazine. Her profile photo was in the corner, along with some images of each of the recipes. I looked down at my half-eaten muffin and suddenly felt sick.

"Sorry," I said. "I'm always being told to eat slower. Guess I still haven't learned my lesson."

She looked at me worriedly but said nothing.

In the distance, I heard footsteps and muffled grumbling. As the person came closer, the voice became clearer. It was Mr. Potter.

"Wendy, I think we should leave now. We're running out of time and I'm getting worried someone will find—" He stopped when he saw me. His face registered an initial expression of surprise, jaw slightly slack. But he quickly regained his usual intimidating stare and lowered his gaze. "Elliot."

"Mr. Potter."

"What are you doing here?"

"He's here for Lydia," his wife cut in, sounding uneasy. "You're right. We should get going."

She circled the counter, picked up the magazine, and pushed it into her bag on the table. I watched as she abruptly left the room, calling that she needed to find "appropriate shoes." Mr. Potter stared at me.

"If you're staying here for dinner, you can order something to eat. Lydia knows where the money is," was all he said before disappearing out the door.

I heard whispering in the foyer area before they left.

"Elliot?"

"Down here," I called.

Lydia appeared a moment later, holding the phone. She put it back on the cradle and went to the fridge, pulling out a bottle of water.

"Sorry about that," she said after she'd had a drink. "That was my aunt. She had me say hello to all five of her cats. Now that I think about it, I'm not sure why she called. I'm sure she had a purpose, but our conversations always circle back to her pets."

"Family, huh?"

"Yeah. Have you been waiting long? My dad didn't grill you about anything, did he? He can be scary when he wants to." She picked up a muffin.

"No, I haven't been around long. Your dad didn't say much. Your parents actually left kind of abruptly."

"They've been kind of weird lately. I think they're just going through a bump in their marriage. They've been going on more date nights." She took a bite from the muffin and licked her lips. "Man, these are some insanely good muffins."

"Your mom's a fan of Alexandra Yanks's creations," I said. "Did you know she has her own segment in a cooking magazine?"

"How could someone who can create such sweet baked goods also create a son who is so poisonous?"

"Beats me. Should we start doing some research?"

She nodded and we headed into the living room. I took the letter from my back pocket and put it on the coffee table. Lydia sat cross-legged on the floor, picking up a notepad sitting among the magazines and newspapers, and finding a pen.

She started by writing the bold words out, trying to find connections: DAILY PROTEST. Then we read through the whole letter again and tried to pick out any significant phrases. Two hours later, the most we had accomplished was finishing a bag of chicken-flavored chips and a bottle of lemonade.

By this time, the only thing we could agree on was some sort of hidden significance behind the phrase "daily protest." Lydia became more agitated the more she stared at it. There was something familiar about it, but she couldn't put her finger on it. It only made her angry.

My phone vibrated on the table and she glared at it.

"Sorry," I said, picking it up and checking who it was. "It's Cass. Hello?"

"Hey, so I've got about twenty minutes before I have to go out again. I just wanted to check in on you and see if you've gotten any further with the letters."

"We've got nothing."

I watched Lydia write on the notepad.

DAILYPROTEST

"Are you guys working on it now?"

"Yeah, but we've had zero progress. Do you have any leads?"

"No, I've been hanging out with the girls," she answered. There was shuffling and distant laughter. She lowered her voice. "Killers and clues aren't exactly things I want occupying my thoughts while I'm supposed to be celebrating my birthday."

"The only thing we've agreed on is that 'daily protest' plays a role," I explained. "We're trying to figure out what that role is."

Lydia scratched her pen against the paper.

D

A

I

L

Y

PROTEST

"I'll be back on Monday. If you don't figure anything out this weekend, we'll go over it again. But for now, I need a break. The only headache I want to experience this weekend is because of a hangover."

"Are you hungover right now?"

"Only a little."

I laughed. Behind me, Lydia swore.

She was never much of a swearer, and whenever I said any remotely offensive word, she'd frown and tell me to use my words more appropriately. Lydia only swore rarely, and by rarely, I mean almost never. When I turned around, she was standing, racing toward the door.

"Cass? Let me call you back."

There was a sound of protest before I hung up, but I tossed the phone onto the couch. I glanced at the notepad filled with scribbles and notes. And then I saw it.

Without hesitation, I ran after her. The back door was open and Lydia was by the single tree in her yard. The tire swing was dusty with age, but she was searching the whole structure, ignoring the dirt that covered her fingers.

"It's an *anagram*," she said triumphantly, searching the inside of the tire. "That's why the arrangement was emphasized. You had to rearrange the letters in the phrase. It spells my name, Elliot. That's why the GIF on that website was of a *little girl* on a tire swing, not a little boy."

My heart was pounding as Lydia pulled up the tire to reveal a letter taped underneath. She took the paper in her shaky fingers, and as she opened it, a coin slipped from the folds and landed on the grass. I picked up the dollar and ran my thumb over the surface.

It almost seemed like a taunting joke. A dollar coin was exactly what I'd let decide my fate.

Lydia held out the paper and took in a shaky breath. "Ready?"

My fingers closed over the coin. *No.* "Yes."

> *Irrationality derives from insanity, and insanity is merely a result of a wild imagination. Perhaps murderers are merely geniuses and the remainder of society lacks the ability to dream. That's why people like me are locked up, because our thoughts are such beautiful creations that the world deems them hauntingly dangerous.*
>
> *There's a little food for thought for you. Now on with the confessions.*
>
> *Colton owed people a lot of different things: explanations, confrontations, apologies, time. Even money. Just ask Lydia Potter. The last letter led you to her, didn't it? When Colton was in trouble, he turned to his loving girlfriend for support. But asking for a thousand dollars doesn't come unconditionally. Something valuable was exchanged for that kind of cash.*
>
> *Ever heard the saying "a penny for your thoughts"?*
>
> *Depending on the individual, the cost of a single speculation should increase—it should be valued according to its worth. It seems like some of Colton's deepest and darkest secrets spilled like blood that night in exchange for that much money.*
>
> *Everything comes with a price, after all—even innocent fun.*

The Ridgemount carnival is always the busiest during summer, but it has a lot to offer. Perhaps you should try your luck there next. The first round is on me. Use the dollar wisely and make sure you're getting your money's worth. Remember, you don't want to lose your head in the process. Because thoughts are just wasted on Severed Heads.

"He asked you for money?" I said quietly.

Lydia's fingers curled around the thin sheet of paper, causing it to crumple. She didn't look at me as she refolded the letter.

"I'm sorry."

"That's all you have to say?"

She shook her head at me and walked away. I stood there for a moment, watching as she slid the door open and disappeared inside. My heart was pounding so hard it felt like my whole body was beating with it, lurching forward a fraction every time.

With deep breaths, I tried to clear my head. Talking to Lydia when I was confused and angry would only make matters worse, and with the killer watching us like a television segment, it would only be extra entertainment they would use to toy with us.

When I was calm enough, I followed her inside. She was sitting at the counter with an untouched glass of iced lemonade. She lifted it, the ice cubes clinking against the glass. Then, without taking a drink, she placed it back down.

"I think we should tell the police about the letters."

"What?"

She turned around and repeated, "I think we should tell the police about the letters."

"Why now?" I asked. "We're so close . . . Just two more to find and then we'll have them all, we'll have answers. We'll unmask the killer and—"

"I've had enough."

"Lydia," I started, but she interrupted.

"It's the right thing to do, Elliot. We'll just tell the police we're being contacted by Colton's killer, we'll have the letters as evidence, and they'll figure out the rest. The killer doesn't want to get caught, don't you see that? Their intentions are to drive us insane by tormenting us with information beyond our reach. The first letter never said we'd directly discover who the person was by the end of this. It just said we'd have enough information to come to an alleged answer. If the person really wanted to get caught, they'd be sending those letters to the police. It's up to us to show the authorities what we have. They've made zero progress on this investigation, and we need to push them in some sort of direction."

"We've been withholding this information for weeks now," I argued. "We could be charged with obstruction of justice—or hindering a police investigation, whatever it's called. We'll be treated as suspects."

"I'm willing to take that risk," she answered.

I pulled out a chair and sat down in front of her. "Does this sudden change of mind have anything to do with what was in the letter?"

Lydia frowned and looked away. Her gaze swept over my shoulder and out the screen door. She took a couple of shuddering breaths as her eyes glistened.

"I'm so stupid," she said, her voice breaking in between her words. "The money . . . I thought . . . I shouldn't have . . ."

I reached over and took her hand. "Hey, don't cry. You didn't know, okay? None of us knew he was going to get killed. Cass wouldn't have given him her motel room, I wouldn't have gotten drunk to a point where I forgot an entire conversation. The killer is just trying to make you feel guilty, to put some blame onto your shoulders. But it wasn't your fault."

Lydia hiccupped and used the back of her hand to swipe away her tears. "I should have told you about the money . . ."

She let go of my hand and reached over the counter to grab a box of tissues. I watched as she sniffled and dabbed at her eyes, waiting quietly until she was ready to talk.

"The reason I didn't tell you was because I didn't think it was related to his murder."

"Lydia, a thousand dollars . . ." I trailed off when I saw the look on her face. She looked hurt and broken, and my judgments were making it worse. "I'm sorry."

She sniffed at me, only half believing my apology. But she continued anyway. "I know. *I know*. But you don't understand. The night he visited me was about a month after he had returned. He was so disconnected when he came back to town, but that night . . . that night he was sweet and romantic and spontaneous. I caught a glimpse of the old Colton. He almost told me everything that night . . . what he was so afraid of, why he'd disappeared. I thought I was losing him . . . but he gave me something more precious at that moment: reassurance. Reassurance that he still loved me, that he still trusted me, that he'd eventually tell me everything. And I desperately clung to that glimmer of hope."

The killer was wrong. Colton didn't give Lydia answers in exchange for money. He gave her something she needed at the time, something more valuable than answers. He gave her hope, reassurance, love.

She took a deep breath. "When he asked me for money, I didn't think twice. I didn't question the amount or the urgency of it. And because of that night, the way he was acting, the things he said . . . I thought he was going to propose. Now it seems completely idiotic to think he would ask his girlfriend for money so he could buy her an engagement ring, but I was filled with false hope. And even now, I still was—up until a few minutes ago, when that letter slapped me with the reality that he'd used that money to pay off his debts. Getting those letters has only made me doubt how much I really knew about him. His second identity, his disappearance . . . I relied on our relationship to be the only constant, regardless of what name he was using. I guess I was wrong."

"Marriage, huh?" I said weakly, unsure what else to say.

Lydia's family was super religious, and she was a hopeless romantic. Even though she'd never talked about a serious commitment with Colton, I knew she adored the idea of a wedding. Sometimes she'd hint at it, leaving magazines with cakes—and dresses that looked like cakes—in his car and at his house, and I'd catch a glimpse of them. She'd always light up like a firefly when he said something about it, even if it was, "Lyd, let's have mini-pizzas at our wedding . . . What do you mean it's not classy? Everything looks classy if it's mini." And even though he was always half-hearted about it, I knew that sometime in the future, he would have liked to settle down with her.

Even if I had said any of this to Lydia, she wouldn't have believed me. Our views on marriage were polar opposites, and I'd never wavered on my opinions when we'd discussed it. After seeing so many failed relationships in my family, I was reluctant to ever tie the knot. We Parkers were infamous for disastrous marriages.

"I think we would have just had a long engagement and then gotten married after university and everything," she answered, laughing uncomfortably before she sniffled into a tissue.

"Do you really want to tell the police?" I eventually said. "If it's something you want, I'll back you up. This affects all three of us, so we'll have to talk about it with Cass, but if you really want to . . ."

She sat there, completely quiet. Time seemed to slow as I waited for her answer.

But eventually, she took in a deep breath, pulled the letter from her pocket, and handed it over. "Just give me a few days to process everything."

Now it was my turn to cling onto a single thread of hope.

Cass came home on Sunday night and I filled her in. We continued making notes and discussing theories, but we didn't do much else. I'd promised Lydia a few days, and we'd agreed not to do anything extravagant until we came to a decision together.

On Wednesday, Cass turned twenty-one. My dad attempted to bake a cake, but when that quickly failed, he bought an ice cream replacement from the supermarket, and we had it in the afternoon.

"What else do you want to do for your birthday?" Dad asked, unwrapping a Freddo Frog chocolate bar from the packet sitting between us.

"I don't know," she said. "But I was thinking Thai food for dinner?"

"Whatever you want. Today's your day." He grinned at her. "Thai sounds good. I think I have a menu somewhere. Write down whatever you want and I'll call and make an order later."

I silently cheered. As much as I loved ice cream and chocolate for two consecutive meals in the span of one day, I wasn't sure I could stomach any more. And although the takeout food wasn't a very healthy alternative, at least it slightly resembled more of the ideal food groups. There would be vegetables, at least.

Other than having dinner sorted, we didn't have any other plans for the day.

"I think I'm going to get changed into my pajamas and watch *Friends* for the rest of the afternoon," Cass announced, standing up to stretch. "Thanks for the present, Elliot."

"Don't marathon it too hard. Take it easy."

"What are you talking about? I'm a certified champion when it comes to series marathons. Ten seasons is a piece of cake."

She grinned and started making her way upstairs, but there was a quick knock at the door. Cass changed directions.

"Who is it?" Dad yelled.

There was a pause before Lydia stepped into view, holding a plate.

"Hi," I said, my voice softer than I was expecting. I cleared my throat and said a little louder, "Uh, what are you doing here?"

Cass appeared by her side. "She came here to wish me a happy birthday. Lyd, you're adorable. Thank you."

"I also brought fairy bread."

Dad stood up and walked over to the plate, picking up a triangle. "Can't have a party without fairy bread."

"Exactly what I was thinking," I said as the girls walked to the table and dropped the plate between us.

"Do you have any plans for dinner, Lydia?" Dad said between bites of bread and sprinkles. "You're welcome to stay. We're having Thai."

Lydia was perched on one of the dining chairs, nervously fiddling with the silver cross around her neck. "Actually, I was wondering if I could steal Elliot and Cass for the rest of the afternoon."

"Oh?" Cass said, surprised.

"I have a birthday surprise for you."

"That sounds like fun," my sister answered with a smile.

"When you're on your way home, call me and I'll place the order for dinner," Dad said, reaching over for another slice of fairy bread.

"Actually, it's kind of an overnight trip." Lydia shifted in her seat. "It was a last-minute idea, a little spontaneous, I know. I probably should have called ahead to see if you had any plans but—"

"An overnight trip sounds like a great idea," Dad interjected, noticing her discomfort. He gave her a smile. "Cass has been acting like a grandma all day. A night out sounds like a much more appropriate way to spend her twenty-first birthday."

"Really?"

"Yes, of course," he reassured her. "I just don't understand what Elliot is for. Aren't you having a girls' night out?"

"Chauffeur." Lydia didn't skip a beat.

"Bring a book or something, Elliot." My dad patted my shoulder sympathetically. "You're in for a long night of waiting. When are you planning to leave?"

"My car has a full tank, so I'm ready to leave when you are," Lydia answered, looking at Cass and me for confirmation.

"I'll pack a couple of things now, and we can be on the road before five."

"In that case," Dad said, reaching over to take the plate of barely touched fairy bread, "I'll just steal this. Drink responsibly. And take care of the girls, Elliot. If I have to drive to the police station at three in the morning, you're taking the blame. Have a great time!" And with that, he headed into his office.

As soon as his door was shut, I looked over at Lydia, slightly panicked. Was I really just roped into a girls' night out?

Lydia caught my expression and she shook her head. "Relax, there won't be any alcohol whatsoever tonight." She glanced at my sister and added, "Sorry."

Cass flippantly waved her hand. "I have multiple regrets from last weekend, don't worry. I'm not ready to party again just yet. What are we really doing?"

"Pack practically. We're driving out to the Ridgemount carnival."

A sense of relief washed over me. I wasn't ready to let go of Colton's case yet, and I'd been hoping Lydia would come around.

"What changed your mind?" I asked.

Lydia dropped her voice, her tone barely more than a whisper. "Someone was in my room."

‡

As soon as we were on the road, we started asking questions.

"What do you mean someone was in your room?" Cass asked urgently.

"I don't know when, or who, or why, but I *know* someone was in there. Something is missing."

"Someone stole something?" I said.

"What did they take?" Cass whispered.

Lydia hit the brakes at a red light. "Something from my childhood. A bear. A blue one. It's a tattered old thing, one of the few things that didn't get lost in the move. Wow, I can't believe how much that still bothers me. I love that bear so much."

Lydia moved states when she was just a child, right before she was due to start school. A few of the boxes had got lost during the move, including the ones that held her toys. She'd always labeled it a traumatic experience, which would be an accurate description for when you're five and suddenly most of your things are gone.

"You know, this is exactly the kind of thing the killer would do," Lydia continued, making a sharp turn as soon as the light turned green. "It's like the person knew I was going to back out, so they planted something that would force me to still play this sick game. Financially, that bear isn't worth a cent. It's battered and stitched up and missing an ear, but sentimentally? It's my early childhood. I've been robbed of my boyfriend, these letters are driving us crazy, and I'm not going to get another thing taken from me."

Cass squeezed her shoulder. "We'll get it back."

Lydia nodded, but she didn't say anything else for the entire trip. The forty-five-minute drive was silent. No one wanted music or chatter or laughter. We were solemn, like three soldiers about to march into battle.

As soon as we got to Ridgemount, Cass directed us to a cheap motel not too far from the showground. We got a single small room that smelled like urine, with one uncomfortable-looking bunk bed and tasteful graffiti on the walls recording sexual adventures. The only plus side was that it was close to where we were headed.

"I'm starving," Cass announced. "Do you guys want to grab something to eat before we scout the area?"

"Yeah, let's grab a burger or something. Showground food is always a rip-off. Six bucks for a corn dog is practically robbery," I said.

"Well, I am a little peckish . . ."

"I'm actually craving some frozen yogurt. And since I'm the birthday girl, I vote we eat that. Besides, I know the perfect place that has the best toppings."

When we got to the frozen yogurt place, there was a Subway right next door, so while the girls got their food, I went in for a sandwich. Cass and Lydia were still loading their cups with toppings when I got back. I started to regret my decision when they came to the table.

"I haven't had frozen yogurt in so long," Lydia said, gazing into her cup topped with granola and strawberries.

"You'll love this stuff," Cass said. "I was obsessed when I first started uni. I came here almost every day."

After one scoop, Lydia said, "I can see why."

"Okay, we need a game plan," I said.

Cass turned her wrist and checked her watch. "It's almost six-thirty. We'll go then."

"Then we'll start searching the place."

"Separately?"

"Together," Cass answered definitively.

"The bear should lead us to the next letter. We'll focus on finding it. We will find it, Lyd."

She didn't say anything else until we set foot inside the showground.

There were four entrances, each with a healthy line of people. Teenagers lingered in groups and families huddled together. You could taste the anticipation in the air. But that excitement didn't extend to us. Lydia, Cass, and I were rigid.

When we got to the front, we paid for all-access passes and entered a random raffle. We all agreed we needed to be able to move freely between rides and games to try to cover as much territory as possible.

"Where should we start?" Lydia asked.

"Let's circle the place first and see if we can find anything."

Together, we passed lines and crowds of people waiting for rides, games, and food. The entire showground smelled like grease and sweat, and as we walked into the heart of the carnival, the odor only intensified.

Screams and chants filled my ears, my vision spinning with lights. Dusk was upon us, and the decreasing amount of sun only made the dazzling colors stand out even more. Everywhere I looked, I was blinded by dizzying motions of pigmented light.

"How about trying your hand at a game?" one of the men asked Lydia when her eyes lingered on the prizes lined up behind the stall for a fraction too long.

"No, thank you."

"It's only five dollars for three tries. Tell you what, I'll even give you an extra go for free if you want."

She shook her head, and I quickly steered her away before he could convince her otherwise. Cass was standing by the gates of one of the rides, looking up as the arms of the structure spun, flinging people in all different directions, making them scream in fright and euphoria.

"Maybe we should have come here earlier," Cass said, lowering her gaze from the sky. "It's hard to see anything without going up close, and I can't even glance at something for a second without being pressured into playing."

"I know what you mean," Lydia muttered, chewing her lip. "I have no sense of direction. I haven't been here in years and I can't see anything. I feel like we've been going around in circles."

Behind Lydia, I could see the Ferris wheel. Its large structure slowly spun, each carriage rocking softly as it neared the top. The colored lights shone brightly behind the dark backdrop of the sky. It seemed almost peaceful amongst the mix of scream-inducing rides and loud carnival workers.

"Speaking of circles, we could get a better picture of the grounds if we go on the Ferris wheel. Maybe we can spot some sort of clue from up there."

When we reached the ride, our wristbands were scanned and the three of us entered the small carriage. We were then locked up and secured, and we slowly went up while another group of people entered below us. The small cage we were enclosed in rocked gently.

"What are we looking for?" Cass asked, poking her nose through the metal bars.

"Clues," I said.

"Yes, but what *kind* of clues? You don't actually expect some kind of bear-shaped arrangement of lights, do you? Or some kind of glowing arrow with your name on it?"

"If anything, we'll at least get an overview of the area," I answered. "Jesus, Cass, cut the sass."

"It's still technically my birthday. I can be sassy if I want to."

"I'm sorry about that," Lydia said softly from beside her. "It was selfish of me to bring you out here on your birthday . . ."

"Hey, it's not too bad." Cass gave her a reassuring smile and a quick shoulder squeeze. "If I forget about killers and confessions, I can almost have a good time. The Ferris wheel is my favorite ride, did you know that?"

Lydia smiled slightly. "At least let me buy you something."

"You already paid for my entrance ticket."

"Something else?"

The wheel spun, directing us higher into the sky.

Cass thought for a moment. "How about one of those jumbo buckets of caramel popcorn? The one with the walnuts in it. But seriously, Lyd, it's not like we're at a graveyard or anything. I can manage a place with lots of food, lots of people, and lots of rides."

Lydia reached over and gave my sister's hand a squeeze. "Thank you."

After a couple more groups were secured in, the ride began to spin. The view from the top was striking. Rides spun and dropped and swerved in all different directions, and the striped cloth tops of stalls rippled in the early evening wind. People flooded the pathways like ants, blurred motions of shadows as they moved from one station to another. The carnival was so full of life, motion, happiness.

It was such a stark difference from the places the killer had been sending us to. It was like a hysterical joke, dangling such joy in our faces.

As the ride did its rotations, the only thing I managed to document was the arrangement of the area. It wasn't very complicated. Each row started and ended the same. The entrance held a lot of homemade craft stalls where people were selling crocheted goods and trinkets and colored garments. Then it transitioned into a combination of rides, games, and food tents. And right at the back was a circus, surrounded by a cluster of what looked like claw machines.

Eventually the Ferris wheel slowed, and one by one, passengers were taken out to let new ones in. The three of us exited through the side and were pushed back into the swarm of bodies.

"Guess we should just circle the perimeter," Cass yelled over the roar of the crowd. "We're bound to find something eventually."

Lydia checked her phone. "It's quarter past seven. I can't believe we've already been here for that long."

"Luckily we came here relatively early. It'll give us some time to look around," I answered. "We're going to have to be home before ten tomorrow."

"Yeah," Cass added. "Our mom is coming back to town for our New Year's party tomorrow night. She's coming over so I can help her with the food."

"Dad's going to follow her like a lost puppy."

"I've already got that sorted. I've got a bunch of party errands for him to do. It'll give us at least a couple of hours to get things sorted."

Cass described her plans to Lydia as we walked deeper into the carnival. I was only half paying attention as I continued to search the area.

We were reaching the back of the grounds where the circus tent was set up. Inside, it was glowing and people were cheering as the final show of the night closed. But outside of the performance, something caught my eye.

"Severed Heads," I whispered to myself. Then I yelled, "Cass! I think I found something."

Lydia was a flurry of strawberry blond hair as she noticed the claw machine titled Severed Heads. She pressed her hands and nose against the glass case where the prizes were held.

"That's it!" she yelled. "That's my bear!"

A penny for your thoughts.

The first round is on me.

"The killer wants us to play for it," I said, digging into my pockets for some money.

Because of our snack break, I had some extra change, so I pulled out a gold coin and pushed it into the slot. A dollar allowed one try. A two-dollar coin scored three.

I took hold of the stick and navigated the claw until it was above the bear. The stuffed toy was a piece of coal in a sea of diamonds. Half of an ear was chewed off, unidentifiable stains dotted its arms, and stitches covered its body. It was a downright mess.

But I was going to get it back.

I was so focused on getting the swinging silver claw in the perfect position that I didn't notice what happened next. Lydia and Cass were quiet, their attention glued to the machine. All three of us were silent, concentrating.

Then suddenly a face appeared behind the machine.

"Oh my God," Lydia shrieked, jumping half a mile into the air as a round of demonic laughter sounded.

With all the commotion, my fingers slipped and slammed against the button. I let out a growl as I watched the claw helplessly grab at nothing before it circled back to its original position.

"What the hell?" I said, directing my attention toward the person.

I was taken aback for a moment when I turned to meet a face of chalky-white paint and a head of blue frizz. The clown's eyes were dotted with black triangles and his mouth was painted to resemble a permanent smile, so even when he was frowning, his artificial features said otherwise. To go with the face paint, he was wearing a bright costume, a collection of random geometric shapes stamped from his neck down to his high tops.

My heart thrummed with the initial shock, beating in time with the upbeat tempo of the carnival music. And the more I stared at the clown, the faster it pounded. Something was wrong. My brain was working in overdrive to figure out my body's initial response.

Then it clicked.

I knew him.

A flash of recognition must have crossed my face because the clown grinned and took off. I instantly left my spot by the machine and ran after him.

Was he the killer, though? Or a distraction?

"Elliot!" Cass yelled.

As I pushed my way through the crowd, the clown didn't once turn back, confident that I'd lose him in the sea of people. But I still had the tufts of his blue wig in sight, and I didn't dare to blink as I forced myself to move faster.

With my eyes set on him, I didn't see the line of people in front of me. Shoulders collided as the crowd tangoed to keep their balance. A string of curse words and angry shouts came from the people, so I said a hasty apology and stumbled forward.

I had lost the chase again. The clown was nowhere to be seen. Balling my fists, I stalked my way back to the circus tent.

"Are you insane?" Cass hissed when I returned, grabbing hold of my forearm like an angry mother scolding a child. "He was just some jerk from the circus! He gave us a scare and you want to hunt him down?"

I shook off her grip. "I knew him."

"So what? One of your friends works at the damn carnival as a summer job. What's the big deal?"

"He doesn't work here."

She faltered. "What are you talking about?"

"He doesn't work here."

"How . . . he's wearing a costume, the makeup, the hair . . ."

"Shoes. He was wearing Converse."

There was a cluster of clowns having a late-night dinner near the trailers behind the tent. Their feet were clad in ridiculously large shoes. One even wore flippers. The show had just ended when we'd arrived, and all the performers were loitering around, still in their full sequined costumes, their faces packed with glitter and color. No one had bothered to change yet. Not even their shoes.

"Oh my God," Lydia whispered in horror, clamping a hand to her mouth.

"Do you think he was the killer?" Cass asked softly.

"I don't know. Whether he was or he wasn't, he's gone now. Let's just get the damn bear and get out of here."

I was in the completely wrong mindset as I went back to the claw machine. I was angry and frustrated and distracted. If it was the killer's intention to distract me so I wouldn't get the bear, it had bloody well worked. But was the clown even the killer?

The clown could have easily been hired by the main mastermind to do a simple job. Maybe to confuse us, distract us, piss us off. Do all damn three. I sighed, slamming my fist down on the button and watching as it missed entirely.

Then I missed it again. And again. *And again*. Cass missed. Lydia missed. It took twenty-three dollars before we managed to get the bear. The girls cheered in triumph and I sighed in relief as the toy was dropped into the chute.

As soon I picked up the small, tattered bear, I felt something underneath its skin. Lydia reached for it with outstretched fingers, but I gently jerked it away.

"Wait," I said, my fingers tracing against a particular stitch. "I feel something."

"Another letter?" Cass asked, appearing next to me.

"No." I pressed both thumbs on either side of the stitch and something sharp protruded from the seam.

"Is that a *blade*?" Cass was horrified.

I gently pulled it out, trying not to cut myself against the jagged edges. "It's a broken piece of mirror."

I looked down at the fragment, catching glimpses of my tired face—the hollows under my eyes, the parchment-like look of my skin. I looked almost dead. The fluorescent lights weren't doing me any justice either.

I let out a tired breath and flipped the piece of mirror. In red marker was a note.

Food for thought provides a fresh perspective.

"The maze of mirrors," I whispered almost instantly. "That's where we have to go next."

†

The maze of mirrors was huge, to say the least. It was a dizzying structure that made you see infinite reflections in all different directions, causing the suffocating feeling of being surrounded by doppelgängers. It sounded mostly harmless in theory—until you were suddenly faced with a million other figures identical to yourself. There was no escaping your emotions in that place. If you got scared, you couldn't hide it. It only intensified.

A quick scan of our wristbands and we were flung into the illuminated maze. The faint sound of music filled our ears, and in the distance, we could hear groans and screams of frustration.

Other than the shard of mirror, we had no other clues. Was our objective to find our way through until we were greeted at the exit with some sort of grand prize? It seemed too simple.

Congratulations for making it through the maze of mirrors! Here's a complimentary letter, a bagful of anxiety, and half

a bloody finger just to shake things up a bit. Enjoy the rest
of your evening!

Yeah. Right.

"Maybe the mirror came from here. We'll just find the place where the piece came from," I suggested, holding up the fragment.

"Oh my God, Elliot," Cass said, swatting my hand down. "You still have that?"

"It's a clue."

"It's a weapon," Lydia whispered. "At least keep it out of view. There are kids in this place."

Cass delicately pinched the mirror with her thumb and index finger, wrapped it in the cardigan she had taken off, and dropped it into her bag. With the blade put away, we started walking.

We'd barely got to the heart of the maze before a couple of twelve-year-old kids turned the corner toward us. They were laughing hysterically, but one look at the three of us had them recoiling in temporary fright. The girl took in a sharp breath before she quickly collected herself, smiled hesitantly, and apologized for running into us. Then she took the boy's hand and they quickly took off again.

"We look ghastly," Lydia said, pressing a hand to her cheek and squishing half of her face.

"We just brought looking like crap to a whole new level," Cass muttered. "Come on, the faster we get out of here, the better."

Left. Right. Straight. Dead end.

We went around in circles, trying different combinations until everything blurred, all my reflections screaming at me to find an exit. I was their leader; they depended on me to escape.

After some more helpless wandering, we managed to find the exit. The black, velvet-covered area was welcoming, and so was the breeze that swept in from outside. Staring at the illuminated mirrors and endless reflections of myself had been harsh on the eyes.

"So much for that," Lydia said, slumping against one of the maze walls as a group of teenagers sped past us out the exit.

"The maze was flawless. No chips anywhere, especially not one that would fit the piece we got," Cass answered.

"That thing was hell. If there's another clue in there, I'm not ready to endure another headache. I need to recharge, and I don't care how overpriced those giant frozen Fantas are. The orange one is calling me and I can't refuse." I started heading toward the exit. "Plus, this stupid song isn't so easy on my ears. This is, what, the seventh time it's played? It's going to be in my head for the next week."

"Wait," Lydia said, placing a hand on my shoulder. "I know this song is annoying, but are you actually listening to the lyrics?"

I paused. As did Cass.

"It's about a carousel."

"Maybe that's our next clue," Cass whispered.

✝

After a headache-inducing adventure through the maze of mirrors, spinning around whilst sitting on a purple unicorn was not the most favorable of tasks. But I kept thinking about a giant frozen Fanta, orange-flavored.

Before the ride even began, we all made a huge deal over which animal to sit on. We ran our hands under the creatures, over their bellies, beneath their feet, trying to find something—*anything*—that would bring us closer to the next clue. But all we found was a piece of fresh gum stuck to the bottom of a pink pony.

The ride was equally as torturous. We tried looking for patterns in the music, the arrangement of animals on the carousel, shapes on the ride. There was nothing. And once the ride was over, I was close to giving up.

"Maybe we misinterpreted the message on the mirror," I said once the ride was over. "We might be following a completely random path right now."

"Food for thought was part of the message. Maybe we're supposed to find a clue in a bag of candy floss or something." Cass tried to give us a smile that said *don't give up yet*, but even she looked like she needed more convincing.

"Whether it's a clue or not, let's get some food. I'm starving. I'll pay for everybody."

Cass turned her wrist and looked at her watch. "I guess we could eat and scout out the place one last time."

The girls got ice cream and Cass's bucket of caramel popcorn. I got my giant frozen Fanta, which wasn't orange. Instead, I'd opted for grape at the last second. It was a good choice and went excellently with my Dagwood dog.

"What time does this place open in the morning?" Lydia asked, licking the melted ice cream dripping from her cone. "Maybe we can stop by before we leave, while it's still daylight and there are fewer people."

"I think it opens at eleven. They'll probably want to set up for the New Year's countdown," Cass answered. "We'll be long gone by then."

As we directed ourselves through a new path, an announcement chime sang. A few groups of people paused to listen in, but most weren't interested in the message. They continued on with their business.

"It's that time of the night again, folks! Another raffle draw. Remember to keep your wristbands on and come to the main entrance if your name is called to collect your prize. Without further ado, our lucky nine o'clock winners are . . . Cass Parker, Elliot Parker, and Lydia Potter!"

Lucky wasn't a word I would have used to describe our situation.

"Wrists, please," said the overly cheery guy who had announced our success at winning the raffle. He held out his hand expectantly and smiled at us with stained teeth.

Lydia hesitantly placed her hand in his while he scanned the band on her wrist to confirm she was one of the "lucky" winners. He gave her a toothy grin and dropped her wrist when a cheerful beep sounded. Cass was next.

"Do you think . . ." Lydia drifted off, unsure of how to end her sentence.

"I don't know," I said, stepping up for my wrist to be scanned.

"Congratulations!" the man clapped his hands together. "We've got some great prizes for you tonight."

He moved from the foldout table and met a bulky security guard a few feet away. They exchanged a couple of quiet words before they moved on to the bin of prizes wrapped in cheap cellophane and flimsy crepe paper. When they returned, our winnings were in their hands.

An oddly shaped blob was passed over to Lydia. She tucked the little blue bear under her arm and reached for the package. Her fingers dug into the yellow paper, creating a small tear in the side.

Next, Cass was given a wad of coupons. As she sifted through them, I caught glimpses of codes that could be used online to preorder cheaper entrance bands, discounts on food, and complimentary passes to play some games. She smiled stiffly and pushed them into her bag.

I was last. My prize hadn't even been wrapped, so there was no mystery behind it. It was a one-hundred-piece jigsaw puzzle of a little cottage in the countryside. The box was taped poorly in an attempt to keep all the pieces inside, and the lid promised "bucketloads of fun."

A piece of tape had lost its adhesiveness and was peeling away on the left side. I gently tugged on it, peeling the rest off. Beside me, Lydia was opening her giant blob. The thin paper had little resistance, so it quickly shed after a few quick tugs until she was left with a giant stuffed bear.

It was pale pink, its fur resembling a huge wad of candy floss. Around the toy's neck was a bow made of magenta silk. It was such a stark contrast, seeing her hold it out in front of her. Lydia was pale and defeated; the bear was big and bright. Lydia's features were clouded with secrets and lies; the bear's were cheerful and innocent.

Slivers of clear tape collected in my hand as I opened the box. Inside, dozens of puzzle pieces were scattered, some facing downwards to showcase plain cardboard backs, others displaying odd shapes and colors. They seemed insignificant individually, but each would contribute to the overall picture.

But then I noticed something else. Taped to the back of the lid was a letter. Confession number six.

Cass sucked in a breath, noticing it too. Lydia's hand circled around my bicep, her fingers squeezing into my skin.

"Again, congratulations on winning our nine o'clock raffle! If you'd like us to hold onto your prizes until you leave, we can store them here."

"No, thanks," Cass said nervously, fidgeting as she pulled out Lydia's car keys. "We were about to leave anyway."

The man shrugged, flashing his stained teeth once more before we headed toward the exit. We heard his overly cheery voice as we left, his animated speech following us on our way out.

"Do you think the killer was in there?" Lydia whispered as we speed-walked to the car.

"Not sure," Cass answered. "But I sure as hell don't want to stick around to find out."

We'd had to park around the block because the crowd was so big, so when we finally got to the car, the letter was already out. I slid into the middle seat in the back, Lydia hit the lights, and then we all read the letter together.

> *Did you have fun?*
>
> *You deserved it. You've come this far, after all. With all the emotional and mental stress you've endured, I was afraid your little mind had reached its breaking point. And I can't have you locked away because of instability, especially this close to the end. Where's the fun in that?*

I hope you had a good time. And if you didn't—well, I'm afraid that was your only chance from here on out. I gave you the opportunity, though, which was extremely considerate of me. I appreciate gratitude in the form of commitment. Stick around until the last letter is found. I can assure you, you won't be disappointed.

Now back to the star of the show: Colton Crest. Are you starting to notice little things about him now that he's gone? Or maybe it's the opposite; maybe you're starting to forget simple things about him. Perhaps you're beginning to doubt what was real and what wasn't, if your memories are real or if they were all made up in your head.

I'm sure there's one thing you haven't forgotten about him, though, and that's his pocket watch. He wore it everywhere, didn't he? It was almost like an extra limb, a natural extension of his very being. It's something that made Colton Crest.

But it's very unfortunate that the pocket watch didn't actually belong to him. I had to reclaim what is rightfully mine.

It was a very special part of him, however. So I did him the honor of swapping it out for a replica.

That's right—the original is still out there.

He was buried with the fake.

Colton's pocket watch was still out there, and it was probably hidden with the final confession. What a finale; the thing he most treasured was in the possession of the killer and was being used as some sort of grand prize. Then an idea occurred to me.

"Maybe that's why he was murdered," I whispered.

The discussion between the girls faded, and they turned to look at me in both surprise and horror.

"The pocket watch. There must be some sort of significance behind it other than its worth. A piece of jewelry seems like a petty excuse for murder, and the killer is way too smart for that. Maybe Colton had the replica made to try to trick the other person. They could have had some sort of deal or something, but when Colton handed over the fake, the killer retaliated."

There was silence as my theory sunk in.

"But the killer is smart," Cass said. "Obtaining that watch wouldn't have been much of a challenge. If they can break into Lydia's house and steal a stuffed toy without anyone noticing, they sure as hell could have gotten hold of the watch. Theft would have been much easier than murder."

The flaws in my theory were starting to emerge, and the more I thought about it, the more senseless it became. I sagged in defeat, already flung back to square one. We were going around in circles.

"Or maybe," Lydia said, "Colton figured it all out. That would explain the replica. He knew the killer was after him, so he had a fake watch made. Maybe the real one will lead us to whatever information Colton discovered. The letter didn't specify whether it was in the killer's possession or not."

"Should we start looking for the pocket watch now?"

"No, we can look for the pocket watch, but our main focus should be on the final letter. We're so close to the end and backing out of the game now isn't going to do us any favors." I ran my fingers through my hair. "Besides, there's no indication of where we should start looking. At least with the letters, we're given some sort of clue, even if it is vague."

"We should get back to the motel and see if we can find anything in the letter—or even our prizes—that could lead us to the final confession," Lydia said, putting her keys into the ignition and turning on the engine.

"We can squeeze in a couple of hours if no one is tired?" Cass suggested.

Even though we were exhausted, no one argued, and no one suggested an alternative. Instead, we went to McCafé for drive-through coffee before heading to our room for one hell of a long night.

✝

There wasn't much room to move. It was practically a closet, with a slim walkway of carpet to get from one side to the other. The double bed on the bottom half of the bunk seemed to have the most space, but the girls refused to spend more time on the mattresses than necessary. I didn't argue.

We opted for the small coffee table in the corner, right under the hanging box of a television. It was small, and we were cramped, but there wasn't a sound of a complaint as we smoothed the letter and started dissecting the words. Lydia sat nearest to the wall, her phone plugged into the charger as she wrote down some notes dictated by Cass.

While they worked, I did too. I went through our prizes from the raffle. Lydia didn't seem bothered when I asked to sacrifice her pink bear for the sake of the investigation. She seemed rather relieved when I managed to find a weakness in the stitching and tore off the left leg.

The floor was covered in stuffing and pink fur when I was done, with absolutely nothing of interest lingering inside. I guessed the killer didn't want to repeat the same tactic twice, but it was worth a shot. As I moved on to sifting through the coupons, I joined in on the conversation at the table.

"That first line of the letter really pissed me off," Lydia confessed as she tapped away at her phone.

"Typical of the killer," Cass muttered in agreement. "I can't believe the point of that carnival was to allow us some 'fun time.' There was absolutely no purpose in the maze of mirrors or the carousel."

"The killer's an asshole."

"Elliot," Lydia warned automatically.

Her swearing radar was particularly strong because of the coffee. Not that it had much caffeine in it. All the energy she was imbued with was due to the caramel syrup and whipped cream.

"Sorry," I said. "I meant asshat."

"Is that meant to be a little better?"

"It's a little funnier?" I offered.

"How is that funny?"

"Asses don't wear hats."

"Guys," Cass said, looking up from the paper, "focus."

But as soon as she said it, her phone went off and she instinctively reached for it across the table. I raised an eyebrow, but she told me to shut up.

"Is it Dad?" I asked.

"It's Trevor."

"Who's Trevor?" Lydia asked.

"Her boyfriend."

"Boyfriend?"

"Yes. And a boyfriend I haven't even met yet."

"Tomorrow's your chance. He's coming over for the New Year's party," Cass announced.

"Are you sure that's the best time to introduce him to everyone? With our mom there and Dad being a goofball, and the Crests floating around being . . . well, sad?" I said.

"The situation can't really get any worse. Besides, Trevor is a big people pleaser. He'll be a great addition to the party."

"Okay," I said, unconvinced. I turned back to the coupons.

There wasn't anything noticeable at first glance. They were just big, brightly colored tickets with deals like two-for-one ice cream cones or a free extra try at balloon darts. Discounts were written in big, bold lettering and images of carnival rides were printed in the corners. I couldn't find anything on my first search, and there was nothing the second time around either.

That left the puzzle. I felt around for any possible openings in the worn box, anything circled on the picture on the lid. I even flipped each of the pieces over to see if I could find any markings or letters that might spell something out.

"There's nothing," I announced.

Cass looked up. "Guess it's just hidden somewhere in the letter, then."

"Have you gotten any leads?"

Lydia held up her phone to show me their notes, which consisted mostly of insults toward the killer for forcing us through emotional and mental turmoil, and a bullet-point list concerning the fact that the pocket watch was a notable aspect. Other than that, there was nothing.

"This has been productive," I said.

"It's not meant to be easy," Cass reminded me. "We were practically given this letter for free at the carnival. This is the last confession we're talking about. It's going to be a tough nut to crack."

I sighed. We continued to work on the letter. But only twenty minutes in and I was already starting to fall asleep. Cass was rereading the letter out loud for what seemed like the millionth time and my mind was drifting. To keep my eyes open, I started doing the puzzle.

> *Are you starting to notice little things about him now that he's gone? Or maybe it's the opposite; maybe you're starting to forget simple things about him. Perhaps you're beginning to doubt what was real and what wasn't, if your memories are real or if they were all made up in your head.*
>
> *I'm sure there's one thing you haven't forgotten about him, though, and that's his pocket watch. He wore it everywhere, didn't he? It was almost like an extra limb, a natural extension of his very being. It's something that made Colton Crest.*

Piece by piece, I managed to get little clusters of the cottage.

But it's very unfortunate that the pocket watch didn't actually belong to him. I had to reclaim what is rightfully mine.
It was a very special part of him, however. So I did him the honor of swapping it out for a replica.

Piece by piece, it started to resemble nothing like the cottage.

That's right—the original is still out there.
He was buried with the fake.

Lydia's fingers curled around my wrist as I reached for a corner piece. I looked up at her wide, unblinking eyes, her parted lips.

"That's Colton's," she said softly.

Cass looked up at the small cluster of pieces I had put together. It showed a cream background and a fraction of a corkboard. Because of the distance and the size of the content pinned to the board, I couldn't make out any of the documents or photos. But it was enough for Lydia to recognize it.

"That's from Colton's bedroom."

"Are you sure?" Cass asked.

"Positive," she confirmed, pointing at the clusters of joined puzzle pieces.

"Crafty bastard."

Lydia didn't bother scowling at me that time. "We have to finish the puzzle. Maybe there's something missing or something added. I don't know, but this should lead us to our next clue."

With shaking fingers, she started arranging some of the border pieces. The puzzle was—thankfully—only one hundred pieces, and each segment was reasonably big. Between the three of us, it didn't take long to finish. The more new pieces were added to the overall picture, the more I recognized the image too. It was the wall opposite the door, where Colton's study desk was. But the picture cut off before it could showcase Colton's stack of textbooks or his pen jars or even the corkboard above the desk. The central focus was something to the left.

His bookshelf.

The last few pieces were placed into the puzzle, confirming the location in his bedroom. Lydia's eyes scanned the overall image, searching for something out of place, but it was hard. Colton was an avid reader, and his shelves were packed. The books no longer had a structure; they were just slotted in wherever there was room. If a novel was missing, I wouldn't have known.

Lydia scowled, making a sound of frustration.

Cass reached over with her phone in hand and snapped a quick photo of the puzzle. "Nothing?" she asked.

We shook our heads.

"Maybe there's not meant to be a clue in the puzzle. Maybe we have to go to Colton's bedroom ourselves. But Mrs. Crest guards that place like a hawk," I said.

"What are you proposing?" Lydia asked.

"We break in."

Cass gave me an exasperated sigh. "No, Elliot."

"Tomorrow night would be the perfect chance. While the party is going on, we'll sneak out in the middle of it, go to the Crests' house and look around. You know Mrs. Crest doesn't let anyone in. It's a shrine, that room."

"Elliot," my sister said, frowning as she rubbed at her temples, "stop being so stupid. Don't you think it would be suspicious if we all just disappeared?"

"I could go by myself."

"No. Too dangerous." She thrust her hand in my face to stop me from talking. "I can't think right now. It's late, we need sleep. We've made progress, guys. This mystery can't be solved overnight. Let's sleep and talk about it in the morning."

There were no arguments there. Not even from me. Sleep sounded good.

After we each had a quick turn in the cubicle they called a bathroom, we settled into bed. Lydia climbed up and slept in the single top bunk. Cass and I shared the double on the bottom. My sister was the first to fall asleep, followed by Lydia.

I spent a majority of the night wide awake. I didn't have to be sleeping to conjure up nightmares.

DEPRESSION

We checked out at nine, Lydia dropped us off at ten, and Cass left the house to pick up our mother from the airport at eleven. We were in for a busy day.

"Does this scream 'sophisticated and sexy' to you?" Dad asked, passing my room. He held up a pea-soup-colored tie.

"What?"

"Or are you getting more of a 'sad and single' vibe?"

"Well . . ."

"Should I just go with my silver tie?"

"Jesus, Dad, I thought you'd burned that tie."

"The silver one? Why should I do that? It's my jam."

"I'm pretty sure it's *stained* with jam," I corrected.

"It's a nice tie, regardless of the"—he paused, trying to think of an appropriate adjective—"questionable stains on it."

"Dad, it has sequins on it. It looked like you'd killed the rainbow fish and tied it around your neck."

"Sequins are disco."

"Sequins are dorky."

He paused, reconsidering. "Was it really that bad?"

"You wore it to Cass's graduation. Your tie alone had more sequins and shine than the dresses."

"That was a great night. So no to the silver one?" I didn't answer. "I'll take your silence and glare as a confirmation of my suspicions. I'll wear the black one, then."

"Who are you dressing to impress anyway?" I asked.

"I have an awful relationship with food, and your mother is bringing meatballs. I don't want to be underdressed for the occasion."

"You're getting fancy for meatballs."

"Correct."

"Okay," I said, swiveling back to my desk. "You'd better go pick out some shoes now. Wouldn't want to disappoint the cheese platter."

As soon as the video had self-destructed and I'd stopped trying to retrieve the footage, I'd started writing down everything I could remember. There were bullet-point lists, highlighted passages from the letters, and question marks everywhere. It was the only record I had, and whenever I thought I remembered something else, I added it to the document.

"I met your mother because of meatballs."

Dad was still lingering by the door. I thought he had left. "What?"

"I met your mother because of meatballs," he repeated. "I was at a restaurant, and she recommended the meatballs. I noticed her reading, so I recommended a book to her. We ended up eating together."

I had never heard the story of how my parents met. It was awkward. Neither Dad nor Mom had wanted to share until now.

"Why are you telling me now?" I asked.

"Sometimes the fondest memories come at the most unexpected times. Moral of the story—food brings people together."

"You aren't dressing for the meatballs. You're dressing for Mom."

"Elliot, however did you come to that conclusion?" He had a mischievous grin on his face as he exited the room.

╪

When Cass and Valerie came back from the airport, they turned the kettle on for tea and started preparing the food. Dad missed them by a mere ten minutes. Cass had strategically sent him to run errands—extremely specific ones. He was instructed to go to the other side of town to buy sparklers. My sister claimed them to be the best, but in actuality, they were no different from the ones you could get at the dollar store close by. Not that my father was any the wiser.

Cass also had plans for me. I was in charge of the drinks, which she'd deemed "extremely important." I tried helping out in the kitchen, as a taste tester, but she hastily shoved me out of the way and told me I'd better head to the liquor store and pick up some drinks before they were all gone.

"I don't have any gas," I reminded her, returning. "Guess I'm destined to be a taste tester."

Valerie stifled her laughter, nervously turning away when I noticed. I shifted uncomfortably. Cass grabbed her keys from the counter and threw them at me.

"Take my car then."

"Okay," I said, defeated. Her tone had me creeping toward the door. "But save me one of those mini-cakes."

The accidental theme of our New Year's meal was food as miniature balls—or, as Valerie had said, "spherical foods." The meatballs were being prepared by Cass while my mother shaped spoons of cake mixture.

Cass shot daggers my way, so I held my hands up in surrender and backed out. I was barely inside the car when my phone rang. Pulling it out of my pocket, I put it on speaker, placed it on the dashboard of the car, and spoke.

"Hello?"

"Hey, it's me," Lydia said. "Are you busy?"

As I put on my seatbelt, I thought about my errand. "Not really."

"Do you think Cass would be up for a little adventure?"

"She's busy, but what did you have in mind?"

"My mom is sending me to the Crest house to see if we can borrow their pasta maker. I'll distract while you look around?" she suggested.

"Lydia Potter, is that rebelliousness I sense?" I teased.

"I may have had more cups of coffee than the average person should."

"Better take advantage of your enthusiasm, then," I said, cranking the engine. "I'll be there in ten."

✝

This was the fifth time we'd circled around the block, trying to come up with a plan instead of spontaneously barging in. This wasn't the right situation to improvise in. One wrong move could get us caught, and then questions would arise. Questions we couldn't answer. Not even to ourselves.

"Here's the plan—I'm going to distract Mrs. Crest and you're going to sneak into the house and look around."

"And how do you propose I sneak in?" I asked.

"Climb through the window?"

"Lydia, I'm not a squirrel. Even if we were lucky to find an open window, there are no trees close enough for me to climb."

She chewed her lip, thinking. "What did you have in mind, then?"

"Going in together? Excusing myself to go to the bathroom?"

"Sure, *that* won't raise anyone's suspicions. What if Mr. Crest is home?"

And although the killer had never threatened or made a move to hurt our families, I didn't want to take the risk. Involving them would just add more pieces to the game board, and things would just get harder. Besides, we were so close to the end now.

I pulled over on the other side of the block. "I'll scope the area. If there's any way to get in, I'll go in. If not, we'll have to come up with a better plan."

"Okay, but why did you park here?"

"I'm driving Cass's car. It'll be suspicious if Mrs. Crest sees it in her driveway. We'll walk."

Lydia nodded before she undid her seatbelt and stepped out onto the road. I locked up and handed the keys to her. Her bag was not only more secure, but it would allow me to move freely without worrying about making a sound. As we started walking, I switched my phone on silent, turning off the vibrations.

"Your mom's making pasta?"

"What?"

"Pasta," I repeated. "Isn't that why she wanted to borrow the pasta maker?"

Lydia hesitated. "Not exactly."

I looked at her, hoping the confusion on my face was enough to make her continue.

She sighed and tucked a piece of hair behind her ear. "She recently got into polymer clay and she needs the maker to flatten it out."

"Clay," I repeated.

"She's crafty."

We didn't say much else as we walked the remainder of the way. The sun beat down on the back of my neck, creating a thin sheen of sweat. The day was meant to reach excruciating extremes, ending the year with what could quite possibly be a bang.

The neighborhood was busy. Kids were loitering on the grass playing games and having water fights, and parents were hauling out lawn furniture for midnight celebrations. But as we neared the Crest residence, it was as if the life had been sucked out of the block, and all that remained was an intimidating structure of melancholy.

Before we reached the driveway, Lydia placed a hand in front of me. She nodded toward the open garage doors, from which dusty objects were being flung out onto the lawn. I lingered by the neighboring house, seeking refuge in their garden. I was close enough to hear.

"Hi, Mr. Crest," Lydia said as she neared the mouth of the garage.

"Lydia," he answered, stepping into view. "What a surprise to see you. I was just doing some cleaning that I've been meaning to do forever. Decided now was a more appropriate time than ever. Why not start the year fresh?"

"I'm sorry, I don't mean to interrupt."

"Don't apologize," he answered. "You're always welcome here. What brings you around?"

"Mom's been having me run errands, and she wanted me to stop by and ask if we could borrow your pasta maker. She talked to Mrs. Crest about it a few days ago, but I'm not sure if—"

"Honey? Who are you talking to?"

Mrs. Crest opened the gate and stepped onto the front lawn as I slunk back farther into the garden. She sported a straw hat and a pair of gloves. She was looking tired, but her fatigue didn't seem to be from sadness or crying.

"Lydia, what a surprise to see you," she said, delicately wrapping her dirt-covered self around Lydia for a hug. "I was out in the back doing a bit of weeding. The garden is starting to look horrific. How can I help you?"

"Hi, Mrs. Crest, I was just stopping by to see if I could pick up the pasta maker?"

"Oh . . . of course," she answered, pulling off her gloves. For a brief moment, her attention extended beyond Lydia, and for a heart-pounding few seconds, I could swear she was staring at me. Thankfully, though, I wasn't what she was looking for. "How did you get here?"

"Walked. Ever since graduation, I don't think I've been leaving the house enough. I thought I'd take advantage of the warm weather."

"You must be thirsty if you've come all this way on foot." Mrs. Crest motioned for Lydia to follow. "Let me make you a drink. Have you had lunch yet? I have enough for a sandwich inside. Tomato, ham, and cucumber?"

They disappeared into the house, which meant that all I had to do was sneak past Mr. Crest. He was still busy in the garage, but I couldn't predict his movements. Sometimes it would take him a few minutes to turn his back. Other times, only a few seconds.

And each time I attempted to step out of my hiding place, he would turn back around to throw something onto the lawn. I was dancing around in circles. I hoped the neighbors wouldn't notice, especially the owners of the large hedge I was creeping behind.

I was wasting time, and Lydia couldn't stay in there forever. I contemplated circling the block so I'd be on the left side of the house. My chances of sneaking past would increase, but I didn't want to waste any more time.

I wiped the sweat from my brow. I'd just have to take my chances and run for the side of the house. As soon as Mr. Crest disappeared inside the garage again, I leaped up from my hiding spot and bolted for the side gate. I reached over and fiddled with the lock for a couple of seconds, but then I heard him step back out.

"Hello?"

My heart stopped for a fleeting moment, until I realized he wasn't talking to me. He was on the phone. He was also a mere three feet away, with his back to me. My heart kicked back into action, pounding so loud I was sure he could hear. Either that or he'd pick up on my breathing. My panic, accompanied by the heat, didn't do me any favors. I felt like I was dry heaving.

I couldn't even eavesdrop on the conversation because I was certain Mr. Crest would turn around and catch me creeping around his garden. However, after a few torturous seconds, he started making his way toward the opposite side of the house to resume his conversation.

Opening the gate as quietly as I could to make my way toward their backyard, I peered around the corner to make sure it was completely abandoned before I started wending my way through. Lydia and Mrs. Crest were in the kitchen, talking on the opposite side. The laundry door would be open if Mrs. Crest had been in the garden, so I tried that door first. To my relief, the handle turned.

Pushing it open without any sound was another story, though. It groaned softly as I inched it forward, and I heard the conversation in the kitchen fall into silence. I kept still, waiting for footsteps, but then I heard Lydia resume their discussion, and everything fell back into place.

I didn't want to risk opening the door any farther, so I squeezed through the gap. Once I was inside, I crept through the hallway. I was thankful for the sound in the kitchen, but I kept my ears open. Mr. Crest could open the front door or the one that led to the garage at any second.

I headed for the stairs, then launched up them, two at a time. Colton's bedroom door was shut, so I gently turned the handle and slipped inside. As soon as I was in, I was hit with a suffocating wave of memories. I closed my eyes and watched them flicker behind my eyelids like an old home movie. Then I crossed the room and went straight for his bookshelf. I pulled out my phone and inspected the picture Cass had sent. It was an intense game of spot-the-difference.

But all I could spot were similarities. It was practically identical.

My fingers ran over the spines of the novels before I quickly withdrew them. I inspected my hand, but there was no dust, there were no spider webs—no indication that I had touched his belongings. I sighed in relief and silently thanked Mrs. Crest for taking such good care of everything. I was extremely careful when moving things, though. I had no doubt that she had tattooed the arrangement and placement of each of her son's things into her memory. So I used the photo on my phone as a guide whenever I nudged something from its spot.

I tried looking for cracks in the wood, any secret hatches. I searched for messages or drawings or little objects. My eyes scanned the spines, looking for hidden words or clues.

Nothing.

I rested my elbow against the closest shelf and sighed. There wasn't enough time to search anything else. I would have to come back at a later time.

Great. I was anything but thrilled.

I texted Lydia, telling her I was about to leave so she could distract the Crests and use my message as an excuse to head out. Then I put my phone back and pushed off the shelf. Because Colton's books were double stacked, I expected everything to be tightly packed. But as my elbow put pressure against the books, they were pushed back, exposing something in the wood.

It was a small, square opening, no bigger than the mouse pad on a laptop. A thin outline connected itself to a half-moon hole, big enough for a single finger to lift up the top of. My temples throbbed as I pried the lid off to reveal a folded piece of paper.

But as I pulled it out, I realized it wasn't that big. It wasn't the regular notebook-sized letter I had gotten so used to. This was a perfectly cut square of textured paper, like something from an art diary. It was uncharacteristic and tiny. How could anything possibly fit on such a small note?

This wasn't the last confession. Or was it?

Taking a deep breath, I unfolded it.

> *Everybody lies, including me. How do you think I managed to get this far without getting caught? There's an eighth and final letter. The pocket watch holds all the answers. Find who it truly belongs to, and my identity will be revealed.*

Everything went downhill as soon as I left the Crest residence. We drove back to my house and I showed the girls what I had found. Cass looked like she wanted to pluck all my eyebrow hairs off when she learned how I'd used her errand as an opportunity to sleuth.

Lydia went home to get ready. But I was tense throughout the whole afternoon, completely forgetting to eat a late lunch, which made matters even worse. By the time evening rolled around, I was standing around glaring at everyone. I was completely unapproachable. The last thing on my mind was a party. And to top it all off, Cass was in a rage because I'd completely forgotten to get the drinks. Tonight was going to be awful.

Cass had never been much of a jewelry person. But tonight, for the party, she was all glamour. She was wearing long crystal earrings that resembled miniature chandeliers and swung with the slightest movement of her head. "Elliot," Cass said, prodding me in the back, "smile."

I obliged.

"Great. Now smile without the I'm-going-to-kill-someone gleam in your eyes."

"I can't do both. How about *you* smile?"

We were both nervous, stressed, annoyed. Seeing the last—or more accurately, the second last—confession had me fuming. Every time someone tried to speak to me, I couldn't help but growl out a poorly thought retort.

After everything that had happened, I had been looking forward to closure. I'd wanted answers and resolution and freedom. I didn't want to go on one last hunt. I was bending backward like some sort of circus animal, and I was sick of the torture.

My sister was a mess. She was planning on introducing Trevor to everyone later on in the evening, and not having the perfect party had set her on edge.

"Mom wants to see you in the kitchen," was all she said.

I disappeared and found Valerie chopping fruit. My dad was, thankfully, nowhere to be seen. I presumed he was entertaining the guests.

"Grab a knife and a board and help me?"

I did as she said, grabbing some prewashed strawberries from the container between us and starting to cut.

"I don't see the appeal of alcohol. We can still have a good time with water."

"We can?" I asked, uncertain.

"Of course. One pitcher will have blueberries, strawberries, and raspberries. The other will have cucumbers, lime, and mint. Besides, we can impress the guests with the food."

"I guess."

She stopped cutting for a moment, looking up at me worriedly. "Something on your mind?"

"A million and one somethings."

"That's not a way to end the year."

I shrugged, mindlessly cutting up the fruit. We were silent after that, the only sound coming from Dad in the living room as he dramatically told another one of his stories. The Crests hadn't arrived yet, and neither had Lydia and her family. Our house was filled with other family friends, some neighbors, and a couple of Dad's old mates from the university.

As I dropped another pile of strawberry slices into the pitcher and moved on to the remainder, my mother dropped something in front of me.

"I said I would."

I looked down at the collection of miniature cakes. There were three of them, each dipped in chocolate and topped with sprinkles.

Before I left, I'd asked her to save me one. It was a half-hearted request. I didn't actually expect her to do it. But she did.

"There's caramel inside. Don't tell your sister, though. Those are the only three. I used the rest of the caramel for something else."

I smiled weakly, the angry tornado inside me settling to a mere gust of wind.

"Thanks."

She smiled at me before turning back to her cutting board.

Lydia and her parents arrived, and then the Crests, and more people too. The house started to fill up. My dad got out some of his old music. Cass abruptly switched it for a playlist on her iPod. The food started coming out, people ate, a couple of people brought drinks, some came with desserts. Then Trevor arrived, and Cass went to greet him outside.

"He's here!" Lydia whispered, trying to peek through the frosted glass panel by the door.

I gently hip-bumped her to try to get a look. But before I could spot their silhouettes, the front door opened, and Lydia and I sprang back like the guilty spies we were. Cass stepped in first, her eyes glued to the figure behind her. She was smiling, all the unease from the day drained from her face. She laughed as she pulled her boyfriend inside.

Trevor was and was not what I was expecting. He was clean-shaven, hair kept well above the collar. His skin was free of any visible tattoos or piercings. But something itched beneath my skin as I looked at him. Everyone was a suspect.

"Trevor, this is my brother, Elliot, and his friend Lydia."

"I've heard so much about you," he said, smiling. His handshake was firm.

I couldn't say the same, so I didn't say anything at all.

As soon as Trevor was done meeting us, his hand fell back to his side and found my sister's. Their fingers entwined. Cass lit up like a Christmas tree.

"We're just going to make a couple of rounds and introduce him to everyone," she said, leading him away.

"It was great to meet you two," Trevor called over his shoulder. "We should catch up later."

I watched as they were engulfed by the crowd.

"He seems nice," Lydia said. She dragged her nails against the inside of her elbow. "But . . ."

"Something is off."

"Oh, thank goodness, I thought it was just me." She looked up at me worriedly. "We've had a stressful day, though. Maybe we just recognize him from the paper or something."

"Or something," I repeated.

Cass looked happy, and she had every right to be. I decided to give her boyfriend the benefit of the doubt. For now.

In the kitchen, I showed Lydia the little cakes my mother had made especially for me. I felt like an extremely proud child, but I didn't care. I didn't get moments like these growing up. I handed Lydia one of the cakes. Her eyes widened as she was hit full-force with the chocolate center. I shoved the remaining two into my mouth, devouring them all at once. Dad sped into the kitchen just as my cheeks were filled. He started waving his hands around, trying to find the words to speak.

"Cass. Boyfriend." His entire expression was emitting exclamation marks.

"She introduced us earlier," I said.

"I couldn't believe my eyes," Dad explained. "I had to touch his face to make sure he was real. He's real, by the way—in case you were wondering. My little girl is growing up . . ."

Dad was delighted by Trevor.

And as the night progressed, everyone was impressed by him. As Cass said, he was a charmer and an extremely fluid conversationalist. He could make people laugh and swoon and tear up. Everyone clung to his every word, his every movement. Trevor had mesmerized everyone.

Every time he did something that pleased his audience, the itch beneath my skin burned with irritation. Even his goddamned voice seemed familiar. But maybe I was just being picky. I tried canceling out my newfound detective voice in my head and tried to channel my brotherly instincts. Unfortunately, the two were practically parallel, so it didn't do him very many favors.

I still didn't like him.

When midnight was close, Dad proposed we take the party outside. Everyone flooded through the doors and out past the pergola. Mrs. Crest and Valerie were huddled together, handing out sparklers. Lydia and I got a couple.

They both seemed tense. Mrs. Crest kept looking at her watch, studying the seconds as they ticked by nearing a new year, one without Colton. My mother kept looking at my father with his googly eyes and goofy grin. I imagined she was dreading the final countdown where everyone embraced.

Once Lydia's sparkler was lit, I used it to start mine up. Then she spun hers around, watching as the sparks danced in the dark. She was fascinated by the movement—how one quick flick of her wrist could cause a temporary pattern of light. I watched as the spark of mine slowly made its way to the bottom. Not matter how old you were, sparklers were always a great addition to New Year's Eve.

It was a single fleeting moment of beauty. The countdown started as soon as my sparks died out. Lydia was chanting, waving her burned-out sparkler. She was living in the moment, her problems taking the back seat. Cass and Trevor were at the edge of the crowd. His hand was on her back. She looked at the beauty of the fireworks. He looked at the beauty of her.

The Crests were gazing up at the sky, holding each other as they sent prayers and wishes, hopes and dreams into the heavens, hoping one of them would get caught by a star.

For the first time, my mother looked comfortable. She looked happy to be surrounded by people, to be a part of that moment. My dad stared at her from across the lawn like she was the only person in the world, like someone who'd fallen in love in under ten seconds.

"One!"

At that moment, everyone seemed content. And so, for the first time in a long time, I allowed myself to be too.

"Happy New Year!"

✝

As people floated back inside, I swung my arm around Lydia and gave her a comforting squeeze. "Any New Year's resolutions?"

"Yes, actually," she said. "I think I want some change this year. I'm going to dye my hair."

"No," I cried defensively. "Not the hair."

She laughed and self-consciously captured a curl between her fingers. "I also plan to do something that scares me."

"Like go skydiving or something?"

"Or something."

"What did you have in mind?"

"University."

Even though I'd known she was going to go, it still shocked me when she said it out loud. We had grown a lot closer over the past few weeks, and it was nice to have a friend. The thought of her moving away caused a small lump to grow in my throat.

"What about you?" she asked.

Just as I was about to answer her, the yelling started. For some reason, someone had switched the television on, showing the news channel. A small gathering of people started to form as the volume increased.

"It's Hailey Carmack reporting live from the Ridgemount Police Department, where only ten minutes prior to this broadcast, Tristan

Yanks, a previously convicted murderer, confessed to killing eighteen-year-old Colton Crest."

The sob from the crowd became a wail, then screams of agony. I pushed through the people, who parted willingly. Mrs. Crest was crumpled on the floor like a wilted flower, the soft fabric of her dress delicately surrounding her destroyed form.

Mr. Crest comforted his wife, but he could barely keep himself upright. Until he couldn't any longer, and he was beside her, crying uncontrollably. But while Mrs. Crest voiced her pain, he held his in and wept silently. I didn't know which was worse.

Lydia was crying too, and I put my arm around her. Even my mother was sobbing quietly. Dad circled his arms around her, trying to stay strong. He looked grimly at our silent guests. Someone switched the television off—or maybe just muted it—and we spent the beginning of the new year in quiet. Everyone drifted into small groups, comforting each other, thankful for the health and nourishing lives of their loved ones.

We clung to each other, trying to give something that words couldn't provide. Then realization dawned on me.

Tristan Yanks killed my best friend. I'm lucky to be alive.

I visited Tristan as soon as I was able to. I needed closure and answers. I needed to face him, to speak to him, to tell him how much I hated his wretched soul.

Paperwork was completed and a visitation time was scheduled. When I arrived, all my belongings were removed from my person. All I had to do was wait for someone to escort me to Tristan. When a guard finally came to bring me to him, I was on my feet in an instant. The muscular tower of a man gruffly nodded at me but said nothing as we walked down the corridors toward one of the monitored visiting rooms. Ahead of us, there were footsteps, and a few seconds later, we were greeted by another visitor.

An angry-looking woman stormed her way through, tendrils of dark hair flying behind her as she trudged down the hall. She didn't bother with polite excuses or making room. Instead, she barged past as her escort followed with furrowed brows and tired eyes.

As she passed me, her shoulder knocked into mine. There was a brief pause in her swift saunter, and she looked at me with wild eyes. Something in her expression softened when she perhaps considered I might be in the exact same position she was. But her brief concern was quickly transformed into disgust as she picked up her pace.

I kept looking at the place where she had stood in her momentary hesitation, but I wasn't thinking about her. I was thinking about a similar situation. The shoulder bump had ignited a memory, something that happened during Colton's funeral. A stranger had run into me. But that stranger suddenly had Tristan's face.

He was there at Colton's funeral. While everyone was grieving and remembering him, this sick-minded killer was glorying in his success. Did he share stories about him? Did he pretend to be a distant relative? Did he—

I paused.

All types of memories started coming back now. Like his brief apology after our shoulders had collided at the funeral. *He had spoken to me.* And that's why he'd seemed so familiar when I first went to the Yanks residence for coffee with Eliza. I couldn't connect it then, but there it all was now. As clear as day. All the things he'd done, like leaving all those slips of paper in my car, with his favorite line: *Colton Crest is long gone.* He'd tortured me, he'd tortured Lydia, he'd tortured Cass.

I was escorted to a guarded door. My heart was pounding as it swung open and I stepped inside. On the left side of the room were a row of desks, each separated by a wall to give each visitor privacy. I was brought over to the farthest desk and sat down on the uncomfortable plastic chair. A glass panel separated me from the prisoner half of the room, and a phone was hung up to my right.

As soon as I saw Tristan, I was overwhelmed by a dozen different emotions. I hadn't seen him since that night. The night he'd threatened to kill me. I couldn't say that was the last time *he* had seen *me*, though.

He was handcuffed and being escorted by a guard. Once he was close enough, he sat down across from me with an easy grin. That single gesture alone made my bones rattle. Tristan watched me with unnerving intensity, smiling as if everything was a huge joke. He seemed utterly pleased with himself.

Without breaking eye contact, he picked up the phone. I followed suit.

"Elliot, right?"

"Tristan."

"Good to see you again. How can I help you?"

I hated how condescending his tone was. "Why did you do it?"

"Do what?"

"You know very well what I'm talking about."

He leaned forward. The grin on his face spread wider. "I want you to say it." I felt a tick in my jaw. "Ask me why I *killed* him."

"Don't give me another reason to hurt you."

Tristan laughed, clearly amused by my response.

"*Answer me*," I demanded.

"Colton stalked me for years. The kid was obsessed with me. He pretended to idolize me in order to gain my trust, but that was only a facade. Answers were what he truly wanted, so I gave them to him. But everything comes with a price. You should know that."

I gripped the seat of my chair with my free hand, refusing to react. I kept my face expressionless.

Tristan's grin returned, seeing through my calm exterior. He drummed his fingers against the table, daring me to challenge him with another question.

"Were answers for his life a fair trade?"

"My answers were. I'm an extremely considerate man, Elliot. I made sure he was satisfied with the information I'd provided. Unfortunately for him, he didn't realize their worth until it was too late. Colton knew too much at that point. He needed to be silenced." He leaned forward. "Do you know who keeps secrets the best?" he said. I answered him with silence. Amusement danced in his eyes as he said, "The dead."

When I finally found my voice, I choked out, "What answers did you give him?"

"The truth."

"Tell me what you told him." My voice came out more harshly than in my previous response. My reaction made him giddy. "What secrets were so precious that you had to kill him?"

He laughed. Without my consent, my brain sucked in the sound and played it on repeat. It was deep and mocking and rattled me, infusing my senses with fear and anger and disgust.

"I don't think you can afford those answers, Elliot."

"How?" I asked. "Colton wanted closure for something that happened eight years ago. How could that information still carry its worth?"

"Oh, it happened more than eight years ago. Honestly, haven't you learned anything?"

"You killed Harrison Noel eight years ago."

My confident tone had disappeared, and I couldn't conceal the confusion in my question. I had accidentally swum into dangerous waters and had lost all direction of where the conversation was going. Tristan noticed, his lips twitching upwards.

"My motives behind killing Noel weren't the only thing Colton wanted answers for. He also wanted to confirm his suspicions."

"Suspicions about what?"

Tristan tossed the question around in his head. And although his contemplation was brief, the wait made my insides churn with anticipation. His fingers tapped against the table. Pinkie, ring, middle, index, thumb.

Then he answered with a single word. "Family."

Behind me, a guard said, "Time's up."

I looked from the guard to Tristan. He seemed indifferent toward our interruption. My heart was still pounding frantically. I still had so many more questions.

Why did he decide to confess now? Where was the final letter? Who does the pocket watch belong to?

Something didn't add up. My anger flickered like candlelight in the wind, on the brink of disappearing and turning into nothing but wisps of smoke. When I'd arrived, I was certain that Tristan killed Colton, but now I had an unsettled feeling in my stomach.

"I have one more question." I nodded toward his hand against the table. "Are you left-handed?"

He let out a howl of laughter. "Observant, aren't you? Not sure why it matters, but yes, I am."

That was all the confirmation that I needed. Tristan didn't write the letters. He was covering for someone. The real killer was still out there.

✝

The summer heat wrapped itself around my sweaty body, only adding to my irritation as I left, sinking back into the shadows by the entrance, trying to cool my flushed skin. I closed my eyes and tried to absorb the cooler air. Visiting Tristan didn't give me answers, everything was vague. I needed more.

Someone was pacing back and forth. Sweat patches had formed at the back of his white dress shirt. I watched as he tugged the collar of his shirt, trying to relieve his saturated skin. A familiar itch found its way under my skin again. There was *something* about him . . . Trevor. It was him. He was talking on the phone, but as soon as his eyes met mine across the parking lot, he gave me an enthusiastic wave. I stiffened, wanting to backtrack, but he was already making his way over.

"Elliot, what's going on? What are you doing here?" He gave me a smile. "We didn't really get to talk at your New Year's party."

"It sucked."

"The fact that we didn't get to talk or the party?"

"The party," I answered, deadpan.

"Cass said you were funny. You didn't answer my question, though. What are you doing out here?"

Under normal circumstances, I would have been nervous. But I was angry and tired and in need of a nap, so instead, I snapped, "What are *you* doing out here?"

He curled his fist and tapped it like it was a microphone. "This is Trevor Keagan reporting live from Berkeley Park, where we have eighteen-year-old Elliot, the younger brother of sensational woman Cass Parker."

Trevor cleared his throat and straightened his tie, looking at me. I'm not sure if he was expecting applause or a mock answer, but I just continued to stare at him, the meaning of his words dawning on me.

"You're a reporter."

"Just for the local news channel," he answered. "It's not much, but if you want to go big, you have to start small, right?"

"Right."

That's where I knew him from. The itch under my skin slowly dulled until it was practically nonexistent, but somewhere in the back of my mind, it was still warning me to be cautious. I wondered if this was now my natural response to meeting new people. Would I suspect everyone? Treat everyone like a potential threat?

I mentally shook my head. I had the right to question people, to be wary of them, to doubt their motives.

But as I scanned my mind for any past encounters, I couldn't find any. I couldn't confirm if he was one of the people in the church the night of Colton's memorial, but I definitely knew he wasn't the clown from the carnival. The only place I truly remembered him from was the local news update at six before all the good shows on TV started to air. At least that's one less person on my list.

"It was good seeing you again, but I really have to go."

"That's okay. My cameraman is on break, but we have a story to report soon. A woman's cat around this part of town had albino kittens."

"Riveting."

Although Trevor's name had been crossed from my mental suspects list, I was still pretty pissed from my conversation with Tristan, so I couldn't help the venom in my voice. If Trevor was offended, he didn't show it. He simply smiled.

"Have a good afternoon, Elliot."

I didn't say anything back.

Anger and frustration had built up inside me since my visit. I couldn't even tell Cass and Lydia what I was thinking—they were both feeling so relieved that it was over. And even if I wanted to talk to Lydia, I couldn't; her parents had whisked her away on a short holiday just after New Year's. I hadn't seen her since then, and with Cass always working or with Trevor, my candidates for company were extremely limited.

In dire need of an outlet, I decided to go to the gym. The burning in my lungs was intoxicating, and so was the pain in my muscles. Working out was the only thing on my mind, not killers or confessions, not lies or letters.

Once done, I picked up my water bottle and took a long overdue drink. The workout had definitely helped my temper, but I didn't want to go back to the house. Now that everyone knew about Cass's boyfriend, she spent a lot more time away from home. She seemed happier, livelier.

I wish I could've been the same despite there being no answers.

We still didn't know why we'd been contacted. Lydia suggested it was just a sick form of entertainment. But why *us* specifically? Or more importantly, why my sister? She had no direct links to Colton, except through me. She didn't fit the puzzle.

I picked up my stuff and headed for the locker rooms. But as I passed the front desk, someone called my name. I turned, seeing Rick's familiar bulky frame. His brow was creased, steely eyes narrowed. I wasn't sure if he was pissed to see me, or if that was his usual expression.

"Hey," I said.

He was holding a clipboard, but he placed it onto the counter next to the computer and walked over.

"I heard about Tristan."

Once again, the murder circled back to me.

"Yeah," was the only response I could offer.

Rick scratched behind his ear. "I'm not sure what to say in this kind of situation."

"Likewise."

We exchanged gruff noises of agreement, the uncomfortable topic of conversation thickening to create even more tension. The air was practically simmering with discomposure. I just wanted to hit the showers, douse myself in cold water, and head home.

"Colton was a good man. I'm glad his killer confessed." He shifted, his eyebrows drawing together. He crossed his hefty arms across his chest and straightened his stance. "I have to say, though, it came as a bit of a surprise."

"I didn't think he'd just turn himself in either. I suppose he got bored by the lack of chase. His sick mind had to be stimulated."

"Sure, that sort of makes sense."

There was something about his tone, his movements, the way he seemed to be too deep in thought after every reply I'd supplied him with.

After a heartbeat too long, I said, "Why do I get the feeling Tristan going to the cops wasn't what surprised you?"

Rick ran his hands over his shaved head. He knit his fingers together behind his skull and his eyes finally met mine for the first time during our conversation.

"No, I meant I'm surprised *he* was the one that was caught."

"What's that supposed to mean?"

Rick's eyes shifted toward the people on the gym equipment, then he nodded toward the doors. I followed him, my head pounding with questions. I wasn't the only one who didn't believe Tristan's story. This got my mind back into the mystery, my veins pulsing with determination, my gut hungry for answers.

When we made it outside, Rick waited for a group of people to finish their sprinting course before they moved to another area. He turned to face me, his eyes haunted with secrets.

"Remember how I told you Colton came here a lot when he returned?" he said.

"Sure."

"One night, someone followed him."

"W-what?"

"At first, I didn't think much of it. The car arrived not long after Colton came in for training. I thought it was just another of those high school couples. They've been abusing my late-night hours and abandoned parking spaces to make out. Knocking on fogged-up windows is more awkward for me than it is for them."

Rick had probably seen an overwhelming number of make-out sessions.

"But as soon as we were done, and he left, an argument started outside."

"An argument?" I repeated, my throat dry. The words scraped against my skin as they clawed their way out.

"I was getting everything ready to lock up when I heard them."

"Heard them?"

"The yelling," he answered. "I couldn't make out much of it, but Colton sounded furious. There was also a lot of crying."

"Did you catch sight of anything? The person's face? What they were wearing? A license plate?"

"It was dark, and I couldn't see much."

My stomach sunk with disappointment. For every step forward, I had to take three steps back. I felt like I was getting nowhere.

"I know one thing for sure, though." Rick looked at me grimly, and with his jaw set, he said, "He was fighting with a woman."

That changed everything. Only a fool would underestimate a woman.

There was a knock at the door. As I passed my father's office to answer it, I saw him standing on his desk chair, conducting an invisible orchestra. The loud instrumental music came from the corner of the room where his old record player was resting. Dad waved his arms with reckless abandon, and then—for the hell of it—started to kick the air too.

I did *not* need to see that. *No one* needed to see that.

I gently shut his office door and walked the remainder of the way to the front door. As soon as I opened it, I was greeted by a smile and my dark little soul shriveled up in defense. It was way too early for me to deal with this shit.

"Hey, Elliot. How have you been?"

"Trevor," was my gruff response.

The corners of his lips didn't dip, but he shifted from foot to foot. He placed his hands in the pockets of his jacket to refrain from fidgeting.

"Is Cass home? I wanted to surprise her by taking her out for a late lunch. She hasn't eaten yet, has she?" he asked.

"She left about an hour ago, but she'll probably be home soon. I don't know if she's eaten."

"Damn. Surprising your girlfriend is a lot harder than expected, am I right?"

Trevor quickly placed his foot in the way as I tried to close the door. "Mind if I come inside?" he said. "To wait for your sister?"

"Make yourself at home."

As soon as the opportunity came, I turned my back and started heading back upstairs. The mere presence of Trevor's overly cheery smile was giving me a bloody headache. Just because he had been crossed off my suspect list didn't mean I had to like him. Maybe he wasn't a murderer, but there was something about him that made me feel uneasy.

"Elliot, do you have a problem with me?"

There was a loud crash from my dad's study, soon followed by, "Oh, my elbow! My favorite elbow too."

We both looked in the direction of all the commotion, then back at each other. Trevor stared me down intently, searching for an answer that I wasn't about to give. Eventually he ran his hand through his hair, his shoulders sagging as he spoke. "You know, Cass is the best thing that's ever happened to me. I don't expect us to be best mates, but I plan to have a future with your sister, and I think we should get used to seeing a lot of each other. What do you say we get to know each other a bit? You'll come to find that I'm not such a bad guy."

I walked back down the stairs. Trevor took my return as an acceptance of his offer, so he followed me into the kitchen and took a seat at the bench. I was opening the fridge, ready to pour him a glass of water, when I saw the shining gold of a perfect opportunity resting beside what I think was last week's dinner.

"Want a beer?" I asked, taking a bottle out from the pack and sliding it across the table.

I watched as he looked at it with disinterest before simply sliding it back. "I'm driving. Wouldn't want to put myself or your sister in danger now, would I?"

"Water?" I asked gruffly, scanning the fridge.

"Actually, do you have any juice?"

There was a small, high-pitched beeping sound, so I looked up. Trevor was pulling a small device off his finger. My stare must have been smoldering because he looked up.

"I'm having a hypo," he explained. My expression didn't change, so he added, "Hypoglycemia. It means my blood sugar is low. I have diabetes."

"Oh. Well, shit," I said.

I returned to the fridge and poured him a glass of orange juice. If he passed out on my kitchen floor, then Cass would kill me with her bare hands. He took a long drink and wiped his mouth with the back of his arm.

"Do you need to lie down or something?" I asked.

Trevor shook his head. "I should be all right in a bit."

The television was on in the living room, the news report a distant hum in the background. Cass must have been watching something before she left. Trevor seemed to be listening to whatever story they were covering.

"So you're a reporter."

"Indeed I am. I haven't been for very long, though."

"Still, you must hear a bunch of crazy stories," I said.

"Not really. Not much happens around here. Well, with the exception of the Yanks family. They seem to be making headlines left, right, and center."

"They're quite a family," I said.

"Tell me about it. I grew up in Ridgemount. I went to school with Eliza, you know. She was one hell of a student. She gave me a run for my money even though she was always three years below me. She had a pretty rough time growing up. I'd probably have a mental breakdown if I was in her position."

"You knew Eliza?"

"Not personally. I wouldn't say we were the best of friends, but there were times when we had conversations."

"I guess you kind of knew Tristan too," I said.

"Not really. He went to prison when Eliza was really young, and was gone all through high school. From what I heard, though, he wasn't a very approachable bloke, even before."

"Yeah, he doesn't exactly have the friendliest personality."

Trevor paused. "The other day when we bumped into each other. You were visiting him?"

I had walked into an inescapable trap. There was no way I could talk myself out of this one, especially when I was trying to squeeze information out of him. To gain something, I had to lose something. He must have noticed the reluctance in my pinched expression because he gave me a quick grin. "I didn't tell your sister, if that's what you're worried about."

"I'd prefer if she was kept in the dark about it. She finally seems at peace with everything. But yeah, I visited Tristan that afternoon. I was just looking for some closure."

"Pretty brave thing, what you did. Not everyone could look into the eyes of the person who killed a family member or a best mate."

Brave. Or perhaps extremely stupid.

Either way, I did gain something out of my visit. Tristan was only a small detail in a much more elaborate picture. He was distracting everyone from something that was in our line of sight, just temporarily out of focus.

The gears in my head started turning, a film reel in my head started flickering. I tried piecing together the information, the facts, trying to find connections. My concentration was mistaken for pain, so Trevor took this opportunity to redirect the conversation.

"Luckily it's all over. It's been rough, even for your sister. The curious case of Colton Crest."

I had a flashback of finding Cass's journal in the motel room, seeing the exact same title printed on the first page.

"It really tore Cass apart. She tried solving his mystery and I helped. I hated seeing her hurt so much," he continued. "Pain sometimes has a domino effect, and she fell really hard. I didn't want to be the next victim of pain because she needed me to support her. We never really went that far into Colton's case, though. Maybe it's because I'm not cut out to be a detective, but his mystery . . . it was impossible to figure out. I have to admit, though, I was relieved as hell when Tristan walked into the police station and confessed."

"Doesn't it seem too easy, though?"

Trevor took this into consideration. "It does . . . but—"

"But what?"

"But Tristan *is* a potential suspect. He has already killed someone. What would prevent him from doing it again? It's no secret that the guy had major anger management issues. He'd snap like a twig at the smallest of things. Getting angry is no big deal for most people, but with Tristan? It was a serious problem, one that put a lot of people in danger."

"Do you really think he did it?"

"I know you want Colton's murderer to pay the price, and I can guarantee that justice will be served."

In the distance, I could hear someone at the front door. Then a moment later, my sister walked into the kitchen.

"Finally got out of bed, El—" Cass stopped when she saw her boyfriend sitting at the counter. "Trevor! What are you doing here?"

"Hey," he answered, crossing the room to give her a kiss. "I came here to surprise you and take you out to lunch. You haven't eaten, have you?"

"I haven't, but I just came back from the sushi bar in town, and I may have ordered enough to feed the whole nation. How do you feel about tempura prawn?" She placed the plastic bag of takeout on the table and started producing boxes of fresh food.

"So much for the surprise," Trevor said nervously, placing his hand on my sister's waist.

"It's a lovely surprise."

She kissed the top of his head—my cue to leave. "I'm sure you two would like to have a romantic late lunch, so I'll leave you both to it."

"Are you sure you don't want some? I got a couple of those smoked salmon rolls."

"I think I'll eat later."

"Okay, Trevor, do you mind setting up? I'm just going to run upstairs and take my shoes off. They're killing me."

Cass quickly kicked off her shoes, took them in her hands, and sprinted out of the kitchen. While she was gone, I turned to Trevor, unsatisfied with the way our conversation had ended.

"You didn't answer my question."

He looked at me, expressionless. His eyes haunted, gaze lingering. "I gave you what you wanted to hear, though, didn't I?"

In a way, he had—he had given me a reason to keep searching. But the way he said it was unsettling, and it buried itself deep into my mind and tattooed itself there.

Colton's case wasn't closed just yet.

"What's wrong, honey?" Valerie asked, placing a sandwich in front of me.

She'd been persistent about taking me on a holiday. Ever since Tristan had been placed behind bars, she'd been subtly hinting that this was the perfect opportunity to get away before his trial. She left little pamphlets about resorts by the coast in my car and travel magazines tucked between my things.

Whenever I visited her at her motel, Valerie rearranged the reading material at the small circular table and made a fuss about going across the street to pick up some "groceries." She wanted me to read the articles about five-star hotels and relaxing activities while she was gone. Then she'd return with bags of freshly made sandwiches, snack cakes, and chocolate.

I felt like I was ten. I wasn't complaining, though.

I was warming up to my mother, and I found myself enjoying her company. The phone calls from her family in Queensland were still really awkward, but she had since learned to switch her phone off whenever I was over. It was a relief.

Valerie pulled out the chair opposite me and pushed the sandwich closer. She smiled at me nervously, waiting for an answer. All I could do was shrug and stare down at my lunch.

I'd decided to go back to the letters. The eighth would confirm everything, so I decided to search for it. But with all the events that had happened, the frustration, the anger, the confusion, I'd been sent into a pit of depression. Phase four had taken its toll on me.

Silently my mother stood and rummaged around in the shopping bag until she pulled out a snack-sized bag of Smith's salt and vinegar chips. She slid it across the table until it rested next to my sandwich and nodded, encouraging me to eat.

"I'm not very hungry."

"What's on your mind?"

"A lot."

"I'm a good listener," she said, handing me a glass of tepid tap water.

"I'm not a very good talker."

We fell back into silence. I felt guilty about turning down her offer to help cheer me up, but I doubted she could do anything to make me feel better. Plus, I was too exhausted to pretend it had worked.

"Have you read the book I gave you?" she asked, changing the direction of the conversation. I was thankful.

"No. I haven't had a chance to pick it up yet."

"Your father studied it in university and so did I. It's an eye-opener," she said.

"So I've been told."

"I was reading it when I met your father."

Dad had reminisced about the exact same thing before our New Year's Eve party. "You recommended the meatballs."

Her eyes widened slightly, her lips parting. Then she contained her surprise with a small forced smile. "He told you that?"

"The day you came back into town."

She couldn't fake her smile anymore. Valerie pursed her lips into a thin line and wrapped her hands around her cup of takeout tea. She delicately picked it up and took a small sip. The thought of my father remembering things about their relationship seemed to make her uneasy. So did the realization that she was doing the same thing.

"Regardless, it's an excellent story."

She dropped the topic after that.

"How about I wrap up your lunch for later?" she suggested, grabbing the takeout container and picking up my sandwich.

"Actually, I should probably get home." I stood up, trying to keep my eyes open.

For the past few nights, I hadn't managed to get much sleep. I had been spending my nights awake, making notes, analyzing words, rereading the letters. It was the time I was most productive—when the world had gone to sleep, and I was levitating on the edge of my dreams, where my imagination was free, and my mind was open to all possibilities. My peak was at five in the morning. Sometimes I would completely shut down in the middle of my work. I'd wake up at my desk, papers stuck to my face. Other times I'd find myself on the floor, highlighters finding a home beneath my exhausted body. Then I'd spend my days stressing, wondering, calculating. I'd mindlessly shift from my everyday routine, floating around until time passed.

"Elliot, I don't think that's a good idea." She placed a hand on my shoulder and gently pushed me back into my seat. "You look so tired. I don't want you driving like that."

"I'm okay," I muttered weakly.

"I'm not letting you leave until you take a nap."

She gestured toward the single spare bed, and I got up with zero complaints. I shuffled over and dropped down like a bag of potatoes. Crawling under the covers, I stared up at the ceiling with unblinking eyes. My mother tucked me in like a human burrito. I remained unmoving. She didn't kiss me on the forehead or tell me she loved me, which was a relief. I didn't want her to think she had to escalate her affection by doing the expected motherly routine for a sleepy child. It would have been forced and awkward, and I liked the pace of our relationship.

"While you're sleeping, I'm just going to pop over to the library," she said, picking up her purse and an oversized hat. "You can stay until dinner if you want. We can go somewhere nice?"

My mother seemed shy about her offer as soon as it came out. We had never extended our visits to more than two hours. If I stayed for dinner, it would have been a record. I just nodded.

"Call me if you need me." She smiled, and left.

I closed my eyes and longed for a sleep that never came.

†

After an early dinner, I was granted permission to go home. My meal had settled uncomfortably in my stomach, and as I drove, it rumbled. I wasn't sure if it was because I was unsatisfied with the amount I ate, or furious that I'd eaten at all and now had to sit through the distress. Either way, the discomfort had occupied my mind to a point where I wasn't focusing on my surroundings. When I unlocked the front door, I nearly tripped.

"Dad!" I cried, grabbing hold of the door to catch myself.

He looked up at me from the floor with a pained expression. He was lying in the middle of the foyer spread out like a starfish. I sighed and gently kicked the front door shut.

"Writer's block?" I asked.

"No," he answered softly. "There are no more cookies."

"You're complaining because we ran out of cookies? Why don't you just go out and buy some?"

"No gas." He sighed, sounding defeated. "I miss your sister."

"That makes two of us."

"I'm not sure I like that Trevor boy."

"Because he deprived you of your cookies?"

He nodded sullenly. "Where have you been anyway?"

"With Mom."

"Oh?" The interest in his tone was hard to deny.

I tossed my keys onto the floor. "Here, go wild. Can you fill up the tank when you're done, though?"

Dad grinned, grabbing my keys and looking at them like I'd just given him a million-dollar check. I headed for the stairs.

"Don't you want to come for a drive?" he asked when he noticed I'd turned to go. "We can get ice cream on the way back."

"I'm actually really tired. I think I'm going to have an early night."

Dad gave my shoulder a tender squeeze, and that single gesture alone spoke volumes. "Want me to buy you anything? How about some Oreos? Tim Tams?"

"No, thanks. I might read before I go to bed, though."

Dad was thrilled. His eyes were wide, his smile uncontainable. He looked like an animated character from a Sunday morning cartoon. I had never been much of a reader, which had always disappointed my father. He wanted his children to appreciate literature the same way he did. Cass enjoyed a good book, but I had always been skeptical.

"I hope you enjoy," he said, grinning. "Promise we'll discuss it when you're done?"

I doubted I'd finish it anytime soon, but I promised anyway. "Okay."

Dad was beaming as he left the house. I listened as the car pulled out of the driveway before I headed upstairs. The book was still sitting on my shelf, surrounded by the required reading I'd had to do in high school. I picked up the bare hardcover and got into bed to read it.

A Madman's Message

A novel by Gregory Everett

The next page read:

> For Jamie. You were my first, but not my last; my forever, but
> not my always.

Followed by this epigraph:

> "And then he was overcome with the most unbearable mel-
> ancholy as he watched his blood pool on the hardwood floor.
> The man screamed in anguish, with so much force that it was
> almost enough to damage his unharmed physique."
>
> —William Harold

I fell asleep before turning the page to chapter one. And I hadn't
slept like that in a long time.

I visited my mom the next day, and we had leftovers from the restaurant for lunch. Lydia had called earlier and said she'd be home later that night, so I had the whole afternoon to kill until we could catch up.

"What are you and Lydia going to do this afternoon?"

I shrugged. "Hang out? Maybe watch some movies."

Maybe even talk.

"Sounds like fun."

"I guess."

"How about we go somewhere today? Get out of this cooped-up room."

"I like this cooped-up room."

"Come on," she encouraged. "The fresh air will do you some good. We can pop into the library, remember—"

"I'm not much of a reader."

"Your father mentioned that when I first came into town."

"Is that why you recommended the book?"

A small, secretive smile played on her lips. "Did it make you sleep?"

"Like a baby."

She laughed a little, tucking a piece of hair behind her ear. "What do you say? The library has audiobooks. With you driving from home to here and back again, they could be just the ticket—they can make car rides much more riveting."

"Even more adventurous than alternative rock?"

Valerie scoffed. "Of course."

I stood from my place at the table and stretched. "I guess we could go."

"There's free air-conditioning too."

"I'm convinced," I reassured her.

She smiled. "Then let's go."

†

As soon as we stepped through the automatic doors, I caught sight of a blur of color and a whiff of something floral and, in an instant, an enthusiastic woman greeted us, her tie-dyed headband slipping to cover her eyes. She quickly brushed it away from her face with a quick sweep of her hand and blew some stray raven curls off her forehead.

"Valerie, I wasn't expecting to see you until later this afternoon," she said. Her attention then turned to me. "Oh, and you must be Elliot. I haven't seen you since you were just learning to walk! Aren't you a handsome young thing?"

My mother squeezed my arm gently. "Elliot, this is Margaret. We used to work together."

"It'd been years since I'd seen your mom, but after reconnecting, it's like time hasn't passed. Are you here to help out this afternoon?"

My mom gave me a sidelong look. "I was just going to show him what we've been working on, and maybe finish up my half while we're here. Elliot, you don't have to . . ."

"What have you been working on?" I interjected.

"Come with me," Margaret said, beaming as she took my wrist and led me into the library. She was practically skipping as we rounded the corner toward the semi-enclosed children's area. Picture books were stacked everywhere, and the shelves had been taken down.

"We've been doing some refurbishments in the children's section. We're going to be moving the shelves from this wall to this wall. We're also getting some new furniture and games for the kids to play. But since everything is moving, we've had this empty wall. Your mother suggested we paint some animals. She's been doing an excellent job here. Very dedicated worker—comes every afternoon from four to six."

I looked over to where Margaret had motioned. The far back wall was completely covered in all sorts of animals. There was a purple elephant with a spotty monkey on its back, a bear wearing a tutu as it danced with a crocodile in a tiara. The entire left side was splashed with color, while the right side was only partially complete.

"It's . . ."

"Not my best," Valerie said, picking up a smock and tying it around her waist.

"No, it's great."

My approval made her glow. She picked up a paintbrush and smiled. "Want to help?"

I looked hesitantly toward the buckets of paints. "I'm not what you'd call 'skilled' when it comes to painting."

Valerie dismissed my excuse, pulled out a stool, and patted it. I slowly walked over and sat down. Now that I was closer, I saw the faint outline of each shape. She explained that it was exactly like a giant coloring book. All I had to do was paint each animal a single solid color and she'd add the detail later.

We instantly got to work.

Since the library was mostly empty, Margaret switched on a small radio and placed it in the corner for us to listen to as we painted. My mother and I were silent as we worked. Occasionally she would hum to a song she was familiar with, but other than that, no sounds were made.

It was strangely comforting.

†

I decided to head home after I'd walked Valerie back to the motel. I wanted to have a shower and a quick change of clothes before Lydia came over. The summer days were only getting hotter. I was sticky and uncomfortable and covered in paint.

When I got into my car, I turned on the air-conditioning to cool myself down. The shade I had parked under had since moved as the afternoon progressed, and my car had been baking in the sun. I placed a hand up to shield my eyes, but it did little to protect me from the glare.

Eventually I dropped my hand and decided to hit the road, but before I could turn my key, there was a knock on the passenger side window. When I turned, I was greeted by a familiar face.

Eliza.

"Hi," she said through the glass. She pointed at the handle.

I shifted in my seat, uncomfortable with the thought of her sitting in my car. Whatever she wanted to talk about, I knew it wouldn't be a friendly topic. Maybe her brother had told her about the letters, about me breaking into their house. There were a million and one things he could have told her, and I had no doubt that some of them had been shared. I reached over and unlocked the door. Eliza climbed inside, cringing at how hot it was. She gently shut the door, locking us in together.

"Hi," she repeated.

"Hi."

"How are you?"

She brushed a damp piece of hair from her forehead, her expression pinched. How was I supposed to answer that? Luckily for me, she spoke again before I could answer.

"I know this is a whole new level of awkward. The last time we hung out, we were technically on an unofficial date. And, well . . . just recently my brother confessed to killing your best friend. I know you probably didn't expect to see me after everything that's happened, and I know you probably don't want to, but something has been eating me up, and, well, I need to confess something."

I swallowed, my heart beating faster. Suddenly the car felt ten times warmer, despite the air-conditioning still running.

"Confess what?" I asked when I finally found my voice.

"Tristan told me he killed Colton."

I ran my fingers through my hair and kept my eyes straight ahead. "How long have you known?"

"Long enough to say something to the police."

I let out a shuddered breath and scrubbed my hand down my face. My fingers found the steering wheel and held on tight, needing to force some physical pain into my system to ensure this conversation was real.

"I know how he followed you," she continued, looking down at her hands in her lap. "I was with him that night."

I turned until my eyes fell on Eliza. The guilt etched onto her face was undeniable, but was it genuine?

"I was with him the night of Colton's memorial. We drove into town to get something to eat, but then he said he needed to do something, so we stopped by the church. He's an electrician, and ever since he was convicted, he hasn't had many job opportunities. The sound system at the church was one of few jobs he'd managed to get."

Eliza took a shaky breath and continued.

"We were in the back room. I was looking around while he worked. But then we heard you come in." Her voice got caught in her throat as she choked back a sob. "His confession startled you as much as it did me. I thought we were in there so he could finish the job, but really . . . he was just waiting for you. We ran for it straight after."

"That was you?"

"I'm sorry," she whispered, using the back of her hand to catch the tears that had collected under her chin. "I was scared. I was in shock. I didn't know what to do . . ."

"It's okay," I answered tightly. "Thanks for telling me."

"I'm not the only one who knew."

My chest tightened. "Who else?"

"Bones . . . Tristan paid him to freak you out at the carnival."

I sucked in a breath. "The clown?"

Eliza nodded. "Tristan said it would throw you off. He said you were looking for something important and that he couldn't let you find it. That same night, he confessed to Bones that he killed Colton."

I had trouble absorbing all the information. Everything was becoming clearer, things were adding up. But that also meant that my suspicions were wrong. Maybe Tristan really was the killer and I was making myself bend over backward trying to find another possible suspect. It just seemed too simple, the way he'd walked into the police department and confessed. I'd expected him to emotionally manipulate me, to force me into mental turmoil, to drag me to the edge of the earth and push me off the surface of existence. He wasn't meant to give up and surrender.

"Like I said, thanks for telling me, Eliza."

She looked at me with watery eyes, the tears on her cheeks already soaked into her skin. She shook her head. "I'm not finished. This isn't why I'm telling you."

"Why *are* you telling me?"

"You have to understand that despite what you think you know about Tristan . . . he's actually extremely caring."

I scoffed.

"It's true," she insisted, her fists curling to contain her anger. "He looks out for his family. He'd never do anything to hurt us."

"That only extends to his family, Eliza. What about Harrison Noel?"

"I admit, Tristan's anger management was never his proudest quality, but Harrison Noel was never an innocent man. The papers glorified him as a hard-working student, an adored hero. Did they mention that he used to abuse his pregnant girlfriend?"

I stayed quiet. I wasn't sure if she was telling the truth, but I wanted to hear the rest of the story since Tristan had been reluctant to share.

"I'm not saying Tristan was right for doing what he did because he wasn't. He obsessively stalked Harrison, he confronted him with direct threats, he ran him over with his goddamned car for crying out loud. They were both wrong. But in Tristan's head, he honestly believed he was doing the right thing."

There was a lump in my throat by the time she'd finished. I still couldn't wrap my head around it.

"That doesn't excuse what he did to Colton."

"He would never hurt his family," she answered firmly. "They were brothers."

"Yeah, I know. They were best friends, closer than ever, thicker than blood, whatever you want to call it. *I know*. This whole town knew before I did." My tone was harsh.

"No, you don't understand!" Eliza's words had a bite as her tears returned. "I don't mean it figuratively. My brother was adopted, Elliot. Tristan and Colton were *brothers*."

I stopped eating. I stopped sleeping. I stopped functioning.

I was an unforgiving hurricane destroying everything in my path. My family started avoiding me. I was unapproachable. My mind was toxic, filled with destructive thoughts, and no matter how hard I tried to erase them from my memory, they would return to become bigger and stronger, consuming me.

Eliza's confession gave me an endless headache. When the Crests had said Colton was visiting family, they weren't lying. And so if Tristan didn't murder his brother, who did?

I was at the lake, sitting at the end of the dock with the seven confessions spread out in front of me, rocks holding them down. I hadn't been there since I'd found Colton dead.

It was extremely morbid of me to revisit the place where he'd been killed. Everything about it gave me nightmares and protruding thoughts of murders and screams. But as traumatic as his last few moments alive were, his last breath—well, I presumed it was his last—was taken here, preserved here. The lake was haunted with memories of him.

Perhaps I was just seeking the impossible for answers. Like the water would whisper the answers I needed, or the trees would show me visions of when he was here.

I was pleading for a sign from the universe. A ghostly appearance from Colton himself. The spelling of the murderer's name in dandelions. Anything.

"*Anything,*" I whispered, staring down at the letters.

Nothing was my response.

At first, I didn't think Eliza was an entirely valid source of information, so as soon as I'd driven home the day she confessed, I started searching for any records to back up her story of Harrison Noel. It was apparently a pretty common name, though, so I had to sift through pages and pages of sites and articles.

But among the mix of trash was a single treasure of proof. A few years before his death, Harrison Noel was arrested from his residential home in Ridgemount after neighbors had alerted the police to a disturbance. Once the authorities had arrived, they'd found his girlfriend at the time, Melissa Doer, brutally beaten. He was charged with domestic violence.

Eliza wasn't lying.

If she wasn't feeding me lies that day, what she'd said about Colton and Tristan was true. They were brothers. The thought couldn't be shaken from my memory. It explained why they looked so similar. It wasn't just a random coincidence. I should have known better, though. Nothing in this goddamn mystery was as simple as a coincidence.

But why would the Crests give Tristan up for adoption?

I tried doing the math in my head, but other thoughts kept worming their way into my train of thought. Time and time again, I lost track of the equation. To stop the numbers from drifting into thin air, I closed my eyes and concentrated. It took a couple of goes before I finally got it.

Mrs. Crest would have been seventeen. Mr. Crest would have been nineteen.

Perhaps it was their age and financial situation that had made them deem themselves unfit to raise a child together. Colton must have found out that he had a brother, and his suspicions drove him toward Tristan. Which must have really messed him up when he'd figured out his secret older brother was actually a killer.

And he had witnessed that murder.

Those two reasons were more than enough for him to venture out and find him. Perhaps their friendship hadn't been forced or held under false pretenses. Maybe Colton really did want to know his brother better, and part of that was understanding why he'd killed Harrison Noel.

But why would Tristan lie about killing Colton? Who was Tristan protecting?

The questions swarmed like angry bees in my head with a constant, infuriating buzz. I wanted so badly to just move on with my life, but I couldn't do that when this mystery was still left unsolved, and I was the only one convinced of such a notion.

From Eliza's story and insistence that Tristan was such a great family man, I figured there was a lot of trust between himself and his adoptive family. Maybe that was why Tristan confessed about killing Colton to two of the most important people in his life: Eliza and Bones. He knew just what to say to make them believe him, so to make his story more legitimate, he made sure to include them in it. And when the time came for him to confess to the police, he already had his accessories to validate his statement.

I laid flat on my back, my arms resting above my head. My theories made less sense as I developed them, but I couldn't help but continue torturing myself. I, along with Cass and Lydia, had been chosen to figure out this mystery for a reason, and I was determined to succeed.

I returned to my sitting position and looked back down at the letters. Silently, I began to read through them for what felt like the hundredth time that day. Maybe I was missing something. But all I was doing was going around in circles. And the only direction I was going was down. I was spiraling into a pit of uselessness.

Beside me, my phone rang. I looked over at it buzzing facedown on the dock. I wasn't in the mood to talk to anyone, so I let it go to voice-mail. But the person trying to call was persistent, so after their fourth attempt to reach me, I finally answered.

"Hello?"

"Hey," Lydia said. "Where are you? I stopped by your house this morning and your dad said you were out."

"Yeah," I answered lamely. "I'm out."

I had been at the lake all day. I was starving and exhausted and dehydrated. The late afternoon summer sun was unforgiving to my skin. I wouldn't be surprised if I returned home looking like a dried-out starfish.

"Come out with me, Elliot. I miss hanging out. I haven't seen you since I got back. Besides, I want to make the most of the summer before I go to university."

"I'm not really up for it." Silence. "I'm sorry," I said when she didn't reply.

Her happiness came out slightly forced when she said, "Hey, guess what?" She took my silence as a cue to continue. "On my little holiday, I got more freckles!"

It was the little things like that that made Lydia such a great girl. "Count them up and tell me the total."

She laughed. "I meant what I said. I do miss you."

"I miss you too. Now's just not a good time."

"I understand. Promise we'll split one last bag of sour worms before the summer is over? It's okay to still be sad, but it's better now that we know who did it, that it's all over."

"Seven bags, if you really want."

"Seven would be great."

"Listen, I'll call you later, okay? I think I might head home now."

"Okay," Lydia answered. "I might stop by later tonight. I need to drop something off."

"What is it?"

"A little surprise I got you from my trip. I'll see you soon."

Finally I was ready to go home. I picked up the rocks that had been holding down the letters and tossed them into the water. Then I bundled up the pieces of paper. But as I looked at them fanned out in my hands, something stirred behind me.

"All the clues, and you still don't get it." That voice. That goddamned voice. A shiver ran down my spine despite the heat. "*I killed Colton Crest.*"

"What *the hell* are you talking about, Dad?"

He waited for me to turn around and look him in the eyes the next time he spoke. My mind was working overtime to catch up with what he was saying, while the speed of my heart indicated my body had caught every word.

I stared at the figure standing in front of me. The familiar face, the ever-present stubble on his jaw as a result of endless nights working and forgotten showers. I looked at his uncombed hair and ridiculously dorky tweed jacket with the leather elbow patches he adored so dearly. But as I continued studying, I noticed a shift deep within his eyes. They were no longer kind. The darkness in them was a riot, like the sea before a storm.

"I killed Colton. Right where you're standing too." He pulled out the pocket watch. Colton's watch. "The watch belonged to me."

What? Why? How?

My head was filled with question marks and exclamations, with jumbled letters making no recognizable words. My stomach twisted as he spoke, my airway tightening.

"I'm surprised you didn't figure it out sooner." My father's usually playful tone had turned to something condescending and cruel. "Honestly, I'm disappointed. The answers were almost spoon-fed to you. I overestimated your capabilities, Elliot."

All the doubt I'd had about my father being capable of murder dispersed in the ten seconds he'd spent speaking. It was replaced with fiery hot rage. It burned my lungs, branching through my chest like poison, heating my temper.

"You sick bastard."

"You were the runt of the family, my boy. I suppose great minds couldn't be given to all three children."

Three.

"You didn't know?" He had the biggest grin on his face as he shook his head. "Tristan isn't just Colton's brother. He's yours too. Didn't you ever wonder why Cass got the letters too? The best friend, the girlfriend and then Cass. She did seem like a random recipient, didn't she?"

I tried to remain as calm as my father, but I was struggling. My hands shook so much that I had to clench them into fists and keep them at my sides. My jaw was starting to ache from biting back my insults.

"You and Megan." It was a question, but I made sure it came out as a statement, a confirmation. My dad and Mrs. Crest.

"We were seventeen. We didn't see our relationship proceeding past graduation. Then Tristan came into the equation. For the sake of an unexpected child, we stayed together until he was born and planned for his adoption. We found a suitable couple from Ridgemount. Alexandra Yanks and her husband, Jasper, were incapable of having children. She was twenty-seven at the time, with a business in pastry, and her husband worked for a big corporation. They willingly took him into their arms. Surprisingly, they had a miracle baby fourteen years later. I believe they named her Eliza."

"So you let your *own son* take the fall for a crime you committed?" I spat.

Betrayal consumed me, and the image I had of my father shifted from that of a loving, caring parent to a heartless villain. He wasn't family anymore. He was a killer. He didn't seem fazed by my outbursts. "He did it willingly. Tristan grew up with the doubt of his origins, but when we reconnected after Colton's death, he was so desperate for parental compassion that he practically *offered* to take the blame. As you know, Elliot, I'm quite skilled with words. It took very little to manipulate him because of the emotional state he was in."

"Why kill Colton, though? What the hell drove you to a point where you *killed my best friend?*"

"He was going to destroy *everything*. Don't you see, Elliot? I did the right thing. I did it all for you. Isn't it better to sacrifice one person than hurt multiple?" The storm in his eyes was electric, a maniac flash of insanity reflecting in his irises. "Ending my relationship with Megan was merely a relief for both of us, but when your mother found out about Tristan, she was hysterical. I had made the mistake of going into a marriage without checking my baggage, and she was unforgiving of such a secret. She was the love of my life and seeing her walk away? I couldn't bear losing the rest of my family because of a secret that should have been kept buried.

"But how could I have told her? How could I have told my entire world that all the firsts we shared together weren't really my first? That in high school, I'd had a child with her newfound best friend? Valerie and Megan were inseparable as soon as they met, and once they had created a friendship, I knew that the longer I waited, the harder she'd take it. I kept the secrets hidden, keep the skeleton in the closet. But as time passed and dust collected, I knew it was time to bury the bones for good and ensure they couldn't be found.

"When your mother left, I was distraught. One night Valerie and Megan decided to open a bottle of red wine, and unfortunately, that wasn't all they opened. First Megan confessed the teenage pregnancy, then who she shared that child with. Do you know what the most heartbreaking thing was about your mother finding out? She didn't yell at me, she didn't throw things. She was hurt and upset in the quietest of ways. I was broken over it. So I decided to start therapy a couple of times a month and haven't stopped going. Did you know that when Colton came back in July, he began therapy too? Coincidentally, we were seeing the same therapist. Our session dates never lined up, so we never passed each other, but on a Thursday afternoon, there he was. He seemed to be focused on his phone, so he didn't notice me in the waiting room. However, in his haste to leave, Colton tipped his journal out of his schoolbag.

"My temper may have gotten out of hand when he threatened to tell everyone those secrets. *My* secrets. Then, in a startling moment, everything had utmost clarity. He had to go. *The boy had to go.* He knew secrets that needed to be buried, and what else do we bury? The dead."

"But the letters . . . I know what your handwriting looks like—"

"Ambidextrous. It's the ability to use both your left and right hands equally as well."

"If you had Tristan helping you, then why didn't you make him write the letters? Why go through all that trouble?"

"Because the last letter was to frame Tristan. He was such an easy target. He was previously convicted for murder and has a history of anger management and violence. People saw him with Colton constantly. It was the perfect plan. Half of the letters were already written when Tristan approached me, desperate for paternal guidance. His adoptive father, Jasper, suffered a heart attack when Tristan was sixteen, and he had grown up as a man without a father figure. I admit, it steered away from my original plan, but it seemed to work out. Tristan would confess to the killing, and you would eventually find the last letter I had planted. The one that confessed Tristan Yanks killed his brother Colton Crest."

Everything slowly fell into place. The blurry picture finally had focus. Events were connecting, so were people. Motives were exposed, perspectives had changed, questions had been answered.

"Why are you telling me this now?" I demanded. "Tristan's trial is in a couple of days, he's already confessed. You practically walked away free and clear."

My father glared at me. "No, someone validated his whereabouts at the estimated time and date of the murder. The police have evidence that he was elsewhere the entire day. They released him this morning and the case has been reopened. I'm not telling you to quench your curious thirst. I'm telling you because now you're my accomplice." He pulled a gun from behind him and aimed it at my temple. "And you're going to help me escape."

Never in a million years did I think my own father would press a gun to my temple and force me into his car. Then again, after his confession I no longer considered David Parker my father. He had alienated himself from that right and replaced his title with "killer."

"It's only a matter of time," he said, keeping the gun aimed at my side as I started the engine.

"You can't kill me," I said, sounding surprisingly calm as I pulled away from the side of the road. I tried to stay indifferent about the whole situation. *Hey, you have a gun pointed at me. No big deal, because you used to feed me microwavable mac 'n' cheese and that has to count as something, right?*

"Of course I won't, Elliot. You're my son. This whole thing started because I wanted to protect you. I wanted to sustain our relationship." He smiled at me, his eyes wild. Then he let out a hysterical round of laughter. The menace behind it was so thick that I could have plucked it from the air and molded it into something monstrous. When he sobered, he pressed the cold end of the barrel harder against my rib-cage. "However, I won't hesitate to hurt you, like I did Colton, to make you bend to my will. We're family. If one goes down, we all go down."

"No wonder she left you."

My eyes were on the road, but his silence was a sure sign of his dis-comfort. I risked a sideways glance and saw a small tick in his jaw. I'd been successful in striking a chord, but I was unsure of the outcome. Would he really put a bullet through my flesh? Would he really sneak in a few cheap hits with his fists?

"You know, if you had read the book she gave you, you would have figured this out much sooner."

It was my turn to be caught off guard. My foot hit the pedal harder than necessary and we made a quick surge forward, nearly hitting the car in front of us. I managed to hit the brake and avoid the collision, but it wasn't a subtle task. The impact flung me forward, my seatbelt locking to try and keep me back. Dad knew the tables were turned once again and he was in control. This made him smile.

"Ah, yes. *A Madman's Message* by Gregory Everett. It was always such a professional alias as opposed to my birth name. I was seventeen when that book was first published."

Answers had been merely a few feet away from me every night. All in the form of a thin hardback book without its dust jacket.

"You said you studied it in university."

"I did. I dissected my own work, looked at it critically, reflected on it. Your mother tried telling you why she left in the form of fiction."

"Jamie," I whispered.

He seemed surprised. "You *did* read some. You didn't get very far, I presume, not that you needed to. That was one of the biggest give-aways. The dedication and the epigraph. Put them together and you get a crucial clue, but those are always the parts that are overlooked by readers."

"Tristan is Jamie."

"We didn't know the gender of the baby. We referred to the child as Jamie because for a fleeting moment in time, we considered raising him ourselves. It was unisex, in case we went through with the idea. *My first, but not my last; my forever, but not my always.*"

"You made me believe my mother was the one at fault."

"I did no such thing, Elliot. All I did was tell you we fell out of love. Her actions of leaving made a mark of their own. I had nothing to do with it."

Taking this into consideration, I realized the truth behind his words. Not once did my father ever manipulate me into thinking she was the one to blame. Her abandonment had caused me to create my own conclusions about her morals. But perhaps I should have given her the benefit of the doubt. There was much more to my father's story, and I suspected the same from my mother's.

I swallowed, redirecting the conversation. "Where are we going?"

And how can I escape?

"Out of town."

"Wouldn't that be suspicious? Tristan is released, and we disappear—"

"You're underestimating my abilities. We'll be returning in a few hours. We just need to dispose of some evidence."

I nearly threw up against the wheel. Was he talking about the murder weapon? The thought of the weapon used to kill Colton made my stomach churn in agony. Was it in the trunk of the car? Was it covered in his blood? I was feeling lightheaded.

"Turn right at the intersection," he instructed.

I did as I was told.

"We're going to have to make a quick stop."

✝

We parked on an abandoned road in the middle of nowhere. Then Dad pressed the gun to the center of my back and propelled me forward through the trees. Despite his claim that he wouldn't kill me, I had a feeling that we were marching toward my death bed.

As we walked deeper into the woods, we came across a small, isolated cabin. My stomach flipped. The barrel dug into my skin.

"What is this?" My voice was weak, and I was furious at myself for showing how scared I truly was.

Dad pulled out a small silver key and unlocked the front door. "Don't you remember this? I used to take you and your sister here when you were just kids. I came out here to write."

The way he reminisced about my childhood was revolting. He spoke as if we were flipping through an old family album and I'd pointed at one of his fondest memories. He was warped if he thought I'd share his nostalgia.

Swinging the door open, he nudged me with the barrel of the gun until I stepped inside. The small enclosure smelled like earth and smoke. Keeping me harnessed in front of him, he started searching through one of the bookshelves. My father muttered incoherently as he sorted through his belongings, being sure to switch his gaze from the task at hand to me every once in a while.

Since he was partially occupied, I started to take in my surroundings. Maybe one gun led to more, or perhaps there was another weapon. But as my eyes swept around the room, I couldn't find anything remotely threatening to use. There was an impressive desk sitting next to the main bookcase, with an old typewriter and a small desk lamp. On the left was an engraved wooden chest, and on the right was a dark leather couch.

It was a writer's heaven.

Unless I picked up the typewriter and swung it blindly, I was toast. And doing so would be too time-consuming. By the time I'd even wrapped my fingers around my makeshift weapon, I would already have a bullet through my leg.

I'd be *deep-fried* toast.

Dad pulled out a tall hardback and flipped through the pages. When he found what he was looking for, I caught a glimpse of a white envelope.

"Let's go."

"Give that to me!" I didn't budge, despite his prodding.

"I've already told you everything you need to know, Elliot."

"There's more than one side to every story. You should know that. You're a writer." His eyebrows rose in response. "I still have questions."

My father seemed to consider, the gears in his mind turning. Judging by his knit eyebrows and pursed lips, he was about to make a proposition, and I could bet it involved using the final letter as a bargaining chip. But he would never admit that my response gave him that idea.

"You'll be rewarded if you act accordingly." Again the gun pressed against my back. "Now start moving."

I took my time, sauntering toward the entrance. I was testing his patience, but I was also trying to buy myself some time. Maybe if I was fast enough, I could slam his hand in the door, snatch his gun, and finally have the upper hand.

But the theory played out much more fluidly in my head when it was just the gist of an idea. Thinking about it realistically yielded more failed outcomes than successful ones. I was not a ninja, and my reflexes were good but definitely not impressive.

Although my father was fifty, I didn't underestimate his ability with a gun. It would be too risky if I allowed myself to believe that his skill was a hoax. Besides, the weapon was only a distraction from what I truly feared.

His mind.

As soon as we stepped outside, there was the unmistakable sound of footfalls. The jogger was obviously oblivious to the fact that only a few feet away, a father was holding his son hostage with a gun pressed to his spine.

Words desperately wanted to claw their way out of my throat. I wanted to yell like a maniac, try to get the person's attention. But I hesitated when a thought crept its way through my mind. What if my potential rescuer was shot? I wasn't letting anyone else get hurt.

While my father was distracted by the possibility of someone catching him, I took the opportunity to bolt for it. I shot forward and swerved around in all different directions, trying my best to keep moving so that I'd minimize my chances of being hit.

Dad yelled out, acrimony in his tone, and started firing shots as he ran after me. The problem with zigzagging in the woods was the ground. Tree roots surfaced from the earth, wanting to catch my shoes and stub my toes. My heart was pounding in my ears until that was all I could hear. My father's yells of fury were drowned out by my rapid breathing, my speeding pulse.

Another shot rang through my ears as I tried to duck behind a tree for cover, but a bullet had found its way into the back of my left calf. I bit back a howl and instead let out a hiss of breath between my teeth.

Son of a bitch.

I could already feel blood pulsing out of the wound. It was hot and fresh and sliding down my leg, soaking into the back of my shoe as my speed became a half-assed run, bordering on a desperate hobble. Fire shot through my muscles, igniting a pain I refused to voice.

I managed to scrape my way toward the closest tree, pressing my back against it and taking the weight off my leg to relieve some of the pain. Sweat poured furiously from my forehead, dripping into my eyes to blind me. I was breathless. My heart was a furious animal beating against my rib cage, demanding escape.

Another bullet went shooting through the trees, managing to hit the very tree I was hiding behind. It skimmed against my wrist, tearing my flesh. Blood instantly pulsed from the wound, dripping into my open palm. I curled my fingers, nails biting into skin as I tried incredibly hard not to yell out in anguish.

"You can't hide from me, Elliot."

I could hear his footsteps, calm and slow. Twigs snapped beneath his boots, leaves crunching softly. He knew I was injured.

Through the hammering in my head and the pulsing of my heart, I could hear my father whistling. "*If you go out in the woods today, you're sure of a big surprise.*"

Fucking bastard. Of course he'd take this opportunity to be a maniac and sing.

"*If you go out in the woods today, you'd better go in disguise.*"

I could hear him slowing down, his steady footsteps getting louder.

"*For every secret that ever was, will gather here for certain because . . . today's the day the family does their killings.*"

I was drenched in blood and sweat, blinded by dizziness.

"*If you go out in the woods today, you'd better not go alone.*"

We were nearing the end. And I wasn't talking about just the song either.

"*It's lovely out in the woods today, but safer to stay at home.*"

I quickly pieced my way around the wide circumference of the tree trunk, keeping myself pressed against it, my footsteps as light as possible.

"*For every body that ever fell, will gather here for certain because . . . today's the day the family does their shootings.*"

I held my breath, as if it would cloak me in the protection of invisibility.

There was no more time to run.

I felt the familiar cold barrel press against my flushed skin, his words right in my ear as he said, "Don't make me shoot you again."

There was no more time to run, indeed.

But I still had time to fight.

"Fuck you." My left elbow got a blind shot and managed to hit his throat.

My father stumbled backward, coughing vigorously. He clutched his neck, and in the process, managed to drop his weapon. With a fire consuming my whole body, burning my muscles, and charring my bones, I lurched forward to grab hold of it.

He quickly saw his fatal mistake, lightning in his eyes as he dove twice as hard to retrieve the gun. We both stumbled forward, a mass of fighting limbs and struggling cries. If you had asked me to hit my old man a few weeks ago, I would have been fucking outraged. But because I had two bullets in my skin, I gave absolutely zero shits.

"Give me the damn gun!" he screamed bloody murder, his fingers digging into the wound on my wrist. I sucked in a deep breath, but the air didn't relieve my lungs. All it did was make me breathless. Blood gushed out and pooled onto the dry ground, seeping into the earth.

He got a cheap shot at my face. His punch caused me to backtrack, but it only made me angrier. My fist shot forward and landed a punch in his gut. He doubled over, gritting his teeth from the impact. I took this as an opportunity to get in another hit. My knuckles connected with bone, igniting an angry roar from my opponent.

While he withered in pain, I managed to take hold of the gun. I hastily scrambled to my feet, my good hand holding the weapon. It was heavy in my palm, but I wasn't sure if it was because of its material or the fact that if I shot it in the right place, I'd suddenly have the weight of someone's death on my hands.

Because of our brawl, my nose was now bleeding. I was starting to think there'd be more blood on the ground than in my body by the time this whole thing was over. If I was even lucky enough to see it through to the end.

I wiped my injured hand across my nose, blood and dirt smearing across my face. I was battered and bruised and fucking exhausted, but I just kept the barrel of the gun pointed at my father. He scrambled to his feet, laughing. He looked at me with wild eyes, a demonic grin on his face.

"Don't move," I warned. I tried to keep my arm straight, my aim unwavering, but it was incredibly hard, and I found myself straining from the effort.

"You won't kill me," he said calmly.

"Very true. But I won't hesitate to shoot you if you try any more of this crazy shit."

"Shoot me?" He laughed. "Elliot, I don't think you could ever hurt me. We're family."

"Didn't stop you from shooting *me*," I said. Then added, "*Twice.*"

"You don't understand! I'm doing the right thing. It's clear, right here." He vigorously pointed at his head, his mind. To him, what he was doing was for the best. To him, he wasn't a villain, but a hero. He licked his lips and laughed psychotically. "Don't shoot me, son."

I wrapped my finger around the trigger.

He quickly realized that I was startlingly serious. "You'd really shoot your old man?"

I remained expressionless.

"You're too much like your mother. You'd never pull the trigger."

"Don't tempt me."

"Okay, then. Shoot me."

I tried to remain calm as he grinned at me. My arm was starting to shake from being held up for so long. I just wanted to collapse onto the ground and sleep on a rough bed of leaves and twigs.

"Shoot me," he promoted, sounding revoltingly eager.

"I'm going to call the police," I said instead.

"You're no fun," he answered. "Let's play a game, then."

With one swift movement, he produced another gun from his person and pointed it at my chest. "Whoever shoots first, wins."

The situation had become much heavier. What if he shot first? In an act of self-defense, would I accidentally kill my own father? My head was spinning, my vision becoming blurry. This was not the time to panic.

But my brain was filled with too many thoughts, all of them running wild, competing for my attention.

"Shoot."

I couldn't concentrate. Time was running out quickly, and I couldn't keep up.

He pulled the trigger, the shot ringing into the air. It startled a few birds and they quickly went fleeing for safety. My heart pounded in response. I looked my father in the eyes, all signs of familiarity gone. He was a stranger.

"*Shoot!*"

With one more breath, I did as I was told. I pointed the gun at his foot.

Just disarm him.

Just injure him.

I pulled the trigger.

Click.

No *bang.*

His laughter consumed me almost as quickly as the dread that followed when I realized I was out of shots. My father simply shook his head, a sweet smile on his lips.

"Foolishness can kill a man."

He stepped forward. I stepped back. He didn't seem fazed by our little dance.

There was a faint crackling in my ears. I was barely able to keep upright at that point. If I wasn't shot within the next ten minutes, I'd be unconscious. Either way, my body would end up on the ground.

My father took another step, but as he did so, a pill bottle fell from his jacket pocket. The pills rattled inside their plastic container. I wasn't aware that my father was on any type of medication.

"It's a painkiller," he snapped, reading my thoughts. "I knew you'd give me a goddamn headache, so I stopped by the pharmacist before I found you at the lake."

He lowered himself to the ground and picked up the pill bottle, keeping his gun pointed at me in case I tried to make a run for it.

"I tried so hard to protect you, Elliot." My father looked at me solemnly, but I couldn't help but catch a hint of hysteria, confirming it wasn't genuine. "At first I didn't think you'd believe anything written in the first letter, let alone venture forth to find the others. But on the day of Colton's funeral when you pulled out your eulogy . . . your expression confirmed that you had found the first one. I did everything I could to prevent you from finding out. I called your mother that same day, and with the power of suggestion, I put the idea in her head that she should take you for a holiday to get you out of town until I came up with a plan. You were stubborn, though, so I issued a curfew, but you were too into the mystery to stop. You were starting to find out too much. I was certain you'd uncover everything. You spent too much time with Colton. His habits were starting to rub off on you. It was so easy for your mother to walk away when she found out . . . I couldn't lose you or your sister the same way. You're growing up, going to university. You'll be starting families of your own. You would have left me."

He continued rambling, continued walking forward, but I was starting to get lightheaded, and my footsteps ceased. The crackling in my ears intensified.

Then I realized it wasn't just a noise in my head as a result of my fatigue. The sound came from someone crunching against the dry leaves and twigs. There was someone out there.

The jogger from earlier.

Now that I had identified the sound, I was able to focus on it. In the distance, I could hear running and I swore it was coming from two different directions. My father suddenly stopped talking. A quick look at the fury in his eyes confirmed my suspicions. There was more than one person out there.

"Over here!" I called, trying to get their attention. It was my last chance at escape. I hoped the person didn't have techno blasting in their ears.

But then I saw a head of strawberry blond hair, and suddenly, my cries for attention dwindled to a desperate plea to let us be.

"No! Lydia! Get out of here!"

My father's head snapped up at the mention of her name, his gun swiveling with his body to try and find her. My eyes were frantic as I tried to guess which tree she had hidden behind. She could be hurt. She could be *killed*.

Goddamn it!

When he couldn't find Lydia, the gun turned back to me. There were only a few feet between us, and the gun was pointed right at my forehead.

"Maybe I underestimated your abilities." I had never seen such a wild look in my father's eyes. It was feral. It was insanity. "How did you do it? How did you contact her? Who else did you tell? Was it the old make-an-emergency-call-and-record-the-conversation trick?"

"I don't know how she found us," I answered, my head spinning. My insides were tying into knots, tightening in fear of the unknown. "I swear to God—"

"*Don't lie to me.*" He was hysterical, his chest heaving as he wheezed out a small, psychotic chuckle. "This is wrong. This is *all wrong*. I planned it all out . . . it was flawless. *How did you do it?*"

Behind him, I could see another person carefully creeping closer toward us. Watching my dad freak out was like seeing him get possessed. I felt like I hadn't recognized him when he confessed to killing Colton. But now . . . now it was like he wasn't even human. He continued to mutter to himself, trying to catch the threads of his rapidly unraveling plan.

The figure behind him stepped into view. My heart got lodged in my throat when I recognized my mother. There were tears in her eyes and her shoulders were shaking. She looked terrified as she trudged forward, my dad's typewriter in her arms.

My father noticed I was distracted by something behind him. He straightened, preparing to turn, but my mother took the opportunity to use all her strength and fling the typewriter toward him. As soon as it left her arms, I knew it wouldn't do much. The momentum wasn't enough to carry such a heavy item far or do much damage.

As expected, it fell a few feet short from where my father was standing. We were fucked. We were absolutely done for.

He looked down at the typewriter, then up at my mother.

"Valerie?"

"It's over, David." She was shaking, tears streaming down her face.

Her words held a double meaning. They were released from her lips like butterflies, delicate and simple. Dad sang the words with the fire on his tongue.

"I never wanted to hurt you, Valerie."

"You're hurting me now."

He hesitated, genuinely confused.

"You *shot our son.*"

My father turned and looked at me like he was finally seeing me as more than just a nuisance. He started seeing me as his own flesh and blood.

"I . . ." He tried coming up with an excuse, a validation of his actions. But nothing came out.

"You spent so long creating villains and demons and nightmares in your head that you eventually became one," my mother whispered, tears escaping her eyes to travel down her cheeks.

"Drop the gun, Dad." Cass appeared a moment later. She was shaking, tears streaming down her face too, but she chewed her lip and tried extremely hard to contain them. Trevor soon stepped into view and wrapped his arms around her waist, pulling her close, promising protection.

"It's for the best, David," he said.

I blinked, trying to clear my vision. How did everyone get here?

Good God, the hammering in my head wasn't settling, and I was starting to crave the painkillers in my father's pocket. I wasn't even sure if any of this was happening. Was I hallucinating? Had I fucking *died*?

My father swiveled around, pointing the gun shakily at no one in particular. He was like a deer caught in the headlights, his eyes as wide and wild. He turned back to my mother, the gun inevitably pointing at her. Cass let out a scream.

"I'm sorry, Valerie. I'm so sorry." He was crying. I could hear the sobs getting caught on his words.

My father thought he was Superman. But all heroes have a Kryptonite. My mother happened to be his weakness. She always had been. He loved her so desperately to a point where it was questionable. Where his twisted idea of affection had compelled him to hurt.

"Everybody surrender your weapons and place your hands behind your head! We have you surrounded."

The police had turned up. The world was spinning. Too much was happening. If a unicorn had pranced into the corner of my peripheral vision, I wouldn't have even questioned it.

Valerie put her hands behind her head. "Surrender, David."

My entire family had him surrounded. Together we stood, united, against someone we had never thought would be an enemy. I'd thought overcoming Colton's murder would be the hardest thing I'd ever have to do, but it wasn't until now that my entire perspective changed.

We place our trust in the ones we love, and sometimes those circumstances have the most hurtful outcomes.

Dad crumpled in defeat, his plans turned to rubble. His shoulders sagged, the gun becoming limp against his side. His eyes were still filled with tears as he placed his weapon onto the ground and turned with his hands in the air.

The police approached him. I couldn't focus on the details of his arrest because the pain of my bullet wounds finally caught up to me, and my attention was drawn to my broken being. My mother appeared at my side as I turned and tried to inspect my leg. A police officer noticed my injury, calling to his team that I required medical attention.

"Where's Lydia?" I asked, searching the trees for her.

"She's okay, she's safe." Her hands flew to my face, pressing against my cheeks like she wasn't sure I was really there in front of her. She choked back a sob. "I was so scared . . . I thought he was going to kill you—"

I propped myself against a tree and ignored the bolt of pain that shot through my leg as I shifted my weight. "How did you know?"

"Trevor," she said. Mom repeated his name a couple of times, trying to recollect her thoughts.

Trevor appeared a moment later, gently patting my mother's arm. "Are you okay, Valerie?"

She nodded, sniffling into her sleeve, but when he noticed she was in no condition to continue talking, he finished explaining.

"I was at the drugstore getting some blood glucose test strips and I saw your dad come in. He was holding a pocket watch, and I couldn't help but think that it looked just like Colton's. Cass had told me about it, and when we had a bit of a chat, your dad didn't seem like his normal self. I don't know how to describe it, he was just so . . . *haunted*, I guess. I called your sister . . ."

"I was in the car, waiting for Trevor," Cass said softly. Her boyfriend rubbed her shoulders. "As soon I heard about the watch, I just knew it was him. We lost him because of traffic, but we finally found you at the lake. You were about to leave, and I didn't know what to do. I called Mom, and she said she thought she knew where he'd take you."

"That little cabin was his sanctuary. I knew if he had any further secrets, he'd keep them there," my mother explained, smiling sadly.

My mother had risked so much to come out here, to confront her ex-husband with nothing but courage and the power of conversation. All because my father had mangled his understanding of protection. He'd manipulated it to a point where he truly believed he was doing the right thing. She had done all that for a son who was almost a stranger. But regardless of our lack of time together, she still loved me with all her heart.

"We're going to get you to the hospital, okay? You'll be okay, I promise. You'll be okay."

I took the arm that wasn't holding me up and wrapped it around my mother. She was startled for a moment, then she dissolved into me and held on tight, frightened that I'd let go. She smelled like fabric softener.

I was home. I was okay.

ACCEPTANCE

The blood loss finally caught up to me as soon as the ambulance arrived. I could barely keep my eyes open, so I welcomed the darkness and fell into unconsciousness. It wasn't until a couple of days later when a light finally brightened up in my head and I was able to stay awake for more than a couple of minutes.

The first thing I noticed was Lydia. She was slumped against the plastic chair in my hospital room, her hand in mine. Her head was resting on the sheets of my bed, tendrils of soft strawberry blond hair surrounding her. I gently squeezed her fingers, and that small gesture was enough to wake her from her peaceful slumber.

"Elliot," was all she said before launching herself toward me. The impact caught me off guard, and I gasped as a wave of sickening pain flooded through my entire being.

"Oh God, I'm sorry," she instantly said, sitting up as she realized what she had done. But I pulled her back toward me, crushing her against my chest.

"I'm so glad you're okay," I said.

"I'm so glad *you're* okay."

Her fingers curled around my shirt, her face pinched in disbelief. Lydia cried onto my shoulder, her body shaking violently from uncontrollable sobs. I buried my face in her hair to prevent myself from doing the same. We stayed like that for a long time.

"I was so scared."

I held on tighter. "So was I."

To be confronted by the revelation that the killer I had desperately been tracking down came in the form of my own father was terrifying. To be aware that he had no limits when it came to hurting people was horrifying. To know that the gun in his hands wasn't the only thing to be feared tied my stomach into knots.

Because, as a writer, he knew *exactly* how to make someone suffer with a single sentence.

Words are weapons, utilized to inflict the most excruciating pain and present the most beautiful of pleasures. They're used to manipulate thoughts, beliefs, motives, and emotions. If my father hadn't owned a gun, his power of persuasion would have defeated me equally as well. The sentiments of a cleverly crafted speech have the potential to get tattooed to our memories, and sometimes that kind of trauma is harder to heal from than a mere bullet wound.

"How did you even know to go down to the cabin?"

"When Cass and Trevor figured everything out, they called your mother. There wasn't enough time for them to pick her up in Ridgemount, so I drove down. God, I almost got into an accident from going twice the speed limit." Lydia shook her head. "I don't even want to think what would have happened if we hadn't gotten there in time."

"I'd be dead."

She shivered, trying to shake the thought away.

"Do you think he really would have killed you?"

"I was testing his patience," I said. "If anything, he would have shot me again because I was being a little shit."

"You really can't help yourself sometimes, can you?"

"It's a curse, to be honest."

We exchanged smiles. Despite the circumstances, it felt so bloody good just to smile. As soon as I had sobered, I turned my head and rested my cheek against the pillow, my eyes wandering around the room. Beside me, I saw a collection of get-well cards and even a foil balloon.

"Who's that from?"

Lydia sat up to look in the direction I had nodded. "Courtesy of Trevor."

"Trevor, huh? I guess I misjudged his character."

"You're not the only one. I was suspicious of him too. He's a great guy, though. He makes your sister incredibly happy. I've never seen her smile so much."

"Where's Cass anyway?"

"At your house, taking care of everything. She was here earlier this morning. She'll be relieved to know you're finally awake."

"Christ, how long have I been out for?"

"Three days."

"I must have missed out on a lot."

Lydia laughed. "Hardly. More happened within the few hours you were at the cabin than the few days you were unconscious." She fell silent, chewing her bottom lip nervously. "What happened out there anyway? You're the only one who knows the whole story . . ."

It occurred to me that everyone was still unaware of what had gone on.

It was a long story, and I wasn't even sure I had all the details yet, but I took a deep breath and told Lydia everything I knew.

†

I stayed in the hospital for another couple of days until I'd managed to gather the strength to haul myself out of bed. On the day I was released, my mother helped pack my things. She insisted that I use a wheelchair, but I was convinced that my crutches would suffice. Lydia also came to ensure that I got home safely. She patiently helped me hobble down to the parking lot. I was bloody exhausted by the time we got to the car.

A gentle hand rested on my other shoulder. I turned and saw my mother. "Let's go home."

Lydia gave her a small smile. "Thanks, Valerie. For everything."

My mother reached out and gently touched her cheek. "No need to thank me, sweetheart. I'm just glad you're both okay."

My mother stepped forward and hugged Lydia, but when she withdrew, she was holding something between them. It was a white envelope.

"In your father's haste to run after you, he let this fall from his back pocket. He didn't notice."

"You didn't give it to the police?"

"That's not his handwriting," she answered. "If he was withholding it from you, I can only imagine what the content is. If you need to take it to the authorities, then do so. But I think you have a right to know what's inside first."

I took the envelope from my mother's hands and gently slid out the paper. As I unfolded it, I instantly recognized the lopsided scrawl.

"This is Colton's handwriting," Lydia whispered, a sob escaping her lips.

"I don't think so, but maybe it will give us more answers than the last letter would have."

We couldn't decide who would take the letter home first. Having to wait for answers when they were within reach would have been torture for both of us, so Lydia took some quick photos of the pages so I could take the original with me.

†

In the car, Mom decided that I needed something to eat, so we stopped to buy some food. She wanted sushi, but she said she'd get me a kebab. It was exactly what we'd eaten when we had our first lunch together.

I was tired and wanted to stay in the car, so she left me in the parking lot, locking the doors and telling me to call if anything happened. While she was gone, I opened the glove box and found the thinly lined paper. It held the answers to all my questions, and I couldn't put off reading it any longer.

Taking a deep breath, I ripped the envelope open and started reading.

My therapist has recommended that I start writing in a journal to help process my emotions. I've never really been fond of writing down my thoughts, and I think it's because I'm afraid that once they're in concrete form, then they're real and I must confront them.

It's only appropriate that I trace back to eight years ago. When I was ten years old, my mother drove me to the train station. There's a post office right next door, and sometimes we'd sit at the front with hot fries and watch the trains speed by. But my mother had a parcel to deliver that day, so I was by myself.

Across the street was a shiny black car. A man was crossing the street ahead of it.

Then I blinked and the two became one: a dark cloud of destruction. There was shouting and tire squeals and the sound of bone hitting metal and glass. There had been a collision, a murder. And I had witnessed the whole thing.

The scene replayed in my head. Over and over and over again. There was no Stop button. You could only pause. Some days, I'd be distracted enough to push the memory back, but I would always be haunted by it again. The nights were the worst. I was surrounded by darkness, my mind completely exposed. And behind my closed eyelids, inklings of my imagination formed nightmares without me having to sleep.

It started with a snowflake and ended with an avalanche. I was the skier, and the only way forward was to go spiraling down. Seeing this type of thing when you're young makes you feel a permanent type of cold.

Every year on the same day, I tell my mother I'm ill and she lets me stay home. If anything, it was just a mental health day for me. I'd play video games, read books, and snack on junk food. But when I was sixteen, I made the decision to take the day off and travel to Ridgemount. I was just a kid. I had thirty dollars in my pocket and a student bus pass to take me around. I had no sense of direction or purpose. All I knew was that I wanted information and I couldn't get it from newspaper clippings or the internet. I needed someone's help.

It must have been chance that brought me to the local market. They weren't supposed to be there on a Monday morning, but the stalls had all been such a hit that the local council had granted anyone with a stall to stay the extra day.

That's where I met Alexandra. I didn't know who she was at first. She was just a woman selling freshly baked goods. But as I passed her stall, she looked at me like she knew me. She called out Tristan's name. She thought she'd spotted her son, I was looking for a killer, and incidentally, he was the same person.

She apologized immediately and explained that I looked like her son. We laughed it off, I bought a brownie, got her business card, and that was the end of our first exchange.

When I went home, I looked up her website and that gave me a name.

She was Tristan's mom.

I kept coming back to the farmers market whenever I had a free weekend, and she was always there. I knew exactly who she was, but she didn't know me. The detective in me introduced himself as Daniel Heckerman. I wanted information without letting her know who I was, and so a new identity was created. I didn't expect it to last for so long, but it did.

Since I was at the markets so often, I eventually asked Alexandra if she needed help on the weekends to prepare baked goods. She was grateful for the extra hand. I formed an unconventional friendship with her this way. However, it wasn't the most genuine relationship. Alexandra found comfort in the fact that I reminded her of the son she had lost. And in return, she told me the simplest of things about her children, like their hobbies and interests and significant moments in their childhood. It helped shape my understanding of a killer.

But it was hard to understand a story from just one perspective.

After some research, I discovered the man who was murdered was named Harrison Noel. He was a twenty-three-year-old and a university student at Charleston University. He was in his third year of an accounting degree, a bright man with a brighter future. His girlfriend was pregnant, and they were ready to start a whole new chapter of life together.

That's how it appeared on the outside. That's how everyone saw it, up until recently anyway. Harrison's girlfriend recently wrote an autobiography that follows her relationship with *him. How their relationship was anything but healthy and suddenly she'd been confronted with his murder. She writes how she's full of conflicting emotions of guilt and sadness and an undertone of resentment. But she always manages to find happiness and pride in her daughter. People say she's money-hungry. I think writing about her struggles was for herself more than anyone, and money was the last thing on her mind. She had a story to tell.*

My mother discovered the pattern in my absences after I turned eighteen. She was hysterical, finally realizing the effects of what I had witnessed. Then the confession slipped: how when she was seventeen, she'd had a baby boy she couldn't provide for, and so she gave him up for adoption. The Yanks family took him in and cared for him like their own. Tristan was her son.

My half-brother.

Containing that kind of secret ate me up inside. May 17 was around the corner—the day Tristan killed Harrison Noel—and with such a revelation, I was destined to crash and burn.

My mother begged me not to leave, so I made her a deal. If I didn't come back in a month, I promised to tell her where I was and why I'd needed to go. My mind was set, there were no further arguments.

Tristan was released during my stay in Ridgemount. But as our friendship progressed, questions surfaced. It was late one night, and we were in his garage. A couple of his friends were coming over for a drink. It was a poor time to reveal my true intentions, but I couldn't contain it.

I told him I'd seen him kill Harrison Noel when I was ten. I told him I had been researching him for years. I told him I needed to know why he did what he did.

Tristan was livid. He accused me of using him for answers. His anger management issues were something I was aware of, but seeing his rage firsthand? It was indescribable. The ferocity in his actions, the poison in his words. He could have killed me with his bare hands.

Then I told him I was his brother.

He knew about my mother. He said Alexandra had told him the names of his biological parents when he was thirteen. That meant he knew who his birth father was.

That's how I found out that my best friend's father had had a teenage romance with my mother back when they were in high school. As a result, it meant that I shared a brother with my best friend.

After I found out, I came back home. And just like I had promised, I met with my mother in the parking lot of the gym. I wasn't ready to confront her, but she was insistent. She was hysterical, her voice shrill. She told me she couldn't lose two sons. But keeping a secret like that was too big for me to just forgive and forget.

I feel awful for not telling Elliot. Keeping this kind of secret from him isn't fair. It isn't fair that his dad is keeping him in the shadows just as much as my mother did. Although some would argue that having a brother that was adopted out shouldn't affect us, Tristan's contribution to both our lives is significant. I have a right to know, Elliot has a right to know, Cass and Lydia have a right to know.

I want to tell them. And I think I will. Therapy has really helped me process my thoughts, really helped me explore my emotions in a healthy way. I'm ready to share, to focus on a better future.

I could have handled a lot of things better when I ran off

in May. For one, it cost me a fortune. I had to ask my girl-friend for a thousand dollars. My stay in Ridgemount had used up the funds I had saved for my travel plans. Asking Lydia for cash broke me. And seeing her do it so willingly hit me twice as hard. Her love was unconditional, and I felt like such a bastard for what I knew I was putting her through.

Emotions can be really messy sometimes. There's a lot of doubt and uncertainty with growing up. But there is one thing I am sure about and that is Lydia. She's so full of love and happiness, and she inspires me to be the best possible version of myself each and every day. There are many things I need to do. I still need to return the pocket watch to David. I have grown to adore it, but it was never my family heir-loom. It's Elliot's. It feels wrong to have it in my possession after learning everything about Tristan, so it's time it was finally returned to its rightful owner.

I'm ready to get up off the ground and keep moving. I'm ready to go forward.

I'm finally ready to live my life.

†

As soon as I finished reading, my heart was thundering, my mind was mush.

The car door unlocked with a click and my mother got in, holding a white plastic bag filled with lunch. She gently placed the bag by my feet and smiled at me, but when she saw the expression on my face, the corners of her lips turned downwards. Her eyes shifted to the letter in my lap.

"Oh, sweetheart . . ."

Just the tone of her voice was enough to shatter my insides completely. For years, I had convinced myself that my mother was a monster, that she didn't care about us, that she visited only twice a year because she couldn't bear to stay any longer. But maybe I had been disregarding her efforts.

"Why didn't you come back for us?"

The question slipped from my lips before I could swallow it down. My tone was curious, as opposed to accusatory. My mother's features slowly melted into a mixture of confusion and hurt and disbelief.

"I tried . . . I didn't want to just leave you. When I went back to Queensland, all I had was a bag full of clothes and barely enough money to last me a week. I had to live with an old friend for a long time. I didn't have a job or a place to stay or food. I didn't want you kids to suffer with me.

"By the time I had found a place to stay and a small office job that paid me enough to provide for you, you didn't want me. You were four, and Cass was almost seven. My abandonment had made you think of me as a monster, and whenever I tried to take you with me, you'd refuse. You two had grown so attached to your father. You'd painted me out of the picture."

All these years, I had reconstructed my vision of my mother. I'd depicted her as a heartless woman who'd torn our family apart and didn't even spare a Band-Aid to try to repair it. I hadn't realized how hard she'd tried to still be a part of our lives, even when she'd known she couldn't be a part of Dad's.

"I understand why you left," I whispered.

She wiped a stray tear from her eye, looking at me in confusion.

"I know about Dad and Megan."

My mother tried to smile at me, to reassure me that she was okay, but it was shaky and strained. "A secret like that . . . it destroyed our marriage. I didn't know what else he was keeping from me. And it was especially hard when I found out that his first child was with Megan. She had been my best friend since I'd moved to town, and knowing their history . . . I couldn't handle it."

"Is that why you gave me the book?"

She nodded, rummaging through her purse and coming out with a crumpled tissue. She dabbed it under her nose. "I wasn't sure if he'd told you yet. By the look on your face when I gave it to you, I could tell he hadn't, but I'd hoped it would prompt him to."

"It didn't."

"I know."

"Mom?"

It was the first time I'd called her that out loud. The look in her eyes spoke volumes, her smile unforgettable.

"I think I'm ready for that holiday."

She reached over and squeezed my hand. "We'll leave as soon as possible."

I squeezed back, thankful.

Family is one of society's strongest creations. Secrets are one of human-kind's infamous destroyers. Together, they counteract each other, and the only product is conflict.

But there *are* resolutions, and it's never too late for them.

For Lydia, her resolution was escape. Our small rural town held too many secrets, too many lies. Leaving it all behind was what she needed, and seeking a place where she would be granted a fresh start was what she desperately craved.

Turns out her family had the same view. All their sneaking around over the past few months hadn't been because of their date nights like Lydia had suspected. They had been looking into moving out of town, and all the events that had occurred with my father and Colton and our families had given them that final push to make a decision.

They were moving back to their hometown in Victoria at the end of the summer.

As for the Crests, they had also packed up and left. A FOR

SALE sign turned up on their lawn a week after my father was arrested. Their marriage was dangling from a frayed piece of thread, but Mr. Crest seemed willing to overcome the obstacles. I wasn't sure if it was inspiring or extremely toxic.

"Aren't you going to say goodbye?"

I turned and saw Cass standing in the driveway, giving me a grin. Despite our solving the mystery, we had found it extremely hard to wrap our minds around the fact that our father was a killer. He had been someone we trusted, that we grew up to love and adore. Now . . . now we were uncertain.

But we were figuring it out, just as much as we were discovering ourselves.

"Bye."

She laughed, opening her arms. "Shut up and hug me."

Lydia and I were heading to the city. She wanted to familiarize herself with her surroundings and discover some "hidden gems" that she could revisit when she started university. Plus, she had just confirmed her accommodation and she was going to be rooming with a booklover all the way from South Australia.

She was ecstatic.

"Call me when you get to the airport."

I'd be leaving Lydia in the city and heading to the airport to catch the next flight out to Queensland. My mother had convinced me that I should meet my half-siblings. Carson, Zac, and Molly were all described as "energetic bundles of joy," which I presumed to be a warning that they'd drain the absolute life out of me.

I'd never really taken the time to appreciate the fact that having an older sibling was a blessing.

Nevertheless, they sounded great and I was looking forward to meeting them. I was expecting some awkwardness for the first couple of days, but I planned on bringing chocolate. Who doesn't love an awesome older brother who sneaks them sugar?

"And you call me if anything goes wrong here." My gaze shot toward Trevor, who was exiting our house.

"I heard that!" he yelled.

I hadn't gotten to know Trevor that much, but during the times we had hung out, I discovered how much of a match he was for my sister. Not only was he one hell of a gamer, but he was pretty skilled in the kitchen. His tacos were the best type of comfort food. But despite all that, the reason I liked him the most was because he made my sister smile. Not only that, but he also made her laugh. The kind of laughter that made milk come out of her nose.

Cass denied it ever happened, but we all saw it.

Anyone who can make Cass Parker laugh that hard makes it into my good books.

I reached out and took Trevor's hand, shaking it farewell. "Take care of her."

Tristan had returned to his adoptive family, no signs of wanting to reach out to his biological parents again. I wasn't sure if he would reach out to his siblings next, but I hoped the thought didn't cross his mind. The possibility of him lurking around the house while I was gone made my skin crawl.

"Take care of *yourself*," he answered. "We're a phone call away if you need us."

"Thank you."

Cass pushed me toward the car. With one final wave, I got into the passenger side and shut the door.

"Took you long enough," Lydia teased. She grinned and started the engine.

"Hey, you took my advice. You didn't dye your hair." I gently tugged on her newly cut curls. They rested just above her freckled shoulders.

"I'm glad I didn't," she answered with a smile as she pulled away from the house.

Driving past each town with the windows rolled down and Lydia belting out the lyrics of the songs on the radio was comforting. It was hopeful, a snapshot of what my future could be.

The last stage of grief was acceptance, and I was on the road to recovery.

ABOUT THE AUTHOR

Olivia Harvard has been an avid reader and writer since the age of fourteen. Since beginning her writing journey in 2011 on the online platform Wattpad, she has accumulated almost one hundred thousand followers and has won three consecutive Watty awards. Her Watty award-winning novel *Confessions About Colton* has garnered over seven million reads and has been published in French by Hachette Romans. Olivia currently resides in Australia and is pursuing a career in education.

When Jane Madarang's neighbor Natalie kills herself and leaves behind cryptic instructions, it's up to Jane and her classmates to unearth deadly secrets.

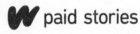

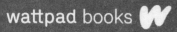

wattpad

Where stories live.

Discover millions of stories created by diverse writers from around the globe.

Download the app or visit
www.wattpad.com today.

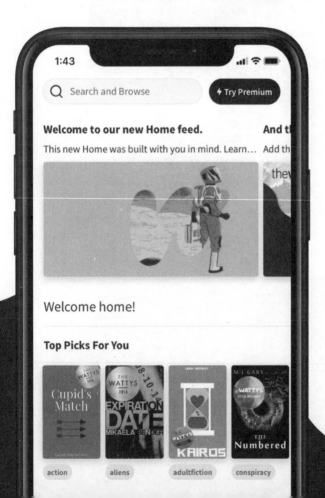

 premium

Supercharge your Wattpad experience.

Go Premium and get more from the platform you already love. Enjoy uninterrupted ad-free reading, access to bonus Coins, and exclusive, customizable colors to personalize Wattpad your way.

Try Premium free today.